Madhavi Mahadevan has published two collections of short stories, *Paltan Tales* and *Doppelganger*, and an e-novella, *Swansong*. Her first novel, *The Kaunteyas*, was a retelling of the *Mahabharata* from the viewpoint of Kunti, the mother of the Pandavas. She has also written fiction for children.

Praise for *Bride of the Forest*

'...a harrowing saga of grace about a woman who managed to be generous, kind and compassionate even while held hostage to the feckless notions of dharma adhered to by powerful men...The author does an admirable job of handling the sensational material with sensitivity even as she infuses it with the gentle beats of a pain-wracked heart.'—Anuja Chandramouli, *The New Indian Express*

'The book is balanced and nuanced. It is defiant and outspoken against a gendered society, without ever seeming out of place for its time of setting. With lyrical prose, interesting characters and side characters and strong philosophical points, this book is a must-read.'—Times of India.Indiatimes.com

'In [*Bride of the Forest*], Drishadvati is a delicately poised figure while tracing feminist lineage...Mahadevan sensitively focuses on Drishadvati's radical character instead of projecting her as a helpless woman, as in earlier adaptations.'—*Hindustan Times*

'This was a delight to read! The writing sparkles with its word flow—there is wit, there is a poetic lilt and a lot of humour tinged with sarcasm...Would recommend this for readers who love Indian mythology, strong women characters and writing that leaves you thinking.'—Wordpress.com

BRIDE OF THE FOREST

The Untold Story of Yayati's Daughter

Madhavi S. Mahadevan

SPEAKING
TIGER

SPEAKING TIGER BOOKS LLP
4381/4, Ansari Road, Daryaganj
New Delhi 110002

First published in paperback by Speaking Tiger Books 2020

ISBN: 978-93-89958-56-0
eISBN: 978-93-89958-57-7

10 9 8 7 6 5 4 3 2 1

Typeset in Sabon LT Std by SÜRYA, New Delhi
Printed at Chaman Enterprises, New Delhi

Contents

The basis of the self is not thought but suffering, which is the most fundamental of all feelings. While it suffers, not even a cat can doubt its unquiet and interchanged self. In intense suffering the world disappears and each of us is alone with the self.

—Milan Kundera, *Immortality*

Prologue

On the seventeenth day of the yagna, just after midnight, a strange thing happened: their ancestor, long dead and risen to Swargalok, floated back to earth. There he was in the banyan tree outside the front door, a dark, saggy silhouette entangled in the criss-cross of branches, clamouring for help. The hullabaloo woke them up. A harvest moon lit up the scene. They managed, with some difficulty, to bring him down and helped him indoors. Dazed by the descent and the excitement of the landing, he said nothing for a while but examined the bruises, crimson and indigo, that were beginning to blotch his skin. Though he was quite casual about it, they were uncomfortable with his nudity. Stark raving naked he was. A bull of a man. Over six feet tall, broad-chested, with a large head, grey shoulder-length locks and matching horseshoe whiskers tracing a prominent jawline.

As the youngest in the family, it fell upon Ashtak to get a loincloth for him. The visitor glanced at it disdainfully and told them that he was used to dressing up as they did in Swargalok: in fragrances, flower garlands and divine ornaments. Please accept this humble cloth as a temporary measure, they said. I want proper clothes, he insisted. We are in the sacred Naimisha forest, he was politely informed, and barkcloth is the appropriate dress code—you will get a new set of garments in the morning. A snort of contempt from him and then the question: Don't you know who I am?

They had all noticed that his feet did not touch the ground but remained about six inches above. Vasuman, the eldest among the brothers, tried to soothe the visitor's irritation by adopting an overly respectful tone. 'O venerable one, as you have come down from Swargalok, you are obviously a celestial being—a yaksha, deva, gandharva or rakshasa. Whoever you are, we are honoured to have you here. Please accept the fruit of our yagna.'

'I saw the smoke from up there,' the visitor said. 'It rose in a thick rope connecting this world with that one. I simply followed it all the way down. What yagna are you offering the gods?'

'The Vajpeya yagna.'

He looked sceptical. 'Only the wealthiest of men have the ability to perform such a grand ceremony. Who among you is the patron?'

'I am,' Vasuman said with quiet dignity.

The old man looked him up and down. 'I am not a brahmin to solicit riches from another man,' he said. 'Indeed, I belong to the class that gives. I am a kshatriya of the Chandravanshi lineage. Yayati is my name.'

Yayati? Can it be?

Observing their awestruck faces, he was slightly mollified. 'You, at least, seem to have heard my name before. No one knew of it in Swargalok, though I reminded them of my title—Maharaja Yayati.'

Vasuman touched his feet. 'You are our grandfather,'

he said respectfully. 'I am Vasuman, king of Ayodhya.' He introduced his siblings as Pratardan of Kashi, Shivi of Bhojanagri and Ashtak of Kankyakubja. These three kings, too, prostrated before the visitor.

Yayati frowned. 'I have several sons,' he said. 'But I recognize only the youngest as my inheritor. Puru is his name. Is any one of you his son?'

By this time the entire household had collected. They were agape at the spectacle. Before Vasuman could reply, a tall, slender woman in the gathering stepped forward. Strands of silver framed the clean, pared lines of her face. She offered obeisance to the visitor and said, 'O noble one, these four are your daughter's sons. My sons.' It was hard to gauge from her expression what she was feeling right then. She looked as she always did, tranquil.

Yayati, on the other hand, was taken aback. Flushing slightly, he sent her a perfunctory nod. 'My memory isn't what it used to be,' he said. 'But I remember something... it was a long time ago...your mother brought you to me. You were...how old? Ten or eleven maybe. She spoke of a prophecy.'

A soft, pensive light gilded her honey brown eyes. 'Yes, Father,' she said. 'That is how it all began—with a prophecy.'

1
Yayati

The forest was already a lush, tangled dream. In the runny light of dawn what appeared surreal to the girl's eyes was the city of Pratisthan—the yellow of its brick walls, the disarray of its streets. The citizens were still abed. The network of narrow, paved alleyways was silent but for the sighs from the night just spent. However, the smells lingered and gossiped of the frenzied drinking and dancing, of clandestine desires and sated hungers, of enticement, seduction and indulgence. In the street of the courtesans, bruised garlands of marigold and jasmine drifted in sluggish drains. A tambourine lay in a pool of vomit. At the city's intersections stood enormous clay lamps that had burned bright all night, but now held curls of blackened wicks, like stillborn worms. The only signs of life were the lean, brown stray dogs scavenging through animal innards and fishbones.

As the sun rose, honeycombs of gold-coloured light appeared on the flat rooftops. The people of Pratisthan stirred listlessly to life. The pious, who had been up long before sunrise for their ritual ablutions, returned from the ghat. Susurrations of grass brooms echoed across courtyards. Mothers yawned as they washed their babies and spooned millet porridge into their pink mouths. Holy men in tawny robes knocked on doors and wordlessly held out their wooden begging bowls. Yodelling calls, from vegetable vendors selling brinjal, bitter gourd, pumpkin, jackfruit and greens, flitted from street to street, reminding the girl of birdsong in the forest.

Her throat felt dry and scratchy. The new cloth bodice wound around her budding breasts chafed against her skin. Sweat trickling down her neck stung like ant bites. She glared resentfully at the woman in whose wake she had trudged these past three days. Some time ago, she had arrived at the conclusion which every child, at a certain age, reaches: that she was a foundling. This woman, she had decided, was not her real mother. The word 'father', however, was a complete mystery to her. She hadn't even known she had one until three days ago, when she'd been abruptly informed, 'You are now going to live with your father.'

'Where does he live, this father of mine?'

'In a web of his own making.' Her mother had laughed but, typically, did not explain.

The girl's face had clouded with misgivings. As one nurtured by the forest she knew that a web was intricate—a spider's web. Beginning with just a single fine silken filament exuded into space, all it announced to the world was an intention. Yet, such was the industry, craft and intelligence of the spinner that from one thread could arise many elaborate creations: a snare for preys, a hideout from predators, a haven for young ones. What web had this unknown father spun? She asked, 'Why do I have to live with him?' When her mother did not reply, a note of anxiety entered the girl's voice. 'Will I ever come back to this forest?'

Speaking as if to herself, her mother said, 'No one leaves entirely. There is always a fragment to return to.' Seeing something, not in the child's face but in the far-off future, she added with uncharacteristic gentleness, 'The forest is yours. It will be here for you.'

The possibility of living elsewhere was scary but also exciting. Ever since her twelfth birthday in the winter past, it had taken over the girl's dreams. On that balmy day, she had gone with her friends to the sandbank in the river. Accustomed only to the dimness below trees, she was at first dazzled by the clarity of the landscape. Under the crystalline blue radiance of the sky her skin had tingled, as if its pores were millions of buds opening up to a new truth. Curving in a broad irregular arc, the river had seemed to her like the longest line in her palm, flowing into the unknown. The fields of wheat toasting in the sun, and beyond them, the grey humped hills receding into the distance...where did this world end? On the rutted dirt track beside the water no one had passed for a long time. Then a young carter singing a song had come by. The jingle of his donkey's harness bells had embellished the warm baritone voice. For days afterwards the lilting melody had haunted her, igniting a longing in her heart for something new. It was coming, she had felt it in her bones, her life was about to change. However, now as they picked their way through the rabble and babble of the city, the girl tucked cautiously into her mother's shadow.

Situated downstream from the forest, Pratisthan lay at the confluence of two mighty rivers. Commerce was its lifeblood. On that morning, as the girl walked through the streets, she saw animal carts piled with merchandise streaming out through the city gates towards foreign lands. Along the riverbank sailboats laden with local goods dropped anchor. Auctioneers ran a quick eye over the inventories. In the improvised marketplace on the waterfront, stalls were set up. Buyers sauntered past nonchalantly, all the while quietly assessing the goods; sellers put on their smoothest smiles; brokers stood to one side in a small cluster; court officials arrived in a flurry of activity. The day's business began. There was a sense of purpose to it all. The girl was struck by the presence of men. They were everywhere. She had never seen so many men in one place, nor so few women—there were hardly any.

'Your father is an important man,' her mother said, using the same scornful tone in which she had first spoken to the girl about him. 'Owns everything you see here.' The child sensed that the words were meant to separate rather than unite. Like everyone else in the forest, her mother owned nothing. Even her skills as a healer belonged to the tribe. There was a seam of tenderness in her, narrow but deep, reserved only for the wild creatures, orphaned or maimed, whom she rescued. On them she bestowed her caresses and softly crooned endearments. She could also, out of kindness, kill with her bare hands an animal that was too mutilated to survive. To humans, however, she had never had much to say, as if their speech itself were absurd. Yet the girl had not lacked for attention or affection in the forest. As an infant she had never gone hungry. There were always a few women around to suckle her at their breasts and care for her in the same rough-and-ready manner they used for all the children of the tribe. It dawned on her that in this teeming city of strangers, where one man owned everything, she was going to be all alone. She would have welcomed a sign of reassurance from her mother, something as simple as a shared smile, or just a slowing down of pace to accommodate her astonishment at the new sights, but, oblivious to her need, the woman walked through the busy streets with her usual detachment. She was like a sleek panther padding through the undergrowth, unmindful of the stir her presence was causing among the citizens. Everyone stopped doing whatever they were at and stared. The virtuous muttered God's name and averted their eyes. One man, a poultry-seller, dropped a cane basket of chicks; the fluffy pale yellow balls scurried away in all directions. Later, when the stories of that day spread through word of mouth, they were embroidered with every telling. Several witnesses were ready to swear that a swan-shaped silver chariot, weightless as a spring cloud, had descended on the river, and a woman had majestically stepped out of it, gliding over the water to the ghat. She was described as a supernatural being—an apsara, yakshi, dakkini or yogini. Slim of ankle, with rounded hips and a narrow waist. Dark hair, loose and lustrous, framing an oval face with a straight nose and a bow-like mouth. Her eyes were slanting bushfires, they said. Everyone remembered the striking tattoo of an antlered deer on the top left of her back. Paeans would be composed to her proud breasts. These renditions would be fanciful, but even the more faithful reports would say that a mysterious woman of ethereal beauty had come to Pratisthan one summer day. And where did she go? No one knew for sure. All they could say was that she was last seen in the oldest quarter of the city near the king's palace. Few remembered that there had also been a petite, raggedy child in tow.

~

Yayati, king of Pratisthan, was under the attention of his barber. The barber came from a long line of professional shavers that was nearly as ancient as the renowned Lunar dynasty, the Ailas, to which Yayati belonged. It was as if the two family trees had grown beside each other, but with a marked difference; the barber's pedigree was unmixed, as his ancestors had all been barbers, whereas the king's lineage was variegated. Beginning with Ila, the transgender daughter of Manu Vaivasvat, the one from whom all humanity has descended, it had the odd apsara, as well as a fierce asura or two implanted in its branches. The inclusion of disparate bloodlines had made the Aila males virile but also unpredictable. They were known to be risk-takers. The dynasty had produced several audacious chieftains who had increased their cattle herds through lightning raids on other settlements, and expanded the kingdom by burning down virgin forests and planting fields in their place. Over time, the Ailas had acquired a mixed reputation. On the battlefield they were heroes and off it hedonists, eating, drinking, gambling and philandering as if there were no tomorrow. Yayati's ancestors had frequently started the day in a foul mood; except for the barber no one had dared enter the king's bedchamber. The barber's forebears had unfailingly attended to their imperial patrons and this had fostered in them an aplomb that was passed down the line.

The barber finished trimming the royal beard. He stepped back, eyed his handiwork critically and gently tilted the king's prominent chin upward. 'Please keep your head at just this angle, Maharaj,' he said. 'There are a few stray hairs in your nostrils that need plucking. Try not to move.'

'I can't move!' Yayati said in a growl. 'It hurts even to open my eyes.'

The barber clicked his tongue in sympathy. 'An oil massage, followed by a warm herbal restorative,' he prescribed. When Yayati did not respond for several minutes, he said in the dry tone of an elder correcting a recalcitrant teenager, 'Self-indulgence takes its toll, Maharaj, even on someone as virile as you...however, you will have to make an effort. Your esteemed father awaits a visit from you.'

Yayati's eyes snapped open. 'What? But I visited him just a few days ago.'

'Several weeks would be closer to the truth,' the barber said. 'Six, to be precise.'

Yayati shot him an angry look, but the man was busy studying his instruments. He chose an ear-pick and began to remove the wax from the royal ear. This too was a delicate operation. Yayati closed his eyes again, seeking refuge from the fierce sunshine that relentlessly pounded his head. After a night of revelries, he had only a hazy memory of the previous day's events. The odour of ghee from the offerings to the fire god lingered in the air, like an exhausted guest who had missed the ride back home. It had been one of those interminable homas that his mother regularly arranged. Hours of mantra-chanting followed by a feast for brahmins, and the giving away of cloth, cattle, gold and gems. What had the ritual commemorated this time? While these frequent ceremonies and the gaieties that followed were draining the treasury, they were apparently earning him merit and fame for his generosity. His mind wandered to the time-consuming duties that had descended upon him with the kingship. They constituted a vast separate realm: of boredom. This visit to his father, for example, would take all day. He could have put the time to better use. There was that new stallion he couldn't wait to try out. He sighed. Six weeks was too long a gap. He would have to go.

Meanwhile, the barber concluded the daily ritual with a head-and-shoulders massage. As the practised fingers danced lightly on the knots around the upper three chakras of Yayati's spine, the wall of pain in his head slowly disintegrated. Half an hour later, when the maids filled the bath with jasmine-scented water and arranged bowls of lentil scrub, a loofah and fresh cotton towels, his mood improved. He invited the three prettiest girls to join him in the bath. After romping with them for a while he felt rejuvenated. Sipping a lukewarm lemon-pepper drink, he called for the chief steward and said, 'Tell the mahamantri that I will not attend the sabha today. I am going to visit Maharaja Nahusha.' There was a virtuous ring to the announcement.

The steward's ear pricked up. He asked in an oily tone, 'Shall I order the cart to be loaded with supplies as usual?'

A chiding glance from Yayati. 'You forgot to include duck's eggs last time.' The steward looked sheepish and murmured an apology. 'One more thing,' Yayati continued. 'Inform the stables that I want the new stallion saddled for the ride.'

'As you wish,' said the steward and backed out of the king's presence.

The barber, still hovering around, cleared his throat. Yayati sent him an inquiring look. 'Please convey my respectful greetings to Maharaja Nahusha,' the barber said.

'Any other message that you would care to send through me?'

Ignoring the jibe, the barber replied, 'Please tell His Royal Highness that despite his long separation from us, the people of Pratisthan have not forgotten him. They remember the good old days of his reign with longing.'

Yayati narrowed his eyes. 'They do, do they?'

'And I, too, miss him,' concluded the barber, plaintively.

Yayati reflected that, for a king, the choosing of personal attendants was just as serious a matter as the choosing of ministers. Loyalty was especially important in the one man who daily wielded the sharp bronze razor across the noble face. He decided to ignore the subtext of the man's words and merely nodded a dismissal.

2

Nahusha

A pale cloudless sky, a stretch of empty road, on either side of it unploughed land interspersed with stretches of thorny babool trees. Yayati would have found the ride tedious if it were not for his mount. He had purchased the stallion from a trader who had connections with the nomadic tribes beyond the Himalayas, in the plateau where the finest horses were bred. Yayati's steed was a perfect specimen; a little over fifteen hands, long and skinny, lean-muscled, with a chiselled head and upright, slim, almond-shaped ears. His grey coat had the metallic sheen characteristic of the breed. Putting the stallion through his paces, Yayati was pleased with the smooth, flowing gait.

Around late afternoon the royal cavalcade reached the spot where Nahusha, the former king of Pratisthan, had taken up residence. This corner of the kingdom was bleak and sterile, as if Nature had run out of both resources and imagination. While the soldiers offloaded the rations from the cart, Yayati made his way across the bare, dry plain to a massive hump of basalt rock. In the outcrop's steep profile were several furrows wide enough for a man's girth. He began to climb one such channel. Despite being in excellent physical condition, it took him an hour to reach the top. Nothing grew on the rock but hardy weeds, a few clumps of wild grass and a lone mango tree that cast a net of cool green shade. He made his way to this tree and peered up. Coiled in one of the lower branches was an ajagara, a rock python, a handsome, majestic creature with a striking skin pattern of creamy blotches on a dark background.

Bowing before the python, Yayati said, 'Respected Father, please accept my humble salutations.'

For several minutes there was no reply. Then a ripple ran along the serpent's looped body and the tail slowly uncoiled, dropping a few inches off the branch. The creature's head slid out gradually from the coil and its forked tongue flickered.

'*I* should be the grateful one, O king,' said the python, with a flash of the mordant humour that had been the former maharaja's trademark. 'How did you find the time and energy, amidst all your pleasures, to visit your poor father who is still languishing in this world?'

Yayati kept his head bowed, trying not to betray the resentment that vibrated in him. As typical, his father was trying to rile him. When he felt sufficiently composed, he looked up and, injecting just the right amount of anxiety into his voice, said, 'You seem a bit weak, Father. I see a dullness in your eyes. Your skin, too, lacks its usual lovely gloss...please tell me, what could be the reason for this sorry state?'

Nahusha was disarmed by his son's concern. A sigh, heaved from the entire sixteen feet of its length, escaped his body. It gusted through the branches like a strong breeze, trembling the leaves. 'I am a bit preoccupied,' he admitted.

'What worries you?'

'I have been struggling with a poem for the last few days. The words just don't come.'

'A poem! What is it about?'

'What should it be about?' There was a dry, quizzing note in Nahusha's voice.

Yayati hazarded a guess. 'Love?'

The tree shook again, even more violently. 'What to do?' Nahusha moaned. 'I am in love....'

'But that's wonderful!' Yayati said. 'To find a companion in this wilderness is a miracle. Who is the unfortunate—pardon me, I meant *fortunate*—lady? What is her name?'

'I call her Champakali.'

Yayati chewed a corner of his lower lip. With a name like that she was probably a simpering village belle—a milkmaid, shepherdess or grasscutter. 'Is she very pretty?' he asked.

'Indeed!' said Nahusha, with a wide smile. 'She is also temperamental. Cares nothing for my verse, or maybe she pretends not to care. It is difficult to say at this stage...I am getting mixed signals.'

Yayati nodded in perfect understanding. 'That is usually how it is in the beginning, but don't give up. Poetry isn't speech's sole offspring. Try jokes...if you can make a woman laugh, that is half the battle won. Does she laugh at your jokes?'

'She laughs all the time. At my verse. *At me!*'

Yayati suppressed a grin. Champakali, whoever she was, had certainly made a captive of the proud Nahusha. *But what does she see in him? There is something odd about a woman who finds an ajagara attractive.* 'Where is she now?' he asked cautiously.

'Sleeping off her meal. The last goat from the supply you left.'

'Goat! She polished off a whole goat? Is she a rakshasi?'

'Certainly not!' Nahusha snapped.

'I meant no offence, Father,' Yayati said contritely. 'But you will agree she has a healthy appetite.'

'She, too, is young...like you.' Nahusha's tone was non-committal. For a while he watched his son's confused, troubled expression with a sly amusement, then said casually, 'If you tiptoe to the edge of the rock and peer below, you'll see her. Be careful not to wake her up. She has a nasty temper if her sleep is interrupted. Whoever called them "the gentle sex" got it wrong.'

Yayati had a sinking feeling in the pit of his stomach. 'Oh no, no!' he said. 'It would not be right to wake up the, uh, lady.'

'Go on, go on. I want you to see her.'

Yayati walked half-heartedly to the edge of the rock, lay flat on his stomach and looked over the lip. A few feet below the surface, in a broad shallow cleft, lay another hefty python. From the loosely coiled yellow rings it appeared even bigger than the one on the tree. Its head was tucked somewhere deep within those circles, but at one spot there was a visible swelling: the undigested remnants of the goat. Utterly revolted, Yayati drew back and quickly retraced his steps to the mango tree. He was breathing hard, as if invisible bands had tightened around his ribcage and forced the air out of his lungs.

'A beauty, isn't she?' Nahusha said. 'Those golden yellow scales are extremely unusual.'

Yayati could not bring himself to speak. He was

appalled by his father's zest. *Not even the horrible punishment he was given for it has quelled his lust!* His thoughts flew to his other parent, the queen mother Viraja, who had always treated her husband's occasional love interests with tolerance. In her view they were a permissible indulgence that did not threaten Nahusha's commitment to marriage and family. However, the latest one, Yayati feared, would be too much for her.

Once again, as if reading his mind, Nahusha said in a sibilant voice, 'You know better than to worry your poor mother. This is *our* little secret.'

Yayati nodded glumly. 'It is safe with me.'

Nahusha sent him a knowing look. 'You have enough experience in keeping similar secrets of your own.'

Flushing to the roots of his hair, Yayati looked away. The dig, about his own chequered past and the absurdity of his present situation, pained him.

Secretly amused by his son's discomfiture, Nahusha said casually, 'You cannot imagine what scandalmongers the parakeets are. I get all the news, but don't worry. I am not judging you. You are not the first man to run two homes and nor will you be the last. Getting caught was bad luck, that's all...matrimony was invented earlier, but infidelity came immediately after. Think of it as a tonic, nothing more. An antidote to the tedium of marriage.'

Several minutes passed without either of them speaking. Nahusha was lost in his thoughts. He'd been born a human, had spent long years obeying the conventions of human society. It had given him a fine appreciation of boundaries: when to push, where, and how much. Yet, at a critical moment his judgement had failed him. Just one slip was all it had taken to bring him down. He let out a heavy sigh.

Yayati shifted his weight from one foot to the other. He sensed that his father's mood had turned morose, a sign that he was brooding on the past.

Here it comes, the same old story....

~

Called 'The Fall of Nahusha', the story had been banned in the court of the Ailas as it was too depressing for them. But everywhere else it was a popular parable—about desire and its discontents. Depending on the raconteur, as well as the audience, it was frequently adapted. Wandering performers, who lived on public generosity, slanted their narration to please the plebs, to whom it made a very satisfying point: King or not, an overconfident man would get his comeuppance. Brahmin teachers told it to their disciples as an illustration of kshatriya ignorance. Kshatriyas, in contrast, saw it as an example of brahmin cleverness. Men interpreted it as a warning against the treacherous nature of women. Amongst women, however, it was regarded as a valuable lesson in how to deal with unwanted male attention.

Yayati's own mother told the same story somewhat differently. She blamed Sachi, the woman Nahusha had coveted, and said this about her: 'As the wife of Indra, Sachi Devi should have understood that her husband, the king of gods, was a role model to kings everywhere. If *she* had put her foot down on his womanizing early enough, Indra would never have acquired the reputation he had. The whole world had heard of his exploits with Gautam Rishi's wife, Ahalya. That poor woman was punished for her sin by her husband. We all know her story because it's meant to be a lesson to us, but does anyone know that

Indra, too, was cursed? Did *he* feel any sense of shame? On the contrary, he bragged about it...my husband was a righteous king, but he, too, secretly envied Indra. When he got the chance to sit on Indra's throne, naturally, he aspired to the same status. Which man wouldn't?'

As if echoing this exact view, Nahusha now said, 'I have always suspected that Indra bribed the rishis who composed the Rig Veda. Did you know that no other god has as many hymns sung in his praise as he?'

Yayati offered no comment. As in the past, Nahusha would not let him leave without listening to the entire tale. It would be the usual rambling attempt at a post hoc explanation of what had gone wrong.

Nahusha began, 'Though they are kinsmen, the devas and asuras have been fighting for aeons over who will dominate the three worlds. We Ailas are connected to both sides; therefore, it has always been our policy to remain neutral. Hence, when we heard the rumours of yet another battle between them, we did not react. But when a delegation of sages came from Devalok to meet *me*, I was quite surprised. The rishis said that Indra had slain the asura Vritra, a creature born of a yagna, therefore sacred. After this unforgivable crime, he had gone into hiding. They requested that I should take over his realm as only I had the merit, wisdom and experience in all three worlds to replace the king of gods. Brahmins are clever with words: Brihaspati, their guru, spoke convincingly. The kingdom of the gods was a place of non-stop enjoyment, he said, and extolled its pleasures. He spoke of mountain lakes and sparkling rivers where apsaras frolicked. Knowing my love of music and dance he said that the celestials were entertained by the finest performers. If I wished to enjoy a recital by Vishvavasu, the first among gandharvas, all I had to do was command. Even the illustrious Naarad Rishi would wait on me. His most promising pupil, Tumbaru, from whose throat song poured out like a shower of perfect pearls, would sing in praise of me. Tell me about the drawbacks, I said. And Brihaspati replied that there were none. Aside from the occasional skirmish with asuras, there was nothing to do in Devalok but enjoy the good life. I asked for time to think it over.

'By now you would know that I consulted your mother. Her view was that it was an honour for a mortal to be invited to govern Devalok. How could I refuse without insulting the sages? Then she began to talk of moving into Indra's palace. She wanted to know if there would be a coronation ceremony. She even planned a new wardrobe to dazzle the celestials.'

Though he had been only fifteen years old at the time, Yayati remembered even now the general sense of anticipation. The people of Pratisthan had spoken of Amaravati as a sister city. They'd conjectured about what this elevation would mean for them. Business communities had hoped that the celestials would be convinced to trade with them. They'd wondered whether Kuber, the lord of wealth, would be persuaded to invest in their businesses. Would Tvashtr, the master craftsman, share his knowledge of weapon-making? Would the divine apsaras dance for them too?

'Do you know the average age of a god?' Nahusha asked suddenly, then supplied the answer himself. 'Sixteen...the sweetest age on the scale of happiness. We mortals have rites of passage to lead us into adulthood, but divine beings don't need such rituals. No one grows old or sickens. They remain adolescents forever...after living in the company of those youngsters for a while, I, too, began to think like them. It may sound odd to you, but despite the imperfections of this world, I had not known discontent in it. Groomed from an early age to think of myself as the future king, I was mindful of dharma. A king must be seen as virtuous and all that stuff they teach you. However, in Devalok, I began to think that my earlier existence among mortals had not been much of a life. It had been a deception. I had always felt inadequate. Though I hid it well, I had been dogged by anxiety. The truth is that no one living in Mrityulok can escape his fears, not even a king. It's not only fear of death that dogs us...I was afraid of behaving wrongly, of failing to do my duty, of losing a war and bringing dishonour to my people, of dying without sons to carry on the family name, of insulting someone who had the potential to harm me—such as a god or a brahmin, of being overthrown by one of my own kin, and ever since that food-taster died of poisoning, of my next meal being my last. When I sat on Indra's throne these disquieting thoughts became irrelevant. In the company of gods, I realized that to be young and healthy *forever* is to be invincible. It was not just that I was walking on the sky, that I controlled the rain and thunder, or that no human had attained higher...it was also the freedom. In Devalok, I felt released from all strictures and structures that apply to human existence. What I failed to see from those lofty heights was that the abyss at my feet had also grown deeper. Hubris does that...ultimately, a man's ignorance of his nature exceeds the knowledge of it. Without stopping to ask what the consequences could mean for me, I took my next step.'

Troubled by what was to follow, Nahusha trailed off. In his mind he had puzzled over different endings to the story: what could have happened, what ought to have happened.

'Sachi Devi, Indra's queen...I have told you about her, but did I tell you how clumsy and ill at ease I felt the first time I met her? She was everything that one imagines about the queen of Devalok. Stunning looks, yes, but every woman there is beautiful. They all have shapely bodies. Skin, teeth, hair, eyes—everything is gold-tinted. Yet, she stood out from the crowd with her air of quietness and refinement. It was evident in the way she greeted me, the new king who sat under the stately columns of her husband's sabha, on *his* throne. There was not a trace of rancour in her welcome but a solemn courtesy. She offered to move out of Indra's palace. I had heard so much about its wonders and was looking forward to living in it, but I felt that it was ungentlemanly to dislodge her so soon. Stay on for some more time, I said. Perhaps there was something at the back of my mind even then—I can't say! Kings who conquer kingdoms own the women of the routed foe. Queens and concubines must obey the new lord. This is how it is in Mrityulok and this was how I began to see it. *I* was the new lord of Devalok. Rambha, Menaka, Swayamprabha, Ghritachi and other divine courtesans were at my beck and call. I spent nights of passion with these women who knew no shyness. If they could be open-minded, why not she? Yet, I did not have the courage...as days passed, my longing became intense. I did everything I could to woo Sachi.

Sent her presents, invited her to the feasts and revelries. She responded politely, always a no. I hinted that I'd like to visit her home; she replied that she led a retired life, as befitted her new status. I had a suspicion that my obsession with her was becoming public knowledge and everyone was ridiculing me behind my back. It made me aware that I, a mortal, was an outsider there. For all the respect they showed, they saw me as a lesser being. The Usurper. The feeling that they were laughing at me should have been a warning. At the very least, it should have made me leave her well alone, but from rejection to rage is an easy step. Constantly thwarted, my ardour was replaced by pig-headedness. I would teach her a lesson, I decided. She would have to receive my suit. I even specified the day!'

It was the point in the narration where Nahusha had come to recognize, with perfect hindsight, the blind spot in his own nature: though he wielded power over the world he had failed to master his own baser instincts. He concluded that the wise sages, too, had seen this weakness. Hadn't they tried to tell him that it was a sin to hanker after another's wife? But he'd reminded them that they had not similarly restrained Indra when he tricked and seduced Ahalya, the sage's wife. Judging that he was in no mood to listen, the seers had secretly fashioned his downfall. On receiving his ultimatum, Sachi had sent a reply: *Come in my husband's golden palanquin—the one that is borne by the seven rishis*. When he asked Vasisth, one of the seers, whether there was indeed a practice so strange—the seven sages carrying Indra on their backs!—the reply he got was even more puzzling. Vasisth said that as the sovereign Nahusha could command as he thought fit. The revered sage never quite answered the question, but Nahusha had not yet realized how much he was disliked. Overcome by shameful memories, he was unable to speak further. Some wounds never heal. He had accepted many things, but could not spit out the taste of betrayal. When the seven seers had turned up at his door that evening—silver-haired, dignified old men, ready to bear the heavy palanquin on their frail shoulders—they, in their wisdom, would have surely anticipated the outcome. They did not deliberately slow their pace, but, at his urging, took the shortest route to Indra's palace. A narrow, uneven and precarious path clinging to the steep mountainside. The rishis had inched along at a glacial pace, till he, Nahusha, had lost his patience with them and ordered: *sarpa, sarpa*...fast, move faster! And then he had done the unimaginable. He had kicked the nearest palanquin bearer, the sage Agastya. For a fleeting moment, just after his foot made contact with the old man's head, he had felt something—a deep, hollow chill. A numbing sense of dread. But it was too late. As he was sucked into the void by a powerful force, his brain barely registered the words of the curse the rishi uttered: *From now on, may you live as a sarpa.*

A serpent.

Flung out of the palanquin, falling from the sky, he had dropped into the narrow chasm a long, long way. While descending, his form had retrogressed. His limbs had shrunk till they disappeared, his spine lengthened, eyes shifted to the side of the skull. His skin lost its hair and developed dark patches. His tongue became thinner and its tip split in two. The vortex that drew him in divested his name of all its glory and rendered it forever a cautionary footnote to other men: No blackness deeper than the one a man falls into when he tries to coerce a woman.

~

The sun had entered the last stretch of its daily journey, the eastern sky was flooded with indigo. Stars sparkled quietly, handmaids to a full moon. The air was cooling. Yayati sought Nahusha's permission to leave. As if still under the grip of the past, both father and son were pensive and the farewell was brusque. Yayati left with mixed feelings. While making his way down from the rock, he reflected that the recent love interest in his father's life only proved that a dog's tail cannot ever be straightened. Though contrite, Nahusha was not one to remain miserable or lonely forever. Living flesh needs a confirmation of its existence, thought Yayati. *Some may call it foolishness, but the moth hovers close to the flame and the peacock performs his shivery dance for exactly the same reason. Touch is the affirmation of being alive. Life is desire.* Even in this cheerless spot, Nahusha had found a reason to be happy. A lady friend who helped him satisfy his lust, to whom he composed love songs and for whom he gave up his food. It was a regeneration of sorts. He made a mental note to send another cartload of supplies soon.

~

It was late in the night when he finally had the time to see the woman and the girl who had waited at the palace gates all day. He was seated on the ancient throne when they were shown in. At first he had no memory of the woman though she reminded him, 'You came many years ago to hunt in our forest.'

'*Your* forest?'

'Don't laugh. It was my mother's before it was mine.'

'And is this girl your daughter?'

The woman flashed him a look. 'She is your seed. That makes her a princess of the Ailas.'

It was ridiculous. He would have openly scoffed, but the defiance in the woman's face—like an evil eye—warned him to be careful. Hadn't a woman's anger shattered his own life? Women, in his view, were strange, unreliable creatures. Could it be possible that this woman was making it up? It was true that he had often hunted in the forest, sometimes staying there for days. True, too, that he had slept with women from the untamed tribes that lived in it. There was something different about those women, an earthiness that he'd found refreshing after the smooth, practised ways of the royal courtesans, the submissiveness of concubines, the claustrophobia of the queen's bed. There had been a period, years ago, when those wild nights of intoxication in the forest had been so many that memory had fused them inseparably into one kind of coarse pleasure. Was this girl an outcome of that time? A princess of the Ailas, he echoed silently. 'Are you quite sure that she is mine?' he said. 'I don't see any of the Aila features in her.'

'If you can't provide for her, just say so. She is no burden to *me*, O king.'

He flushed at the scornful tone. The woman studied him for a long moment then, without another word, turned around to leave. He noticed the lifelike tattoo of a deer on her back and had a flash of a memory, of tracing it in kisses. A recollection arose of a forest-dweller he'd met, a shaman reputed for the efficacy of the spells she cast to ward off evil and the good-luck charms made from feathers, claws and bones of dead birds. The woman had not lied; the girl was following her mother out of the hall. He felt oddly disturbed by the sight of her trailing like a submissive foal. It was as if the ancestors were suddenly crowding him, whispering in his ear, raising a clamour. He could not make out what they were saying, but he sensed the urgency. 'Wait!' he cried.

They stopped, but only the girl, rearing her head as if struck, turned to look at him.

'Come here,' he said.

She stepped from the shadows into the pool of light shed by the flaming torches that surrounded the royal seat. He saw that she was on the cusp of womanhood. Her body had the bony gawkiness of a child, but in the straight-backed posture, the slender long column of her neck and the developing angles and planes of her face there was a forecast of beauty. Her eyes gravely returned his gaze. They showed no awe but were cool and watchful. The quality of stillness in one so young struck him as unusual. He had a feeling that he had seen it somewhere before—a kind of bred-in-the-bone poise—but he couldn't say where or when. Had it been a dream, a carved image or a real face? Had it been a human or an animal?

He was searching for something to say when her mother spoke. 'She will be fruitful. Her womb will bring forth males. Four sons.'

'Is that what her stars say?'

The woman gave a mocking laugh. 'It is what *your*

stars say, Yayati. When the time comes her sons will ensure your safe passage into the next world.'

He frowned. What did she mean? Sons were what a man needed to ensure that his lineage continued. He, Yayati, already had sons. Five. He had paid off his debt to the pitris, his ancestors, so that when the time came for him to leave this world they would welcome him into their golden heaven, Pitralok, instead of banishing him to Put, the hell reserved for men who had died sonless. Yes, he had done his duty. The woman was clearly mad, and he was foolish to fall for her nonsense talk. He regretted the impulse that had made him call the girl back, but the woman was gone…now there were only the two of them in the room, the girl and he. What was he to do with her? Should he request the queen mother to accept the child in her household? He could probably persuade her, but she had troubles enough of her own.

~

An angry brahmin's curse had transformed Nahusha from a human to a serpent. The transgression had been his alone, but Viraja, his chief queen, too, had paid the price. While he waited in the wilderness to be freed from the curse—by a far-off descendant named Yudhisthir—she had been at a loss about what to do with the rest of her earthly life. There had been a fleeting suggestion that, as a devoted wife, she could share her husband's fate and that she could do this by requesting the powerful rishi who had uttered the curse to repeat it for her as well. The idea was novel, but Viraja had a horror of snakes, an absolute phobia. To assume the form of one was unthinkable. Kill me this instant, she had pleaded, and became so hysterical that she had to be sternly reminded that she was a manasi kanya, the born-of-the-mind daughter, of the pitris themselves and, therefore, faultless. As such, she was expected to lead the way when it came to feminine virtues like submissiveness, chastity, devotion and prudence. Besides, there was the more practical concern of bringing up her six sons, ranging in years from eighteen to eight. Viraja, much to her secret relief, had stayed on in the palace.

Soon after Nahusha's banishment to the rock, a second tragedy had devastated the royal family: Eighteen-year-old Yati, who was Yayati's elder brother and the crown prince, had refused to ascend to the throne. I am taking the vows of brahmacharya, he'd declared. From his father's example, he said, it was clear that power, combined with a decadent lifestyle, could destroy a man. He'd decided that he wanted neither. He was firmly reminded of his duties—a long life of renunciation is *not* the duty of a kshatriya—but no argument could undermine his resolve. He insisted that his locks be shaved, jewels and rich garments exchanged for the single white loincloth of a sanyasi. Armed with a begging bowl, a water pot and a sturdy wooden staff, he had set off for the forest without a backward look. Nothing was heard of him ever again.

Now the question that is the bane of the rich and the powerful loomed large: who would inherit? The mahamantri and the council of ministers had pressed Yayati, the second in line, to ascend to the throne; it could not lie empty, they insisted. The raw fifteen-year-old boy was bewildered by this abrupt change of direction in his hitherto carefree life. In the days preceding the coronation, the deference he received from others filled him with a strange sense of fatalism, as if he were a sacred bullock being prepared for ritual slaughter before the goddess. The coronation itself was not a happy event for anyone. When the gem-studded gold crown was placed on his head, and he was led by the rajpurohit to the throne, Yayati couldn't get rid of the feeling that he was an imposter. The sight of his mother weeping copiously throughout the ceremony had further shaken his confidence. He could have used her support, but Viraja seemed barely able to hold herself together.

In time, however, she had come around to the view that Nahusha's rock-bound existence was a metaphysical conundrum, a duality. Her husband was both dead and alive. Twinning her lifestyle with his, she alternated between the pared-down existence prescribed by the shastras for a widow, and the entitlements of a royal consort. Over the years, she had slowly become a relict, still living in the long-ago, but haunting the here and now with her eeriness. There were periods of seclusion, dietary restrictions, plain dressing and devotional song. And there were other days when she did up her hair, flaunted her fine jewellery, celebrated festivals with royal pomp, gave elaborate feasts, donated generously to brahmins, sat in the sabha and issued diktats. She managed her dual life with aplomb, but Yayati was never quite sure which persona he was likely to encounter from one day to the next. He considered his mother harmless, but also felt that she would not be the right mentor for a child who seemed more a feral creature than human. That left him with just one option, the queen. Yayati's face clouded. He didn't relish the idea of broaching the matter with his wife. Glancing at the girl who had been foisted on him, he asked in a loud, irritated voice, 'Do you even have a name?'

She caught the note of contempt and flushed. Yes, she wanted to yell back at him. I have a name, the one my mother gave me. The name of the river that flows by my forest.

Fists clenched, giving no indication of how close she was to tears, she said, 'My name is Drishadvati.'

3

Drishadvati

So here I am. All alone. Trapped in the Spider's Web. A sprawling, shadowy labyrinth full of nasty surprises, I suspect. I do not like the palace.

He wants to know my name. I tell him. He gives a derisive snort. 'Sounds strange,' he says. 'It'll have to be changed. Your mother claimed you have a grand destiny. A royal destiny. Your name shall be…I'll think of something, or maybe the queen will.'

After staring at me morosely for a long time, he gives a grunt and stands up. How tall and broad he is, with the girth and shoulders of a jungle buffalo and a face as big and menacing. Instead of a pair of wide horns on his head, he has a thick moustache trailing down the sides of his mouth. I cannot see his eyes clearly, but I sense that they are hostile. What should I do if he comes near me? I could bite him…but no, wait! He claps his hands together as a signal. Separating himself from the shadows a man emerges. A dark, thin, bare-chested dasa, who stands before him with his head bowed, the picture of submission. The king tells the slave to inform the queen that he is bringing someone to meet her. I assume that someone is me.

Behind her regal back the maids say unkind things about her, this is what I will later learn. However, when she turns her lethal gaze on one of them, it is like petrifaction. Instantaneous. At the very least, she can reduce one to a weeping wreck. Some have even turned white-haired overnight. I do not exaggerate. Those who survive the queen's stare through the first year stay in her service. As if branded by fire, they become members of a cult. A supercilious air, a stately walk and a way of speaking without moving the lips set them apart. Like her, they give an impression of being stone-hearted, but the truth is that none of them has what *she* has: a heart broken. A shattered heart, its fragments reassembled and soldered with hatred. Possessed by the past, it beats steadily, drumming up the red fury that is needed to energize her soul while she waits for—what else?—the next betrayal.

On the night we first meet, after looking me over, she says to the king, 'So! This one, too, is your love child.' Her tone drips honey, her eyes are gleaming dagger points. 'Are there any more waiting to crawl out of the forest?'

He starts to protest, but changing his mind, merely says, 'No.'

She gives him a long, hard glare, then abruptly turning her attention to me again, asks, 'Who are your parents?'

'Don't know.'

'Where is your mother?'

'Don't know.'

She sends him a mocking sideways look. 'Where have you picked her from? Does this creature even have a name?' She turns to me. 'What are you called?'

'Drisha—

'Madhavi,' he cuts in loudly. 'Her name is Madhavi. A fitting name for a rajkanya...richness, good luck.'

'Really?' The queen's voice is cold, disbelieving. She looks at me through narrowed eyes. 'It's clear that she's had no upbringing, royal or otherwise. No one has taught her how to speak to her elders.' Glancing at the king, she says flatly, 'I don't want her.'

'At least give her a chance.' His tone is half-humouring, half-pleading. 'You used to say that after two boys, you would have liked to have a little princess of your own.'

'And you always give me what I want, don't you?'

Are they always like this? She stern and he wary. They don't like each other. Are they enemies? I watch them slowly circling each other, creating ripples of tension that spread through the web, so that its very air trembles. I cannot decide who I dislike more in this odd pair. Odd, yes...she is older than him, much, much older.

Snapping her fingers as if she has suddenly had a brilliant idea, she says, 'That asuri Sarmistha can look after her. '

'King Vrishaparva's daughter is a servant now,' he says evenly.

She sends him a mocking smile and asks with fake gentleness, 'Does that grieve you?'

He glowers at her, then bites out the words. 'Do as you please.'

She lifts her chin as if to say, 'And you, too, will do as I please.'

With a muttered oath, he turns around and leaves. She stares at his back. Her smile has vanished. She is lost in thought. Except for the muscle twitching near her mouth she is as still as death. After a few moments she calls for a maid, and one appears immediately. Without so much as a glance at me, she says to the woman, 'Take her away. I never want to see her again. She probably has lice. Shave off her hair. Burn her clothes. Then send her away from here. Send her to Sarmistha.'

Fear, mixed with fury, swells inside me. Bite, claw, scratch. *Run!* But I am frozen. The maid bobs her head and sends me a sidelong glance, as if she expects me to follow suit. Something in her face alerts me that it would be a really bad idea to ignore her hint. This is a tangled universe that I know nothing about. I bow my head briefly.

'Come on!' The maid jabs me hard in the back, then grasps my neck. She half drags me off towards the servants' quarters.

'Let go!' I cry, as soon as we are out of the queen's hearing.

To my surprise she complies but with a warning. 'Don't even think of running away. She lets the tigers loose at night...you'd better believe it.'

'I don't believe everything I hear.'

'Oho! So you can speak our tongue, can you?'

'Yours and several others...I know tiger-speak as well.'

'Really?'

Her mocking drawl sounds exactly like the queen's. It makes me want to impress her. Taking a deep breath, I focus on the fifth chakra, Vishuddha, from where sound emerges pure and true. Slowly, the energy called Tiger, takes shape, expands...as I exhale, it begins to vibrate, filling my body with its power, acquiring smoothness till, finally, it emerges from my lips as a steady, low-pitched, menacing growl. Her eyes widen in shock. I am beginning to enjoy the performance. I take another breath, this time to amplify the effect, but simultaneously something happens. A deep answering growl—a real one!—emanates from the dark garden around us. A cold shiver runs along my spine. The maid, too, freezes. Several minutes pass before she puts a finger to her lips and, walking as if on eggshells, leads me away by hand. We cross a courtyard and several passages before she can trust herself to speak normally again. There is only the faintest tremor in her voice. 'So, what did you say in tiger-speak?'

'That I was hungry.'

She sends me a darting look, beady-eyed, like a startled squirrel, and asks, 'When did you last eat?'

'Yesterday.'

She purses her lips. 'The cooks will be asleep, but I can give you some milk. There may even be a handful of puffed rice and a banana or two…will that be enough for now?'

When I have finished my meal, Sulabha—that is her name—takes me through a maze of long, dimly lit passages and then up a steep flight of stairs. Suddenly we are in the open, under the stars. A fat butterball of a moon smiles down at us. Its cool milky radiance floods the terrace and I see that we are not alone. There are many people, all asleep, riddling the quiet with their discordant snores. Sulabha hands me a woven grass mat, a pillow and a sheet, and silently points to an empty space. I make my bed, lie down on it. The mat is surprisingly soft. Like a stone dropping into a well, I sink into slumber.

~

Another dawn, another journey. But this time we travel by bullock cart, Sulabha and I, away from Pratisthan. I am glad to leave. I have been given a new set of clothes, and my hair, after being examined for lice, has been allowed to remain.

The route we take is lined with amaltas trees. Above flies a canopy of yellow blossoms, and below lies a carpet of fallen flowers; together they create a golden tunnel. We turn towards the open countryside and the river. A fisherman on a boat in the middle of the water draws in his net and the silver glitter of the catch, the twist and turn of fish in their death throes, attracts my attention. Storks, back from their early morning dip, dry their wings on the blackened skeleton of a tree struck by lightning. I turn to Sulabha. Her eyes are closed, but I sense she is not asleep.

'Who is Sarmistha?'

After a while she repeats, 'Sarmistha? A woman.'

'Why does the queen hate her?'

She frowns, opens her eyes and stares at me suspiciously. 'How do *you* know that she does?'

We could play this boring game all day, answering a question with another question. 'Is she more beautiful than the queen?'

Sulabha looks away. 'Hmm....'

I spend several minutes trying to decipher her response, before giving up. Sarmistha, the princess who became a maidservant, is a mystery for now. What makes her of great interest to me is that the queen hates her.

~

Hate dances in the queen's heart, but in Sarmistha's house songs scent the air. Exile has liberated her vocal chords. Her voice is rich, deep and smoky. It reminds me of the sky in a thunderstorm. She sings in broad daylight, crooning to the cows in the byre as she milks them, cleans out their stalls and mixes their feed. She serenades the pumpkins growing in her kitchen garden so that they puff up as big as the full moon. She even sings to the ill-tempered rooster who perches on the jackfruit tree overlooking the backyard.

On the day I arrive at her house, she is squatting beside the cistern, cleaning fish, humming softly to herself. Fish scales fly around her in an iridescent swirl, festooning her hair and bare shoulders. Fish blood smears her brow. Sarmistha beheads a mahseer on the curved blade between her feet and, with a casual flick of her hand, tosses the severed head into a shallow earthenware bowl. She notices Sulabha and me, pauses in her task and her song, raises an eyebrow in question.

Sulabha pushes me forward. 'For you,' she says, with a smirk. 'A present from the queen.'

Sarmistha's lips tighten into a thin line. She takes her time looking me over. I hold my breath. Is she going to say yes or no? After a moment she returns silently to the task at hand, slicing the fish. For some reason I am disappointed. Will I be cast out of this place too? What now? Where will they pack me off next?

On a string cot nearby sits a very old man quietly watching us. Sulabha goes to him and, to my surprise, ruffles his shock of white hair and asks in an affectionate, familiar way, as if speaking to a child, 'How are you doing, my Puru?'

He is the oldest man I have ever seen. A shrunken, dried-up heap of bones. Skin webbed with lines so fine that even a touch might crumble it to dust. His eyes, bleached to a dirty pebble-brown, are like the windows of a derelict building. Hollowed cheeks, no teeth. Yet, his pink gummy smile is unexpectedly sweet. 'I have been expecting you,' he says in a slow, croaky voice. I get the feeling that his words are meant for me.

'Meet your half-sister,' Sulabha tells him, nudging me forward.

Sarmistha gives a startled laugh and stops in mid-action. She looks at me with renewed interest. 'You are certainly very direct,' she says to Sulabha.

'She is one of his all right,' Sulabha says. 'Her mother stopped by last evening and dumped her on us. The queen wanted her removed from the palace immediately.'

Sarmistha clicks her tongue. 'That is her way of dealing with anything unpleasant. Devayani has always been short-sighted.' Turning to the old man on the cot she says, 'She doesn't look like much to me, but what do you say? Shall we keep her? I could do with some help around the house.'

Why does everyone talk about me as if I am not there?

'She is my sister.' The old man beckons me with a feeble clawing motion of his hand. When I go to him, he reaches out for mine. His fingers close over it and I feel a gentle pressure. His touch is dry. Something passes from him to me, a tingle of warmth. 'Don't be afraid,' he says, amiably. 'This is your home now.'

I am touched by his defence of me and his kindness, but also astonished. How does he know that I am secretly worried of being cast out of this place too? Who is he? How can someone so ancient be my sibling? Are there any more around, waiting to surprise me? Do I come from a family of freaks? What is going on?

Devayani and Sarmistha. Friends who became bitter enemies. Their stories, I will learn, are two strands in a twisted rope, separate but criss-crossing in places, running in opposite directions. One was born in a brahmin's hut and the other in a royal household. The first ended up in a palace, the other was consigned to a hovel. There is no happy ending to either tale though both are nested in the age-old war between the devas and the asuras.

Tragedies, I will learn, are a long time in the making.

4

Devayani and Sarmistha

Like princesses everywhere, Sarmistha had enjoyed privilege from birth, was called beautiful and basked in the reflected glory of her father, Vrishaparva, the king of the danavas. Her troubles began when her father asked her to entertain Devayani, the daughter of their guru Shukracharya.

'Please, Father! Not that tragedy queen,' said the princess inelegantly.

'Do it for me,' Vrishaparva said. 'Invite her for a picnic by the lake or a trip into the countryside...you were quite friendly with her once.' His smooth, jowly face crinkled with charm.

Unimpressed, Sarmistha shook her head slowly from side to side. 'We were good friends, I agree, but you have no idea how aloof she has become lately.'

'At least invite her for a meal.'

'And what shall be the menu for this meal?' Sarmistha asked, with a saucy grin. 'Not love and fresh air. From the latest reports I have heard she is off *that* diet.'

Vrishaparva stopped smiling. 'Clearly, you know the reason I make this request,' he said with a hint of censure.

Sarmistha, unrepentant, waggled an eyebrow. 'Are

you referring to the great romance between Devayani and Kachh and its sad, bad end? Let me tell you that everybody is talking about nothing else these days...you can't blame us. Nothing exciting ever happens in your kingdom. It is too orderly and well-run!'

'Not for much longer,' Vrishaparva said. 'Now that our enemies, the devas, have got what they wanted.'

Sarmistha looked alarmed. 'But isn't it true that Devayani has put a curse on Kachh? They say he will never be able to use the Mritasanjivani vidya that he stole from her father.'

'There are other ways of getting around that hurdle,' Vrishaparva said. 'She cursed him, he cursed her... she loved him once, now she loathes him.' He sighed tiredly. 'It is not the girl but her father who causes me concern. Shukracharya's well-being is important to us. He is worried about Devayani. Life isn't easy for a single parent, but a father can do little when his daughter has made up her mind to pine her way to an early death because she was jilted.'

'What would you do if that happened to me?'

'Let you cry for as long as you want to and then introduce you to a man who would love you for what you are, and not for what he imagines he can get out of you. Such a man would teach you the true meaning of love.'

'What is that?'

'Letting go.'

'Do you mean stop loving?'

'I mean stop being resentful about it.'

'But love isn't a choice...it takes one by surprise.'

'As does a blunder,' Vrishaparva said acidly. 'Devayani

loved Kachh, but when she understood that he'd never had any intention of marrying her, she should have written him off as a lapse of judgement.'

'Kachh deceived her, Father.'

Vrishaparva dismissed her words with a brusque gesture. 'He claimed that he did not. I am inclined to believe him...when he first arrived here, we suspected that Kachh had been sent by the devas to acquire the Mritasanjivani. However, Shukracharya assured us that the vidya was solely for our use and no one else would benefit from it.' Vrishaparva stopped abruptly. It still upset him to think of how cleverly Kachh had duped the danavas.

~

The danavas, like other asuras—daityas, nagas, dasyus, pisachas, rakshasas—were sworn enemies of the devas, which has led to them being vilified, in all accounts, as demons or 'anti-gods'. However, they didn't see themselves as the villains; rather as an older race, sons of the soil, who had ruled the forests, oceans and mountains when the world was still in its infancy. Today no one remembers Hiranyapur, Pragjyotishpur or Nirmochan, but all three were once magical cities built by the pre-eminent magician architect, the asura Maya. The danavas regarded the devas as usurpers. A war between the two sides had been going on for aeons, with both losing their numbers. Then, Kavya Ushanas, also known as Shukracharya, guru of the danavas—and therefore, a rival of Brihaspati, guru of the devas—went away to perform tapas. After long years of meditation and austerities, he obtained from Mahadev the mantra known as Mritasanjivani, an incantation that resurrected the dead. As the one who could resist death, Shukra became the most important man in the world. He was now invaluable to the danavas. Their dead, raised again, continued to fight the devas, whose numbers kept on falling. Desperate to level the advantage, the devas hatched a plan whose executor was a handsome scholar named Kachh.

When the news had spread that a brahmin had arrived from Devalok seeking an audience with Acharya Shukra, there was immediate unease among the danavas. Vrishaparva was not so presumptuous that he would ask Shukra not to take Kachh as his apprentice, but he hoped that the preceptor would see the risk and turn away the aspirant with a good excuse. However, Shukra, for all his wisdom, was not free from the fault of stereotyping. The erudite but haughty guru, like the rest of his ilk, was perennially in search of the 'ideal pupil'. Kachh's brilliance as a scholar was already known. His impeccable pedigree—he was the son of Brihaspati—had only added to his aura. Shukra was flattered that a personable young man with such fine credentials was asking to be his pupil. There was also the added satisfaction of knowing that he was being magnanimous to the son of his arch-rival. He had admitted Kachh into his household.

The danavas, however, were under no such illusion. They guessed that the chink in the acharya's armour was his daughter Devayani. Getting close to her, they predicted, would be part of Kachh's strategy. Immediately, spies were planted around Shukra's hermitage to watch and report on daily interactions between Kachh and Devayani. It came to be regarded as the dullest of tasks, for Kachh was a priggish fellow who took his celibate state seriously. In the beginning, he paid scant attention to the guru's nubile daughter. As time passed, this indifference changed to a discreet, respectful distance. For a long time, the spies had only trivia to report: *He fetched kindling for homa and durbha grass from the forest; she offered him a tumbler of buttermilk*...some more time passed and the tenor of the reports changed. The spies diligently noted how Devayani watched Kachh when she thought he wasn't looking, and how she found some excuse or the other to be near him, while pretending to be busy. *She saw that he had returned from the grazing ground and quickly rearranged her hair. He bashfully presented her with a few stems of pink lotuses, which she coyly accepted. He held her gaze for a few seconds, a faint smile on his face. She blushed, turned away....*

The frequency of looks exchanged between the couple increased. He set up the ritual of bringing her a small token every day: a bunch of wild flowers, a peacock feather, a polished pebble, a small leaf basket of sweet berries plucked from the thorny bushes in the grazing ground. She would shyly accept; if it was a flower she'd caress its petals slowly, and if it was a peacock feather she would nestle it against her cheek. He let her know he composed poetry, she let him know she loved listening to poetry. Between them the two young people concocted enough reasons to spend many hours in each other's company. The danava spies lurking behind the bower and the byre—where mosquitoes feasted on their blood—yawned from the sheer boredom of this assignment. They joked darkly about putting together a handbook for lovers titled, *How to woo a woman in 60,000 easy steps.*

But all this had happened before the theft. Later

Shukracharya said to Vrishaparva bitterly, 'If your henchmen had not murdered that boy, the theft itself would never have happened.'

Vrishaparva did not disagree with him. The danavas had brought the disaster upon themselves because of their impetuosity. Their view was that the long-winded romantic saga of Kachh and Devayani was not going to reach a finale without some external help. They asked one another: is there a better way to immortalize lovers—or to end a love story—except in a tragedy? They were aware that killing a brahmin was a crime. In fact, it was so heinous an offence that there was no punishment prescribed but death and eternal damnation. Yet, a few young hotheads conspired to murder Kachh. They knew that he took the guru's cows to the grazing ground every afternoon and followed him there. While he struggled to compose a new poem, they did the evil deed. Being thorough professionals, they cut up the corpse into bite-sized pieces which they threw into the forest where hyenas, jackals and vultures gormandized on this unexpected bounty all afternoon. Meanwhile, the cows sauntered back home in a leisurely fashion at sundown, but there was no sign of the cowherd.

The moon—only a quarter that night—peeped out timorously. The crows and parrots roosting in the orchards settled down. Devayani waited a while, anxiety hollowing a pit in her stomach, then set out to look for Kachh. She called his name. Except for the high-pitched cries of sated jackals and the pounding of her own frightened heart, there was absolute silence. She was swamped by a new fear that spread like a dark stain through her being. *Something really bad has happened to him*...a suspicion that had been lying in wait in a dim corner of her awareness now stepped centre stage. *Those damned asuras are behind this.* It occurred to her that, for a while, there had been several mysterious men lurking around the hermitage; a decrepit beggar who showed up for alms, a wood-cutter who had offered to lop off the branches from a jamun tree overhanging the hut, a snake-charmer who had sworn he'd seen a king cobra in the compound. Also, pilgrims, bangle-sellers, wayfarers who, inexplicably, had lost their way. What business did they have so far from the thoroughfare? She had not paid attention to these strangers earlier, as Kachh had become her main preoccupation, but now she wondered whether they had all been part of a diabolical plan to get rid of him. She had gone to Shukracharya and shared her hunch.

'He has never been this late before. This is not a minor calamity, Father. It is something more sinister. It could—it could even be premeditated murder. Coming from Devalok, he was a threat to the asuras. But what did he actually do? He was innocent. My poor Kachh did nothing to deserve this. He has paid with his life for being your pupil...it is your duty to revive him. If you don't, what else am I to conclude but that you, too, are responsible for this crime? Please bring him back! If you don't, then you will have to account for two deaths, because I simply cannot live without him.'

Shaken by her outburst, Shukracharya had stormed into Vrishaparva's palace. He was livid. 'People do not go missing in broad daylight,' he said to the king. 'Don't try to excuse yourself by saying that you were unaware of what was going on. You are the ruler and that makes you accountable...you cannot condone this act. You know very well that killing a brahmin is the worst possible crime. There is no pardon for it. Do you want to incur the sin of brahmahatya? I am a man of dharma. Why did you doubt my word when I said that Kachh would never get the vidya from me? I assured you that I would use it only to raise dead danavas. Your men were overconfident, hence this ill-conceived action. It leaves me with no choice...I came to tell you that I am going to restore Kachh to life.'

Vrishaparva tried to calm him down. He explained that the manner in which Kachh had entrenched himself in Shukra's household had made the danavas nervous. Of course, they relied on their guru implicitly but they did not trust Kachh an inch: he would betray Shukra and his gullible daughter as well. 'Restore him to life if you must,' Vrishaparva said finally. 'But having done that, send him away immediately, Gurudev. It is in everybody's interest.'

Shukra had appeared pacified. He left in a thoughtful mood, and the danava king got the feeling his words had found their mark.

The spies had been celebrating the demise of their foe by getting drunk in a tavern. They were dragged out, ordered to sober up and return to their posts. This is what they reported: *Kachh entered through the wooden gate and went towards the kitchen. Devayani had just finished cleaning the ashes from the hearth, her eyes red from weeping. He cleared his throat. She gave a start. Turning pale, she grabbed a rolling pin and said in a quavering voice, 'Go—go away, preta...' To which the brahmin replied indignantly, 'I am not a ghoul. I am real...kindly put down that weapon, I beg you. There's been enough violence for one day.' She fainted clean away.*

After this incident, Devayani did not let Kachh out of her sight. Having been instrumental in his resurrection, she acted as if she owned him. Kachh's meek submission to her bossiness made the danavas even more nervous. Taking it as a sign of his tenacity, they resolved to finish him off in such a thorough manner that there would be no question of Shukracharya bringing him back to life. They had to wait several months for an opportunity. One day during the rains, Shukracharya sent Kachh deep into the forest to pick some rare herbs found only in the wet months. The assassins, with knives sharpened, were waiting. This time they did not bother with cutting up his body, but carried it to a cave, lit a fire and cremated it. Several hours later a servant from the palace arrived at the hermitage with a silver flagon of wine. 'With compliments from the king,' the retainer said.

Kadamba flower wine was Shukra's sole weakness. He immediately poured himself some. The flavour was more astringent than normal, he noted, it left an interesting tingle on his palate. Before he knew it, he had downed the entire flagon. Outside his window, a full moon came into view. It sailed across the sky like a fragile bamboo raft braving a river in full spate. For some unfathomable reason the sight stirred a strange sense of unease in Shukra. Being a teacher, nomenclature was important to him. Though he was drowsy, he tried to classify the unfamiliar feeling. Melancholy? Not quite—it was darker than that. Bitterness? But he had no reason to feel bitter. Self-reproach? Yes, he thought. That was more like it. A tinge of self-hatred. *Where does it come from*?

Like slowly advancing storm clouds, an array of dark emotions gathered in him: disaffection, disloyalty, deceit.

They were alien to his nature. They roiled inside him and his stomach almost buckled under the upheaval. I've had too much to drink, he thought groggily. I am going to throw up. But just as it had arisen, suddenly, the sourness subsided. He was shaking like a leaf in a thunderstorm, dimly aware that something had changed...the rhythm inside him had altered, become dual, a reverberation. A new heartbeat below his heart. *How is it possible*? I need to sleep it off, he thought, and lay on his mat, falling into a restless, troubled slumber that, after a while, was broken by a high-pitched keening like the plaintive cry of a lapwing.

Fatherfatherfather...oh, wake up. Seeeee...eee...what they have done. Againagainagain...

He sat up in shock. The anguished cries continued. The noise had entered his room. Like a long yowl from a trapped beast, it was emanating from his daughter's mouth. Hair dishevelled, eyes aglitter, face aflame with anger, Devayani stood before him shrieking, 'Bring Kachh back to life. Now!'

He had a strong urge to tell her to shut up. He wanted to say: 'Go join Kachh, wherever he is. I'm fed up with the pair of you. Kachh's motives are dark. Something tells me that he has, all along, played a dirty little game—with your encouragement, ignorant girl!'

But, of course, he didn't say that. Devayani was his daughter, he reminded himself woozily, his flesh and blood. A motherless mite. It wasn't her fault.

'Restore my beloved,' she said, alternately pleading and ordering. 'Bring Kachh back from wherever he is.'

Shukracharya closed his eyes and allowed his inner vision to direct him. *Where are you, Kachh?*

At first he thought it was wind rising within him, a powerful sour burp, but no expulsion occurred. Instead, what he heard was a familiar voice saying, 'I am right here, Father, inside you.' The instant he heard it, Shukracharya's lurking hangover took to its heels. He was stone-cold sober.

Devayani, too, was silently staring at him in shock and confusion. Her lips trembled. 'How...how?'

Shukracharya avoided eye contact. After an age, he muttered sheepishly, 'I...er...imbibed him.'

There was an immediate endorsement from within. 'They cremated me and dissolved my ashes in kadamba wine. You drank it to the last drop, Gurudev.'

Shukracharya sent his daughter a look of helplessness. She, too, was confounded and for once bereft of words, but the question still loomed over them like a hangman's noose. *What are we going to do now?* Several seconds dragged past. Shukra's gaze grew fixed. As the meaning of that glazed expression on her father's face dawned on her, Devayani was horror-struck.

'No!' she said in a strangled cry.

'There is no other way for the vidya to work,' Shukracharya said, with a stoic look on his face. 'I have to destroy my body for him to come back to life.'

She began to shake her head violently from side to side. 'I cannot live without either of you. You cannot die for him, nor can he...*Father, find a way out of this mess!*'

Shukracharya sent her a sad, resigned look and asked, 'Is there any other solution?'

The answer came from inside him. 'This is the solution, Gurudev. Bring me back to life and I will return the favour. I, too, have the Mritasanjivani vidya now.'

Shukracharya had never before heard this ring of confidence in Kachh's voice. *Return the favour!* He was outraged at the youth's audacity. His ears had caught the hidden note of triumph. *So it was the vidya, after all*... but the saner, practical side of him also recognized that Kachh had proposed a viable solution. In fact, it was the only way out.

Devayani looked at her father with shining eyes. 'Oh, isn't that such a clever idea! Why didn't it occur to me? Of course, Kachh has the vidya now. He will revive you, Father. Trust me. Don't worry.'

Shukracharya did not say a word. *It is thanks to your stupidity that we are in this predicament.*

Once again, the entity within him let him know that it was privy to all his thoughts. Kachh's voice, a little louder, a trifle impatient, said, 'Don't you understand, Father? This is war. One does what one must, in love and in war.'

Love. Trust. They were strong, weighty words, but coming from the mouths of these irresponsible young people, how flimsy they seemed to Shukracharya. They had been rendered worthless by another, more sinister word: Betrayal. *Kachh, having used my daughter, will now betray her; my daughter will use me again to save him because she loves him; I will back-stab Vrishaparva by giving away the vidya to the devas, but isn't he to blame, as well? Ashes dissolved in wine—who else but a base, arrogant creature, an asura, would have thought up a plan so depraved? Didn't Vrishaparva realize that by swallowing the ashes I, too, would be culpable of brahmahatya? What can be worse for a brahmin than destroying his dharma, becoming an outcast, damned for all eternity? After all that I have done for him, Vrishaparva has put my reputation at risk...but am I not at fault too? I was aware of the dangers of taking on Kachh,* yet *I couldn't resist the chance to show up Brihaspati...ah, vanity!*

Meanwhile, Devayani's face was wreathed in confusion. 'Why is Kachh calling you Father?' she whispered.

Kachh heard the question and, when Shukra did not respond, took it upon himself to answer it. 'Our relationship is about to change, isn't it, Devayani?'

It took her a moment to understand his words. As their meaning dawned, her face coloured in bashfulness. A small joyous smile trembled on her lips. Turning to Shukracharya, she put her hands together in a silent plea. However, he still balked at the thought of suicide. An inner voice was cautioning him that it would not be wise to rush into things. He needed more time. Suddenly he gasped and doubled up as if he had been kicked in the stomach. Kachh's voice rang out, sharp with panic. 'Please don't delay. Your digestive juices are at work on me even as we speak.'

'Yes, yes, yes,' babbled Devayani, in a panic. 'Hurry up, Father.'

A bleak feeling settled in Shukracharya's heart. *Annihilation...so be it.* 'Leave the room,' he said tersely to Devayani. Shooting him a frightened look, she obeyed without protest. Shukracharya was shaking. He took a deep breath to steady himself and said, 'Realize this, Kachh, I am doing this for Devayani.'

Without missing a beat came the answer. 'Yes, Father.'

'No one can come out alive from my stomach, but a brahmin cannot be killed. Therefore, accept the knowledge

I give you. Return to life as my son. When you emerge from my stomach, with the vidya that you have gained, O son, always act in accordance with dharma.'

~

In the days that followed, a tense silence overhung Shukracharya's household. He went about his daily routine as before, but refused to speak with anyone. It was assumed by all that Kachh would now leave, but only Devayani laboured under the impression that so too would she, that they would go away together. The belief was her buoy through the difficult days, her protection against the sense of shame that gnawed inside whenever she made an overture to her father—only to be rejected.

Shukracharya spoke to Kachh one last time. As was customary for a scholar who'd concluded his studies, Kachh offered him gurudakshina, and that he flatly refused. 'You are freed of all obligations to me,' Shukra said. 'Go with my blessings.'

Kachh bowed his head and stepped back. Then Devayani came forward. 'Bless me too, Father. My destiny is now joined with that of Kachh,' she said.

Ignoring her, Shukracharya looked at his former student with mild curiosity. 'Are you going to make her your wife?'

Kachh shook his head. 'How can I? Rebirth is renewal. All relationships acquire new names.'

Devayani's mouth fell open in shock. 'But you haven't been reborn,' she interjected. 'The vidya revives.'

Not quite meeting her eyes, Kachh said, 'It revived others but *I* was cremated. There can only be rebirth for me. A teacher is like a father, but having emerged from Gurudev's body, he is my mother too.'

'What are you trying to say?'

'What else? I am your brother.'

She drew in her breath sharply and glared at him. 'How can you call yourself my brother when your father's name is Brihaspati?'

Kachh replied very gently. 'Gurudev's imprint is now in me, just as it is in you, sister mine...it would be adharma for me to think of you as anything else.'

Forcing herself to adopt a more patient tone, as one would with a five-year-old, Devayani said, 'Kachh, you came here as my father's disciple, as a brahmachari. However, as you were a foreigner in our land, it was my duty as the hostess in my father's house to see to your comforts. I made a special effort to ensure that you were not homesick by spending time with you. Seeing you daily and spending hours in your company, love sprang naturally in my heart for you. I feel no guilt and neither should you.'

Kachh held up his index finger and shook his head. 'That was then,' he said solemnly. 'Let us talk of now.'

Devayani's voice rose to a shrill pitch. 'You are alive *now* because I begged my father to bring you back to life. I did it because I believed you understood my feelings for you and returned them. You may not have uttered the precise words, but in a thousand gestures, in innumerable glances you did communicate your feelings....' She faltered, unable to catalogue before the two men the signs she had read as proof of Kachh's attraction towards her. Had she got them wrong? Had he misled her? She was no longer sure. She sent him a hard, bitter look. 'Beware, Kachh. Lying is against a brahmin's dharma.'

'Sister, if I have unwittingly hurt your feelings, I

apologize.' Kachh's tone was polite and measured, but there was an undercurrent of toughness in it. 'Don't accuse *me* of transgressing dharma. You may call your feelings towards me love, but when did I utter even one word to make you believe I had anything except respect for you in my heart? Even when you contrived it so that we were alone together, I always kept an arm's length between us, as you have just acknowledged. I resisted your feminine wiles. *My* behaviour has always been in accordance with dharma. I came here to study under a venerable sage. My purpose is accomplished, and now my life's work must begin.'

Devayani was dumbfounded. Her eyes raked his face, searching for that earlier topography whose main feature, the tender goofy look, had made her pulse race. There was not the slightest trace of it. Instead, what she saw was his pity and, worse, an aversion to her. Strange that her father's expression was a mirror image of his. Seeing those similar expressions on the faces of the two men she loved most, something inside her curled up in shame. Her mouth trembled as she called Kachh cruel and accused him of playing with her emotions. He remained calm and unrepentant. Finally, she lost her temper and spat out the words: 'My love, that you reject so offhandedly, is worth more than all the knowledge and power you crave. I curse you, Kachh! May you never use the vidya you have gained through treachery.'

Sending her a withering look, Kachh replied, 'You want me to marry you. The shastras advise that when a woman approaches a man, he should not turn her down. However, I have refused—for the sole reason that, in the light of our new relationship, it would be a sin. The fact that your father, a man whom the whole world respects as the embodiment of dharma, has not made any such demand only strengthens my belief. Consider your own action. You have cursed me not from anger but out of desire. You say I will never be able to use my new-found knowledge, fair enough. But the curse will not stop me from passing on this knowledge to another person who can use it. On the other hand, *your* desire will never be satisfied...you will never find a brahmin ready to marry you, sister. Not after this story gets around.'

As if he was tired of watching them bicker, Shukracharya coldly intervened. 'That is quite enough of melodrama! Be gone, Kachh. I cannot wait to see the last of you. As for you, Daughter, find something useful to do with yourself.'

~

Devayani was quick to realize that she had been exploited. While it gave her grief a sharp twist of rage, she was acutely aware she'd become a laughing stock if she didn't do something to salvage her situation. No half-measures for her, she began a fast unto death. If fate had meant her for the part of a tragic heroine, she would play it to the hilt. The spies had been permanently removed from the scene, but there were still enough witnesses to the daily drama her new role provided. As news got around that Devayani had chosen death by grief, her name acquired a certain morbid glamour. Starving suited her. She lost weight and looked more tall and shapely. Living only on fruit and water cleared her skin. As its fine bone structure emerged—the clean, classic lines of nose and chin, the sharp angles of her cheekbones, the deep-set, dramatic eyes and high forehead—her face became more arresting. A melancholic, faraway look in her eyes added to the mystique. In fact, everyone said she had never appeared more beautiful, almost ethereal. Though her father had little sympathy for her, other men were moved by the air of grief that she gave off. The asuras admired physical beauty in a woman as much as they did fidelity. As for the asuris, they were bilious with envy. They asked each other: what does one need to do—other than go on a berry diet—to get that interesting pallor, those deep resonating sighs that spoke of unbearable anguish, the mournful gaze that answered desertion with constancy, the air of vulnerability that cried out to be protected?

Though he maintained an outward coolness towards his daughter, Shukra was sick with worry. 'She hasn't eaten a normal meal for days,' he confided to Vrishaparva. 'Leaves her hair undone, insists on wearing white, mopes all day in the garden nuzzling her pet deer. What am I going to do with her?'

With these words still ringing in his ears, the danava king had approached his daughter Sarmistha. 'Distract her,' he said. 'Take Devayani on a day-long jaunt. Maybe that will cure her.'

~

Anger hungers. It needs to be fed. Devayani's slow burning fury craved a rich supply of food and drink. The trouble was that, out of sheer cussedness and nothing more, she had taken to brandishing the word 'no', like a cobra's raised hood, every time she was asked, requested or begged to eat something. It gave her temporary power that she defied her father with her refusal to take in even a morsel, but it also left her with a growing emptiness in her mid-region, as if her body, deprived of nutrition from outside had started cannibalizing itself. She was convinced her liver and stomach were slowly liquefying, turning into a gurgling alkaline brew of despair, loneliness, frustration and fury that sloshed around every time she moved. Kept awake all hours by the constant hunger in her belly, she fantasized about driving a spike through Kachh's heart, skinning his body, carving it into small portions and feeding it to the wild dogs, or coating it with honey and tying him down with stakes to the ground where legions of soldier ants would feast on him alive.

Fearing she would do herself harm if left on her own, Shukracharya hired, as temporary help, a village girl named Ghurnika. Her orders were to never let Devayani out of her sight. He also employed a cook, whose job it was to prepare delicacies to tempt her renegade appetite to return. The cook's professional skills were inspired. Devayani's senses were the first casualty, buckling immediately under the assault of the wonderful, mouth-watering aromas that emanated from the kitchen: of rice cooking in cardamom-flavoured milk, gram flour roasting in ghee, lentils being seasoned with cumin and fenugreek seeds. Her hearing developed an extra dimension and hitherto ordinary sounds—the dull thud of a mango falling from the tree, the sizzle of colocasia frying in oil—were amplified. They conjured in her imagination full-fledged feasts. The sight of a roasted sweet potato or even a portion of raw white radish, grated and seasoned with lime juice, sugar and salt, sent her off in a trance. Her tongue became a hotbed of desire. As starvation slowly choked them to death, her taste buds remembered with longing everything they had ever tasted: the gritty sweetness of wheat-flour laddu, the piquancy of lime pickled with spices in mustard oil, the indescribable juiciness of an onion slowly grilled on glowing coals. The remembrances of meals past—ending always, always with a cool, fragrant paan—reduced her to tears of pining. Her whole being ached to seize with both hands the dishes that Ghurnika paraded before her for inspection, even as her tongue repeated with the hollowness of a death knell: No. No. No.

'I suppose you will refuse to taste this lovely dish too,' the maid began to say as a matter of course while offering Devayani a tantalizing glimpse of yet another delicacy. Ghurnika's face would convey, in anticipation, her deep disappointment at the refusal, but it also managed to express admiration and encouragement. If martyrdom was Devayani's avowed goal then she had Ghurnika's full cooperation. The dish would be whisked away—to be polished off later in the kitchen—before Devayani had a chance to change her mind. Her expression would be read as brave, silent devotion to a lost love. 'I would never have your courage,' Ghurnika would say, and return with yet another platter of berries. Thus, when an invitation from the princess arrived, it was expected that Devayani would refuse it as well. But to prevent precisely this from happening, Sarmistha herself appeared at the hermitage.

'Please say yes,' she said to Devayani. 'We are going on a picnic to the forest that belongs to Chitraratha, king of the gandharvas. Father's men are putting up swings on the trees by the lake. The water is perfect for a swim. The menu includes—' She bit her tongue in dismay. No talk of eating and drinking, she had been warned.

Devayani sighed deep and long but keeping to the vocabulary of stoicism, uttered not a word. Sometimes, even to live is an act of courage, her silence said. Sarmistha seemed to appreciate this noble sentiment. Adopting the sombre mien of one who had come on a condolence visit, albeit prematurely, she squeezed Devayani's hand, and murmured with just the right note of regret and farewell, 'I had so hoped you would agree, *dear* Devayani, but if you don't feel like joining us, I will quite understand.'

'You are my only friend,' Devayani said, barely above a whisper. 'I don't want to disappoint you, but....' She gave a shrug of helplessness and trailed off. Her tight-lipped look indicated that her torment was beyond the understanding of someone who had not likewise suffered.

Though secretly amused, Sarmistha said with a show of sincerity, 'But I will be disappointed. In fact, I think I may give up this whole idea of an outing. Without you it will not be complete. If only you would change your mind.'

Devayani lowered her head. A teardrop trembled on a long eyelash. After several moments she said with a soft gulp, 'If you insist.'

~

On the day of the outing rain clouds menaced the sky, and it even rained for a bit. Then a September sun obliged the world with its benign presence. Ghurnika dressed Devayani's hair in a thick fishtail braid that demurely revealed her nape. The slightly mussed up look, achieved by leaving a few long strands loose to frame her face, heightened the aura of sorrow. Devayani was not displeased with the look. She was studying herself in a polished bronze mirror when she heard a slight commotion outside the gate: the jingle of bells mixed with the laughter of young women. A procession of two bullock carts had arrived, accompanied by a mounted guard of soldiers. As soon as Devayani made an appearance, however, the merriment died down. She was in yellow. So was the princess Sarmistha. They were both wearing an identical shade—a light saffron. Devayani looked like a waif, emaciated, fragile yet luminous with the otherworldly beauty appropriate for someone on the road to martyrdom. Sarmistha, on the other hand—dark-skinned, strong and energetic as a heifer—suddenly felt she looked like a gaffe. Something that had so far tenuously bound her with Devayani, perhaps a fellow-feeling or goodwill left over from what their respective fathers shared, was severed in that moment. It was the beginning of a new relationship, more deep, complicated and lasting. For a split second Sarmistha's cheeriness slipped, but only for that briefest instant. She managed to recover and greeted the newcomer with a slightly supercilious, informal waggle of her fingers.

'There's space for both you and your maid in the next cart,' she said imperiously, making it clear to all that the empty place beside her would not be filled by Shukracharya's daughter. Disappointment flitted across Devayani's face, the shadow of a kite-tail over an empty plain, but she complied without a murmur. The women in the second cart looked at one another uncertainly, then moved aside to make place for her. There was an awkward silence as they determinedly looked away, not wanting to be caught staring, but after a while they began to steal looks at her. Finally, one girl could not help herself and addressed Devayani with shy admiration, 'Your hair looks very nice.'

'I dressed it,' Ghurnika piped up, full of self-importance. Without waiting to be asked, she went into the details of the hairstyle. Devayani listened to her prattle with a lofty look on her face. The breeze played with her hair; the bracing air brought a pinkish tinge to her cheeks. She didn't speak a word, but whenever anyone else said something, she cocked her head to listen, and the speaker felt inordinately flattered. Soon jokes were being shared and songs sung. Everyone vied for her attention, which she gave with a goddess-like impartiality.

The short spell of rain had left Chitraratha's sylvan glades with a freshly rinsed, shining look. A flirty breeze danced the leaves on trees and hurried the green ripples of the lake to cover the shore in light kisses. Boats painted in bright colours with white sun umbrellas on board openly invited the picnickers. Sarmistha declared that she would swim first. She was known to be a strong swimmer. Her entourage too shed their clothes and draping them on the lower branches of the trees by the lake, entered the water. The few admirers lingering around Devayani looked at her expectantly. They were torn between staying with her and joining the frolickers in the lake. She stood by the water's edge, on the smooth pebbles, wetting her toes. Ghurnika, ever loyal, said once or twice, with yearning, 'The water looks lovely, doesn't it?' Devayani did not reply. Soon everyone was in the water but for the two of them.

'Join us!' the girls called out.

'Unless you want to stand guard over our clothes,' someone added. There were peals of laughter.

Devayani looked away. The day was not going well for her. She was puzzled by Sarmistha's behaviour, but told herself resignedly that it was just one more way in which the world had let her down. After a moment or two she began to undress and said to Ghurnika, 'You stay here and look after my clothes...I'm going in.'

'Then I'll have to join you,' Ghurnika said virtuously. 'The acharya said I must not let you out of my sight.'

'Do you even know how to swim?'

'Not as well as the princess, but I can manage to keep afloat.'

Someone had introduced the idea of having a race and the girls quickly made two teams. Devayani waited to be invited, but no one called out to her. She swam away from the group towards a small island with a white pavilion. The dissatisfaction brewing in her for days suddenly drained out, leaving her very tired. She had been secretly flattered when Sarmistha had come to see her, had rather hoped to find in the princess the kind of female companionship that might have led to an unburdening of her heart. With this step towards decoding the past she might have made room for a future. The truth was she was more lonely than unhappy. It was the neglected feeling of a single child who had been deprived of intimacy with her own gender. Her mother had passed away when she was seven. Her brothers were considerably older and lived their own lives. Shukracharya, a dry, scholarly man, had not remarried simply because he hated the idea of change. Besides, his personal needs were few and Devayani had been groomed to take care of them. Though he was attached to his daughter, he was unaware of how lonely she was. Devayani's romantic feelings for

Kachh had been born of this isolation. The fact that her father, too, enjoyed his company had fuelled her simple dreams of how her life could turn out to be. She had been brought up to believe that to become a wife and mother was to achieve the highest social standing a woman could hope for. She, the daughter of an illustrious guru, would become the wife of a sensitive, noble and handsome young brahmin who would surely make his mark in the world. She would be the mistress of a household to be run as she pleased, and the matriarch of a flourishing family. As if sensing the scale to which she had enlarged her dreams, Kachh had chosen his parting words to her with a particular cruelty. *On the other hand, your desire will never be satisfied.* The implication had chilled her. No husband, no children, no love.

A large bluish grey cloud had covered the sun. The wind had become more punishing and the water had turned choppy. Whitecaps appeared on the lake's surface. Devayani was suddenly aware of the absence of human sounds. The race was over and the women had returned to the shore. They were changing into their dry clothes. With a pang she realized they had forgotten all about her. She swam back quickly, stepped ashore and, without a word to anyone, searched for her clothes, but they were gone. She looked for Ghurnika but the maid, too, was nowhere to be seen. Noticing a dasi from the palace, a woman with a pockmarked, sullen face, hurrying away, she asked, 'My clothes, have you seen them?'

The woman shook her head, but there seemed to be a look of malicious amusement in her slanted eyes. *Is this another of their childish games?* Devayani chewed her lower lip in consternation. The dasi pointed to a branch on which hanging limply was a lone yellow upper cloth. The lower garment had landed on the forest floor. It was soiled and muddy.

'Those are not my clothes,' Devayani said contemptuously.

The woman gave her a sour look and slipped away.

There was a shout from a grove of ashoka trees. A gust of laughter. Were they mocking her? In the distance, near an arbour, she spotted Sarmistha in pale yellow. Filled with an uncontrollable fury she barged towards her.

'Why did you do it?' Devayani asked heatedly.

'Do what?'

'Don't pretend ignorance.'

Sarmistha rolled her eyes. 'I have no idea what you are talking about.'

'You are wearing my clothes.'

'I'm not—' Sarmistha stopped and looked down. She grew slightly flustered. 'It was a mistake,' she said curtly. 'I didn't see exactly where my clothes had been kept. These looked like they were mine, so I picked them up. You can have them back.'

'You think I'm going to wear them now, Asuri? Don't forget whose daughter I am! How did you have the nerve to touch them?'

'*Nerve?*' Sarmistha echoed incredulously. 'Where do you get the nerve to speak to me like this? Your father sits in my father's sabha, but on a seat lower to his. Your father chants the glories of other men and is given alms in return. I belong to a family that gives, while you—you come from a family that accepts.'

Devayani froze. She stared at Sarmistha levelly for a

long moment. 'You seem to have forgotten your manners, Asuri.'

'So? What do you intend to do about it?'

The smack, a tight, open-handed crack, left a red mark on Sarmistha's face. For a few moments everyone was too stunned to react. Then, as if responding to an invisible signal, the women from the palace fell on Devayani. She was slapped, punched, scratched and thrown to the ground. Hair pulled, clothes torn off—all to the accompaniment of abuses. Even with the clamour, she recognized Ghurnika's voice pleading *Nononono… don't hit her.* The attackers turned on the maid, raining blows on her too. 'Shut up or we'll teach you a lesson as well.'

Unable to defend herself against so many, Devayani curled into a tight ball to avoid the blows. After a while she grew aware of a change. A cessation of noise. Was it over? Had the fierce tide ebbed? The whacks and punches had stopped, or maybe she no longer felt their impact. Either way it was a reprieve. But she was not ready to open her eyes yet. She waited till she was sure something *had* shifted. It was not the absence of blows and the abuses, but the horde itself. Gone. Where? Why? However, instead of a sense of relief, she felt a tight knot in her lower belly, a feeling that the nightmare was about to get worse. Something terrible was about to happen to her. A few minutes later she understood the reason for her disquiet.

One of the women had spotted the well on the other side of the arbour. Someone, no one could say precisely who, issued the clarion call: 'Throw her in.'

~

Thirst had brought the hunter to the well, but what he found inside it was a young woman. It was the kind of heroic rescue that he had fantasized about as a teenager. In those fantasies he had fearlessly performed wondrous feats, but this afternoon, peering into the gloom from where the piteous cries for help came, he was less sure about risking life and limb.

'Who are you?' he called out. 'Where are you from?'

Moron, thought Devayani. Instead of coming to my aid immediately, he wants to first determine my pedigree. Controlling her irritation, she shouted back, 'I am a brahmin kanya.'

'How did you fall in?'

After a few moments of silence, she replied. 'I slipped. There is a young tree growing out from a crack in the wall, I am holding on to a branch...have been in here for hours. I don't know how much longer...please help me!'

The wobble in her voice convinced the hunter of the precariousness of her situation. 'Hold on for a bit longer,' he said. 'Let me think of something.'

'Don't you have a ladder?'

'I came to the forest to hunt, not on a rescue mission.'

'A rope?'

'It's not long enough. Wait....' The hunter had suddenly seen the means of rescue—an old ficus trees with rope-like roots that looked strong enough to support the weight of a full-grown man. 'I have a plan, but it might take me a while to execute it,' he said apologetically.

'I'm going nowhere,' came the doleful reply.

An hour later she emerged from the well, bruised and bleeding from several scratches, in tatters. To him she looked ravishing. His openly appreciative smile made her aware of her state of undress. She turned away uncomfortably. Still smiling, he took off his upper cloth and silently handed it to her. She draped it around herself, feeling its fine texture. It occurred to her that her rescuer was no ordinary hunter. He did not, for instance, seem to be from the forest tribes who trapped birds for a livelihood. He was tall, broad-shouldered and light-eyed. There was an air of breeding about him as well as authority in his stance, the way he held his head, as if he were used to being instantly obeyed. A nobleman obviously. Who could he be?

'It is very late and this is a lonely spot,' he said. 'Your family must be worried about you.'

'My…family?' she repeated, as if the words were foreign to her. 'It is *you* who saved my life.'

'I did what any honourable man would have done in the same situation,' he said. 'Now allow me to escort you home.'

She lowered her head and murmured, 'Of course. You must speak with my father. It is the right and proper thing to do. After what just happened.'

He shot her a puzzled look. 'But what did happen? You were trapped in the well. I pulled you out.'

Her face turned pink. 'You pulled me out by my right hand. I am a kanya…it was the marriage hand.'

'The marriage—' He stopped abruptly. The meaning of her words and the piquancy of the situation dawned on him. A twinkle appeared in his eyes, but he lowered his voice and said solemnly, 'There is no one around to contradict us. We can gloss over these minor details of whether it was the right or left hand.'

Widening her eyes she stared at him. 'But *we* know the truth….'

'What I am trying to say is that, under these unusual circumstances, I am not, er, staking a claim.'

'But—you cannot reject me now! You have an obligation!'

'I have? Beautiful lady, you don't know what you are saying. What I mean is....' The man ran his fingers through his hair distractedly. 'You don't even know my name!' he said, shaking his head in wonder. 'You know nothing about me...I am not a brahmin.'

'Marriage for every woman is a gamble,' she said firmly. 'No one can say how it will turn out. Good intentions are usually all one can hope for in the beginning. And you are an honourable man.'

'You are ready to believe that?' He looked amused. He was used to women offering themselves to him, but a brahmin kanya had never been so bold; for her, marriage to a man who was not a brahmin was unthinkable. 'What is your father's name?' he asked curiously.

'Kavya Ushanas.'

He sent her a startled look. 'Acharya Shukra, who—?'

'...brings dead asuras back to life,' she completed the sentence, and gave a little nod.

'All the more reason for us to forget this nonsense about grasping the marriage hand,' he said robustly. 'My name is Yayati. Shukracharya comes from an illustrious line of rishis. He is far superior to me in his knowledge of dharma. I revere him. Leave alone what the shastras say on the matter, he will never permit this alliance.'

She stuck out her chin slightly. 'No man has ever held my hand except you. I accept you as my lord.'

He shook his head. 'The shastras are clear that such a union would create disorder. Your father will never agree.

Do you have any idea of how destructive a brahmin's wrath can be? No weapon can match the power of his curse. It can ruin whole kingdoms. I do not want to invite this misfortune.' He frowned as another thought came to him. 'I am a kshatriya, a king. What of the sons born of our union? They would be known as half-breeds. How could they rule?'

'As you said, my father is the very soul of dharma. When he himself is going to bless our union, no one will call it unacceptable,' she said. 'Our sons *will* be kings.'

~

'Of course, a match between a brahmin kanya and a kshatriya is less than ideal,' Shukracharya said irritably. He was in a private audience with the danava king. 'But what can I do? Devayani wants it.'

'Personally, I don't care about any of the taboos that your shastras impose,' Vrishaparva said. 'They go against reality and only complicate our lives. In the earlier instance with Kachh...it was but natural that two lonely young people who were thrown together should have developed a fondness for each other. However, you had other constraints and denied your daughter permission to marry him. I would humbly suggest you don't withhold it a second time. Also, it is worth remembering that the young man in question is no ordinary kshatriya, but Yayati, a scion of Aryavarta's most important royal clan. More to the point, he is a king.' Vrishaparva paused, gave the preceptor a sidelong glance, then said, 'I admit, though, that it will be a bit strange for her. With all the dos and don'ts about ritual, purity and pollution that you, in particular, follow so strictly, how does she intend to fit into a royal household with its meat-eating and wine-drinking culture? And what about the children born from this union?'

'You don't have to worry about them,' Shukra said shortly. 'A marriage that *I* solemnize cannot be considered illegitimate.'

Vrishaparva accepted the implied rebuke with equanimity. 'Quite right. As long as they have your blessing, it will work out fine,' he said. 'I have heard that Yayati is a likeable young man. It must be love, Rishivar.' He was openly smiling.

Shukra gave a derisive snort but said nothing. His mind was more on what the effect of his next words to the danava king would be. Taking a deep breath, he began, 'There is something else that Devayani wants....'

Vrishaparva looked at him with a slight frown. 'What?'

'Your daughter, as her maid.'

'Acharya!' The king was not a man to be easily rattled, but now he turned pale.

'I know, I know.' Shukra cut him short testily. 'Listen, my friend. You and I get along well because we did not allow differences such as status, power and wealth to come in the way of our relationship, but women...they don't have the same clear-headed thinking as us.'

'We did not allow it to come in the way till now,' Vrishaparva said heatedly. 'But that has changed, hasn't it? Why else would you bring this ridiculous demand of Devayani's to me? You are putting a petty quarrel between two immature girls above our relationship.'

Shukracharya's eyes turned flinty. 'What the princess said and what her maids did was unforgivable. My daughter could have died.'

Vrishaparva lowered his head. 'I have already taken Sarmistha to task for her mistake. Her mother, too, gave her a mouthful. She has expressed remorse. She will apologize to Devayani. Furthermore, I am ready to make reparation in whatever way I can, but this punishment is too severe. Be a little merciful, Acharya.'

'It is too late for that. Devayani is adamant.'

'You are her preceptor as well as her father. You could remind her that forgiveness is a virtue.'

Shukracharya looked embarrassed. 'I tried…"Shed your anger," I said to her. "Nurturing it will only bring you grief. Don't take the cruel words of the princess to heart." But she was not convinced. She, too, has her self-respect. Your daughter's words have wounded her more than the blows. She reminded me that it was my duty, as a preceptor, to chastise a disciple who behaves disrespectfully. Power has gone to your head, O king. It has brought out the worst in you danavas. You have become arrogant and short-sighted. Because I bring back your dead soldiers to life, murder means nothing to you. Understand this: sinful acts do not yield fruit immediately, it takes generations. Like rich food that takes a long time to be digested, they reveal their consequences much later. First Kachh and now Devayani. It has gone too far! You forget that I, too, have been insulted by your daughter. For a lesser misdeed than hers, men more powerful than you have been destroyed by a brahmin like me…I am forgiving and generous because I still think of you as my friend.'

Vrishaparva sent him a bitter look. 'Don't call it friendship, Rishivar. You came here today to settle a score.'

Shukra remained silent.

'And if I refuse to give in to your daughter's demand?' asked Vrishaparva.

'Then I must, with regret, leave your kingdom for good.'

Vrishaparva smiled mirthlessly. 'You have just demonstrated that you are only thinking as a father and not as our guru. We have been associates for a long time, but clearly that means nothing to you. It is not a demand you have stated, but a precondition. Pardon me for saying this, Rishivar, it is outright blackmail. I, too, am a father but I am first and foremost a king. Your departure will mean obliteration for my people. We will go back into the depths of the ocean.' He spread his hands in helplessness.

'I don't care whether you go back into the ocean or fly across the skies,' Shukra said. 'My daughter is dear to me. And you danavas have seriously wronged her—twice. What Brihaspati is to Indra, I have been to you, Vrishaparva...my prayers, my penances, my purity have been harnessed solely by you. You danavas would have been wiped out if it were not for me.'

Vrishaparva brought his palms together in a plea. 'I acknowledge it, Gurudev. My kingdom, its people and its wealth are at your feet.'

'Then give Devayani what she wants.'

'This is unfair, Acharya.'

'In Devayani's eyes it is justice.'

~

It was not the usual grand public wedding that monarchs have but a simple, spare and quick private ceremony. Yayati was in a hurry to get back to Pratisthan. He was aware that he would have to answer for this new development to his kinsmen and the queen mother, but he reckoned that presenting it to everyone as a fait accompli was his best course. His mother would take it the hardest. He could already picture her expression: a frozen look of disapproval. She would most likely give him the silent treatment for a few days and follow that by citing chapter and verse the scriptures he had disobeyed. It would not occur to her to ask him for his side of things, but he would tell her anyway. He would emphasize that he was now related by marriage to the most powerful man in all three worlds, the keeper of the Mritasanjivani. It was something he could hardly believe...he had never met a man whose austere look so completely belied his authority.

In a private chat with his new son-in-law, Shukracharya had said, 'I have bestowed my daughter on you knowing that you will do your best to keep her happy.' The words were spoken in a mild, dry tone, but Yayati's ears detected the quiet force of a decree. 'I sincerely hope that you, too, will learn to be happy with her. She is a bit headstrong, but if you can win her love, you will never find a more loyal partner. Children, family, companionship...life in all its plenitude. Give her this, but above all, let her feel the security of your affection. I understand that you are a king and women throw themselves at you. You may take concubines, even other wives, but never let Devayani feel that her rights as your chief queen are threatened. She must retain her position as your sole official consort. In time, her firstborn son must become your heir.' Shukracharya had fallen silent as if weighing his next words. 'You may have heard that Vrishaparva's daughter is now her dasi for life. Unfortunate, but that is how it is.' He shrugged to convey his regret, then directing a sharp look at Yayati he added, 'Whatever happens, you must not take the danava princess to your bed. Indeed, it would be best for everyone if she and Devayani were kept as far apart as possible.'

~

Bridal leave-taking usually has a poignancy to it, but this one was different. No musical instrument was tuned, no songs sung nor goodbyes said. The hour of departure had been kept secret, but word somehow got around and the danava population turned out in full strength. They had come not only to wish the bride an auspicious start, but also to mourn the ignominious departure of their princess. Nobody knew precisely which one of the covered wagons leaving through the city gates bore Sarmistha, and the passage of each one was accompanied by loud lamentation. Hearing them, Sarmistha wept silently. As for Devayani, she remained stone-faced.

This is where I bid you farewell, Kachh. In this grove where we walked every day. By this lake where you picked pink lotus buds for me. In this abandoned shrine where, one full-moon night, you sang to me a song you'd written about the chakor bird's yearning for the moon. A terrible composition and I don't remember a word of it, but that clean, pure love shining in your eyes...how can I forget that? Did I stumble into love or did I simply fall deeper? Here, and here, and here too, in these fields and forests, I looked for you. To the winds and the sky, to the far corners of the world, I went everywhere in search of you, calling out your name, because I thought you were lost to me…and when I got you back, alive…the relief! What was it if not love? All I know is that what I felt for you was beautiful, it should not make me hang my head in shame, it should not make my eyes burn. But it does all that…you have broken my heart. And now, look at all these pieces I have gathered of my broken self. Each one carries your name…goodbye, Kachh. Here is where I leave you. I am free of you, free of any desire to possess another again. Free of this sickness called Love. A hate word really.

~

It turned out to be a fruitful marriage. A son was born to the queen within a year. Eighteen months later, another arrived. Pratisthan rejoiced in the birth of the next generation of rulers. The royal astrologer drew up the natal chart for the elder boy, Yadu. He studied it with a frown that turned before long into a look of chagrin and worry. What was he going to tell the king? Fortunately, Yayati was only interested in the broad forecast about the babe's future—he will be a great king, he will have a long life, he will bring new lands under cultivation, increase the cattle herds—and declared himself satisfied. The queen mother, however, was more probing.

'New lands cannot be acquired without a fight,' she said. 'Does that mean we are about to enter an age of strife?'

'Let us say there will be unsettled times,' said the astrologer, hedging.

'Adharma, the learned brahmins tell us, leads to unsettled times,' said the queen mother sombrely. 'The rituals are not performed or, which is perhaps worse, not performed in the right manner. The wicked and ruthless thrive. If the king does not set the limits, then the strong would wipe out the weak. It is only fear of punishment that prevents them from doing so. The king alone has the power to punish. To establish dharma, to protect the innocent and the weak, he must use that power wisely. Will the boy be of a steady mind?'

'Rest assured on that count,' the astrologer said. 'His chart is strong. He will live a long life. He will be a man of discernment, a path-breaker, a leader.' Aware that she was still seeking reassurance from him, the astrologer said with more confidence than he actually felt, 'He may establish a new capital.'

The look of tension on the queen mother's face remained. She said, 'These Chandravanshis have always been unpredictable. Who would have imagined that Yati—such a quiet, level-headed boy—would do what he did? I accept that his father's fate came as a shock to him, as it did to all of us, but isn't Maharaja Nahusha bearing the consequences of his action? Instead of drawing the lesson about the importance of self-control, Yati overreacted, rejected the throne altogether and chose the path of a wanderer. That, in my opinion, was very unwise...Yayati, his younger brother, who had no training for the role, had no choice but to fill his shoes. Since then I have been plagued by this fear that some kind of equilibrium was disturbed and—' She broke off and asked plaintively, 'When dharma is there to sustain us, why cannot these men behave in accordance with it?'

'All men are not born equal and hence cannot have the same temperament,' the royal astrologer said. 'It is why we have dharma to guide us. However, it sets a stringent boundary, especially for a king. The tussle is unfair. On the one side, there is one's inborn nature, the baser instincts that are whetted by the absolute power that comes with kingship. On the other, a ruler has duties and obligations and that calls for self-restraint. He, above all, must always maintain equipoise. He must think of the consequences because he is responsible for everyone.'

'One's inborn nature is the source of one's desires,' the queen mother said. 'Men have the luxury of indulging their instincts, and they, too, decide what is and is not dharma, so why cannot they resolve the conflict?'

The astrologer gave a dry smile and said, 'To discover the answer to that I would have to give up this profession and become a truth-seeker.'

~

Devayani's fervent wish was to rearrange her life, put it back in order and within her control. She threw herself into the role of a queen with so much passion and diligence that even the queen mother was impressed at first. The running of the palace had over the years become slapdash. Dust under the furniture, leaks in the roof, cobwebbed corners, ceilings blackened by smoke. The servants were laid-back. Besides gossiping and shirking work, they frequently stole. The household accounts were a horrible mess. Like the proverbial new broom, the new queen swept away the past and seeded a new order. She made a fetish of cleanliness and scrutinized the dasis for dirt-free nails and clean hair. She would descend for surprise inspections in the kitchens, the cowsheds, the palace granary—there was no saying where she'd turn up next, poking her nose, asking uncomfortable questions, issuing orders, stirring up things. It shook the palace up, but it also led to change. The floor was polished, the gardens were weeded, old, heavy, worm-eaten fixtures were removed and replaced with new pieces of furniture. The kitchens were extended to include a separate, pure vegetarian section, and snooty-looking brahmin cooks were inducted. A rigorous training programme for palace servants was introduced. The queen mother watched it all with mixed feelings.

'That cot you ordered to be chopped up as firewood belonged to my grandfather-in-law,' she said. 'It was a part of this family's heritage.'

'It was also a nest of termites,' said Devayani.

'I understand that you've had a very different upbringing, Daughter-in-law, but now that you are one of us, shouldn't you show some respect for our tradition too?'

'Not when it occupies disproportionate space.'

The queen mother sent her a baffled look. 'But this is our world! Tradition links us to our ancestors. It tells us who we are and how we should live.'

'I am not destroying the link, merely rearranging it... or don't I have the right to do even that?'

The queen mother retreated into a wounded silence. She was in her 'austere' phase. Her head was tonsured, she was about to set off on a pilgrimage. Engaging in something as indecorous as a power game with her domineering and sharp-tongued daughter-in-law did not appeal to her present mood.

With the births of the princes, Devayani's tempestuous nature was somewhat bridled, and her softer side emerged. She was a concerned if not an overly loving mother, as well as a firm one. Etiquette was important to her. She was forever admonishing the boys—*Speak a bit slower, Turvasu, and remember not to repeat yourself.* Though she was outwardly impartial in her affection, Yadu, the eldest, was her secret pride. He was a reserved, self-possessed child, whose prim and proper nature reminded her of Shukracharya. Even Yayati, whose love for his sons usually took the form of horseplay with them, was somewhat daunted by his elder son's grave demeanour.

Passion, which many believe essential to a happy marriage, had fled permanently from Devayani's life. It had been replaced by an asset more important to the day-to-day running of a domestic set-up: reason. Thus, as marriages go, Devayani's union with Yayati bore all the hallmarks of success. Its defining feature was stability. The running of the kingdom was, to Devayani, an extension of the management of her household. She took her place in the sabha, where she was the king's eyes and ears and, according to some people, his brains as well. When one expects high standards, one gets them. Devayani demanded. Consequently, exemplary order reigned in most aspects of her life. This was the closest she would be to her ideal of marital happiness.

~

Late one evening, Yayati was returning from a hunt. Passing by a grove of ashoka trees, he turned into it. It was one of his favourite spots. Among the tall trees, the light was a muted green shot with gold, tremulous and ethereal. In such a setting it seemed entirely natural to him that she was waiting, as if for forever, a yakshi, an otherworldly being, whose shapely figure, soft full lips and large kohl-rimmed eyes seemed inspired by a dream. Her dark hair was pinned up, exposing the long column of her neck and her strong shoulders. She watched him approach. Stillness in her posture, but on her face a coquettish smile and a resolve, an inner strength that she did nothing to conceal. She was the huntress and he the hunted. When he was close enough she brought her palms together in a greeting, bowed her head and addressed him in a low, intimate voice. 'Though you don't know me, O king, I am your servant. I have not lived in your inner apartments, but I have, on the queen's orders, lived in a seclusion even deeper.'

His face became grave. He dipped his head slightly, as if acknowledging with regret the truth of her remark—that she was living as an outcast. 'Is there anything I can do for you, O princess?' he asked gently.

She raised her eyes to meet his. The look in them was sad yet sensual. 'Don't mock me, Yayati...I am no longer a king's daughter. Neither am I a wife and mother. You are aware that I am of noble birth and can only wed a man of equal status.'

He nodded, waiting for her to go on.

'I want you to make me a mother.'

He did not look at her directly, but focused his gaze on her curly hair, black as a monsoon sky. There was a creamy yellow magnolia tucked behind her ear. It gave off a sweet, heady scent. 'You come from an ancient and proud race,' he said in a courteous tone. 'You are beautiful...I would dearly love to make you my queen. In fact, an ancestor of mine, Ayu, married a danava princess. But I am not free to do so. I gave Shukracharya my word that I would stay away from one woman—you.'

A smile, resigned but also mocking, curved her lips. 'I know. It is the reason why I have approached you... Devayani insisted you marry her because no brahmin was prepared to do so.' An acid note entered her voice. 'Her father, who is otherwise a stickler for convention, quickly gave his blessings so your fear that the union would be sinful was allayed. He also imposed this ridiculous condition on you. He is a powerful man, but so are you.'

'I must bow to his superior knowledge,' Yayati's voice trailed off.

'You have been educated in the dharma shastra too,' she said with more spirit. 'No one questions that integrity is a measure of a righteous man, but it's not necessarily a lie if one doesn't own up to the truth. Only a fool practises truth without knowing the difference between truth and falsehood. The wise understand that there are nuances between the two. It has been said that lying is excusable—even necessary—on five occasions: when one is playing a joke, when one is in a relationship with a woman, when marriage negotiations are on, when one's own life is in danger and when one is about to lose one's wealth.'

'I like your frankness,' said Yayati. 'All the situations you mention are for ordinary men. I am a king, my behaviour has to be exemplary. Others may lie, I dare not.' He fell silent, but it was a troubled silence. Seeing that he was incapable of breaking it, she laid a hand on his arm. He still did not look at her directly, but was acutely conscious of her gaze trained on him, imploring but also inviting. He felt like a horse that had stepped into a quagmire, struggling to be free, yet every movement only pulling him in deeper.

Sensing that he was weakening, she said, 'My lord, Devayani serves you. As her dasi, I serve you too. I am yours as much as she is. You have every right to enjoy me. She chose you as her husband. I am, by extension, your wife too. As such, I am within my rights to ask this of you. Do not be anxious. Nothing will change, I promise. If you fulfil my wish of becoming a mother, my virtue will remain protected, as other men will not bother me with unwanted attention. I request you, O king, absolve me of sin.'

Having said this, she did not wait for his reply, but came even closer. He felt the magnetic pull of her womanhood. It was in her eyes, the full lips, the abundance of curves, the subtle, warm scent she gave off. She seemed to fill in a shape of his self that he hadn't known till now as incomplete. She is taboo, his brain warned, but his senses were inflamed. Desire blazed in him. He was torn between beating a retreat and drawing her close. In no such dilemma herself, she rested her head on his chest as if it was the most natural action in the world. He sensed the depths of despair and the loneliness in her. He was deeply moved. Of their own volition, his arms encircled her and drew her into their shelter. Nothing existed outside their embrace.

~

Armed with gifts for the newborn, but without warning, Devayani arrived at Sarmistha's doorstep. She swept aside the flustered words of greeting and, with barely a glance at the humble surroundings, made straight for the cradle where the infant lay swaddled in a covering made from old used cotton cloth. It was frayed in places, but very soft to touch. She gazed a long time at the babe's peaceful sleeping face, the set look on her own dissolving involuntarily into one that was almost benign.

'So you, too, are a mother now!' she said, with a frosty smile at Sarmistha. 'A beautiful baby, but tell me who is the father?'

Realizing that the suddenness of the question was meant to catch her off guard, Sarmistha, despite her pounding heart, remained collected. 'A brahmin rishi,' she said.

'His name?'

'I did not find out.'

'Oh?' Devayani arched an eyebrow. After a while, she asked in a deceptively gentle voice, 'Did he force himself on you?'

'No.'

'So...it was consensual.'

Sarmistha shot her an unreadable look but remained silent.

'If the infant's colour and features are any indication, his father is from an aristocratic lineage,' said Devayani.

'The noble rishi had the resplendence of the sun. To question him about his family tree—when he was blessing me with a child—would have been presumptuous.'

Devayani considered this. For some reason the reply quelled the senseless anxiety that had risen in her when she first heard of Sarmistha's pregnancy. A playful, amused smile appeared on her face. 'Yes, that would not have been seemly,' she said.

Sarmistha caught the half-smile and responded spontaneously with one of her own. It was a strangely complicit exchange, reminiscent of their younger days, when competition, though present, had lain low. The exchange of smiles did not dispel the hostility, but it did serve to remind them that they were compatriots in a land that was, despite their years of stay in it, still foreign to them.

Eyeing Sarmistha critically, Devayani said, 'Motherhood suits you. You look radiant.'

Sarmistha merely dipped her head in response. 'May I offer you some buttermilk?' she asked in a friendly tone.

Devayani accepted. She glanced around the hut, taking in the earthen floor and walls, the scant furniture and the simple cooking pots of clay. *I reduced her to this*...despite herself, she was moved to pity. How far a cry this was from the danava princess's earlier life. 'It must be lonely here,' she said, after a while. 'Would you like to live in the palace? The child will have company.'

Sarmistha shook her head. 'I am accustomed to living here now.'

Devayani tilted her chin upwards. 'I could order you to move.'

'Yes, you could.'

The quiet resignation of that 'yes' deepened Devayani's sense of guilt. 'I leave it to you,' she said in a brittle voice. 'If he is, as you say, the son of a highborn rishi, the boy should be properly educated...let me know when the time comes.' She got up to leave.

Sarmistha stood outside, watching the queen's chariot roll away till it was no longer in sight. She went back into the hut and examined the gifts: a shawl, baby clothes, a rattle and some other toys. She fingered the soft woollen shawl and draped it on her shoulder. The baby woke up and started to cry. She lifted him and held him close to her bare breast, covering his head with the shawl as his mouth began to tug at her nipple. Looking down at his rapt face, her features softened, a film of tears covered her eyes and she began to croon softly lullabies from her own infancy.

~

It was soon after this meeting that the nightmare began to haunt Devayani. Darkness, an unbearable weight on her chest, a pressure on her eyelids, a creeping numbness. A loss of will, energy, love, memory, her very soul. Everything she had lost and would lose in the future pressed her down. Her face slowly turning into a carved mask. There was no freedom to be anything else…night after night, the heft of her days and the secret life that sluggishly flowed below them slowly stifled her. Her tortured cries rang out, jerking her upwards from her pillow. In those pain-wracked moments, she asked herself this question: *Will I never heal?* And the answer always came in the form of another question. How can I heal when the most vital part of me is lifeless? When I feel nothing…there *is* nothing except for the slow march of Time to tell me that I still exist. Devayani is a preta, a wandering soul, doomed never to complete its journey.

Daylight, however, did bring reparation if not repair. *She* was the queen. It was not necessary to be loved, only to be honoured and implicitly obeyed.

~

Wanting what is forbidden can become an obsession. Sarmistha, abandoned by her father to a lifetime of slavery, had craved the respectability of motherhood, while Yayati had wanted her. Their passions fed on each other. The more careful they had to be, the more they were drawn to each other, and the more intense was their pleasure. After a while neither foresaw an end to the relationship. Love's truth is rooted in its indestructibility. Discretion was the key to its longevity. *As long as we are careful, we can go on.* Thus, theirs became a commitment deeper than either had originally envisaged, a shadow union more rich in its intimacy than its overt twin. However, as the relationship, predicated on secrecy, ripened, so did their secret, till one day, fully grown and saturated with its own juices that were perhaps about to sour, it exploded in an ugly, sorry mess.

The day had started innocuously, with the king and queen setting off on a chariot ride to the countryside. It was that time in late spring just before harvest, when Nature had transformed the earth into the multihued richness of brocade. Ears of wheat ripened in the fields, and the first lime-green blossoms had appeared on mango trees. The koel sang sweetly to announce the arrival of summer. Devayani, too, knew a certain contentment. Her elder son had returned from the gurukul after completing his years of study. Yayati had announced that Yadu was to be made yuvaraj. The ceremony to declare him as the successor would be held in a few days. Shukracharya had confirmed that he would preside over it; he was expected to arrive any day. From all over Aryavarta, noble families with marriageable daughters had begun to send feelers. The royal astrologer was busy studying the horoscopes of princesses.

'It is a good time for Yadu to be married,' Yayati said. 'There is peace on our borders, and with this new harvest, the third good one in a row, prosperity too is assured for some time.' After a moment's reflection he added, 'Yadu is the marrying kind.'

'What do you mean?' Devayani asked curiously.

'Only that he will make a good king.'

'Well, the queen mother would certainly like to see him married,' said Devayani. 'She consults the astrologer all the time. It's as if she were anxious about the future.'

Yayati sent her a sidelong look. 'Aren't you?'

Devayani hesitated, then shook her head. 'Just as you see no threat to your kingdom, I see none to mine.'

'I am glad to hear that,' Yayati said calmly. 'But why the pause? Are you unhappy about something?'

'I was very unhappy once.' Devayani faltered. Intimacies had never come easily to her. With the passage of time she had become better at simulation. Forcing a smile, she said, 'Why talk of the past? Let us look towards the future...I, for one, cannot wait to see Father!'

At the mention of Shukracharya, Yayati's heart began to beat faster. To hide his nervousness, he said casually, 'Do you think that Acharya will stay long? I mean, it would be a blessing for the kingdom to have such an eminent seer honour us.'

'It would be good for me too,' said Devayani. 'I know he is well cared for and probably does not miss me, but I still worry about him.' She shook her head. 'He will not stay long. I know that too.'

'Unfortunately, I will be rather busy during his visit,' Yayati said, hiding his relief. 'But I will try my utmost to spend some time with him.'

Devayani glanced around. 'How far we've come,' she said. A note of dissatisfaction entered her voice. 'We should return. There is much to do in the palace. The provisions for the rituals have to be weighed out. We must arrange for more ghee and milk. With so many priests participating in the fire sacrifice, I have a feeling we may run short.'

'Mix a little water in the milk,' Yayati joked.

She frowned at this flippancy. Yayati meekly turned the chariot around. She is a good wife, he told himself. A good queen, conscientious, thrifty and just. Her children are well brought up. I should be grateful to have a consort like her. But then I, too, have tried my best...marriage is a sacrament that binds us for life, but it kills desire.

At one time he had felt something for Devayani, a youthful ardour in response to her physical beauty, to which she had responded spontaneously, in the way of young flesh. However, that fire had all too quickly burned out and had become conjugal duty. He was a sensual man, an experienced and ardent lover. Though nothing had changed outwardly, he had intuited that she did not look forward to his visits to her bedchamber. His touch was unwelcome. But, he wondered, without touch how was pleasure possible? It was his view that mutual arousal had to precede gratification. One's existence may be temporary, but one's pleasure was real. It was rooted in the body. Sexual desire was just as essential to the proper maintenance of the body as was a healthy appetite for food. He had discreetly found his pleasure elsewhere. They had never spoken about it, but the gaps between the nocturnal visits to her bedchamber had increased and neither could remember when the visits had completely stopped. She had turned a blind eye to his dalliances. On his part, he had understood that she must never feel as if she were the object of ridicule.

It was not unusual on these drives into the countryside for Yayati's people to approach him directly with their problems. He encouraged these interactions. In contrast to the formal, long-drawn sessions in the sabha, the impromptu meetings were informal, even friendly; disputes were usually resolved in an amicable manner. When a group of villagers approached him with folded hands to request his intervention in a matter about taxes, he stopped the chariot and stepped off to meet them.

After a while, bored of waiting for him to return, Devayani too got off and walked to the ghat on the river. She sat down on the lowermost step and dangled her feet in the icy water. Boys from the village were playing a ball game close by. They ignored her and went on with their play. Some time later, she noticed that she wasn't alone on the steps. A shadow appeared above her. A boy of about eight or nine, small, thin and gangly, with bushy dark hair, a narrow face. Framed by long curling lashes, his large brown eyes had in them the sparkle of intelligence. He shot her a shy smile and turned his attention to the river. She wondered who he was. There was something about him, a sensitivity that struck her as different from other children.

'Don't you like playing ball with the others?' she asked.

'I got out early from the game,' he said placidly. 'It is nicer to sit by the river.'

'I agree.'

In the upper reaches of the Himalayas, from where the river emerged, the ice had started to melt. The water was a deep green, flecked with foam where the swift current was tripped by underlying boulders. Like the new buds on the amaltas trees along the bank, the river too celebrated the rebirth of the season with replenished energy. In an explosion of colour, a kingfisher flew down to a white marble rock on the edge of the water. Its plumage shone in the sunlight as if it had just received a fresh coat of paint. Like the woman and the boy on the ghat steps, perhaps the bird, too, was a seeker of solitude. Watching it, a rare kind of tranquillity entered Devayani's soul. What was this strange dance called life? Who was its choreographer? Whose palette had picked those perfect shades for the bird...the dazzling blue, the fiery yellow? From whose imagination had her destiny emerged? She had believed that she could bleach the past and repaint her life in new shades. But no matter what she did, the past percolated down her bloodstream, tainting her present. Why was she never entirely happy? What was it that she lacked? Was it her father's impending visit that was raising the spectres of the past with these sombre thoughts? Why did she imagine that the river, this water in which one day her ashes too would be immersed, was singing a dirge? Whose end was it mourning?

With a high-pitched squeaking cry, the kingfisher took off, flying low over the water towards a tree. Her reverie broken, Devayani stood up to leave. Climbing the steps, she paused on the one above occupied by the boy. He stood up as well.

Studying his face she asked, 'Are you from the village?'

He shook his head silently.

'Then?'

No reply.

'Who is your father?'

The boy turned around and pointed to the circle of men in the distance.

Devayani looked in the direction and knitted her brow. 'His name?'

The boy flinched at her harsh tone, but remained silent.

She realized that she had spoken a little too sharply. 'Don't be afraid,' she said, forcing a smile. 'All right, tell me what is *your* name?'

'Puru.'

'Puru…son of—?'

'Sarmistha,' he said.

A silence. Then Devayani said evenly, 'I know your mother quite well.'

He looked up with a flicker of interest. 'Really?'

'Yes, Puru, I do know her. I came to see you when you were just born. It was a long time ago.' She paused as if trying to remember, then shook her head. 'No, it was not you, you are too young. It must have been your elder brother. Do you have one?'

Squinting his eyes against the sun, he said, 'I have two.'

'And what are their names?'

'Anu, Druhyu.'

'Nice names. Who chose them?'

'Father, who else?'

'So, you are Puru,' she prompted. 'Son of—'

'Yayati,' the boy filled in.

There was a longer silence this time. The child wondered whether his reply had displeased the lady. Why had her face sealed up? Without another word she turned away, climbed the steps and walked briskly towards the chariot waiting under the tree on the road to Pratisthan.

5

Yayati and Shukracharya

The tongue is a source of delight. After the feast, the road from Pratisthan was crowded with sated brahmins. Like a romance that had ended, they relived its flavours by talking about the food. 'I had two helpings of everything,' said one. 'All twenty-one dishes.'

'Twenty-one? Were there really that many?' The fellow who said this had thin, bloodless lips and a long nose. Its function, besides breathing and smelling, seemed to include speaking as well. 'There could have been an additional sweet in the menu, don't you think?'

'You are, as usual, nit-picking, Agastya,' retorted the first brahmin. 'There was payesh, and two types of laddu, one made entirely of dry fruits.'

Agastya sniffed. 'Yes, but did you see the size of it? My father used to praise sky-high the king-sized laddus that were served at feasts when Yayati's father Nahusha was on the throne...it seems with every generation the laddu shrinks.'

'It could also be, that in *your* family, with every generation the stomach enlarges.'

This remark was greeted with a shout of laughter from everyone. When it had died down, Agastya said,

'What I would like to know is why Acharya Shukra ate so sparingly? Was the food from his daughter's kitchen not to his taste?'

'I noticed it too,' said one of his companions. 'It could be the result of one of those long penances that great rishis like him perform from time to time. Sure to give one acidity. That would explain the sour look on his face.'

An older brahmin commented, 'He is by nature an austere man. Very clever, but with no social skills whatsoever.' While talking he glanced at the sky and, noting that it had darkened considerably, said in a chivvying tone. 'Talk less, walk faster...we are still a long way from the ashram. There is a storm brewing.'

As if to lend weight to his warning, a vein of lightning throbbed across the heavens, followed by deafening thunder.

In the palace at Pratisthan, a different storm was breaking, but with less fuss. Yayati had made a half-hearted attempt, motivated more by social correctness than any real warmth, to invite Shukra to stay longer. The sage had refused. He did not like being away from his hermitage, he said. He would leave right after the ceremonies were over.

Not a minute too soon, thought Yayati. He had been riven with anxiety all through the rishi's stay. The memory of what had happened to Nahusha was still alive among the Ailas, and everyone was terrified of displeasing the brahmin guest who said little and maintained a dour expression. The tension in the palace had been palpable. In all the flurry, it went almost unnoticed that Devayani was acting strangely, there was a kind of passivity in her. One person who did notice the change was the queen mother. She attributed it to Shukra's arrival. *Finally, there is someone she is afraid of.* This made her think well of the rishi. The dasis were merely thankful that the queen did not berate them for the minor mistakes they made.

Devayani's attention was divided. What was going on inside her head had no connection with what was outside. She did not know which world was real and which false. She examined her memories, tasted again the bitter and sweet feelings they evoked. The emotions had not changed, yet the flavour of betrayal was the one that was now the strongest. Betrayed by the same man she had served dutifully...it left her stunned. Her tongue gave orders and responded with the right words when an answer was sought from her; her limbs, too, moved as if automated. But all her vitality, she felt, had been used up. It was as if she was trying to swim in a sea of oil: too much effort. *What is the point of it? How did I become who I am today? Where did I go wrong? Was it the choices I made? Didn't I try hard enough, every time, to make them work?* However, as she watched Yadu going through the ritual bath of herbal oil, turmeric water, sandalwood paste, curds, milk and honey, as the chants of the priests vibrated in the air, as the ghee was poured into the fire and the smoke rose to the heavens, as the newly proclaimed crown prince sought the blessings of his guru, his parents and his people. As he was made to sit on the seat reserved for him, as he sat there, with a sharp young blade-straight posture, head held high, his countenance grave—a wave of happiness rose in her. *Yadu was born for this*...she felt a rush of energy and reached a decision. Now she waited only for the right moment to announce it. With Shukra's impending departure that hour had come. The chariot that would take him back to his ashram stood at the entrance. Yayati and Devayani saw him to it.

'Father, I will not stay here,' she said in a low voice.

Shukracharya, preoccupied with his own thoughts, did not at first hear her. But the drawn look on her face caught his attention. He stopped. 'What is it?' he asked. She raised her eyes to meet his. He was struck by the desolation in them. She repeated the words, a little louder this time. His expression remained calm. 'Daughter, this is your home now,' he said.

'That is not true, Father.'

He frowned. Her tone had not changed, but he recognized it from old as one preceding an outburst. 'Why do you say that?' he asked gently.

'You too believed, like I did, that Yayati was an honourable man,' said Devayani. Her face was suddenly ablaze. 'How wrong you were! Virtue has been crushed by vice—yet again. And why? Because those who are lower than us have risen...and the high have fallen. That asuri Sarmistha, who is my slave, enticed my husband to her bed. When I asked her to name the father of her firstborn, she, typically, lied to me. But having learnt the identity of her children's father recently, I confronted her, and her words to me were: *You chose Yayati as your husband. Since I am your slave, that makes him my lord too*. Yes, these were her exact words. She further said that the relationship was with mutual consent—a gandharva vivah, she called it—as sacred and virtuous a union as *my* wedding, that you, Father, the soul of dharma, had blessed. Despite the promise he made, he has betrayed me with her—repeatedly. He has given her sons. *Three* sons...

She was always jealous and, just as she stole my clothes once, this was her way of stealing what I had. When I reminded her that she was my dasi and that her very life depended on me, she said that whatever deference she had been required to show me had stemmed from my being of higher birth. But having married a man whose birth was lower than mine, I had, in fact, lost that superiority. She had—*she had the temerity to call me a pariah*. She also said that my sons were no better than chandaals. It is unpardonable, Father. I cannot forgive these two who have hurt me so deeply...I can no longer stay with this man who does not treat me with dignity. I cannot live in this edifice of lies that he has built. Far from such lofty ideals as upholding dharma, he could not even protect my right as his wife...because he is nothing but a cheat.'

Shukra heard out his daughter without any outward display of emotion. For a few moments he was silent, then he trained his gaze at Yayati, as if asking the question: is this true?

It was not the most agonizing moment of Yayati's life—that was yet to come—but it was still terrifying. He was appalled at Devayani's sense of timing and her manner of making the disclosure. Why bring her father into it? Why did she choose this moment when the sage was just about to leave? Cheat? What sort of language was that to use for him? Wasn't he her lord? Did she have no loyalty towards him? She had been behaving strangely the past few days. Who had influenced her? Was she possessed by some evil spirit? How on earth had she found out? Aware that Shukra's face was beginning to look like thunder, he collected his wits and tried to speak with a confidence he did not feel: 'Revered one, when a woman beseeches a man in the way that the danava princess approached me—I mean, she was desperate—and I....' He fumbled for the right words, but they, like his courage, seemed to have fled under the sage's icy glare. 'I could not, erm, turn down her request. The wise say that a man who refuses a woman, when she is in her season, is guilty of the sin of slaying an embryo...I wanted to save myself from that sin and, of course, save her virtue too. You bestowed her on me, she was depending on me.'

'Maybe that is why you forgot that you were dependent on me,' said Shukra.

Yayati had no answer.

The sage spoke without rancour, but with a dry note of criticism: 'You should have heeded my warning to you and stayed away from Vrishaparva's daughter. If you were in a quandary, it was your duty to seek counsel from those wise in the ways of dharma.' He paused, then spoke even more slowly to drive home the point, 'A man who experiences the sweetness of mountain honey on his tongue just once craves for it thereafter. But when a man is ruled by his appetites alone, such is the craving that it soon outstrips his common sense. With complete disregard to the fragility of his situation, he is prepared to risk his life on the cliff's edge. Obviously, he can fall—any time. So it is with the pleasure-seeker. The senses align us towards a honeyed life, but the man who depends on his sense organs for his happiness is trapped. Chasing after enjoyable experiences, he loses equanimity and wisdom—one needs these two qualities to perform the right actions in this life, especially when one is a ruler. What such a man does not understand is that the body will not remain invincible forever. Flesh decays. Hearing, touch, colour, taste, smell...everything goes. For a seeker of sensory pleasures, old age does not bring wisdom. It is only about loss. From now on, O king, may extreme decrepitude be yours.'

When does youth end? When does old age begin? It depends on the age one is now.

Though his adolescence ended on the day he was crowned king, he had always felt youthful. Ageless. The idea of growing old had remained incomprehensible. Hunting being a passion of his, he was no stranger to death. In the eyes of a quarry, and later, in battle encounters with enemy tribes, he had seen it many times, always taking its victim by surprise. Death was an accident, he had come to believe, and all one had was the moment—its fullness. A fistful of gold dust that would slip away, uselessly, if not spent well. Pleasure scented life, gave it sweetness and delicacy, uplifted it...the senses were the gateway through which life's brevity was made worthwhile. With the curse of decrepitude, they were in decline. All that gave him pleasure had been stolen from him. He had lost entire decades, so how could he say what his age was? Ninety, ninety-nine or a hundred and ten years, it was all the same. A deprivation. At first, he could not comprehend what exactly he'd lost. Immediately after the curse had taken effect, he'd felt nothing. Then he started to notice the changes in the texture of his skin. It had become wrinkled, mottled and flaky. A tremor appeared in his hands, even at rest. When he tried to speak, the words did not form clearly on his tongue. Irritated by the bewildered, frightened faces of his servants, he had gestured for a mirror to be brought to him. The image that he saw—and he could see it only when it was very close—was weak, blurred, as if he was looking through a mist at a crumbling monument. Even his distinguishing features, the prominent jaw, the curved nose, had faded into oblivion. Convinced that the feeble-looking creature imprisoned in the mirror was not him, but an illusion, a piece of magic, he had laughed out loud. The sound that emerged from his throat was unfamiliar. It was a dry, scratchy, off-key croak. Panicking, he had touched his face, the forehead and the bushy white eyebrows. The creature in the mirror parodied every move. He thrust that mirror aside in anger and asked for another to be brought to him. But the image he was searching was not in any mirror. It was nowhere to be found, except inside him. Trapped in him was its very essence, unchanged. The self that had been nurtured by life's garden of pleasures remembered each one and hungered.

A few weeks later, he journeyed to Shukracharya's ashram. He did not go alone. Devayani insisted on accompanying him. Yayati's transformation had come as a shock to her, cooling her rage. Though at first repulsed by him, she had realized that this decrepit, impotent creature was still her husband. Like it or not, they shared a fate. By punishing Yayati so harshly, her father had cursed her as well. When admitted into the seer's presence, Yayati, purblind, frail and bent, brought his shaking hands together. An obeisance, a plea. The illustrious brahmin asked him what he wanted.

'Rishivar, though *you* know the antidote to death, the truth is that no one lives forever. However, while one is alive, a strong, healthy body is most precious. It enables a man to pursue the aims—dharma, artha and kama—that make his life meaningful. By cursing me with senility, you have, in fact, cursed me twice. You have taken away everything that brings quality to my life, but the one thing that lies at the root of this body.'

'And what is that?'

'Desire itself...you should have taken away that too.'

'No one can do that, Yayati, not even I. Craving is intrinsic to human nature. If you don't wish to be enslaved by it, *you* have to root it out.'

For a few moments Yayati was very quiet. He sighed, then slowly spoke. 'If you already knew that, Rishivar, then pardon me for asking the question: what was the purpose of this punishment?'

'It looks like you have learned nothing from your father's example,' the sage said drily.

Yayati flushed. Trembling in anger he said, 'My father was equal to Indra...the punishment he got was just as unfair as the one you have given me.'

'Why do you say that?' asked Shukra in a mild voice.

Yayati took a moment to collect himself, then said, 'My elder brother Yati abandoned his duty at the last minute because he perceived the world and its pleasures as false. He gave priority to his inward journey. Yet, moksha is only one among the four meaningful aims. Yati neglected the remaining three—dharma, artha and kama. On the other hand, I, who had kingship thrust on him, was made to learn that material well-being was the most important. I had to add value to my legacy by creating wealth for my kingdom and livelihoods for my people...I took every opportunity to enhance my kingdom's prosperity. Whatever life gave me, I grabbed with both hands. This is what I have learnt: to lead a balanced life, a man must pursue all four aims, including pleasure. Desire energizes me. It enables me to act. One needs a healthy body even to perform good karma. Without desire, the five senses are superfluous because everything that exists is, anyway, insignificant. I have understood that you are a teacher and wanted to teach me the lesson I had neglected to observe, of tempering power and pleasure with self-discipline. But, the body too has its natural processes. Time brings everything to fruition. Even a starving animal, having consumed his fill, refuses the next morsel. My point is this: what has to be shed falls away naturally. Desire too burns itself out. Why then did you give me such a hard punishment?'

'Because you did not understand that kama is an intoxication,' said the sage. 'Its influence is much more than that of artha or dharma. As long as there is an attachment to the object of desire, not even Time can uproot desire. It is the very nature of desire to grow immoderately, to exceed one's capacity to satisfy it, to become indestructible. When that happens, common sense oozes out, like water from a pot with holes. Kama is innate, but one must always remember that anger, ego, fear, anxiety and confusion are also the offshoots of kama. It has to be reined in through mental discipline. Inordinate pursuit of pleasure leads to an unruly mind. It cannot be the foundation of a truly dharmic life...if one wants to lead a righteous life, it is dharma one must keep uppermost, even before wealth...desire is the lowest.'

Though Yayati tried to speak calmly, there was an unmistakable edge in his voice. 'I repeat my earlier question, Rishivar. In disciplining me, didn't you go too far? Is your world view limited because you live the life of an anchorite? An ashram is a kingdom too, but its reality is very different from the one I govern. Renunciation is the cornerstone of an ashram, but it is the richness of life that matters to my people. The external world, the one I govern, is understood only through the senses. Prosperity must make itself visible in the pursuit of pleasure, celebration, the sweet life you hold in such disdain. To you, my lifestyle may have seemed profligate, but for me it was important to live as befitted my status...I am a samrat! My people look up to me. Mere existence is barrenness, devoid of hope. It is cruelty. In the past few weeks, I have learnt what it is to be denied pleasure. The maids who help me out of bed and wash my body are all young. I experience their touch, it brings back memories...the younger self that lives in me craves. Night after night, I command women to warm my bed, to stimulate me, because I want to experience once more that remembered delight...I fail. Yet, it only makes me want it all the more. The body never forgets a pleasure that it experienced all too briefly. That thirst is never quenched. You may say that an attachment to the senses is false, but now that I have all but lost them, the channels through which the life force flowed in me have narrowed to a trickle. You may argue that old age is only a phase in life, but having entered it when I was unready, I am like a prisoner in solitary confinement. The world is all around me, but I am no longer in it. Life calls out to me, I feel the urge to respond, but how do I go out to meet it when I am trapped in a worn-out body? Is there any other way to know this world but through the senses? With my awareness of the everyday world reduced to nothing, my insights have gone, so has my discernment, *so have I*...all that is left is this shell. An atma chained by breath alone to this lacklustre existence.' Wracked by a coughing fit, Yayati stopped speaking.

Shukracharya watched him imperturbably for a few moments, then stood up and poured a tumbler of water from the pot in the corner. Placing his hand on Yayati's bent, shaking shoulders, he held the tumbler to his mouth. Yayati sipped the water slowly, took the tumbler in his own hands and placed it to one side. He murmured a word of thanks to the sage. For a while neither man spoke. Then Yayati said, 'I am a king...I understand something about justice. The seven sages were unnecessarily harsh on my father, but that punishment will one day end. In my view, you, too, have awarded me a punishment that far exceeds my crime, but there is no end in sight. Rishivar, I request you, either you give me back everything you took or take all my remaining breaths too. I do not want this type of life.'

Shukracharya's expression remained inscrutable. Yet Yayati felt that he was listening to every word and was not unsympathetic. Finally, the sage spoke. 'I have not forgotten that you saved my daughter's life...though I cannot retract my words, I can offer you some relief. If one of your sons is ready to bear the curse on your behalf, then you could regain youth.'

'Regain youth?'

'...In exchange for this curse of old age.'

Yayati was aghast. 'That would hardly be fair to my sons!'

'A son is obliged to honour a parent's wishes. When it was your turn, didn't you do what was asked of you?'

'Yes, but how can a father ask his son to take on such a terrible curse? It does not seem right! Isn't there any other solution?'

'Don't bargain with me, O king. I am not a merchant.' The quiet reprimand subdued Yayati. As if to take the sting out of it, Shukracharya said in a kindlier tone, 'It will only be for as long as you want it. Once you are done with your enjoyment of the world, you will go back to being old again and your son will revert to his youth.'

'Ah!' said Yayati, with obvious relief. 'So, it is not irreversible...that does change things.'

'Does it?' Shukracharya looked amused. 'Do you think your sons will agree to the barter?'

Yayati gave a nod. 'They are loyal to me. Besides, Rishivar, I know human nature well enough. Society runs on a covenant: give and take. In return for having lived my old age for me, I will give my kingdom as reward to whoever agrees to the exchange.'

'*Your* kingdom?'

Yayati caught the note of irony and flushed. He felt a deep irritation. Crushing it, he said evenly, 'I have built on what my forefathers left me. My kingdom is what it is today because of my vigour and effort. I have extended its borders, brought forests under cultivation, increased the herds, planted groves, dug wells, developed important trade routes, maintained friendly relations with other kingdoms. My land is well governed. It is peaceful, prosperous and strong. I am a samrat.' Having said these words, he felt better than he had for days.

'So you see yourself not merely as Pratisthan's custodian but as its owner...'

'It was my duty to nurture my inheritance. It is my duty to protect it. This gives me the right to choose my successor. In my view, a son who honours his father's wish—difficult though it may be—cares about his father's welfare. He will care for his subjects with the same empathy. He is fit to be the next king.' As an afterthought, Yayati added, 'With your blessings, of course.'

'You have five sons from two wives,' the sage said. 'The son who gives up his youth for your old age will become the inheritor of your throne. He shall have all that a man desires: a long life, wide fame and numerous progeny.'

Yayati bowed before Shukracharya. 'I am grateful to you.'

The seer had the faraway look of one in deep thought. An enigmatic smile appeared on his lips. 'Let the play of light and darkness go on,' he said, half to himself. There was a tinge of irony in his words, as if he were engaging in a game of dice with an opponent who had, for now, outwitted him.

~

'It's only for a few years,' the father said. 'Time flies.'

'Does it?' asked the eldest son, the crown prince Yadu. His face was bland, but his voice was spiked with disdain. 'Just yesterday you said that old age was a curse.'

'Forget what I said yesterday. I was depressed. Old age is inconvenient, that is all.'

'Is it really all?' The crown prince pursed his lips. 'I recall you complaining that, with your teeth fallen and your digestion weak, you could neither eat your favourite meats nor drink your favourite wine. I also saw how cheerless and disinterested that deprivation made you. Your apathy has affected the running of your kingdom. If an enemy were to attack us now, you are no longer capable of leading the men into battle. Why, you even lack the strength to sit in the sabha for more than a few minutes.You are deaf to the petitioners, you do not care to listen to the advice of your ministers, you begin a sentence only to forget what you wanted to say, unmindful of the fact that the courtiers are fidgeting and openly sniggering at you...I have seen how age has dulled your mind, Father. From your example, I have reached the conclusion that old age is inconvenient for ordinary people, but, for a king it has serious consequences. I hope never to reach that age, *your* stage...I do not want it. You have other sons who are more dear to you than I... exchange your decrepitude with one of them, if you wish.'

'Is that your final answer?' Yayati asked coldly.

'It is.'

'Then you are not just thankless, but undeserving of being my successor. You have forgotten that you owe your very existence to me. Any fame that you achieve in your life will be on the strength of the name I have given you. I disown you. Leave now, go away wherever you wish, or if that is too much for you, stay on. I can afford to keep you, but only as a dependent. You will never be the king. Nor will your descendants ever wear a crown.'

~

He went to his second son and made his offer.

'One can only be young once, Father,' Turvasu said. 'That is how it has always been. What is being young? It is experiencing the pleasures of the world for the first time; the first tiger one kills, the first wrestling match one wins, the first horse one tames, the first woman...there is nothing to match the novelty. Youth is fleeting, I accept. I am not clinging to mine, but neither will I give up the normal progression of age. Life has its seasons, and one must accept the changes each one brings with equanimity. I want to experience all the seasons of life, but only in their proper sequence. Therefore, I must refuse. A man in your condition should be thinking of the world to come. What you are asking of me is not just unreasonable, it is also unnatural.'

'Nothing is more unnatural than *you,*' said Yayati. 'You have disappointed me bitterly. You were the one closest to my heart. When your elder brother turned down my offer, I was secretly happy that you were going to be my new successor. But all that has come to nought. This season, that you will not part with, is all the joy you will have. If you ever become king, your subjects will be men and women of impure thoughts and immoral behaviour, without dharma. Your kingdom will be doomed from the start.'

He went to the third son. Druhyu, Sarmistha's firstborn, had inherited his maternal grandfather Vrishaparva's strong physique and bluff nature. He had a way with animals and spent most of his time in the royal stables. Yayati found him nursing several nasty bruises that he'd got from breaking in a stallion. Though he was in considerable pain, Druhyu sat up when his father arrived and listened to the request he made. Then he spoke.

'At this moment, Father, when every bone in my body seems to have been broken and the agony is terrible, I would gladly exchange it for the aches and pains of old age. After all, how much worse can they be? But there is one problem.'

'What is that?'

'Since my body is young, it will recover fast. I will be

back in the saddle tomorrow. If I were to become as old as you, I would never be able to ride a horse again. That would be as good as death.'

'Are you even of royal blood?' Yayati asked contemptuously. 'Forget horses and elephants, you yourself are nothing but a donkey. Your thinking is so retarded that you deserve only to rule over a land that will forever remain undeveloped: no roads fit for chariots and palanquins, but only mule tracks. No bridges over rivers, but only the crudest of rafts. No prosperity, no custom or culture...that will be your lot.'

Though tired and disheartened, Yayati approached his fourth son, Anu. 'Take my weakness and old age,' he said. 'Do this for me, son. Do it because I, your sire, ask it of you. It is your duty to respect my wish, but I, too, will show my appreciation. I will make you my new heir.'

'I never imagined that such a situation would come to pass,' Anu said frankly. 'I have never aspired to be your successor, Father.'

Yayati sent him an earnest smile. 'I mean it.'

'With three others ahead of me, it was not even a remote possibility.' Anu gave a light shrug.

'Those three are not fit to rule this kingdom,' Yayati said. 'A king must have a vision, but they cannot think beyond their own immediate concerns. I am sure you will be different.'

Anu scratched the side of his nose. 'Father, had I not seen your state as it is now, I may have agreed,' he said. 'But when the rishi's curse transformed you overnight, I saw the degeneration. From a powerful king, you became—what?—just another doddering old man. Where you once strode through the palace like a lion, you now barely manage a slow shuffle. Your mouth drools. You need to be spoon-fed like a small child, your teeth are rotten and your breath foul, you suffer from incontinence, you break wind frequently and with embarrassing loudness. Truly, Father, old age is just another word for rot. What good are you? In this condition, you can no longer even sit for a yagna, nor can you—'

'Enough!' roared Yayati. He was trembling with rage. 'You have listed all the bodily changes one has to endure in old age. I was what you are today, and what I am today will one day be your fate. May you experience each and every one of my vicissitudes with no mitigating joys. You will never see your grandchildren grow, because none of your sons will live long enough to provide you with any. Your line will end with you. As for those yagnas you consider so important, with your sons dead, they too will be meaningless.'

~

Yayati was dejected. A man who has sons is considered blessed, but each one of his sons had belied his hope. Before the curse he had appeared strong and glorious; not one of his progeny would have challenged his authority. Now that he was old and bent, they had all risen in their own estimation; not one would bow before him. Somewhere in the dimness of his memory he recalled that he had a fifth son. What was his name? Ah, yes, Puru. How old was he? Not more than ten or twelve...what good would he be? Why would he be any different? Nevertheless, he called for the boy. When the child appeared before him, he was disappointed to see how scrawny he looked, like a solemn-eyed monkey.

'Son,' he said, bringing his eyes on level with the lad's. 'A rishi named Shukracharya has cursed me so that I, a strong man, became weak and old instantly. Sages have these powers, you see. Later, Shukra regretted it, he felt bad, but he can't change me back—unless you agree to, er, let me borrow your body. It is only for a very short while.'

'But if you borrow my body, where will I live?' the boy asked anxiously. 'Will I have to be a preta atma and hang upside down from a tree in the cremation ground?'

'Oh no, no! Who has filled your head with such nonsense? You will live in mine, of course.'

The boy looked him up and down. 'Yours?'

Yayati was mortified, but he shook off the feeling and said robustly, 'Don't mock it. This is the body of a samrat. How many boys of your age would get the chance to live in a samrat's body?'

'But *why* do you want to exchange a samrat's body with mine?'

Realizing that the boy was no fool, Yayati said candidly, 'I just want to enjoy a little longer all those things I was forced to give up.'

The boy looked surprised. 'What were you forced to give up?'

Yayati was at a loss for words. How could he explain to one so young and naive that decrepitude robbed you of everything: your charisma, your freedom, your virility, your very identity. Old is just old, nothing more to it.

He asked the boy, 'Do you know who you are?'

'I am Puru, son of Yayati.'

The child's proud tone, more than the answer, surprised Yayati. He gave an approving nod. 'That's right. Through me, you are the grandson of Nahusha, great-grandson of Ayu. Your great-great-grandfather was Pururavas, the founder of our dynasty...did you know that Pururavas was so renowned that he was invited to Indra's court? Our ancestors, mine and now yours too, were strong, bold men. They never turned away from a fight, they bore hardship with stoicism, they understood where their duty lay.' He was rambling. He sensed that the boy was bored but too courteous to show it.

'Druhyu likes wrestling and Anu enjoys cockfights,' Puru said. 'But I don't like either.'

Yayati's hope fell. 'What do you like?'

'Stories,' Puru said. 'I love to hear the sutas when they sing the gathas of our kings. I already know the story of Pururavas. He fell in love with an apsara named Urvashi.' He grimaced. 'I don't like love stories. What I really like is the story of Nahusha and how he became a *huuuge* ajagara. He is still there, you know, on a rock far away. He can eat a whole deer in one go. Cartloads of food go from the palace every week to keep him alive. The suta said that when they run out of livestock, they would have to start with humans. *Live ones.*'

Yayati sent him a sour look. 'Young boys about your size will be the first to be sacrificed.'

Puru's mouth fell open. After a moment, he said confidently, 'He will not eat me.'

'Why not?'

'I am his grandson. It would be adharma.'

'Adharma,' Yayati repeated. He was silent for a while. 'Isn't it adharma to refuse your father's wish?'

The boy nodded. 'My mother always says that the child must not disrespect the parent. Do you know my grandfather Vrishaparva?'

'No, I have not had that honour, but I have heard of him. He is a good king.'

After a moment, Puru said, 'He sent my mother away. She became a slave because that was what he asked of her. He told her that it was for the welfare of his people.'

'A king has an obligation to his people. He must think of their good before he thinks of himself,' Yayati said. 'Therefore, I have put my sons to test, and they have all failed. It is now your turn. I know in my bones that you are the right one. But I must still put you through the test. You come from a line of kings on both sides...would you like to be the next king? '

The boy looked confused, but gave a tentative nod.

'Then you must do as I ask,' said Yayati firmly. 'It is your duty.'

6

Drishadvati

In the forest where I lived for twelve years, there was no need for doors. In the palace where I spent one night there were too many, all guarded. In Sarmistha's house there is just one. I am allowed in. My new life is a litany of household tasks. In the forest, we spent some of the daylight hours looking for food. Here I slog from dawn to dusk: milk cows and goats, mix cattle feed, gut fish and fowl, tend to the vegetable patch, sweep the floor and yard, clean the cowshed, fetch pots of water from the river and firewood from the forest, wash clothes, churn butter, pound millet, give alms to the stream of wandering ascetics who knock at the door. Housework is good for the hips and haunches, Sarmistha tells me, and strong haunches are good for childbirth. Her own are ample. She works me to the bone, this woman, watching me with a hawk's eye. Everything must be just as she says, or else a smack across the back of my head, a painful twist of my ear. I learn quickly. How to grind herbs and spices to exactly the right texture, how to use the knife efficiently so that no part of the vegetables is wasted. But things are not so bad either. Sarmistha is like the jackfruit she loves to cook, hard and spiky, difficult to cut open, but tender inside. One of the nice things about my new life is the wonderful food. The kitchen is stocked with spices I have never seen. My nose learns to recognize new aromas. We eat at fixed hours. There is always plenty to eat. The frequency and plenitude of meals, the certitude of the next meal—all this is new to me.

When we are at last done with the day's work, she sits me down before her and rubs oil into my scalp, then weaves my hair into tight braids that I stealthily loosen the minute her back is turned. She seems to enjoy this time we share. We are both exiles. Her loneliness speaks to mine. She tells me stories from her earlier life, hums a tune or two from songs she once sang, asks me to give her feet a massage. About a year after I come to live with Sarmistha, I feel a dull pain in my lower belly. My body begins to leak. When I see the thin red line, sticky to touch and smelling of iron, running down my thighs, I ask Sarmistha, am I dying?

To which she says, 'It is not a sign of death, it is life's blood. You are blessed. You will give life. A woman is born for childbearing. Your body is getting ready for its main purpose.'

It hurts, I whimper.

'Pain is not an option for us women,' she says. 'And this is good pain...like the one that accompanies childbirth.'

I inform her that I do not want babies—if I have to suffer this cramping pain.

She smiles thinly. You will change your tune, she says, as if she knows it all. Her words make me resentful but also a bit anxious. In her own way, Sarmistha is as inscrutable as Devayani. It is hard to think of one without thinking of the other. Ejected from her father's kingdom, a lifelong slave to her rival, yet Sarmistha has attained a woman's highest destiny: *putravati bhava*. May you have sons. She has three. It is no mean feat, her smile conveys.

Angered by her belittlement of my discomfort, I say, 'Two of your sons have left home. And the third, with a curse on his head, is an old man who needs to be fed and cleaned like an infant. When I wasn't around, you did your own work; now I do it for you. So what good are sons?'

Sons are what a man dreams of, she says.

Why does he dream of sons? Why not daughters?

She sighs. Slowly, as if imparting a lesson, she replies. Of all the things a man pursues in his life, a name is the most valuable. Name is power. Name is blood. Name is flow. Genealogy connects the visible to the invisible. It is the line drawn, segment by segment, from father to son to grandson. A straight line is preferable. It is an arrow shot through the heart of time, the story carried forward. A fence against non-existence. Man needs the fence because immortality is denied to him. He is not a god. Thus he hungers for sons—and isn't this an irony?—*his* body has no space in it to carry a child. Only a woman has the capacity for procreation. That is her fate. She must provide a man with sons—the perishables he needs in his pursuit of the imperishable.

I tell her about my birth mother. In the forest they would say that the bones of the dead sang to her. Every creature—predator and prey, male and female, rival and ally—sang the same song. My mother called it the song of the tooth and the claw. *Stay alive, stay alive*. A short song, because all too often, life for most beings in the forest *was* short-lived. The fastest deer could only hope to outrun death for one more day. But here, it is as if men want to beat it forever...I ask Sarmistha another question: 'A man wants sons, but what does a woman want?'

Silence. The stillness of a dragonfly trapped in amber. Then she says, I was you once, even though looking at me now you may not believe it. I, too, can no longer remember my younger self. It seems like she was a different person—that princess! Everyone called me beautiful. To be adored was all I wanted...she trails off with a wistful look in her eyes. Then, in a dry voice she tells me: You are no longer in the forest. Here lives are longer. Too long perhaps. Just as I was you once, one day you will be me Look! Look at me carefully...this sagging stomach, these drooping breasts. A tired womb. Three babies survived, but two died when still inside me...how did I become this way? Why? To men, women are young or they are old. Other than that we are just women, undifferentiated. All must obey their rules. Our value lies in what we can do for them: warm their beds, bear their sons, care for their families, extend their influence in the world through the connections we bring. Then how can we want anything different from what they want for us? To breathe, to breed. This is all that gives meaning to a woman's life. To become a mother, the mother of sons, that is her highest destiny.

But what does she want? What do *we* want?

Her eyes become sad, reflective. I don't know, she says. Maybe no woman ever knows because no one ever asked her. The question itself is not pertinent...who knows, she adds, one day we will become brave enough to ask ourselves, to dream up an answer. Imagine living in a world where there are other possibilities.

What will we do then? How will we choose? Will women still choose to warm their beds, run their households, bear their sons? I ask.

She laughs and says, 'Probably. It's safer, believe me.'

How dull it is to be a woman!

There is an antidote to dullness, she says. Our songs. They bear witness to our lives. They seep into everything we do: the rows of rice we sow, the grain we thresh, the cloth we weave, the food we cook, the lullabies we hum. It is enough for now to sing our secret songs. Everything may be taken from us but not our melodies, made up from odds and ends as only we know how to use them—scraps of our mutilated selves, the wounds and the tears. An ensemble of sorrows strung together on our tongue. Names do not matter, only the truth counts. It adds up. We pass it on...we return from the dead when we sing of our lives. We love ourselves again in the only way we know, by singing our pain away. We absolve the world with our music. With our blood we wash it free of sin. We make it look human again. We renew this world. We do it every day, with nothing but the chorus of all our lives.

On Purnima, when the full moon swims slowly in the dark skies and fireflies pirouette on trees, Sarmistha abandons her daily cares. She drinks a fermented juice mixed with barley and ghee that powers her flight. All night she sings only love songs, overflowing with dejection and misery. *Do not go, do not go. I will cry if you are gone, I will die if you are gone,* is a favourite one with her. But it's an empty threat. Though Yayati never visits her now, she carries on living, singing, cursing...I find such compositions meaningless, and say as much to her.

You are a Chandravanshi, she tells me. You belong to

the moon. It is ensconced in every cell of your body, it is that secret tide in your blood. One day, not too far away, it will rise and romance will melt your bones. You, too, will know moon madness.

What comes with the madness?

Yearning. A senseless longing to unite. Merge, in flesh, mind and heart. Become nothing.

Sounds like a prison sentence, I say.

She does not speak for a long moment. Then she says sadly, 'There is no happily ever after.'

Moon madness is followed by noon madness. Even in broad daylight, our lives have become senseless. Though we live more or less in seclusion, we are not immune to the changes sweeping across this land. Yayati reigns unchallenged. All rules are upside down: a son in his dotage, while a father celebrates his second youth. Yayati enjoys it with the greed of one whose hunger is visceral. It lives in his memory. *That never-to-be-forgotten hunger.* How can that be satisfied? With glands now in overdrive, he is a confused, sweaty, rebellious adolescent, filled with dreams of a revolution. Euphoric one minute, dejected the next. Everything is a test of strength. There is not a race Yayati will not run, no wrestling match he will not join, no maiden he will not bed. His seed is propagating all around us, evident in the prominent jawline, the strapping body, the thick shock of hair. Sons everywhere.

Meanwhile, the son who exchanged his youth for Yayati's old age languishes on a string cot, drooling, dribbling and leaking like a helpless baby. It is my job to keep Puru clean and tidy. That bag of bones, my half-brother, with his sad, watery eyes, is the future king of Pratisthan. Be careful with him, his mother says to me. Shukracharya's curse has made his bones brittle.

Says Puru: Sometimes, I get the feeling that, like the dreamer's dream, I don't exist.

If you are the dream then you won't feel the pain if I pinch you, I say, and bring my forefinger and thumb threateningly close to his arm.

He chuckles quietly.

How old are you now? I ask.

Your guess is as good as mine, he says.

I have another question: What did it feel like to become old overnight?

The self never ages, he says grandly. (Being old, he makes out, is being a fount of wisdom.)

I roll my eyes and tell him I wasn't talking about *that* self but this body.

This body is a garment, he says.

An old, soiled garment—I mutter—that it is my luck to wash.

He laughs and says that the garment analogy is all worn out. Shall we replace it with masks?

Masks?

That Time makes us, who pass through it, wear.

His face is a map of fine lines, some wandering off into eternity. I ask: Why does Time make us all wear the same mask?

Because we mortals are all under its command.

But you are Puru. And I am Drishadvati. One day you will be a great and glorious king...our journeys are very different.

We make the same journeys but under different names—so that we understand our personal truth.

But I have two names, I remind him. Drishadvati and Madhavi. So what will my journey be?

Two journeys for you, he says. One will end, the other will not. Does a river end when it flows into the ocean?

Another eye roll from me. Puru, stop being old and wise, I say. Your answers are more confusing than my questions.

He peers at me with a strange animation that is completely at odds with his appearance. Young eyes in a crumbly face. Bedridden, all he can twitter on about is journeys. In this mad world, where Time shuttles—back for some and forward for others—creating not waves but whirlpools, my own life seems closed off, sealed within a casing of ordinariness. I long for freedom, my feet run towards it. Twice I take off, but each time I am brought back.

Even fledglings break free, I grumble. Their dreams unfurl. They fly.

But they must still return to earth, Puru says. That is the law. Birds are netted for their feathers, meat and bones. No part of them is wasted. For their beauty, their songs, and for their eggs they are caged.

Birds and women too…is that also the law?

He is silent for a while. Then he says distantly, 'Cages keep birds in, but they also keep predators out. They keep birds safe.'

'Not from those who cage them.'

He cocks his head to one side and looks at me. 'You are too clever for your own good,' he says. It sounds like an admonition.

~

One day an old wandering ascetic comes to the house. Sarmistha is not at home, so I make the offering of grain and fruit as she has taught me. There is nothing unusual about him at first glance. Nor do I act any different from what I have done in the past. However, while leaving, instead of the customary blessing, he says, 'You have no need of my blessing, Daughter. It is ordained that you will be the mother of sons. However, I will give you a boon instead. After the birth of every son, you will be as you are now.'

When I tell Sarmistha about the old mendicant's visit, she thins her lips and says sharply, 'Tell me the truth... did anything else happen? Did he touch you? Ask you to touch him?'

I shake my head and repeat his parting words. A mocking smile curves her lips. 'You must not believe everything you hear.'

7

Garud and Gaalav

There was an unusual rush outside the gates of Vaikunth. A cloudburst in the mountains was the cause. Trailing puffs of smoke from the funeral obsequies, the dead souls queued up, clamouring to be allowed into this, the most prestigious of addresses in Afterlife.

Although they had shed their bodies, habits acquired over a lifetime were harder to discard. Once inside, they began to note the drawbacks in the new home. Breaking free of the cycle of birth and death, they were plunged into confusion. In Vaikunth, formlessness was the norm. The crystal mansion, their new home, presented a peculiar challenge. Though there were walls, doors and windows, there was no privacy. The older inhabitants of Afterlife told the newcomers that it would take a while for them to understand the new reality, that as pure energy, souls can flow through anything, from water to walls. Such is the Lord's leela, they said, what you saw of it in Mrityulok was only a preview. But the newly arrived souls continued to carp. Everything is imprecise and it's causing us enormous stress, they said. We were promised Everlasting Bliss. You are still trapped in the five-sensory reality, the old souls explained patiently. Everlasting bliss lies within. Even so, Vaikunth is not bereft of its charms. For instance, just look at the gardens. The flowers are always in bloom, the fruit you want is always within reach. In this place you don't have to wait for summer for the mangoes to arrive. The wish-fulfilling Kalpa trees provide you with every kind of fruit all year round. In fact, fruit salad is a popular request, and you can have any combination of ingredients you like. The Kalpa trees give optional dressings too, all sattvic, of course.

Please don't speak to us of food, the new souls cried. The funeral feasts cooked in our names still weigh us down. That's another advantage of living in Vishnulok, they were informed, no obesity. Having reduced our grosser selves to the five constituent elements, we are all weightless; besides the fact that there are no joint pains to suffer from, it is easier for us to be absorbed into Lord Narayan. Ah, that was our goal too, the especially pious among the new arrivals said. *Oneness with the Lord....* All the same, a few cynics were heard to mutter, that was what we were told to aim for. It was the reason why one had to lead a virtuous, if rather dull, life in Mrityulok. All those rules, never steal a cow, never covet another's wife, and so on. Then there were the series of good karmas one performed: the endless homas, charity donations, feeding the poor, rigorous fasts, annual observances of rituals to honour dead ancestors, the continuation of the family line through the begetting of sons. That was the toughest: one must, somehow, anyhow, obtain at least one son, if one aspires to Eternal Bliss.

The birdman eavesdropped openly on the various conversations. This was a good way for him to catch up with the news from Mrityulok. It had been a while since he had travelled there. Usually, only a few souls were deemed pure enough to make it to Vaikunth, but the latest batch was bigger than usual. It was made up almost entirely of pilgrims who had been on a circuit of the teerthasthanas in the Himalayas when the cloudburst had occurred, leading to flash floods in the mountain rivers. In Mrityulok, the dead were still washing up along the banks. The rulers of riverine states had ordered and paid for mass cremations. More souls were expected to arrive and lengthen the queues at the gates of Vaikunth.

One of the new arrivals said to its companions, 'While we were rushing away from the waters, did you notice the brahmin who was rushing towards them, shouting, *I want to die*?'

'No,' came a terse reply. 'I was too busy trying to cling on to my earthly existence.'

A third newcomer interrupted. 'That was Gaalav. He was from my village. I was acquainted with him slightly.'

Hearing a name that he knew, the birdman's ears pricked up. He edged closer to the three and said, 'Pardon me, but I couldn't help overhearing…I am friendly with a brahmin youth named Gaalav, who is the disciple of Rishi Vishwamitra. Are you talking about the same person?'

'That's the one.'

'Has he departed from Mrityulok too? '

'Probably. He was certainly keen on leaving it.'

'That's strange!' the birdman said. 'Was he in some kind of trouble?' The newcomer hesitated, wondering if gossip was permissible in Vaikunth. Reading him correctly, the birdman said, 'I am only asking because Gaalav is my friend and I am concerned about his welfare.'

'All gurus test their disciples, but Rishi Vishwamitra is known for setting especially difficult tasks.'

'What task did he set Gaalav?'

'The rumour was that he asked Gaalav for a gurudakshina of eight hundred horses.'

'Eight hundred!' The birdman frowned. 'Why would a sage want so many horses?

'Vishwamitra is a complicated man.'

The birdman turned away, lost in thought, unaware of the interest his presence had caused in the gathering. When he was out of earshot, the newly arrived souls asked the older members of Vaikunth about him. 'Was *that* an example of the Lord's leela, a man with oversized wings? Who is he?'

'Haven't you heard of Rishi Kashyap's son Garud? He is known by other names: Suparn, Garutman, Tarkshya.'

'Ohhh...*That* Garud. Yes, we chanted his 108 names in Mrityulok...Is it true that he flies the Lord around the worlds?'

'That is one of his duties, yes.'

'Well, if he is here, that means the Lord is in residence too. Do you think we'll get a glimpse of him?'

'*A glimpse!* Did you chant the thousand names of the Lord every single day while you were in Mrityulok?'

'You must be joking!'

'Answer the question.'

'Well, sometimes one rushed through them, maybe skipped a few. You know how it is in that world. Never a moment to oneself.'

'This is Eternity. You have all the time now. Start by chanting his name. That too is a manifestation.'

~

It was still raining in the mountains. Diving into the sea of clouds, Garud felt the chill wind in his face.

He rode the air currents like a seasoned charioteer, his golden wings opening and closing in perfect synchrony. Every now and then lightning crackled and there was a crash of thunder. His glee knew no bounds. This was the life he was born for. Reminding himself that he had a mission to accomplish, he flew out of the turbulence and descended. There was a break in the clouds and he could see the aftermath of the storm on the ground. Everywhere his gaze travelled, it saw only scenes of devastation. Mudslides had uprooted a whole forest. Young trees lay buried, their limbs poking out of the debris like accusing fingers; entire villages had been crushed to grey rubble. In the narrow valleys, the torrents raged, whipping up waves that broke the riverbanks and swept away the rope bridges, rocks, walls and roofs of homesteads. Uprooted trees, carcasses of animals and human corpses floated downstream as one macabre parade: Death had been fair in its randomness. Flying low over the scene, Garud reflected that from the heights he inhabited the world of mortals looked toy-like, but the tragedy it had endured was real, colossal and crushing. He navigated through the valleys in a box pattern, narrowing every circuit towards the centre. While he was completing the last course, something caught his attention. In the middle of a river, there was a rock, and spreadeagled on it, face up, was a figure he recognized. He swooped down and lifted the unconscious man with his strong talons.

~

At last, Gaalav stirred and opened his eyes. He was disorientated and could not remember exactly what had happened. There had been a loud rumble and the hillside he had been standing on had slipped into the river, then water had come snarling at him with the ferocity of an angry tigress. If only it had taken him away, he moaned. If only Garud had left him on the rock, instead of lifting him up and bringing him to the safety of a cave on the hillside.

'Be like me,' Garud said, flapping his wings to dry their feathers. 'Nothing can keep me down. Challenges energize me. I am born again and again.'

'I want to die,' Gaalav said with quiet misery. 'Please, let me die.' He sat in a huddle against the cave wall, resting his face on his knees. He was in his early twenties, lean and tanned, with a curved nose, and extra-long eyelashes that gave his face a slightly feminine look.

'That is foolish talk,' said Garud. 'Only the Supreme One decides when one is to die.'

Gaalav looked even more glum. He repeated dully, 'My life has no meaning now. I only want to end this miserable existence.'

'And embark on an even more miserable one as a bhoot-preta,' Garud said with asperity.

'What else can I do?' Gaalav snapped in sudden anger. 'Where will I get eight hundred white horses?'

Garud gave a start. '*White* horses?' After a moment he asked uneasily, 'Did your guru insist on the colour white?'

'*White as moonlight*...with one black ear.'

'A white horse with a black ear, a shyamkarni.' Garud grimaced. 'You may find one or two, but eight hundred! It is an unreasonable request. Did you do something to annoy your guru?'

'On the contrary, I went to his aid!' said Gaalav indignantly.

'You are talking in riddles, my friend. You had better tell me the whole story.'

Gaalav shook his head in a helpless, apathetic way. 'O Garud, what good will it do now?'

'O Gaalav, it may do no good at all,' Garud mocked. 'But it will help us get through this night.'

'Where does one start?' Outside the cave the rain fell steadily. After a while Gaalav began to speak.

'Guru Vishwamitra...I will never forget the first time I saw him. It was the summer I turned twelve. My thread ceremony had been performed that year. My family waited for the monsoon to get over, and then, as my father had promised, he would leave me at the ashram. Seeing my tonsured head my sisters laughed at me, but I liked the new look. The tuft on my head and the thread across my shoulder made me feel important. But what made my chest swell with pride was the memory of my mother's face. It had shone with joy when news came that I had passed a rigorous entrance test and been accepted as a pupil by Rishi Vishwamitra. She said, "He is the greatest guru of all, the guru of kshatriya princes!" *Gaalav, disciple of Vishwamitra*. I loved the sound of it. That was how I would be known for the rest of my life. There was no greater honour, I thought.

'After the rains my father accompanied me to the ashram. It took us two days to reach it. I had never travelled that far before. My father wanted to return home immediately. As he said goodbye, I sensed a discomfiture in him, a keenness to get away. It puzzled me. He was a simple, affectionate man, but he did not so much as pat my back or stroke my head. All he said was that I should study hard, obey the guru and live peacefully with my fellow-scholars...I realize now that he, a humble purohit, was both awed and intimidated by the renowned guru, and that was the reason for his stiff farewell. You have seen Rishi Vishwamitra. The first impression is one of immense strength. He is over six feet, his strapping frame marks him out from other men. But there is something about Gurudev that sets him apart from other sages as well. I don't know how to describe it.'

'It is a combination of arrogance and dogmatism,' Garud said matter-of-factly.

Gaalav looked offended. 'My guru comes from the Chandravanshi clan of Kanyakubja. His father, you may know, was the ruler, Raja Gadhi. His grandfather was—'

Garud interjected, 'But what does all this have to do with the demand for white horses?'

Slightly annoyed, Gaalav said, 'Be patient, Garutman. I was just trying to give you the background. Gurudev is an unusual man. A rajrishi. He has the blood as well as the upbringing of a kshatriya. Kshatriyas are proud of their stables. When they aren't riding horses, they are dreaming about them.'

'Your guru is suffering from phantom pain,' said Garud. 'Yearning for what he gave up long ago.'

Gaalav said sternly, 'Allow *me* to tell my story.'

Admission into Vishwamitra's gurukul was sought by all the royal families of Aryavarta. His students came from well-off homes. Gifts of fruit, grain, ghee and spices arrived daily by the cartloads. The princes ate very well and had comfortable living quarters. However, Gaalav, whose family did not have the means for lavish gifts, had to pay for his tuition and boarding with his services. These included lowly household chores. He performed the tasks efficiently, without grumbling, and became quite the favourite of Vishwamitra's wife.

'After a while Gurudev too began to notice me,' Gaalav said. 'He would ask me to assist him. In the beginning it was only with preparations for the rituals, but later he even allowed me to sit behind him during the sacrifices. In fact—' He stopped speaking, feeling a little self-conscious.

'In fact, you became known as the teacher's pet.' Garud suspected that Gaalav's conscientious ways and prim manner had not won him many friends among the boisterous and pampered royal princes whose lives had been very different from birth from that of the priest's son. In a mild tone, he observed, 'You couldn't have been happy there, Gaalav. Perhaps Rishi Vasisth's gurukul would have been a more suitable place for you.'

'There's nothing special about that place,' Gaalav curled his lip. 'How can it be when *everyone* goes there?'

Garud was secretly amused. The rivalry between Rishi Vasisth's older, more egalitarian school and Vishwamitra's select gurukul for princes was well known. Its origins lay in a running feud between the two gurus themselves.

The quarrel between the two men had sprung many years ago, when Vishwamitra was still a king and his name was Vishwarath. On a visit to Rishi Vasisth's ashram, he had accepted the hospitality offered by the rishi's wife, Arundhati. To his surprise, it was not the simple repast that a brahmin household might be expected to offer, but a lavish meal with several dishes, each better than the last, and all superior to what the king ate in his own palace. Not just the quality, but the quantity too surprised Vishwarath; his sizeable entourage also had eaten very well. Curious to know how his hostess had managed to feed so many people, he inquired if she had special cooks in her kitchen. To his surprise, she took him to the cowshed and pointed out a white cow, bedecked with an orange silk cloth, a string of tiny bells attached to her horns, and a garland of flowers around her neck. This is Kamadhenu, she said. She is a gift from Indra bhagwan. Thanks to her powers of giving, I feed all the ten thousand disciples in the ashram, as well as the visitors who drop by. No one ever goes hungry.

I could do with a creature like this, thought the king. I need it more than these brahmins, as I have many more mouths to feed—a whole kingdom, in fact. He made a polite request to his host to hand over the magical cow to him. When this was turned down, he tried to take her by force. But Rishi Vasisth, whose own supernatural powers were legendary, thwarted him. Shamed, King Vishwarath cast aside his crown, saying that the royal authority he had inherited and the army he commanded were nothing compared to the spiritual powers a brahmin obtained through his tapasya. That was real power. Everything else paled in comparison. Vishwarath abandoned his throne, spent several years in the wilderness engaged in meditation. When he returned from the forest, the world recognized him as a consciousness transformed, an eternal power, a rishi. Specifically, a rajrishi, kingly seer. Vishwamitra was his new name. Friend to the world. The gods, however, saw him as the very opposite. Through tapasya, an ambitious human may acquire those powers of Nature that the gods consider their own. Such a human is a threat not just to them but to the entire universe and the maintenance of its innate order. Vishwamitra had proven his mettle to the gods, but the fire that had been ignited in him had not burned out, despite their periodic efforts to douse it. Being a rajrishi wasn't enough for Vishwamitra. He could not forget that his rival, Vasisth, was a notch higher in rank as a brahmin rishi. That was the status Vishwamitra aspired to.

'Competition is food and drink to a kshatriya,' opined Garud with a deadpan look.

The gods had constantly tried to test Vishwamitra's will. In one such instance, the god Dharma had come to the ashram in disguise: he had adopted the appearance of Rishi Vasisth. Gaalav, an eyewitness to the incident, said, 'Of course, we didn't know the god's real identity when he appeared. That revelation came later.' Though taken aback, Vishwamitra had welcomed the illustrious guest in the customary manner. He had offered Vasisth hospitality, which was accepted.

'Usually, whenever we had an important guest, Gurudev would ask Guru Ma to make something special, but on that day, he decided, that even her cooking was not good enough. He wanted the offering to be perfect and said that he would cook the sweet rice himself.'

'Perhaps he still remembered the food that Kamadhenu had produced magically,' quipped Garud.

Gaalav ignored him and continued with the narration of events. 'Several hours went by. The guest was shown around the ashram and invited to give a short discourse that we all attended, but still there was no sign of the meal.'

Finally, the guest, tired of waiting, had walked into the hut of another brahmin in the ashram and partaken of his hospitality. He was washing his hands after eating when Vishwamitra emerged from his kitchen, holding the steaming dish he had prepared. It was clear from the rajrishi's expression that he was proud of his creation. No one had the courage to tell him that the guest had already eaten. I have eaten, he said, very casually. It seemed at first that Vishwamitra did not understand. Then, as the meaning sank in, he flushed deeply. He looked down at the pot that he was still holding. Without even so much as glancing at him a second time, the guest said just two more words, 'Stay here,' as if he would be back in a minute.

'*And then*,' said Gaalav with slow emphasis, '*He left that place for good*.' His hushed tone reflected the shock he had felt that moment. 'He walked away without a final salutation. No one spoke. No one dared…it was not just an appalling breach of good manners but an insult. When it finally sank in, we didn't know what to say.'

'What did your guru do then?'

Vishwamitra had immediately understood then that he had been tricked into believing that the guest was Vasisth. This was a ploy devised by the meddlesome gods: another of those tests to destroy his tapasya, because it challenged their need to be constantly venerated by mortals. They had attempted this sort of trickery before, but had not succeeded. This time too, he resolved, they would not. Obeying the command to remain in the same spot, he had raised the pot of kheer and placing it on his head stood immobile like a pillar. That day and the next and the next. Like a sacrificial post dug into the ground he had stood for a day, a month, or maybe each hour felt like day, and a day like a month. 'He looked as if he would stand for a century,' Gaalav's voice was muffled with emotion. 'My guru, the man I respected above everyone else, suffering like this. No one dared go near him, not even Guru Ma. An anthill came up around his legs, weaver birds built a nest in his beard. Shoulders caked with bird droppings, nails long and twisted, face contorted with pain. But he did not lower his arms holding the pot...I couldn't watch it without going to his help.'

Gathering his courage, Gaalav had approached the guru, at first to offer him sips of water, then to clean and care for him. He had untangled the rishi's locks, trimmed the nails and beard, bathed his body, changed his garments. From no other motive but the reverence and love he had borne his guru, he had tended to Vishwamitra, participating in the guru's ordeal with care and solemnity, as if this too were an important yagna. Then one day the god reappeared, as Vasisth. Thank you for waiting, he said, I'm ready to eat now. He had eaten the sweet rice to the last grain, and even remarked on how warm and delicious it was. To Vishwamitra, he said: 'O, Brahmin rishi, I am pleased with you.' Saying that he vanished into thin air.

'When this happened, I was the sole witness,' Gaalav said. 'There was an expression of disbelief mixed with joy on gurudev's face. He looked at me and said, "Gaalav, did you hear what he just said? *Brahmin rishi.*Do you know what that means? Now the gods too recognise me as a brahmin. No one has been bestowed *this* honour".'

'And then?'

'And then?' Gaalav echoed. 'And then he said these words to me: "O Gaalav, no son could have served his father better than the seva you have performed for me. You have my permission to go wherever you want".'

Garud looked at him in surprise. 'But that is good news, Gaalav. What did you say?'

Gaalav had said, 'I am not yet free of my obligation to you, Gurudev, not till you accept a dakshina. Please be good enough to tell me what is it that you desire from me.'

'You have done enough for me,' the guru said. 'I want nothing more.'

Gaalav looked at him in confusion. Everything had happened too quickly for him to comprehend, and now this sudden dismissal. The guru-shishya bond was sacred, a covenant. It had to be ended formally. How could he just leave? 'Gurudev, I have a final duty to fulfil,' he said. 'I cannot leave without paying the fee.'

Once again the guru asked him to leave, but Gaalav persisted.

Leave, the guru said. Yet Gaalav did not go away.

Then the guru commanded, 'Give me eight hundred horses white as the rays of the moon, each horse having a single black ear. Go, Gaalav. Do not delay.'

'Since that day, I have not had a wink of sleep,' said Gaalav. 'A brahmin who cannot keep his vow is tarnished forever. Tell me, Garud, how can a man like me, who does not have even a single rich friend, get these eight hundred horses without gold and silver? Why did my guru ask for something impossible?'

To teach you a lesson—because you failed to distinguish between perseverance and pig-headedness. But Garud could not bring himself to say such harsh words to a friend.

'Hasn't my life been utterly destroyed?' Gaalav moaned. 'Then, what is the point of remaining alive? I am indebted to my guru...if I fail to keep my word to him, I will lose respect in the eyes of everyone. Worse, I wouldn't be able to live with myself. I may as well go to the Lord's feet in Vaikunth and beg for refuge. Surely, *he* will not turn me down.'

'Don't be in such a hurry to reach the Lord's feet, my friend,' Garud said with mock severity. 'The Lord himself has sent me here to help you. That is my mission, O brahmin. Don't fret. I can help you...sleep now. Tomorrow will bring us something good.'

~

The rain had stopped. A clean tranquillity pervaded the world. The sky above the snow-clad peaks was a deep sapphire blue. The cool pine-scented air smelt of freshness. It sent Garud's blood rushing. His feathers shivered in excitement. He shook Gaalav awake. 'It's going to be a beautiful day,' he said. 'Let us make an early start.'

Gaalav stared at him silently through sullen, sleep-filled eyes.

Undeterred, Garud asked, 'Where would you like to go first?'

'Wherever I get eight hundred white horses,' Gaalav said curtly. 'That is my only wish.'

'In journeying, it is not one's wish that counts but one's intention,' said Garud. 'Intention is the most important of all. We have to start the search somewhere. East, south, west or north. Where?'

'Um...'

'Let us consider east,' Garud said, forcing himself to be patient. 'All the gods live in that part of the world. It is the direction of sunrise. The gates through which the day begins its journey lie there. There, at dawn, the pious offer prayers and water. All beginnings lie there. All auspicious tasks are begun facing east. There the Immense Being, Brahma, who created all the worlds, first chanted the Vedas. It was in this quarter that the first sound, Aum, was created, and the mahamantra, Gayatri, was manifested to a mortal, none other than Rishi Vishwamitra. It is for these reasons that this direction is known as Purva, first.'

Gaalav blinked a few times. 'You seem to know a lot about the world,' he said.

'Shall we go eastwards?'

'I only want to go in the direction I can be sure of getting the horses.'

'We will get to that in a moment,' Garud said. 'Before you decide, hear something about the other directions too. Facing east, on your right is the quarter that the sun, Vivasvat, having performed the first sacrifice, gave away as dakshina to his guru. Hence, Dakshin. It is a direction everyone must travel towards, and you, too, will journey there one day.'

'Will I get my horses there?'

Garud winced. 'Stop thinking about horses for a few minutes and listen to me...Dakshin is where the Vaitarini flows. It is the river that the soul must cross when it leaves the body. Dakshin is the path of grief that every mortal must eventually travel. Now, do you wish to follow that route?'

Gaalav hesitated then said, 'It doesn't sound like a place where one can make a start. What is the next direction?'

'Next comes the realm of Varun, lord of the waters. It is called Paschim, because it is where the day ends, the sun sheds his rays, and the mountain named Asta accepts them. Thus, suryasta, twilight, spreads, bringing in its wake night and sleep, when living beings enter the half world of dreams. Here lies the ocean where all rivers end, and where they begin their new journey. Ananta, the king of serpents, resides in the waters, and my own lord, who is without a beginning or an end, has made the west his permanent residence. This, then is the western path. Shall we head there?'

'There is one more,' said Gaalav. 'Tell me about the north, O Garud.'

'The northern route is supreme among directions,' said Garud. 'Only people who have exercised self-restraint all their lives can go there.' He paused to allow these words to sink in. Gaalav, who was not unintelligent, understood that the jibe was meant for him, and blushed. After a while Garud continued, 'In the north stand the Himalayas, home to Mahadev. Raja Daksh's daughter, Uma, performed austerities among these mountains so she could obtain the great god for her husband. There are many beautiful hermitages in that region. There are clear lakes filled with rare lotuses. There are pristine forests, high-altitude meadows and sacred groves. The north is also home to Dhruv, pre-eminent among the Lord's devotees. Such is his honour that the sun, moon and stars circle around him...O Gaalav, I said right in the beginning that this was the supreme among all four regions. That is why it is known as Uttar. Now, tell me where do you intend to go?'

'Everywhere!' Gaalav cried. 'I want to see *all* these places, but first take me to where the gods live. I am keen to meet them...maybe they will help me. A man who can obtain the blessings of the gods cannot fail in any endeavour. Take me to them, Garud. Take me east.'

'I like your keenness,' Garud said. 'However—'

Gaalav brought his hands together in a plea but he was smiling. 'O Garud, please not another lecture.'

'I was merely going to ask you, have you ever flown before?'

Gaalav's eyes widened. In his haste to be on his way, he hadn't considered how he would travel. Fly! Speechless at the prospect, he merely shook his head. Compassion, an emotion he did not often feel, flickered in Garud. He had a sudden sense of the narrowness of an earthbound existence. *Humans are captives in their way of life. Like birds with broken wings.* 'Climb on my back,' he said gruffly. 'Don't worry, you are safe as long as you hold on to my neckband.'

He soared straight towards the rising sun, his wings lit by the rays. Every feather glinted. He looked as if he was on fire. The gold-plated light blinded Gaalav, he tried to shade his eyes with his hands but, in the process, lost his grip on the neckband and almost fell off. Hurriedly grabbing it again, he tucked his head inside Garud's soft, warm plumage.

Chortling to himself, Garud sailed in the strong tailwind. 'I am just using the thermals to push us along,' he said. 'Flying is the easiest thing in the world.' After a while Gaalav felt emboldened enough to peer over the side. The landscape—a patchwork of fields, forests, tiny hamlets, stitched by the meandering rivers and their tributaries—looked placid, inert. It was nothing like the teeming, troubled world he inhabited. 'Now watch what happens when I flap my wings to propel us ahead,' Garud said.

The effect was immediate. They entered the eye of a storm. Around them, for miles the hurricane created by the rush of Garud's wings knocked down trees, lifted off the thatched roofs of homes and the freshly stacked hay in the fields. Pillars of black clouds began to build up in the sky. The wind roared, it whistled eerily. Greyness all around. Lightning split the firmament. There was a clap of thunder that nearly knocked Gaalav off his perch. Everything flashed past in a blur. Then came a new sound, a snarl deeper than thunder and even more ominous; it was a warning growl of an ocean on the boil. In a flash, islands were covered in giant waves. Seashores submerged. Fish, serpents, crocodiles, whales, octopi, sabre-tooth tiger sharks and swarms of pale jellyfish rose in the sprays and were flung sky-high. An electric eel landed on Gaalav, squirmed down his back and leg, giving him a strong shock before it dropped back into the water and darted into its depths.

'Please slow down,' cried Gaalav. 'I can hear the terrible bellow of the ocean. Its mouth is wide open. It will swallow me. It's so dark, I can see nothing. O Father! O Mother! Save me...stop, stop, O bird! I cannot bear it. I am soaked to the skin. My chest is weak from birth! I cannot breathe...you are frightening me to death. Is there no land in sight? Take me down!'

'Don't be so timid,' Garud said.

'I will die without fulfilling my pledge,' wailed Gaalav. 'Where will I get the white horses now?'

'*Horses, horses, horses!*' Garud's face became a fiery red. He turned his head to one side so that an eye glared balefully at Gaalav. 'A while ago, you were willing to travel everywhere. A mere storm has scared you off,

Brahmin, and now you don't want to see the world! No human has ever sat on my back, but you are too fearful to appreciate that I was doing you a favour.'

'I beg you...just put me down on the nearest shore.'

'I will,' Garud said testily. 'I spy a mountain in the distance. We'll rest there, and get something to eat before heading back.'

'And the horses?'

'Yes, yes...you will get your horses.'

~

The fang-shaped mountain known as Rishabh rose out of the peninsula. The summit, enfolded in grey clouds, was like a woman in veils. It was raining on the top, but when the rain stopped and the fog rolled away, the view unspooled like time without end. The blue of the ocean soared to become the sky dome. The steep slopes of the mountain were thickly forested. There were trees here not seen anywhere else, covered with sturdy vines that bore delicate bell-shaped flowers in the colours of a tropical dawn. Droplets gleamed on their petals. The forest was covered in moss and fern. Ripe mangosteen fruit lay on the ground, their purple skin split open by the fall, revealing the soft white flesh; litchis hung in bunches of fuchsia. Cascades tumbled down the mountain's flanks, glided past the tangled roots of wild fig trees. The steady sound of flowing water amplified the snatches of birdsong. Sunbirds, bee-eaters, hornbills, treepies and nightingales rummaged in the foliage, the flutter of their wings creating a clandestineness, like a woman's anklets.

'This place is beautiful!' Gaalav declared, eager to wipe away the shameful memory of his panic just a short while ago and to establish that he was a bold traveller. 'But it is lonely. Does no one live here?'

'No one.'

'I do,' said a new voice behind them.

The visitors turned around in surprise. The woman was tall, lean and firm of body. Though her curly hair was lightly silvered, it was hard to tell her age. The tresses rose in a widow's peak and fell all the way down her shapely back to her knees, partly concealing the smoothness of her skin, which was bare, except for two strips of barkcloth. Her face was narrow and unlined, with a high brow, clear brown eyes and sharp features that gave it an austere beauty.

Gaalav recovered first and greeted the woman. She returned his salutation with a blessing.

'I am Shandili,' she said. The name had an air of neglect, as if it was an artefact from an earlier era, lacking a meaning in this one. They waited for her to say something more by way of introduction: who were her kinsmen, whose daughter, wife or mother was she? She merely looked at them in silence. Gaalav turned to Garud, expecting him to lead the conversation, but the latter looked on, still nonplussed.

Finally Gaalav said, 'We were returning home…there was a storm out at sea.'

'I know,' she said, and glanced pointedly at Garud. There was a hint of reproof in her look.

'We need a dry place to lie down for the night,' Gaalav said. 'Also, something to eat.'

She nodded. 'Come.'

She turned around and began to walk. There was no path through the forest, but she led them with the surefootedness of a wild goat to a cave on the edge of the mountain. A torrent flowed down the mountainside near the cave. Below, at the end of its sheer drop, the ocean rose and fell with a constant hissing noise. Gaalav looked down once at the seething waters and shuddered. Dusk had fallen, the wind began to rise. Though the spot was bleak, within the cave's cosiness, Gaalav felt, at last, comfortable. He sent up a silent prayer of gratitude to the gods for delivering him from a watery grave.

Shandili's home was simple, functional, yet complete. Gaalav wondered if she lived by herself in this wild and lonely place, and immediately dismissed the idea. It was unthinkable for a respectable woman to live alone. Probably her husband wished to live like a hermit, and she, poor woman, had to go along with his wishes. Among the scant personal goods in the cave were several storage jars, clay plates, bowls, tumblers, cooking pots and crude wooden ladles. The earthen fireplace was big enough for a family. There was also a good supply of kindling. All this led him to believe that the brahmin woman had kinsmen to protect her, but for some reason they were not at home that evening. Meanwhile, she soon got a fire going and there was something cooking in a deep round pot. It appeared to be a concoction of dried roots and fresh herbs.

'Mother, may I help you with the cooking?' Gaalav said. 'I have some experience in the kitchen, having helped my Guru Ma quite often.'

'Thank you, but I prefer to cook by myself,' she replied, softening her refusal with a quick, warm smile.

'Please tell me then what's cooking? The aroma, though tempting, is new to me.'

She smiled again but did not reply.

Her lack of response discouraged questions, but Gaalav was eager to make conversation. 'In my guru's ashram, we grew our own vegetables,' he said.

'Then you will find the flavours in this preparation quite different,' she said. 'It is made entirely from wild plants. They speak in their original flavours. If your palate deciphers their language correctly, you may even appreciate the dish.' She peered into the pot, stirred it and added, 'It's almost done.'

Something strange was going on. Garud was being moody. He had not spoken a single word since the woman had appeared on the scene, although he had cast several darting glances at Shandili, as if assessing her. While she cooked the meal, he sat at the entrance of the cave with his back to the rest of the company, seemingly absorbed in his own thoughts. He heard Gaalav offering to help with the cooking, and also Shandili's reply, as if feeding stranded travellers was something she did every day. He wondered who she was? Why was she here? Why did she live alone?

The moon came up, bathing the sea in its silver light. Inside the cave the fire crackled merrily. Finally, Shandili served the chunky aromatic gruel to them in clay bowls. Gaalav ate, praising every mouthful. 'It tastes so fresh and light,' he said. 'Of the sea's song and the soil's strength.'

'Not enough salt,' Garud said, too loudly, without looking at their hostess.

Frowning at the note of belligerence in his friend's voice, Gaalav said to him, 'O son of Vinata, it lacks nothing.' With seeming artlessness, he added, 'Maybe *you* are used to excess salt in your food. That would certainly explain your angry nature.'

Garud sent him an outraged look but said nothing.

When the meal was over, Shandili took away the bowls to wash them in the waterfall. She returned them to the stack on a ledge and carefully cleaned out the ashes from the fireplace. These she placed in a clay urn just outside the entrance. Then she handed thin mats and rough blankets to the visitors, blew out the lamp and lay down herself. Once again, Gaalav's curiosity was aroused. The dark made it easier for him to speak. 'Is there no one to take care of you, Mother?'

'There is no danger on the island,' she said.

'Does no one ever come here?'

'They do. All the time. Mostly fishermen who stray too far from the mainland. This island is just off a shipping route, sailors stop to replenish their fresh water supplies and to seek refuge from hurricanes.'

'But isn't that a danger to you? All men are not the same. And seeing you without a chaperone....' Gaalav trailed off.

'I know how to look after myself,' she said.

~

Vinata, his mother, came to Garud in a dream that night. It was a dream he'd had before. At first his mother was not in his line of vision, but her voice reached him, low, unemotional yet sharp enough to carve the words on the inside of his skull.

'We are slaves, O son, Kadru's slaves. The wise learn from their history, so listen. Kadru is my sister. Daksh, our father, married us off to Rishi Kashyap, who had several wives. A great soul he was, of measured speech and manner, yet he had an unmistakable eye for feminine beauty. In our company he spent many happy hours. One day, quite without warning, he asked us to dust his tiger skin, rinse and fill his water pot and fetch the wooden staff. I'm done with dalliances, he said. Just like that. Dusting *us* off too, as if we were nothing. We were fearful of the future. One male of any age is enough as the guardian of a dozen women, but without even one male, a dozen women of all ages cannot get on in this world. Though widowhood is a curse, even a widow is respectable—as long as she has a son. Then how were we to live without a husband or sons?

'Seeing our dismay, Kashyap took pity and asked us to choose a boon each. Kadru wanted to be first—that was always her way—and I allowed it because she was younger. Kadru asked for a thousand sons, all equal in splendour. When it came to my turn, I asked for just two—who would be as great as her thousand. With his magical powers Kashyap generated a thousand eggs for Kadru, oblong, with leathery shells. He told her to fill clay jars with moss and dirt and place the thousand eggs inside them. As for me, I had just two beige eggs that I placed, on his instruction, in a nest woven from tall grass. Watch over the embryos, he told us and left. We never saw him again.

'The wait begin. Kadru would count her eggs every single day. If I so much as glanced in their direction, she'd dart towards me, spitting fury. Then she'd make a big show of counting the eggs again. It amused me to irritate her. Five hundred years passed this way before Kadru's eggs hatched. Her babies, a shiny black mass of serpents, writhed all over the floor. They slithered up the walls, crept into the kindling, curled up in kitchen pots. I even found one in the nest where my embryos still lay unhatched, as I tended to them. Kadru never lost an opportunity to drive it home: her plenitude, my paucity. Pitying smiles and fake encouragement were what she doled out, while pretending to be preoccupied with the mothering of her own brood. Watching her, my anxiety grew by leaps and bounds. What if my two babies were dying inside? What if they were already dead? I spent sleepless nights alone with my fear, till I could bear it no longer. One morning, I woke up very early and before I could change my mind, cracked the shell of one of the two beige eggs. I looked into the contents. There he was, your elder brother—with an upper body that was perfectly formed, but the lower part still undeveloped. He drew his first breath and said his first words. Such angry words they were. "Since you could not curb your envy of your sister, you broke the egg ahead of its time, and so I am born to suffer as a cripple. A curse on you for your rashness, Mother. You will become your sister's slave." I wept not just for myself but also for him. Perhaps my grief mellowed his anger, for he said, "If you can curb your impatience and allow the second egg to hatch, my brother, who is destined for great things, will set you free. If you want him to be strong, take good care of the egg this time." Saying this he flew straight into the sun. Arun is his name. He is Surya's charioteer. I see him every day crossing the sky, the carmine glow of dawn reminds me of his fury. How can I blame him? Motherhood—one learns it only through becoming. Then, how can I blame myself?'

The restless energy in her had reappeared in him. He relived that time inside the egg when he had dreamed about breaking out and conquering the world. Garud knew what would come next but he still hated the sound of it. His mother could reach him wherever he hid, in sleep, maybe even in death. He would not be at ease as long as the dirge played in his head: *Birth is death too. A creature born only exchanges one crypt for another. We are prisoners, O son, slaves to my sister…*

Vinata said, 'Around this time, while I waited for the second egg to hatch, something happened. The seven-headed horse began to come to the beach near our hut. His name was Uchhaishravas. He was the first horse in the world, created when the Ocean of Milk was churned by the devas and asuras. Made entirely from amrit, he belonged to no one, only to himself, and wandered wherever he willed, admired everywhere for his grace and strength, that proud white radiance he gave off. I loved to watch him. One day, Kadru squinting hard—she was one-eyed—asked me: "What colour is his tail?" It was a harmless question. White, I said. She merely smiled, that slow, superior smile which should have warned me, but left me feeling, as always, inferior. Shaking her head, she said, 'It's black.' Egged on, I challenged her. "Take a bet. The tail is white. If I'm wrong, I will be your slave; if not, the other way round." Yes, these were my exact words. It was tempting to think of Kadru as my slave. She who acted like a maharani when we lived with Kashyap. Never lifting a finger, yet bossing over me as though she were his favourite wife.' Another long silence and a sigh. Then Vinata said in a tired voice, 'Why blame her? Kadru is who she is because I am who I am. Sisters are like that, the love and its opposite are conjoined, but when is it not so? We were rival wives, too, you must remember. Vying for one man's attention can wreck the best of bonds. So, after making the bet, we waited together for the next dawn. The horse rose from the horizon like milky foam, the silk wind blowing through his mane. And when he was close, so close that I could see the steam emerging from his nostrils, the gold in his eyes, the droplets of salt water, like fresh pearls forming on his skin and falling off, the sparks where his feet touched the ground...I also saw that his tail was covered with fine black hairs...I looked at Kadru. She smiled at me. She knew that I had lost the bet, and with it my freedom. And so it is with you, O son. Born to a slave mother, you too, are Kadru's slave. Her offspring, the nagas, see you as a vehicle that can ferry them from island to island. But let me say, before you think that *I* made a mistake—it was Kadru who did not play fair. This is what she did: she asked her sons to wrap themselves around the horse's tail so that it appeared black. They refused to be a part of her plan. After all, wasn't I their aunt who had always been nice to them? So, she, their own mother, cursed them. Their species would become extinct, she said. This is their punishment for disobeying her.'

And now Garud asked the question that always troubled him: 'But why didn't she take her curse back when they obeyed her?'

'It is their punishment for refusing in the first place. A mother's wishes must be obeyed immediately, without question. Kadru's sons obeyed only because they were afraid. Even so, Kadru, being who she is, went too far. During the yagna that will be conducted by King Janmejaya, Agni, the fire god will consume all of the world's serpents.'

'Must something so far in the future come true? Cannot the course of the curse be changed?'

His mother's voice floated across the darkness. It was the same answer as always. 'A curse, just like a boon, is only the result of an action. While actions come from within us, curses and boons magnify their consequences. Thus do stories make us aware of our nature. Our ignorance. They tell us that with ignorance comes arrogance. Janmejaya will be born in the final age of man—when virtue will be on its last leg. Janmejaya, a child of his times, will succumb, as mortals invariably do, to hubris. He will hold the sacrifice to exterminate all snakes because a snake bite will end his father's life. The desire for revenge so quickly becomes a blaze that it cannot be controlled. Janmejaya, son of Parikshit, grandson of the Pandavas, the five who will kill their hundred brothers. And that too will be because of a rivalry from birth, like this one between you and your half-brothers, the nagas—an enmity born of envy and desire. Born of fear. Anger and fear, these grow in secret within us. Like a hidden sickness in the blood, they are passed on from one generation to the next. Janmejaya will hear the story of the great war that his ancestors fought. Maybe he will understand.'

'Understand what?'

'The value of self-restraint.'

Rancour, fatigue, disgust. He was never free of them. The serpents demanded that he fly them from island to island. You have to do what we ask, they said. He hated them. On land, in water, wherever he spotted a serpent, whenever, he would hunt it down, tear its flesh with a mercilessness he could not explain even to himself, and feed on it....

'So, it's all up to you,' Vinata's voice in the dream said again. Garud felt the burden of her words descending on the narrow space between his shoulders. She had ground him down. 'I ask this of you because you are my son and I your mother...buy my freedom and your own as well, for you too, born to a slave mother, are not free. Only you can choose a different life for us, for yourself. Do you want to live like this always, in thrall to your cousins and seething in anger?'

Garud was tired of hearing the bitterness in Vinata's voice. It flowed beneath the story but was like a current in the opposite direction, a drag. Envy, enmity, vengeance, destruction. Was this her only bequest to him? He asked fretfully, 'What must I do to be free?'

Vinata replied, 'Steal amrit from the devas and give it to the nagas...Kadru's sons want immortality. They want it more than others since she has cursed them with extinction. And now the same curse that enslaved you will set you on your path to greatness. It will write your story. Gather your courage. Go!'

'But I am hungry,' he said. 'I want to eat before I start out...what is there for me to eat?'

'On your way you will see the Nishadhas: hunters, fishermen, bird trappers, rodent catchers...eat them, if you must. But don't make the mistake of swallowing a brahmin. A brahmin must not be killed.'

'What does a brahmin taste like?'

'Like a burning coal.'

~

The same dream but somehow stranger than before. Garud woke up with a bitter aftertaste coating his tongue.

A suspicion rose: had there been something in that broth that the brahmin woman had served them for dinner? He saw that Gaalav was already awake, staring down at him, wide-eyed.

Gaalav asked hesitatingly. 'O bird, what happened to you?'

'What? *What*?'

'Your wings....'

Garud looked down. His body had shortened so that he was barely a foot above the ground. However, it was not the shrinking that horrified him so much as the sight of his wings lying in a pile of ashes, a few charred feathers the only reminder of their former glory.

'Why have your lost your wings?' Gaalav asked. 'Why have you become so tiny? Is this island enchanted? Is it a curse? O deva! Just look at yourself...how are we going to leave unless you get your wings back? Garud, such bad things happen only to those who seriously transgress dharma. What have you done?'

'Nothing! I didn't do anything'—he stopped mid-sentence. *Is she a daayan, a dakkini? Who is she?* Thinking was an act too. Had she read his thoughts? He had been thinking about her ever since the moment he first saw her. After a while, he said as if making a clean breast of it, 'I had no evil intention, Brahmin. None...I....' He stopped because he could not find the right words to describe what it was that he had felt. She mesmerized him. He burst out, 'Look at this place, its utter desolation. *We* can't wait to get away from here. How could anyone, leave alone a woman as beautiful as she, live here without any thought of safety? It is not appropriate for a well-born woman to live without a male...I just thought that we could take her along with us.'

'Take her along? *Who?* Are you talking about Mata Shandili?'

'Why not?'

Gaalav's face became stern. 'Take her where?'

'It was merely an idea I had. There is a hut in the mountains where I could have kept her...kept her safe, I mean.'

'What did you intend to do with her?'

'Nothing...I mean, it would have been better than this. Have you ever heard of a respectable woman living alone? It is wrong!'

Garud stopped speaking. For he had suddenly noticed her presence. She was sitting by the hearth, watching him silently. There was nothing in her face to show that she was angry, but he sensed a strange, powerful nimbus around her.

'Don't tell me what is wrong,' she said softly.

'I was only thinking of you,' he said, looking in her direction but not meeting her eyes. Would she burn him down entirely? What was his crime, other than having a wish. *I wanted only to shelter you from the world.*

She sent him a look of scorn. 'You believe that there is something shameful about a woman who has no man to protect her...perhaps you also believe that a woman cannot leave her home. Unlike men, she is not allowed to go away alone to the forest.'

Garud had a beleaguered look. 'I apologize—I was only concerned about your safety.'

'Your *concern* is wasted on me, O king of birds. I live alone in this wild place, but don't misjudge me. I am not a destitute widow. I may not have a son, but I am no object of pity. Nor does my living alone imply that I am of easy virtue. I prefer solitude because I have chosen the path of liberation. The path does not distinguish between man and woman, it welcomes every true seeker. Righteousness has no gender. All I saw were two fellow beings who had lost their way and needed shelter for a night. With humility I shared whatever I had by way of food with you. I have always done this. Men who are honourable thank me and leave. Those who are not end up there.' She inclined her head towards the clay urn by the entrance. 'I don't need to do anything to protect myself. My tapasya takes care of me. Maybe you should ask yourself why *you* saw only a woman alone, and felt the need to bend her to your will.'

Garud flushed deeply. 'Forgive me.'

After a moment she inclined her head to signal that she accepted the apology. 'You will get your form back. Go wherever you wish, but wherever you go, don't judge a woman for how she looks or the way she lives—if she does not fit your ideas of a woman.'

He got his wings back, but they were not the same wings. These were bigger and stronger. The return journey was quick and uneventful, as both Garud and his passenger were lost in thought.

They touched down in an open field. Gaalav saw a figure sitting under a tree on its edge. His relief at returning home vanished. He approached the man slowly and bowed low. His heart was thumping. *Has Gurudev come here to tell me that I am forgiven?*

Vishwamitra remained in meditation for several minutes. At last, he opened his eyes and sent Gaalav a level look. 'Well?'

Gaalav lowered his head wordlessly.

'O brahmin,' said Vishwamitra. 'You promised me a dakshina, though I did not ask for one. The time has come to keep your word. You understand what a brahmin's vow means, therefore do as you think fit. Meanwhile, I have waited this long, I can wait a little more.' Saying this he stood up and walked away into the forest.

Gaalav was trembling. The enormity of the task before him and the consequences of failing—it was all too much to bear. He sent Garud a look of total despair and said, 'I served him with complete devotion. Why is he hounding me?'

Garud, too, had seen and heard Vishwamitra. Any remaining doubts he'd had about the absurdity of the gurudakshina disappeared. Gaalav has reason to worry, he thought. Not a moment's rest for this unfortunate brahmin till he has given his guru what he wants.

'Gold is what you need,' he said. 'Without this precious metal you cannot get those horses. Created inside the ground, purified by fire, it is only obtained by those who are fated to be rich. There is no other way to get it but to approach a king. Not any king, for a minor one would tax his subjects to get the gold. You must ask a king who is rich enough and comes from a long line of royal sages.'

'I don't know any such king,' said Gaalav bluntly. 'Do you?'

'Yes. He belongs to the Chandravanshi dynasty and is the richest man on earth.'

'Rich enough to give away vast amounts of gold just for the asking?'

'You have a lot to learn, Gaalav,' said Garud. 'Kings are not like ordinary humans. They love flamboyance and vie with each other even when it comes to bestowing gifts.

The grander the better. Yayati is known never to turn down a request. He takes pride in fulfilling his obligations as a king. When the news spreads that he has given away enough gold to buy eight hundred of the rarest horses to a brahmin, the bards will go mad composing paeans to him. No quicker route to fame, I assure you...that is what every king wants—to be remembered forever. To be sung about forever.' He paused for a few moments, then added with a show of casualness, 'Besides, Yayati and I are old friends. Though we haven't met in a long time, I think he will give it to you—if *I* ask.'

~

Twenty years had passed since Yayati's barter with his youngest son. The second puberty he'd gained was running out of steam. Pratisthan, too, was in a decline. The rivers had flooded several times; with siltation, trade had dropped. Occupations gone, lawlessness was on the rise. Officials were corrupt, the population disenchanted, pieces of the kingdom were being snatched away by hostile tribes and cattle raiders were a growing menace. Sensing troubled times ahead, those who could were leaving the land. The rest asked questions: Where are we heading? How can such a king give stability to a kingdom? When he displaces his anointed heir and appoints another for a purely personal reason, isn't he setting the wrong precedent? This is how kingdoms break up. Adharma rises, cracks appear within families and wealth is divided unfairly. The seeds of strife are sown thus, much in advance....

As if to lend support to the fears of commoners, Yadu, the embittered eldest son, without seeking his father's blessings, quietly saddled his horse and left the land with a small personal retinue. One by one, his brother and half-brothers followed his example.

'This is not the end,' Devayani said. 'My son Yadu will be the patriarch of a new line. But *you* have destroyed your family.'

'No. You did that for me,' Yayati retorted.

'All this for a mere dasi?'

'Careful...she is not your dasi any more, but the mother of the next king.'

Devayani's face turned pale. 'This is my home. You cannot make me leave it.'

Yayati made no reply. A deep weariness had come over him. He would not admit it to her but the departures of his sons had deeply grieved him. Yet he understood their reasons—how else were they to keep their self-respect?—and blamed no one. If blame was to be apportioned, he acknowledged privately, then his was the bigger share. He had wronged each one, even if he had not meant to. He felt defeated. Ever since he had regained his youth, he had tried to be a conscientious king. But he was aware that the damage had been done; his people saw the leap backwards, from old age to adolescence, as unnatural. The story when narrated down the generations would portray him as a reprobate. There was also this other thing: he had begun to understand the accuracy of Shukracharya's words that desire, by its own nature, was indestructible. It spawned new hungers but also left one jaded. The experience of living a lifetime again, traversing the same old terrain of desire and its gratification, was using up too much energy. It had become a nightmare and he did not know how to free himself from its clutches. How thin the life of the pleasure-lover was. The songs were no longer pleasing, nor was the wine, nor were the female bodies he used night after night. No matter what he did to fill his hours, he could not fill the emptiness within. He had begun to look forward to an end.

~

Despite his diminished resources, when it came to hospitality the king did not stint. The two guests were welcomed in the proper way. First their feet were washed, then they were offered refreshments and finally, after an oil massage and a bath, a well-cooked meal was served to them in dishes of silver and gold. Only after the servants had cleared away the dishes, did Yayati ask Garud the reason for this visit.

'O son of Nahusha,' said Garud. 'My friend Gaalav, who was till recently a student of Rishi Vishwamitra, is in a strange predicament and his only hope is you.' He gave Yayati an edited version of the events, emphasizing on Gaalav's perseverance, the guru's strange demand and the dilemma that it had caused. 'You know, O king, that among all the transgressions, the worst is that of not keeping one's word. Gaalav cannot repay his guru, and that is why he seeks your aid. Give him, as daan, the gold he needs to repay Vishwamitra. You will be doubly blessed, by your very act of kindness, as well as by Gaalav's gratitude and goodwill. A share of the merit obtained from his austerities will come to you. It will attract good fortune all around.'

Hiding his dismay, Yayati invited the guests to rest for a while. He was in a quandary. One of the reasons his fortune had declined was all the wealth he had been required to give to needy brahmins. The line seemed to only grow, till he had begun to feel needy himself. He was struggling to keep up a semblance of his former lifestyle. He did not have even a decent stable any more. Feeling remorse for the way he had treated his sons, when they left he had given away much of his gold, as well as many of his horses, elephants and cattle herds as the wherewithal on which to start a new life. Yet, how could he turn away a brahmin who had sought refuge in him? *These two have come to me instead of going to any of the prosperous Suryavanshi kings in Aryavarta. It is those rajas who are likely to have the priceless shyamkarni horses in their stables, not I. Garud and Gaalav don't know how destitute I am, but I cannot tell them that; they will not understand. If I disappoint this brahmin, then he, too, may curse me...what can I give him that will send him on his way a satisfied man? It has to be something that is even more invaluable than gold, so that he can trade it for the horses.*

After thinking the matter over for several hours, he hit upon a solution. It would appear unusual he thought, but anything born from desperation is bound to be drastic. Gaalav, who was in a difficult situation himself, would understand; he would accept what was expedient.

'Shyamkarni horses are the most expensive in the world,' Yayati said to his guests. 'I do not have sufficient gold for you to exchange for eight hundred such horses. But I'm prepared to bestow on you something even more precious—in fact, she is of incomparable value.'

'*She*?' repeated Gaalav, frowning. 'Who are you referring to?'

'My daughter Madhavi. This daughter of mine is

a gem. For her beauty alone, devas, asuras and rajas have solicited her. Moreover, she is well-trained in the household arts and has a sweet adjusting temperament. But, what makes her truly invaluable to kshatriya families is a prediction in her horoscope—that she will have sons who are destined to become chakravarti samrats. *Four, no less!* Thus she will enrich four royal lineages. If that were to become known, kings will offer entire kingdoms as bride price—what to speak of shyamkarni horses! Accept this daughter of mine, O brahmin. All I have ever wanted is to marry her off into a well-to-do family where my grandsons will get the right kind of upbringing as future kings.'

For a few minutes Gaalav was speechless. 'Are you giving your daughter *as daan*?' he burst out, panic-stricken. 'What am I supposed to do with her?'

'Do as you think best.'

Gaalav had spent the last few hours in an almost euphoric state, with visions of himself striding triumphantly into Vishwamitra's ashram filling his head. His eyes narrowed as a suspicion arose in his mind: was the king stretching the truth about his daughter? After all, that was Yayati's reputation. He had fooled his wife and his father-in-law for years. The story about Shukracharya's imaginative curse had become well-known in Aryavarta. It had become a case study. *Boons and Curses: How, Where and When to Use Them* was a popular subject for both discourse and debate among brahmins in ashrams across the land.

Then a fresh misgiving bothered Gaalav. *If this daughter of his is all that he says she is, then why hasn't Yayati married her off till now? The bride price he's talking about would have helped* him. *It's quite likely that, being an opportunist, he is trying to please me and earn merit for himself, as well as get rid of a daughter he can't, for some unknown reason, marry off...maybe the bit about her beauty is a gross exaggeration, and she is squint-eyed or worse. Who is her mother? Is her character blemish-free? Should I or should I not accept? If I refuse, I have to do it very tactfully. I cannot risk offending any more powerful personages.*

But before Gaalav could choose the appropriate words in which to decline the king's offer, Garud intervened. 'This is really quite unexpected, O king! My young friend is awestruck at your generosity. When he recovers his power of speech, he will no doubt thank you for helping him out of his difficulties, but I will do so right now.' He brought his hands together and bowed his head in gratitude.

Yayati couldn't believe his luck. Trying to look suitably modest, he said, 'Oh no, no...it's really nothing. It is my honour that I could be of service to the brahmin and yourself, O son of Vinata. Please remember me to your lord.'

Recognizing a cue and taking it, Garud said, 'That reminds me...I must return to Vaikunth now. They really can't manage without me for too long. I will take your leave, O king. Thank you for your kindness.'

'What?' said Gaalav, sitting up with a jerk. 'Are you leaving?'

'Yes,' said Garud, shortly. 'And so should you, my friend. We must not impose on Maharaja Yayati's hospitality any longer. Besides, you still have to accomplish your task and obtain those horses.'

'Yes, but I thought you would help me.'

'Haven't I done exactly that?'

'But—'

'Gaalav, you are no longer a scholar in an ashram, but a man of the world. You have to become self-reliant. With all the support I've given you, flying you around the world, introducing you to a generous king, you still seem to be at a loss. Grow up, my friend. Get rid of these paralysing fears of yours. Stop bemoaning your fate. Go out and do something to help yourself.'

With a smooth smile, Yayati interjected. 'You are by all means welcome to stay, Munikumar Gaalav. My kingdom, its wealth and I myself are at your disposal.'

Gaalav thought to himself: Which kingdom and what wealth? Hiding his consternation, he said brusquely, 'No need for all that. I, too, must be on my way.'

'Of course, of course.' Yayati nodded. 'The palanquin is waiting outside. An escort of soldiers will see you till the borders of my land.'

'Palanquin?' Gaalav frowned. 'I don't need one. Nor do you have to send an escort to see me off your land.'

Ignoring the bite in the brahmin's words, Yayati said, 'It's only fitting that, in her own country, a royal woman should travel in a palanquin, under an escort.'

'Oh! Ah...I see.'

Garud well understood Gaalav's new predicament. The brahmin's travails were by no means over. And now this extra baggage. Taking pity on him, he said, 'Maharaja Yayati is an astute man. His suggestion is excellent. And I have one of my own for you. Go north to Ayodhya, kingdom of the Ikshvaku dynasty. Treasuries, granaries, stables, armies—the Ikshvakus have it all. Besides, they are a pious family, which always helps. The king respects dharma and knows what is expected of him. He is famous for his largesse, especially towards poor brahmins. Ask him nicely. He may well accede to your request...and now, I really must leave.'

Bowing in farewell to first the king and then Gaalav, Garud flew off.

8

Drishadvati

When this story gets told, they will surely edit this bit—about how I left Pratisthan. Choosing bland words, they will make it look as if it was an orderly and formal leave-taking with my father handing me over to the brahmin, all new, nice and tidy. It was anything but that.

This is how it begins: *Bam!* A hard thwack on the back of my neck, at that precise spot where the lowest part of my skull meets the spine. Aahh! The pain...a river that flows both ways, down the ridges of my backbone and up, to the very top of my skull, the crown lifting itself completely off. How did this come about? *What happened*? The last coherent memory I have is of digging my teeth into flesh. Human flesh. A hand attached to a man—an ugly, brutish fellow with yellow eyes. His accomplice was the one with bad teeth and foul breath. These two ruffians came along by the river.

But what was I doing there—by the river?

Wait, it's all coming back...Sarmistha had sent me to pick greens for the evening meal. There was a stretch on the riverbank where the most tender shoots were to be found. But I went there for a special reason: a pair of swans had made it their private patch, weaving into an everyday scene a new intricate beauty. I loved to watch them glide gracefully through the water. They were never far from each other. They paddled through the shallows, diving for food, occasionally calling out to each other. They seemed supremely content to wake up together every single day and live their entire life this way. Sarmistha called it *love*, adding that swan pairs never separate...after a while, I heard a faint jingle-jangle of bells. Two men carrying a covered palanquin made of cane hove into view. They looked like they were from the palace. *The queen?* Gooseflesh prickled up my arms. I hadn't seen Devayani since that night four years ago, but the feeling, that she was watching me, her face frozen with antipathy, had imprinted on my mind.

One of the palanquin-bearers said something I couldn't clearly hear. '...the way to...?'

Which way was he talking about? There was only the river here. Where did he want to go? Reluctantly, I went closer to hear him better. Big, big mistake. They grabbed me. One pinned my arms back while the other one lifted me by my feet. I fought in all the ways I could. Screamed, bit, scratched, kicked. My foot made contact with his belly and he doubled up in pain. I felt a fierce joy. Then, one of the scoundrels, the one with bad breath, hit me at the back of my head. That is the last thing I remember clearly...the rest is a blur, a horrible blur of sensations: nausea, pain, dizziness, gut-wrenching fear... was I dead? I could feel my toes when I flexed them, my fingers too seemed all right. So...not dead. My stomach lurched suddenly. This terrifying swaying movement. It struck me then that I was being carried in the palanquin.

A prisoner. Bound hand and foot, gagged, blindfolded for good measure. Where were they taking me? Why? Who were they? Darkness came over me again, blanking out thought.

~

My eyes are being pried open. A long howl of protest. Mine, I realize, when someone says, 'Stop it!' The command is followed by a splash of cold water on my face.

Spluttering, I surface and yelp, 'No...don't!'

Nothing happens for a few moments. I open my eyes a crack. There is a shadow bending over me...a man. One of those two louts? *O deva, not again!*

'Don't!' I beg. My eyes well up.

'I am not going to harm you.' The voice is unsteady, as if its owner is about to burst into tears.

I am in his arms. Smooth, warm skin. Wrapped in sandalwood oil. His face is so close that I can feel his breath fanning across mine. His lashes are long and curling. Reflected in his brown eyes, I see my own bruised, dishevelled face. *Who is he?* There is a moment of total stillness...as if we are the two edges of a flame that has just been lit. I am suddenly conscious of my bare state. Those men tore my clothes. They roughed me up. A new fear grips me: What *else* did they do to me? Is he one of them? I struggle to sit up, push him away. He removes his arms from around me and steps back. My head hurts. I can't think...I can't...he is looking distraught. He couldn't be one of them...then who is he? I take a secret inventory of him. A brahmin. Thin but not frail. A coiled strength in his arms. Clean-shaven, with the tuft of hair atop the tonsured head, symmetrical narrow face with high cheekbones that emphasize the austere look. Dark melancholy eyes, the colour of warm melted jaggery. *Those eyelashes!* A firm square jaw. No, I will not look at his lips or his eyes. Not at his strong hands, the lean wrist, the fine hair on his muscular arms. Yet I cannot pull my gaze away from him. I compose myself, search for the right phrases to couch my gratitude. But my tongue, carrying an aftertaste of fear, is unruly. A fit of stammers gives the thank you speech a hysterical punctuation. 'I don't kn—know what—what would have hap—hap—happened if you hadn't resc—rescued me. Those men wou—would have ru—ru—ru—ruined me.' It sounds so ridiculous that I decide to keep my mouth firmly shut. I make myself look straight into his eyes. There is a halo of light around him, as if the sun were rising for the first time. I am lightheaded, as if I'm floating...something momentous is going to happen in the next few seconds. To me. To us. I hiccup.

He clears his throat, as if he, too, is nudging his vocal chords into action. 'Are you all right?' His voice is husky. 'Did they hurt you? I didn't know those men would stoop so low. They were the king's servants...I don't know them. When we reached the border of the kingdom, they returned...the king's orders, they said.'

'The *king's* orders?' My voice rises. 'Why? What have I done now?'

My question alarms him. After a moment, he asks abruptly, 'Who are you?'

'I—I—' *What should I tell him?*

'My name is Drishadvati.'

He narrows his eyes in suspicion and asks another

question. 'Drishadvati? Then you are not Yayati's daughter. You are not Madhavi...who are you?'

I am unsure about where this line of questioning is leading. 'I am the...king's daughter.'

'I don't believe you,' he says flatly. 'You don't look like a princess to me.'

'I was abducted,' I say, gathering whatever shreds of dignity I can.

He walks away a short distance to sit on a rock under a tree, pulls up his knees and buries his head in his arms, a picture of dejection. After a while he lifts his head and sends me a stony look. 'We are at the border of your father's kingdom. I will show you the way back. Then you are on your own. I refuse to be responsible for you.'

My head is in a whirl, but one thing jumps out: he was being so nice to me. Why has he stopped? Unaware of the threshold I am crossing, I say the first thing that comes into my head. 'I don't want to go back.'

He looks appalled. '*What?* How can you say that? You are Yayati's daughter. Where else can you go?'

~

Yayati's daughter. The words tether me to my fate. But I am ready to fight. I have been restive for a while. Twice I have attempted to leave, but I lost my way each time and was caught before I could get very far. The second time, I was thrashed. It is not that I am miserable in Sarmistha's house so much as bored. Though she burdens me with the housework, she is not unkind. Besides, there's Puru. On his good days—when aches and pains do not make him grumpy, when memory does not falter—he is tolerable company. He likes to tell me stories about events that happened long before either of us was born; he has a storehouse of such gathas. Some of them are so fantastic that I think he makes them up just to look knowledgeable. Do you? I asked him once.

He replied: Did you make me up? Did I make you up? Who made us up? We too are stories.

Yes, I said, with a mock yawn. But where's the end? Can you see it? I can't.

We will be our own storytellers, he said grandly. We will make our own endings. We will write the songs that others will sing about us. When I become the king, all the gathas about me will make me brave, handsome, generous and wise.

What about my gatha? I asked.

Gathas are only about kings, he said.

Feeling snubbed, I turned away.

But, it's true, isn't it? How different this world is from the forest...here, I am an outsider. Despite the long years she has spent in Yayati's kingdom, Sarmistha too remains an outsider. No one pays attention to us. Maybe they pretend not to, for fear of the queen. Our existence is marginalia. This is a home for the decrepit and the discarded. We live as if lost in a dark, confusing maze, with not a star to guide us out of it. Who are we? What is our calling? When will we know? Who will tell us? It is the king, my father Yayati, for whom we wait. We wait with longing for the day Puru will wear the crown. Meanwhile, Puru, with a faint air of martyrdom, calls it his destiny to grow old before his time. I wonder what he will call it when he goes back to being young again. Will he, too, live like Yayati, a compulsive pleasure-seeker? Somehow, I think not...Sarmistha waits for life to turn full circle and return her toothless, bed-wetting *old* son to his youth where a crown awaits him. She has never forgotten that she was born a princess. And now she hopes to be the queen mother and live in the palace one day. Just like Sarmistha, I too, am the fruit of royal loins, but, unlike her, I have never been a princess or lived in a palace. Though my birth mother still comes to me, as a shadow in a dream—a crowd of shadows, actually, since her birds and animals are always with her—these appearances are becoming rare. Till a while ago, I remembered the forest clearly. When the rains came, the lush green scent of soil and vegetation reawakened my senses. The forest came alive in my bloodstream. The dance of light and shade, sunbursts of birdsong, the sound of water flowing, the deep green vines twining around dark trunks. Then the memory remained only as an ache, a hankering, a residue on which I planned my escapes, but I could never get clean away. So now there is only Sarmistha's brown hut in which we live our dull brown lives, the exhausting monotonous round of chores, the waiting. In fact, this kidnapping has been quite the most exciting thing that has happened to me, and now *this*—being rescued by the best-looking man I've seen. I could look at him all day, a month, a year. A lifetime.

'I cannot go back,' I say to the brahmin.

'But—'

An ending is also a new beginning. I offer him my sweetest smile. 'I am now in your care...*your* responsibility. You saved me from those ruffians.'

He is startled. 'It wasn't quite like that,' he mumbles. A shifty look appears on his face again. He sends me a quick, assessing sideways glance like a fox's, then defiance...

why? I feel a strange prickling along my skin. An exciting new thought takes my breath away. Did he see me before, fall secretly in love and plan my abduction? That's how it happens in the best stories. Did he hire those two thugs for the job? I wait for him to say something, declare his intention as honourable, recite a love poem, but he disappoints by looking even more glum than before. The silence stretches, going nowhere.

'Please tell me everything,' I say, finally. 'Tell me what is really going on.'

He looks at me and then starts to speak slowly, in a voice thick with emotion. 'I am Gaalav, a disciple of Rishi Vishwamitra…there is no one more unfortunate than I.'

9

Gaalav and Drishadvati

'An honourable end is all I seek,' he said. A vision of the hair-raising flight over the ocean came back to him. His guru's words rang in his ears. He shuddered. 'I *have* to get those horses at any cost.'

After a while the maiden asked casually, 'Tell me, have you ever actually seen a shyamkarni horse?'

He frowned, shook his head. 'No. Never.'

'Then how do you know it exists?'

'What a question!' He shot her an angry look. 'Would my guru ask for something that isn't even there?'

'He could be testing you.'

His expression hardened. 'If he is, then I have to pass this test.'

She studied him for a few moments, then said softly, as if reaching a conclusion. 'It's not only about passing a test.'

'What do you mean?'

'It's a contest. *You* challenged the illustrious guru, and the great man has given a reply.'

What incensed him more, her tone or her words, he couldn't say. 'Challenged my guru? How can you think that? You are just a girl...you know nothing about the relationship between a guru and his student. It is—it's an unbreakable bond.'

She sent him a half smile. 'Stronger even than the father–son bond?'

'Yes!' he burst out, then corrected himself. 'At least, it's as strong.' A memory of his father's mild and self-effacing nature came back to him. Rephrasing his answer with obvious irritation, he said, 'The two cannot be compared.'

She nodded solemnly as if she understood.

He pursed his lips and turned away. Ever since he left the ashram his emotions had been in a turmoil. But, with the passage of days, a certain clarity had come. He had been putting it off, but now her question forced him to mull over the true nature of his relationship with Vishwamitra.

Born in a brahmin household, Gaalav had been brought up to believe that the link between a guru and his shishya was sacrosanct. Aimed to pass on a sophisticated tradition, it was predicated on complete trust from the side of the shishya, in whom the guru recognized a worthy inheritor of the truth he represented. Gaalav had venerated his guru and worked to win his trust. As time passed and his persistence paid off, his aspiration had grown: from wanting to be a credit to his guru, he had shifted to craving honour for himself—as Vishwamitra's most famous disciple. Was that *all* that he had secretly wished for? Was there such a thing as too much ambition? It was beginning to dawn on him that he had perhaps overreached. When Vishwamitra had rewarded him for his services by freeing him of the obligation of gurudakshina, he should have simply accepted and left. Instead he had mulishly insisted on repayment. What had prompted it?

Was it the fear that if he did not observe this all-important formality, he would never really be free? If he could not pay his debts in the world of men, how could he ever hope to enter the world of gods? Or had it arisen after the period of intimacy he had shared with Vishwamitra as his caregiver? In that time the line between master and disciple had temporarily blurred. However, following Vishwamitra's enhancement to the status of a brahmin rishi, the hierarchy had been reintroduced. He should have remembered that and been respectful of his guru's wishes by not harping on the fee. But settling his debt had dominated his mind. While he recognized his mistake, he was not convinced that his stand was wrong. What he found impossible to stomach was the memory of the most recent encounter. Vishwamitra's words had cut deep: *You promised me a dakshina, though I did not ask for one*. The guru had been needling him. Beneath the fear, dejection and the sick feeling of humiliation Gaalav had felt something else—a spark of anger. It was growing, energizing him in a new way. *After all that I did for him, how could he treat me like this? I will show him what I am made of*.

His reverie was disturbed by the sound of a throat being cleared, politely but pointedly. The maiden was standing before him. She had made some effort to tidy herself. 'Listen,' she said in a measured tone. 'I can see that you are upset by how events have turned out. Yayati gave you the impression that he was handing you a treasure. And you now feel he fobbed you off with a false promise.'

He stared at her in astonishment. 'You call your father by his name?'

'My father only fathered me,' she said angrily. 'As he has probably fathered dozens like me. I am his seed but not his child. He has never been overly concerned about my welfare. In the four years that I spent with Sarmistha, he never once inquired about me. And look at the way he got rid of me, packed me off with you.' Resentment vibrated in her voice.

'Still, there are more respectful ways of referring to him. You were brought up as a princess.'

She shook her head. 'He sold me to you as a princess, but the truth is that I have only spent one night in my entire life in a palace.'

'But he said that—'

'I would give birth to sons who would become great kings.' She smirked. 'My mother told him that. I heard her say it. I was watching his face. He wasn't quite sure whether to believe her or not, but he remembered her words all right when you demanded the shyamkarni horses from him.'

The crook! He has fobbed me off just as I suspected. Gaalav was stung to anger. 'I've been listening to your nonsense for a while,' he said coldly. 'If you don't wish to go back home, then go wherever you choose. You are released.'

'But *you* are not,' she pointed out. 'If I go away, there is no possibility of you getting those horses. I am your only hope.'

She's right. What am I going to do? 'What do you want from me?' he asked.

She chewed her lower lip and thought: I don't know anything except that I will not go back.... 'What do *I* want?' she said, pretending to mull over the question.

'Well, for a start, you could be nice to me. You could learn to smile. It doesn't hurt, not one bit.'

He did not deign to respond.

'How far is this place your friend Garud advised you to go to?' she asked.

'Ayodhya,' he said. 'I don't know anything except that it's to the north of Pratisthan. It may be very far.'

'I have an idea…Druhyu, my half-brother, is mad about horses. If there are black horses with single white ears anywhere in this world, he will know.'

'No, no…white horses with single black ears. They are called shyamkarni horses.'

'*Whatever*,' she said impatiently. 'I think we should go to him first.'

He could no longer drum up the energy, in spirit or body. 'I am tired,' he said.

Her eyes rounded in surprise. '*You* are tired? Let me tell you, Munikumar Gaalav, being abducted is exhausting.'

'How far is your brother from here?'

'It's only a short way,' she said. 'We need to spend the night in a proper shelter. There will be beds to sleep on and food to eat in Druhyu's place.'

~

Druhyu said, 'Haryashva, the ruler of Ayodhya, has shyamkarni horses. I have heard of a deal he made with the only horse trader who knows where to get them. A man who used to supply us Ailas once.' Remembering the good old days, he sighed deeply. 'Pratisthan is no longer the place it used to be.'

'Is that why you left it?' Gaalav asked curiously.

Druhyu chortled. 'You have been listening to gossip,

Munikumar.' Before Gaalav could deny this, he added, 'Sometimes a curse is a blessing in disguise. My father is a progressive man. He wants roads, ports, markets. Anything that will make trade easier and enrich the treasuries. But I am not like that. I prefer a quiet, simple life and a bit of wilderness around me. When my father threw me out—because I was not interested in that bizarre exchange he was trying to make—he cursed me. I would live in a backward place he said. "No roads fit for chariots and palanquins but only mule tracks, no bridges over rivers but only the crudest of rafts. No prosperity, no customs or culture," he said.' Recalling that memorable exchange, Druhyu smiled in amusement. 'Believe it or not, Munikumar, I saw the light at that very moment. The picture he had painted was exactly the one for me. I could have kissed his feet for uttering those words. In cursing me, he set me free of any obligation to remain in his kingdom and live my life in a predictable way. I could now shape my own destiny. As soon as I could get away, I sought my mother's blessing and left.'

'What did you do next?'

'Wandered around for a bit, saw something of Aryavarta...then I found some land. Good pastures with plenty of water. Now I breed horses for war.'

Gaalav sent him a puzzled look. 'War horses? Who needs such animals?'

'They will be needed in the future,' Druhyu said. 'This is a land of plenty. Kingdoms are growing. Not just in size but in numbers too. New dynasties seek to become prosperous through acquisitions of land, a rush for cornering natural resources—rivers, forests, mining rights. There *will* be wars, Munikumar, bigger and more deadly than those in the past. The newer chariots are being designed as battle vehicles, to be used as archery platforms. They will be lighter, swifter, manoeuvrable, pulled only by two horses. Of course, horses have to be trained to pull them. Horse-mounted warriors, whether bladesmen or archers, will be an elite force...I have obtained a stallion and some mares from that horse trader I just spoke of. He told me about Raja Haryashva's stable. Apparently, the raja is horse-crazy. He has a special stable for the shyamkarni horses that is as grand as his palace. He cares more for the horses than he does for all his queens and concubines, but that is conceivable...a horse understands you better than any human can.'

'Will Haryashva part with the shyamkarni horses?'

Druhyu didn't answer immediately. After a while, he said, 'If I owned a shyamkarni I would *never* part with it. Not even if a god came to me and asked for it. But I am not as wealthy as Haryashva. Never will be.' He gave a short laugh. 'Rich men see the world differently. The anxiety of having is worse than the anxiety of losing. A man who gathers these rare and precious horses in large numbers is interested only in acquisition. It boosts his self-importance, but does not engage his heart. He may give away a few...the trick is to offer him something he wants even more. A man may have everything but the one thing that he most desires. And believe me, Munikumar, *that one thing* is always there. The moment you give him the feeling that you can supply it, the desire only grows.'

Gaalav listened with close attention. He cleared his throat and asked in a seemingly casual tone, 'Does Raja Haryashva have sons?'

Druhyu shot him a knowing look. 'The question you

are asking is, has he been blessed with an heir?' He shook his head slowly. 'And the answer is no.'

'How old is he?'

'Irrespective of the king's age, a kingdom without the succession in place is in a precarious situation. The Ikshvakus are particular that only the eldest son has a right to the throne, but there is something in their lineage that makes the begetting of sons a problem. These Suryavanshi families are like that.'

Gaalav said, 'Then I have no choice but to go to Ayodhya.'

A pensive look came over Druhyu's face. After a while he said in a quiet voice, 'She is of royal blood, all said and done. In the king's household in Ayodhya, she will lack for nothing. Even so, it's anyone's guess how long she will remain there....'

'What do you mean?' Gaalav asked, alarmed.

'She is a handful. Though she has lived with my mother for nearly five years now, the idea of domesticity, the drudgery of a routine within four walls, chafes. She may have left the forest, but it has not left her. My mother has tried to tame her...in the last year alone she ran away twice, was found and brought back. Beaten too. '

Gaalav felt uncomfortable, but he couldn't say exactly why.

As if sensing his qualms, Druhyu said, 'Giving birth is empowering...some mares are difficult to break in, but foaling quietens them. Maybe motherhood will rein in her wilful nature. '

'I have lived as a brahmachari till now,' Gaalav said. 'But even I find it hard to believe that she is a princess. I cannot imagine why any man, leave alone a king, would look at her twice the way she is now.'

Druhyu laughed. 'Oh, that...it can be remedied in no time. Solah shringaar, the women call it. The sixteen arts of beautification. When applied together, they turn any woman into a goddess. I will get the women to see to it.'

~

They set out at daybreak, the brahmin scholar and the princess. Her half-brother loaned her the use of a covered chariot, and gifted a black mare to Gaalav. The brahmin accepted the gift reluctantly. He had never sat on a horse before. His trepidation increased as he listened to Druhyu describe the mare's quirks.

'These desert horses are very good for long distances. She is a steady mover, will give you a smooth ride, but watch out for a few things. Never present your back to her, she can't resist taking a bite out of a rump.'

'Are you serious?'

'I am. She's a grumpy old thing. If she pins back her ears, it's a sign something has annoyed her. She may kick. Best to stay out of range.'

'Don't you have a horse without these, erm, quirks?'

'Quirks are a sign of intelligence, Munikumar,' Druhyu said. 'Also, make no sudden movements. She doesn't like surprises.'

'Thank you. I'd much rather not—'

'Think nothing of it,' Druhyu said, with a grand wave of his hand. 'It's a parting gift. One last point that I'd like to make: you, too, are young and speed will excite you as much as it excites the mare...she can fly like the summer wind, but like the same cruel wind, she'll leave you covered in dust.'

Gaalav's voice quavered. 'In dust?'

Druhyu nodded. 'Yes. That's a trick of hers. Stalling suddenly and dropping the rider. I warned you she was quirky.'

'Maybe it's better I walk.'

'All the way to Ayodhya?' Druhyu raised an eyebrow. 'In this season, it will take you three to four days. She'll get you there by midnight. You should start moving, Munikumar. Make use of the early morning coolness before the heat of the day slows your pace. Come, let me help you up.'

Before Gaalav could say another word, Druhyu lifted him and planted him on the horse's back. The creature snorted and shook its mane vigorously as if in protest. Gaalav, too, tried to register his dissent, but his vocal chords were as stiff as his legs had become. He was terrified of falling off. The mare shifted suddenly and it startled Gaalav so much that he tumbled off his perch.

'Sorry about that,' Druhyu said, helping him back in the saddle. 'Like I said, she is a handful.'

Gaalav had an uncomfortable sense that his benefactor, as well as the mare, were conspirators in a practical joke being played on him. He felt the mare's flanks ripple powerfully under him, a reminder that she was in charge now and not he. Druhyu gave her rump a brisk, friendly pat by way of a goodbye and she was off. Just like the wind.

If the flight on Garud's back was an ordeal for Gaalav, he discovered that it had been a mere appetizer. The flavour of a full-blown nightmare now came to him; the dryness in his mouth, the dark fear burbling in his stomach, the stickiness in his palms. Bump, bump, bump, he went down the dust track, bouncing along till all his joints felt askew. Whitish grey, clayey dust covered his eyes, making it impossible to see anything. With Garud he had communicated his fear through words, but what could he say to this creature insensitive to everything but the throes of her delight? Her mane flew like a banner as she galloped along a smooth stretch, whinnying her joy to the world. How many hours to Ayodhya? Would he arrive there in one piece? Maybe they would recover the fallen parts of him at different spots along the road and build a memorial at every spot, the way they did with gods and goddesses. For some reason even that thought did not improve his mood.

After a while the mare appeared to have worked off the excess energy. Her stride became slower. She would occasionally cast up her head and give him a look through the corner of her eye, as if asking: 'Is this good for you? *Is it?*' He felt oddly grateful for this little kindness, as well as a little more reassured. She is not evilly inclined, he thought, and began to relax. When his heart had stopped racing and his breathing returned to normal, he remembered that the royal maiden had been travelling in the covered chariot and that he had been entrusted to look after her and deliver her safely to her new home. But where was that chariot? He turned and craned his neck as far as he could. There was only the bare dry landscape burnt to amber, the white dust trail, fallow fields, and in the distance the thin silver thread of a river. As if sensing his anxiety, the mare slowed to a standstill under a lone tamarind tree. He slid off her back and tried to stand on shaky legs. Impossible. Lowering himself to the ground, he reached out to grip the tree's trunk. His limbs felt disjointed, like pieces of wood. Reclining against the trunk, he stretched his legs out and slowly massaged them. A deep sense of fatigue came over him and, after a glance to see that the mare was grazing peacefully nearby, he closed his eyes and went off to sleep in the same half-sitting position. He had no idea how long he slept. When he stirred at last, the sun was past its high-noon mark. A feather was tickling his nose. He brushed it off and sat up with a groan.

'Awake, Munikumar?' the maiden asked with mock tenderness. 'If you keep taking long naps, we are going to take a week to reach our destination.' After a moment, she added, 'Not that I have a problem. My ride was quite comfortable, thank you.'

Her speech struck him as gratuitous and he scowled to show his displeasure. He did not look at her, but focused his attention on the chariot standing some distance away, the team of bullocks grazing quietly and the charioteer who was stretched out with a thin wet cloth towel covering his face.

'We didn't want to disturb your nap, so we ate our midday meal,' she went on, unaware of how much her chirpiness was annoying him. 'Your portion was packed and kept aside right in the beginning. Do you want it now?'

He did not reply, refusing even to glance at her, though he saw through the corner of his eye that there was something different about her today. After waiting a few moments for him to respond, she got up and went to the chariot. When she returned it was with a stitched leaf plate on which there was an offering of fruit, parched rice grains mixed with roasted gram and pieces of jaggery.

'Please eat,' she said. Her tone was cool, no longer as friendly as it had been. 'There's a pot of buttermilk too.'

He was very hungry and in no time the meal was eaten, the buttermilk downed. The charioteer was awake by now; he rounded the bullocks and hitched the chariot to the yoke. Gaalav remembered his own ride. He looked around in alarm and asked, 'Where's she?'

'Who?'

'The mare.'

The maiden looked at him blankly. 'How would I know?' The question was an innocent one, but he detected the hidden mirth bubbling below. He sent her an angry look. This time he could not help but observe her. The change stunned him. His first reaction was fear, a chill. This cannot be the same person. The wild, ill-kempt, raggedy girl was gone. In her place, as if by enchantment, was a slender, graceful young woman with a heart-shaped face, sparkling eyes and a wide pert smile that revealed a perfect set of teeth white as jasmine buds. He could not take his eyes off her. She, too, held his gaze, warily, but also as if she were issuing a challenge. Something leapt up in him to meet it, a spark of a new, reckless joy. A smile, tentative and bemused, appeared on his lips. He was overcome with a strange sort of shyness. But the wave cresting inside him crashed as suddenly. In its wake came confusion, a sense of dismay: this should not be happening. The maiden broke away from the contemplation first. Her colour was high. What had passed in that mutual scrutiny was too much for either of them. Was this possession? Then who had acquired whom? Do we even belong together?

Her thoughts in a muddle, she grew flustered and stood up abruptly. 'I don't know where your mare is,' she said. A faint charge of anger made her voice shrill. 'Did you leave her loose? Why did you do that when any fool knows that—' She bit her tongue as if realizing that she'd gone too far and said sulkily, 'She would have run away quite far by now...no way of getting her back.' Saying this, she turned her back on him and flounced off towards the chariot.

After a few minutes, as if in a daze, he slowly followed her. The charioteer, a muscular sunburnt man, bare-bodied but for a white lower cloth and a matching turban, was waiting patiently. We could stay here all day, his attitude suggested. All year we could stay, or even forever. There is no need to go anywhere. Not to Ayodhya. Not for the horses. They don't matter, never did. Gaalav stared at the waiting chariot, as if it were a strange, otherworldly object that had descended on that spot. The mystery was inside, behind the cloth curtain, shielded from even the gaze of the sun. As a princess should be...*Where else does she belong but in a royal household surrounded by luxury? What else is she herself but a piece of high-value property? Not prized for itself, but for what it will yield*...a fallacy to think that there was a distinct entity in her. She was meant not for ordinary men, but for kings and emperors. A royal womb: dynasties would emerge from it. A repository of dreams, but none of them his. They belonged to another man—a king who would, in exchange, give him the horses he needed.

'We've wasted enough time' he said peremptorily to the charioteer. 'I'll share the seat with you.'

The man was aghast. 'How can that be? A noble brahmin like yourself...'

'It's all right this one time,' Gaalav said curtly.

~

Ayodhya, the Unconquerable, was the capital of Kosala, the kingdom of the Ikshvakus. It had been established by Manu, the founding father of the Solar dynasty, aeons ago. Its rise to power matched the sun's glorious ascent in the sky. The Golden Age of King Ramachandra was still far off in the future, but its foundations were being laid. Imperial style dictated that the avenues be broad and lined with flowering trees, the parks be spacious and filled with deer and peacocks, the mansions grand with frescoed facades and carved entrance doors. Of course, the most splendid building was the palace. Gaalav noted its magnificence: the tall pillared halls, marbled floors, the water channels with oil lamps floating in them. Someone was playing a flute. The air was cool and scented. He was welcomed graciously by beautiful smiling women who washed his feet, led him to a cushioned seat, fanned him with a peacock-feather fan, waited on him to know what he'd like to eat and drink. They behaved as if they were taking part in a well-choreographed dance, their expressions smooth and movements graceful. But everything he saw and all the attention he was given only made him, for some reason, irritable. It was partly due to tiredness, but it may also have been that something marred his satisfaction at reaching Ayodhya, and made him impatient to conclude his business there and be gone.

'Where is the king?' he asked. 'How long will he keep me waiting?'

'Maharaj will be here in a while,' an attendant said. Her manner was polite but somehow managed to imply that 'a while' could also mean a very long time.

~

Haryashva, the king of Ayodhya, had an imposing physique. Brawny but also tending to middle-age corpulence, he seemed to take up more space than ordinary men. From his firm stance, the square jaw, the full lips, the well-groomed beard and silver-streaked shoulder-length locks, to the glitter of gold and precious stones from the jewels that adorned his body, he gave off a larger-than-life aura.

'I apologize for keeping you waiting,' he said. His voice was deep and rich, his manner courteous but also patronizing. 'I hope they have taken good care of you... was the food to your taste? It was? Excellent. Now, please tell me, Munikumar, how may *I* be of service?'

Gaalav was impressed by Haryashva's direct manner. It was the opposite of Yayati's obsequiousness, a style that he now associated with phoney men. Yayati had laid out a welcome too, but it had been nowhere near as grand as this. In the end, he'd failed to give Gaalav what he had asked for. Everything about Haryashva suggested that he would be different. Encouraged, Gaalav said, 'O king, my request is not an easy one for lesser sovereigns than yourself, but I am confident that you will grant it.'

'One is gratified to hear that, but what makes you so confident?'

'You are regarded as Indra among mortals, and your city rivals Amaravati in every way. You are a chakravarti raja whose fame has spread even beyond the distance covered by your chariot wheels.'

Haryashva sent him a sidelong smile. 'Ask, Munikumar.'

Despite himself, Gaalav hesitated. 'I need...shyamkarni horses.'

'Really?' The look of amusement deepened on the king's face. His tone begged the question: why does a brahmin like you need something meant only for kings? Then a second thought struck him and he narrowed his eyes. '*Horses* you said...how many do you want?'

'Eight hundred.'

Haryashva's eyebrows shot up. 'Hmm...that is an unusual request.'

Gaalav gave a short laugh. 'Let us just say that my guru is an unusual man.'

'I have heard that,' the king said, stroking his chin. 'And you are this unusual guru's favoured disciple. That, too, one has heard. You stood by him in his hour of need and this is the way he rewards you.'

Gaalav responded with a stony silence.

Haryashva sensed his embarrassment and gave a disarming smile. 'Please don't misunderstand me, Munikumar. I don't wish to mock you. But I get the impression that Vishwamitra has put you through a particularly difficult test. Perhaps he sees you as a threat. I find that interesting. It means that you are destined for great things.'

Gaalav frowned but continued to look at him silently.

'You do know, don't you, that a moon-white horse with a single black ear is sacred,' Haryashva said. 'It is sacrificed to the gods in the rite of Ashwamedha, which only the greatest kings have the ability to perform.' He paused to let his next words sink in. 'Just the price of *one* shyamkarni horse can seriously dent a royal treasury.'

'For a minor raja, yes, but not for you.'

'I appreciate your confidence in me, Munikumar,' Haryashva said drily. 'However, the fact is that I cannot just give away what is so hard to come by. I am not the owner but the custodian of my kingdom's wealth. Ask me for something else.'

'I am not asking you to give them away.'

Haryashva raised an eyebrow. 'Then what did you have in mind?'

Gaalav felt a rawness in his throat. 'An exchange.'

'And what, in your opinion, is a fitting exchange—for eight hundred priceless horses?'

'Sons…you need heirs.'

'Careful, brahmin. Don't insult me.' Like a snake struck with a stick, Haryashva's demeanour had changed.

Though inwardly rattled by the transformation, Gaalav forced himself to speak calmly. 'I would never do that, O king. However, it is well known that the ancient bloodline of the Ikshvakus has reached a dead end. The citizens of Ayodhya have started asking questions, as is their right, about the future of the dynasty. You need a royal bride who will remedy the situation for you. I have one to offer. Give me the horses as bride price and accept her as your wife.'

'There is no dearth of royal women in my palace. I have three wives. How are you sure that this rajkanya will give me sons?'

'Because that is *her* destiny. She is Yayati's daughter, born of an apsara it is rumoured. Precious though your horses are, there is no maiden in the land like her. Her beauty is certainly extraordinary, but her birth chart is even more so. It reveals that she will be the mother of chakravarti rajas…not one but four.'

Haryashva shot him a look of disbelief. 'And you expect me to hand over eight hundred shyamkarni horses to you on the mere probability that this prediction may come true?'

Gaalav met his eye levelly but did not reply.

Haryashva studied him for several moments. 'I will have to take a look at her first.'

'*Take a look at her*? She is a rajkanya.'

'She was given to you as daan by her father. *You* own her now. She is no longer entitled to special treatment.'

Gaalav nodded curtly. 'Make your decision after seeing her, but do not take long. I cannot wait any more.'

'I will not delay you,' Haryashva said and left.

When he returned, there was something different about him, a new kind of light in his eye, a change in his tone. 'She appears to be of royal blood,' he said. 'But she is more than just a rajkanya. She has all six high points.'

Gaalav knitted his brow. 'Six high points?'

Haryashva sent him a superior smile. 'Nose, eyes, ears, nails, breasts and neck...her body is deep in the places that should be deep, and slender in those that should be slender, meaning waist, ankles, wrists....' As if unaware of Gaalav's discomfiture, Haryashva went on blithely. 'Red in those places that should be red: her palms are like lotus buds, as are the soles of her feet...a sign of good health. Her tongue and lips have the right pallor. Her navel too—'

'What!'

'The royal astrologer was with me during the examination. He corroborated that she is, indeed, a virgin. Her hips and thighs are strong, perfect for childbearing. And she has several auspicious marks such as a mole on her....' Haryashva did not complete the sentence. Instead, he glanced askance at the brahmin. 'Forgive me. I keep forgetting that you are a brahmachari,' he said half-mockingly.

Gaalav's nostrils flared in anger. 'So what have you decided?'

'Your offer interests me, but what I had in mind was something slightly different.'

'Different? What do you mean?'

'Let me explain.' The king's manner was almost friendly now. 'For this rajkanya, I would have gladly parted with eight hundred white horses—if I had them.'

'What do you mean *if I had them?*'

'Please be calm, Munikumar Gaalav.'

'I am calm.'

'No. You are not...your face is crimson, your fists are clenched, your breath is short. I can see your anger and disappointment. I think you should have some water.' Haryashva called out to a dasi to bring some water for the guest.

Brushing her away with a wave of his hand, Gaalav said coldly, 'I do not wish to stay here a minute longer. If you do not have the horses, why did you not tell me right in the beginning?'

'Did I say that I didn't have the horses?' Haryashva asked, widening his eyes. 'I never said that.'

'Do you or don't you have the horses?'

'Of course, I do.' After a moment Haryashva added, 'Let us go to the stables so that you can see for yourself.'

'I am ready to take your word for it.'

'No.' Haryashva held up a finger to reinforce his point. 'A trader must check the goods.'

Stung by the insult, Gaalav retorted, 'I am not a trader.'

'Pardon me,' the king said calmly. 'But you have come here in order to make a transaction.'

'The custom of bride price is yours, O king, not mine.'

As if conceding the point, Haryashva sighed. 'We

can spar like this all night, but what good is that? I am sympathetic to your difficult position just as you are to mine. I am ready to give you the horses, but you should see them first. Come, let us go to the stables.'

It was evident that the king was very proud of his stables. He insisted on showing Gaalav every aspect of them, pointing out special features like the stone drain that ran through the length of the building so that the urine would not stagnate, the clean water troughs, the storage bins for barley, the spacious stalls, the exercise area. He rattled off the names of the breeds he owned, identified by their places of origin—Kamboj, Gandhara, Bahlika—and pointed out the desert horses, like the one that had abandoned Gaalav just a few hours ago. Then he came to the Arab steeds, his beauties, as he called them, and spoke about bloodlines, temperament, stride length, till Gaalav felt benumbed.

'And now,' Haryashva said with the air of a showman bringing his performance to a much awaited finale. 'And now we come to the shyamkarni horses...but we need to see them from a viewing platform.'

Gaalav had a sense of déjà vu. He was looking again at the heaving sea from a height. Frightened, but also trapped in a bewitchment, he could not take his eyes off the flowing manes and tails, billowing white waves leaving trails of luminous pearly foam. He was mesmerized by the beauty of the long necks, the shapely heads, the mysterious intelligence in the eyes. The horses belonged in a dream. Even a single one would have been spellbinding, but the combined effect of so many was that of a powerful energy, pure and elemental. Sacred. There was no creature in creation as perfect. Nothing could compare with this splendour.

Haryashva was watching his face, a faint smile on his lips. 'I come here at night sometimes,' he said softly. 'When no one else is awake, I spend hours with them.' His voice suddenly trembled with emotion. 'But Munikumar, it is nothing compared to seeing them in the open, thundering across a plain, swimming in the river, rolling in the grass. Free. They are Varun's children, untamed as the element from which they were created. They are my secret joy, like no son born of my loins will ever be.'

Despite himself, Gaalav was moved by the king's emotion. He looked down again at the expanse of horses; it didn't seem endless as it had first appeared. He did a quick rough count and asked with a frown, 'How many are they?'

'All I own,' said Haryashva and stopped. After a while he said, 'Two hundred heads.'

Gaalav closed his eyes momentarily as though the words were a physical blow. Swallowing the bitterness in his mouth, he said, 'Keep them, O king. They will not do for me.'

'Munikumar, why don't you understand? You will not find eight hundred horses in a single stable anywhere,' Haryashva said. 'There is only one man who knows where to obtain these horses. He is a strange man. He sells only to select buyers and does not sell more than two hundred to one person. Quote your price, I said to convince him to change his mind. I was ready to give him enough gold to build a city, but he did not agree. My suggestion to you is this: for these two hundred horses, leave the royal maiden with me for a year. I only need *one* son from her, not four.'

'I need eight hundred to repay my guru,' Gaalav said forcefully. 'Where am I to get the remainder?'

'The horse trader said that there are other kings in Aryavarta who would take care of these horses as they deserve...you will have to collect them slowly, Munikumar.'

'But the royal maiden?' Gaalav sent Haryashva a troubled look. 'Is it right to subject her to—what I mean is, she is high-born and the role you are suggesting for her is—is....' He trailed off.

'I am a practical man, Munikumar Gaalav. We both know that we need this transaction to go through. There is too much at stake. Are we going to talk of the maiden's feelings now?'

Gaalav looked at him uneasily but said nothing.

Haryashva sighed. 'I am a king and my duties are manifold. When times are hard or when one faces a particularly difficult choice, the usual notions of right and wrong don't apply. Yayati has lost much of his wealth, yet he cannot turn down a brahmin's request. Therefore, he took the unusual step of handing you his daughter. Likewise, I must think beyond myself. My kingdom needs an heir...I am obliged to provide one. And you too, if I may say so, have an important obligation to fulfil, to your guru. We can help each other. Isn't that more important?'

Gaalav thought: It could be that *I* am the one who is confused. A man must be clear about his goal and go after it. That is what gives life direction. Haryashva is ready to give up what he loves in exchange for something that will bring value and true meaning to his life. It is his duty to produce an heir. He has the mental strength to be obedient to his dharma. I, too, must be clear and focused. I cannot deviate from my obligation to my guru. But what of her? No, no...I cannot think of that. There can be no space in my life for her—if I want to make a place for myself in this world.

After a while, he said, 'We both have to gain from this arrangement if it is to work. Your suggestion ensures that you get what you want, but my need is only partially fulfilled.'

'Can you think of a better solution?'

'No, but I cannot ignore the maiden's welfare either. Her father placed her in my care.'

Haryashva sent him a sharp, assessing look, then said, 'Rest assured, she will be well cared for as the mother of the royal heir in the time that she is here.'

'What happens after that?'

'You will get your two hundred horses.'

Gaalav gave a start. 'What! You want me to wait a year for the horses?'

'I belong to the Ikshvaku lineage. I will honour my word, but only after my heir is born.'

'But...she too must agree to all this. '

As if following his train of thought, the king said, 'Speak to the maiden. As she is of royal blood, she is no doubt trained to bear her responsibility. Remind her that she is bound to you now by her father's word, that she must uphold the honour invested in her. You could even tell her that this is in *your* best interest...I have a feeling she will do her part.'

~

He did not see her at first.

The oil lamps set in niches made hushed pools of light, but the hazy air blurred his vision. As his eyes grew used to the lay of the room, he scanned it slowly. Something moved at the far end, a very small shift, like the rustle of leaves. He noticed the window, wide open, framing the darkness outside. He felt a twinge of alarm. Had she fled? Then he noticed the faint silhouette standing to one side of the window. He approached her.

She did not turn around. 'Have you seen the night?' she asked, after a while. 'Amavasya. A night without stars. The moon reduced to its bare skin. As I was a while ago.'

'I regret—' He began stiffly, stopped and muttered, 'I...am sorry.'

'So, Munikumar, did you get what you were after?'

'No.'

'*No?*' She spun around to face him. 'You mean he will not give you the horses?'

'Not in the number I need. Two hundred are all he has.'

'Then?'

'He wants to keep you in his palace.' He cleared his throat. 'It's only for one year....'

'One year,' she repeated slowly. 'What does that mean? Does it—does it mean that he will not marry me?'

He did not reply.

'But, if I am not to be his wife, what am I to be?' An edge entered her voice. 'After one year, what happens to me?'

He replied woodenly, 'I will return to take you away.'

Her disbelief was a starburst. 'You mean that after one year I will be *free*?'

He caught the scattering shower of hope and let it slip through his fingers.

'Only *one year*!' she said. 'And I had thought I would have to live here cooped inside this prison till my dying day...a year is *nothing*. It will pass. I will count the days, their hours too, so that it is precisely measured. Not a minute more!' His face remained a blank wall, but she had detected something, a queer line of pain, that he was willing himself not to cross. The joy died on her face as a false dawn. In a voice filled with trepidation, she asked, 'What is it, Munikumar? Aren't you happy?'

'Drishadvati, this is very difficult for me to say....'

After what he had just said she was not listening to him any more. 'My name,' she whispered, coming a step closer to him, so close that he could see the delicious burn rising up her face, the soft glow in her eyes. 'It sounds—I don't know how, but it sounds *different* when you say it. As if you are presenting a new me to myself.'

And then he told her of the arrangement Haryashva had proposed.

How still the night had turned. As if it had ceased to breathe. Passed on in its sleep...how cold and distant the stars now that their cruel design had been revealed. That carelessly discarded peel of moon—who flung it out of the window?

'I don't know...what this means,' she tapered off, looking deeply troubled. 'I will be neither wife nor mother—if they keep my child and send me away. Then what will I be?'

He looked at her in silence, then looked away.

'Isn't there some other way out? Surely there must be...'

'Like what?' His tone was brusque.

'I don't know,' she said uncertainly. 'Are *you* prepared to go wandering around the land, maybe for years, searching for shyamkarni horses till you get your eight hundred?'

'Do I have another option?'

Let us invent a new life for ourselves, she wanted to say. A whole new world that exists nowhere but in us. A life that keeps us forever on the road. That, too, is an option. But she could not bring herself to say it. Instead she asked, 'Why can't you go back to your guru and tell him the truth?'

He stared at her in horror. 'What truth? That I have failed?'

'That Aryavarta does not have eight hundred white horses.'

'How do you know that? There are so many kingdoms....' Sudden anger sharpened his voice. 'Do you know everything about each one of them?'

She flinched at his outburst. 'Don't snap at me. I am trying to help you. Do you think that it would make a difference if I...take me to your guru, Munikumar. I want to meet him.'

'Why? What business do you have with him?'

'None. I have nothing to do with Haryashva either, or with—with the disgusting proposition he has put before you.' Her voice rose in a plaintive cry as, despite herself, she beggared herself before him. 'I do not want to be parcelled out between different men, Munikumar! My father gave me to you, but he at least did what was within his rights...what right do *you* have to pawn me repeatedly? You will gather your precious horses but what about me? What will I become? Do you want to know what I went through earlier this evening?'

A look of discomfort mingled with disgust came over his face. He did not want to know. But she, it appeared, was bent on telling him.

'I was brought into this room by four dasis. Then two men came in. The brahmin told me to remove my clothes. When I said no, the king ordered the women to remove them forcibly. I fought but they were stronger. They pushed me to the ground and pulled my clothes off. Then they made me stand up without a stitch to cover me...I have never felt so degraded. I was a mare on sale. The men circled around me. My hips, waist, eyes and ears were inspected carefully. I was revolted! The way that puffed-up king with his enormous head, and that skinny old bearded goat of an astrologer talked with one another as if I wasn't there, about whorls and lotuses and other auspicious signs on my body. The astrologer studied my teeth. He came so close that even by the light of the oil lamps, I could see his own dirty yellow set. He kept licking his lips. Then he held my palm and, under the pretext of examining it, began stroking and rubbing the wrist with his thumb. When he came to my feet, he ran his hands over them and up my calves and all the while his eyes took sly little nips at me. His gaze was slime, his touch is branded on my skin. Filth! These men... they are worse than those two louts who abducted me. They are like vultures eyeing flesh.' Her voice trembled and dropped to a whisper. '*My* body. *It is mine*,' she said. 'What else does one have? No one should take it from me. It is sinful. Don't do this to me.'

He lowered his head. 'What can I do? I am helpless too. It is a greater sin for me, a brahmin, to fail in keeping my word to my teacher. Death would be preferable. After everything that has happened, it seems that I have no choice but to end my life...Garud, Yayati and even you, Yayati's daughter...all of you gave me a false hope.'

After a while she said, 'I don't want to make things worse for you than they already are.' To his relief, her voice was more in control. 'Take me to your guru, Munikumar. Let me speak to him just once. If he is all that they say he is, let *him* tell me why this cost is being demanded of me. He was a king once. A king can be both arrogant and benevolent. He was arrogant with you earlier, he will surely be kinder now when he understands my position...he is a brahmarishi, you said. No one understands dharma better than one like him. I would like to know from him what is the dharma he practises and what is it that he expects his disciple to follow. Are they not the same thing? Is it not adharma to turn a human into an animal for breeding? It's my life that is the sacrifice, but *what* is the killing block? Don't worry, I will ask him politely. Your guru will surely give me an answer.'

Her suggestion was insane. She was hysterical. 'Please calm yourself, Drishadvati,' he said. 'Do not get worked up like this. I—I will take you to my guru, if that is what you want, but it will do no good.'

'Why not? Will he not listen to me?'

'You are right,' he said with a quiet born of despair. 'My guru was a king once. Even though he gave up all that, a man born in a noble lineage will not tolerate what he perceives as a slur. Anger made him challenge the gods. Then what are you or I before him? I know this because I remained with him when he was alone. I know him very well. By my thoughtless insistence on repaying him, perhaps I ignited the dormant rage. And he does not forgive easily. You ask, will he not listen?' He took a deep breath before continuing. 'Vishwamitra *will* listen and he will gloat. He will remind me that I am a brahmin who failed to keep his word. He will tell me to do as I think fit. After that, there will be no other way for me but to end this existence and damn my soul forever. I would have done it too, if Garud had not saved me. I could still do it. It would end my present troubles—and yours as well. I did tell you to go back right in the beginning, to save yourself and leave me to my fate. But you did not listen. Please don't blame me now for this situation.'

To her there was something lonely and tragic about his whole speech. Heroic and heart-breaking. She lowered her head as if to acknowledge her blame. 'I am answerable for this—I accept it. I am a dreamer, a fool. I came away with you because I wanted us both to live. Life for you, a new life for me. I never imagined that it would come to this.' She broke off and turned away. Then with a deep shudder she said, 'How foolish I was...*I am*. Even now, for a moment, I had thought that after one year I would be free. But if I have, indeed, dug my own grave, then *you* want to bury me alive.'

'You agreed to this,' he said tonelessly.

'No! This was not what I—I don't know—maybe you are right....' She turned her face away as if she could not bear any longer to be in the same room as him. 'Go and search for your horses, Munikumar. Who knows, when you come back you may not find me here?'

He shook his head. 'You are mine, Drishadvati. You will be here because I will come back for you exactly after one year.'

10

Drishadvati

You can keep your palaces. They are not for me. Not for me these lofty arches and spacious rooms, neatly laid gardens filled with flowering trees, and ponds covered with plate-sized lily pads on which frogs congregate. Not for me these preening peacocks and stately swans, the elegant pavilions with silken swings, this dreaming, scented air that whispers of body love. And definitely not for me this singsong at daybreak, the stringed instruments thrumming out wake-up melodies. Kings are sung awake. But I only wish to bury my head deeper into the soft pillow and drown the noise. Who cares about dawn? She shows up every day.

In the walled garden outside my chamber is an amalaki tree. Scattered at the base are round pale green fruit. A maid who works in the vaidyashala collects them every morning. She always leaves a handful on my windowsill. I love their sour, clean taste. Does the maid sense my loneliness and feel sorry for me? Though I do not leave my room now, around me the palace hums like a beehive. I can feel the swirl of activity, the early morning goings-on as blinds are raised, sleeping mats rolled up, brooms put to work and incense lighted. Life in the palace goes on but no one calls my name any more. For all the fine things it holds, grand halls with painted walls, gilded ceilings and carved pillars, this palace is a trap. A rambling network of desires. Entangled in it is the scion of an ancient line who worries about his legacy. The Ikshvaku lineage *cannot* end with him. There is a long line-up of pitris who will not let him into their heaven unless he does his duty by them. Haryashva, with his hairy face and thick fingers, like a bunch of raw bananas, must leave a male successor before he dies. Too tight, too tight, he muttered all night as he tried to thrust into me on the first occasion—that first full moon. Yes, they made an occasion of it.

It started with a homa at sunset to propitiate, if you please, the deity who controls the opening and closing of wombs. Apparently, this divine being is particularly fickle. There was an air of listlessness about the proceedings, the priests looked bored. While I listened to them chant mantras and sing hymns, my leg went to sleep. However, as dusk rolled in over the plains, anxiety gripped everyone. The stars began to reveal their positions in the heavens, as if they were maids waiting for the queen's grand arrival. The chanting picked up in volume and pace, bells rang, the fire blazed, a trail of thick, strong-smelling smoke from the dried banyan twigs burning in the havan kund made its way to the skies, carrying the desperate pleas. *A son, a healthy son!* To continue the Ikshvaku name, for the future of the kingdom, for peace and prosperity. Did the shining ones see us and laugh? Or did the gods shut their eyes, as I did mine, to keep out the smoke? The flames billowed, the heat was so intense that I felt I was melting—that all our bodies would turn to water and what flowed from this homa would be a deluge of desires with us, a hapless lot, caught in it. Just when I thought I was about to faint or drown or both, the nightmare ended. The moon appeared: a creamy, plump, dehiscent fruit that looked as if it were about to burst and send forth a harvest of little moons. There was a collective sigh of relief, a quiet ripple of joy. It was a good omen. They then whisked me away for another bath. The maids scrubbed me from top to toe with turmeric followed by sandalwood paste, bathed my body in scented water, painted my palms and soles in red, drew buds and curlicues on my breasts, lined my eyes with kajal and dressed me in soft new linen. My hair was braided with flowers of gold, a single ornament of moonstone and pearls placed at the top. Gold armbands, bangles on my wrists. All this under the command of the courtesan who, for the longest time, had been the royal favourite.

Supriya was a woman of indeterminate age with a firm body and a charismatic face. Her allure lay in a cleft chin, full lips and high cheekbones, but most of all in the slender arch of her eyebrows, the look in those eyes, heavy-lidded, slanting upwards, provocative. It was hard to read them, but they seemed to know everything there was to know. Swallow this, Supriya said, and a spoonful of honey flavoured with cinnamon was held to my mouth. I swallowed. Chew this. I chewed the betel leaf and areca nut that made my lips a glistening red. She looked me over critically and grimaced. 'Don't act like a baby goat being led to the slaughter,' she said. 'This is not going to kill you. It's an honour to be called to the king's bed.'

'Then let him honour those who think it's an honour.'

Her smile mocked me. 'He will, but for tonight it is

your turn. Delight his heart, please him in every way. Make him your slave in bed.'

Disgust bubbled up in me. 'You make me sick.'

She reached for my chin and tilted it up. 'You may be a princess, but don't take that tone with me,' she said. After staring into my eyes for a moment, she let go and playfully tapped my cheek. 'Though you've grown as tall as a bamboo, you seem to be a child. I get the feeling you are afraid.'

I lowered my gaze, not wanting her sharp eyes to penetrate my heart: the confusion, despair and the strange excitement mingled with anxiety. A look of comprehension came over her face. 'Listen!' she said, half smiling but also half exasperated. 'This moment comes in every woman's life. It may seem difficult, but there is a way you can make it easy for yourself.' I looked at her. She saw that I was paying attention and brought her mouth to my ear. Her warm clove-scented breath fanned across my face. 'A bit of free advice for you: don't resist. Find that stillness within yourself, and let the body relax, to be itself. A woman's body has its own instincts that run contrary to the restrictions put on us. Just give yourself permission to feel.' She studied my face for a long moment, then said, 'Haryashva is an experienced lover, he learnt from the best. Permit him to guide you. Love-making is all about timing. The first time may be a little painful, but don't make a fuss. The trick is this, be present. Your womb will open willy-nilly, but your heart needs to open as well.'

'How can my heart open when I don't love him?'

'Love!' She grinned, displaying a perfect set of pearly whites. 'That's a fatal disease for women like us. We must be all things to all men.'

'I am not like you!'

She didn't contradict me, but looked at me in silence for so long that I felt slightly ashamed of my rudeness. 'Is it a rule that a woman should only dream of becoming a bride?' she asked.

'Isn't it?'

'Neither of us will marry him,' she said drily. 'And even if you were to become his next queen, do you imagine that he would never lie with other women?' She gave a scornful laugh. 'In this world the rules are made by men for men. When it comes to sharing her bed, a well-born woman has no alternative; whether she wants him or not, she must submit her body to her lord and only to him. But women like me are not enslaved. We are free to act on our desire. We have the power to be all things to all men. Think about it: wives bring a moral code to their marriage bed but husbands do not place themselves under a similar obligation. Because men know that nothing kills passion as thoroughly as the tedium of fidelity. Without shared passion, it is not pleasure but duty...without mutual pleasure, what is it but a degradation of one's body?'

Her words shocked me. They made me uncomfortable but I sensed an ally in her, my only ally in this place, one I did not want to lose. As if divining my thoughts, she said, 'You don't have to love him, but if you allow yourself, you can still enjoy what you are about to do with him.'

'I don't want anything to do with him! I—I am not ready for this.' I faltered. If I was not ready why had I ever consented?

As if in reply, she led me by the hand to a full-length mirror. At first, I saw only the blank-eyed inhuman look of a small wild creature in a trap screaming *Save me!* Then the image shifted and I noticed the changes. Not me but a mask. A different woman, armoured and cruel. Older, sophisticated, in command of herself but also mysterious, her silhouette suggesting new possibilities. Somehow she fitted well in this palace, the languor of this night and what lay ahead. She exuded a kind of heady power that I knew nothing about. Supriya was watching me with those half-hidden eyes. She had a curiously impersonal expression. Suddenly, she gave an indulgent smile and said, 'You see? There *is* another woman inside you. Not one but many versions of yourself...and each will bloom at the right time. Look at yourself! Tonight you are the jewel and all this finery only complements your beauty. Be grateful for this youth, this good health, your lovely body. It will not last forever. It too is clay, one day to be dust. But while it is there, we cannot help but know what longing is and what is desire. Tell me, what good is this body if it lacks vigour, if it does not bring you happiness?'

Something of my qualms must have showed in my face because she rolled her eyes and said, 'Those who treat the body's pleasure with disgust are ignorant. They do not honour it. Tonight you are irresistible. Don't resist. Don't think about the past or future. Allow your body the sweet joy of your lover's touch. There is nothing lovelier. Once you experience it you will go back to it again and again, because you will know yourself so much better.' Her words fell on deaf ears, they did not reassure me. The tumult in my heart only increased. I did not have her sophistication or her expertise. What did I know? But then what did she know about being me? Without quite understanding what I was doing, I had tied my fate to a man I barely knew...I was panic-stricken, but I was even more afraid to let anyone see it. Where was Gaalav? Would he return for me? Would *I* be here for him to return to? As if choosing her next words with care, Supriya said, 'See this necklace.' She lifted the five strands of pure pearls around her neck. 'It is from the king. An honourable man pays for his pleasure. Perfume, splendid jewels, fine cloth, my own elephant and even my own chariot and bodyguards. Yes, the lord of Ayodhya has been generous to me. But, if you give him an heir, you can ask him for anything.'

'Anything? Will I be free?'

She sent me a pitying look. 'Why ask for something no one can give you?' Kissing me gently on the forehead, she said, 'Try to be satisfied with all that destiny *has* given you.'

With her words ringing in my ears, I entered the vast gilded bedchamber. Despite my effort to calm it, my heart was pounding. The bed was bigger than anything I'd seen, with a headrest carved in gold and studded with gems. A realm in its own right, with its own rules, it did not look inviting so much as inescapable. How many times would I have to lie on it? I might die in it, ungiving, unpleasured, unhappy, unmourned. Everything was about to change and it was all happening too quickly. I fled to the furthest corner of the room where the window framed the full moon. It was hanging low in the heavens, bleeding its plangent light on the fields and farms, on the river Sarayu just beyond the palace's walls, on the trees and shrubs that had laid down their shadows in the garden, as if in sacrifice. Nothing moved, not a breath.

After a while the door opened. The lamps in the room

flickered desperately. The door closed with a slow sigh. A deathlike quiet. I heard footsteps making their way across the room, felt a hand on my back, a warm heavy pressure on my waist, guiding me gently but firmly to turn around and face him. Though inwardly quaking, I stole a glance at him. Alone, shorn of the fine jewels, in a simple linen lower garment, he seemed less threatening, less repulsive. Though he did not smile, his expression was not grim so much as reflective. Bringing his hand to my brow he stroked it gently, then ran a finger along the outline of my face and tilted my chin so that I was forced to look into his eyes. Dark, calm, but with an expectation smiling up from their depths. 'It is destiny that brought us together,' he said. His voice was rich, deep, intimate.

Dropping all modesty, I turned on him. 'I curse that destiny!'

He removed his hand and said in a level but offhand tone, 'Nevertheless, you cannot escape it and neither can I. I am chained by my duty to my noble name.'

His words made me angrier still. 'Your noble name is going to make a mockery of mine.'

He took his breath in sharply. 'Though you look as fresh and tender as a lotus bud plucked at dawn, you are full of thorns,' he said. 'I have heard something of your story. I agree destiny has been particularly cruel to you. I cannot change that, but I can offer you a reprieve. For a year, I will treat you like a queen, as my love, if you will let me. Everything I have, I will share with you.'

'I want nothing from you. Instead, it's you who desperately wants something from me. Because you cannot get it any other way, you have reduced me to this. But neither are you exempt from shame, O king. Don't think your name will emerge in letters of gold from this whole episode.'

His eyes became cold chips of stone. 'I will not tolerate disrespect,' he said, his tone the cut of a sharp curved dagger. Without another word, he undid the knot of my bodice, loosened the slim gold belt around my waist so that the lower cloth glissaded down my hips and thighs, pooling at my feet. He took his time, trailing his fingers slowly along my naked thighs, my buttocks, and finally my breasts. Eyes trained on my face all the while, he touched the tips of my nipples. His hands picked out the gold flowers from my hair and dropped them on the floor. The heat of shame rose in me. My will deserted me. I could not summon the spirit to resist. What good would it do me? That night I did whatever it was that he commanded me. I did not utter a single word. There was no place for communion. He was trapped in his form, and I in mine. Neither of us forgot that. Sarmistha had once said to me, 'You are a Chandravanshi. It is ensconced in every cell of your body. Love will happen. You, too, will know moon madness.' What I knew instead had no method, no madness and no meaning. It was emptiness. Though I offered myself up to him, it was an empty package, the gift missing. Like a body at its own funeral, I was only *present*. My soul had made its escape. It had fled the scene. Away from those initial whimpers of resistance that rose in my throat, from the strange sensations where his fingers trailed, kneaded and forced open, from the loosened strands of hair sticking to my sweat-covered skin, from the weight of darkness descending on me, the force of his thrusts as my body involuntarily resisted. His lips were pursed, his face a mask of intense concentration as he hacked his way in, reaching for the gold of his dreams. He grimaced, made a funny sound between a growl and a groan, and he plunged deeper. There was a look on his face now, as if the mask had fallen off. Who was he then, eyes glazing over with dampness, tasting a sweet pleasure? It was his alone; for me there was pain, the slicing burn of a sword. A flood of despair. Then, without warning, it was over. He went limp, rolled off. There was blood on me. Blood mingled with a pale stickiness that had come from him. Shame mingled with disgust.

Later, when our limbs had disentangled and he had turned his back to me and fallen asleep, breathing noisily, I slipped from the bed and lay on the bare stone floor, cradling my violated body. It began to shiver uncontrollably. Never had I felt so bereft in my entire life as I did then. Where was the tenderness, the passion that the love songs went on about? I had seen animals mate, but none of those couplings were marked by the callousness that had made this one so bestial. Was this how it would be from now? Cold. Lonely. Dark. A lifeless night, with only my strangled sobbing for company. Outside, riding the heavens, cradled in the arms of the full moon, my renegade soul looked down. It smiled.

That moon waned. It is a habit of the moon. Blood appeared in a ruby trail down my thighs. It, too, is regular in its arrival. In the palace they did not bother to hide their disappointment. Try again, try once more. There is still time...but they said it without much hope.

~

A month passed. The rains came. This was not the rain I knew, the rain of the forest and the countryside, where the earth celebrated by sprouting forth. This was city rain, thin, miserable and tired, leaving damp in the walls, clamminess in the air and spawning a clutch of illnesses: sniffles, fever, boils, dysentery. I, too, developed a severe cold and a mild fever. It gave me temporary relief from those dreadful nights in the royal bedchamber. I slept in my own room, on my own bed. Strange how I, though still in captivity, had begun to think of my cell as *mine*.

For days, I had been having a disturbing feeling that I was being watched. Though I was rarely alone, this feeling of being encroached upon became the strongest at those times that I was. At night I would jerk out of sleep, convinced that someone had entered the room and was standing by my bed looking down at me. There were moments when I was sure that someone had touched me in my sleep, running fingers along my limbs, fondling my breasts and hips. I put it down to the restlessness from my fever. There was no one I could speak to about this feeling.

One rainy dusk, when I was by myself in my bedchamber, waiting for the maids to bring in the lighted oil lamps, I had once again a vague impression that someone had entered the room. I looked towards the open window into the drenched garden beyond. The rain had stopped. A smoky mist covered the scene, water dripped off the glistening leaves of trees. There was no one in sight. Yet feeling uneasy, I went to shut the window when a hand suddenly appeared from nowhere and grasped mine. Before I could scream, the other hand clapped over my mouth. I heard a whisper in my ear, 'Shh…don't make a noise. I am your well-wisher.'

I stopped struggling. When I'd become absolutely still, the intruder removed the gag on my mouth, and I saw who it was: the royal astrologer.

'What are you doing here? What do you want?'

'Only to make you happy,' he replied, a leery smile appearing on his thick lips.

'Nobody can make me happy,' I snapped. 'Get out before someone comes in.'

'Don't be in such a hurry to get rid of me,' he said. 'You will be interested in my scheme.'

'I am going to call the maids.'

A vicious look entered his eyes. 'Listen, silly girl, you need to know this. The king will not give his horses to that brahmin who left you here.'

'*What?* That's not true!'

'True enough,' he said. 'Haryashva will never have a son.'

I stared at him in dismay. 'How do you know that?'

'It's common knowledge. His seed is not potent enough. Daughters in plenty, but no son. He will never beget a male heir, unless—'

'Unless what?'

'Unless *we* help him.'

I stared at him silently.

'I'll tell you how.' He edged close, so close that I had to turn my face away from his foul breath. 'No, no, don't move away.' He gripped my hand and said fawningly, 'Come to me, my little mynah. Don't be afraid. See, it's very simple. You and I—' He glanced towards the bed in an unmistakable way. I gasped. He grabbed my shoulders and drew me into a vice-like grip. I struggled to free myself. His hands wandered to my breasts. Pressing himself against me so that I could feel his tumescent member through his dhoti, he muttered, 'I cannot stop thinking of you ever since I first saw you. My heart overflows with love. Give me a chance to make you happy.' He turned my head forcibly and brought his mouth closer. Before he could plant it on mine, I managed to wriggle out of his grasp and scampered out of reach. He lunged, blocking my path to the door. 'Listen!' he cried out. 'I have three sons from my first wife and two from the second one. I can give you a son! No one will know the difference.'

'You've gone mad!'

His face clouded at the rebuke. 'No, I'm being practical. It has been done before, it will be done in the future, so why not this time?'

I stared at him speechless. Mistaking my revulsion for anxiety, he hastened to reassure me. 'Everyone will think it is his. No one loses, everyone benefits, don't you see? Besides, I must tell you one more thing: our birth charts presage it. Mine says I will have only sons, and so do the lines of your beautiful little palm. I studied them very carefully that night...sons for you, sons for me. We can have at least *one* together, no?'

'No!'

'Why not?'

'Because—' I stopped. He was a loathsome little man, but caution warned me not to say anything of what I thought to him. He was not above pettiness. Moreover, he had influence with the king.

He gave me a slow, fat smile. 'Are you afraid? That night when I first saw you, you looked like an angry tigress, but actually you are a timid little thing...don't worry. There is no danger. It's a simple act of switching. You will be the mother of monarchs, this much is ordained. My son a chakravarti samrat. What a thought!'

'I will not do this.'

He sent me a hostile look. 'You will do as I say.' He tried to grab me again. I evaded his hands and ran towards the door, but he managed to stop me from reaching it. Twisting my arm behind my back till it hurt, he hissed, 'Don't make even the slightest sound. If anyone hears you and comes in, it will be your word against mine. Who do you think they will trust? Now, be absolutely still. I'm going to bolt the door.'

Where were the maids? Should I shout? Would they even believe me? He was the royal astrologer, a trusted man. It would be his word against mine. Bolting the door from inside, he turned back to face me. There was a faint smile twisting his lips. 'You will be a good girl,' he said, running his hand down my arm and gripping my wrist. 'You will obey me.' The glazed look in his eyes as if he'd stopped seeing me altogether as another human being was a familiar one. I shuddered and turned my face away. 'Be good to me,' he said hoarsely.

I had to be able to breathe, to calm down in order to do what I wanted—it was the only way out. Willing myself to grow still, I waited...slowly the energy uncoiled. It rose within me. Dark, glistening, twisting, expanding, fanning out its head. An angry, attacking energy that made itself known to the world through sound. A warning. A hiss so real that I saw—as I had once before in the forest—the eyes, bright as black beads staring fixedly at me. A faint rustle, like the shifting of dry leaves in an autumn breeze, emanated from my unmoving lips. The beastly man froze. I felt cold fear dart through him.

'Did you hear?' he whispered quaveringly. 'Heard that sound?'

'It comes for the milk,' I whispered back and shifted my head towards the covered brass tumbler on the stool in the corner. 'Don't be afraid. And don't move. *Not even an eyelid.*'

'What? What?'

'A king cobra,' I murmured. 'It's a sign of good luck, isn't it?'

His eyes widened in horror. His breath was coming in shallow gasps. He opened his mouth to say something but no words emerged. His glance flitted in desperation towards the open window from which he had entered. I could see him calculating the distance to it. Could he make it to the window in one leap? Where was the snake? I shifted slightly. 'Don't—don't move!' he whispered panic-stricken. In reply, there was another hiss, louder this time. 'It's very close,' he said. Before I could respond, he sprang for the window. In a split second he was out of it.

After he'd gone, I shut the window and lay in bed trembling. It was relief but also a sense of exhilaration. I was not as helpless as I'd thought. After a while, I began to review my situation. I had got rid of the astrologer but my problem remained. Two months had passed. Though it was still unpleasant, I was no longer squeamish about what took place regularly in Haryashva's bed. However, I had not conceived. What would happen to me if I did not become pregnant? And what if I did and gave birth to a girl? Would they keep me here forever as a dasi? What would Gaalav do? Where was he? Was he thinking of me? He had promised to come back for me after one year. Though we were virtually strangers, I *had* agreed to help him. Yet, everything that had followed made me feel unreal. As if I were a hand puppet, inert till someone else gave shape to my existence. Another thought came to me: What if I died in childbirth? There was always that possibility. Gaalav's search for horses would end with me. Would he then kill himself? Would the storytellers sing of us as lovers who died for each other? If I didn't tell my own story, I would be adrift in someone else's version, eventually lost.

~

Haryashva does not order me to his bed any more. His duty is done. I am now with child. The royal midwife has confirmed it. However, the severe nausea I go through worries everyone. They wonder, is it going to be another girl? There are already four from the first two queens. From my window, I frequently watch them at play in the garden. Whatever they may say about Haryashva's seed not being strong enough, I think it produces healthy children. The younger two, whose mother is the second queen, are just five and four, and always together. Sometimes they sneak into my room and amuse me with their games and stories, till one of the maids whisks them away. The eldest is about thirteen years old, a rather bossy girl-woman who would be more attractive if she took herself a little less seriously. Her younger sibling is about ten, a mousy little girl with big eyes. The mother of these two, the chief queen, is known for her deep piety. She never moves an inch without consulting the astrologer first. A short, plain woman, she still manages to convey queenly authority. She runs the palace household, proclaims the days of fasting, leads expeditions to the sacred groves and teerthasthanas near and far, and organizes food kitchens offering free meals to brahmins passing through the city.

Despite her good works, or maybe because of them, the chief queen wears a long-suffering air.

During the initial months of my stay in Haryashva's palace, though I was not ill-treated, the royal women avoided me. I ate alone, spent all my time on my own. The clothes I was given to wear were rough and simple like a dasi's. My status was ambiguous. I was neither queen nor concubine nor slave. I was not a free-spirited woman like Supriya who, I discovered, was envied for her independence as much as her wealth. I was assigned no identity and hence had no status. I was not a nobody, but no one knew what I was. It rankled to be ignored. If nothing else, wasn't I of royal blood too? Yayati's daughter...but, I realized sadly, even that was no longer me. Yayati had given me away. I was Munikumar Gaalav's acquisition, loaned for a year to Haryashva.

There was always something going on in the women's quarters but I was never asked to participate. It would usually be a festival celebration with all its attendant activities. Every now and then itinerant performers were invited to entertain the queens and concubines. Sometimes vendors, too, were permitted inside to sell beauty scrubs and medicinal oils, pieces of jewellery and semi-precious stones, amulets for good luck and other knick-knacks that attracted female fancy. From my room, I'd hear the sounds of gaiety, the light banter and feel more miserable than ever. However, when the midwife confirmed that I was pregnant, the situation changed very quickly. First, Haryashva's three queens came to bless me.

They made a ceremony of this too, slipping a pair of ornate gold bangles on my wrist and gifting new garments of the finest cloth. There was something slightly unhinged about the visit. Amidst the polite chitchat they kept looking at me with a predatory curiosity, never directly, but in swift, sideways glances as if trying to assess from the glow of my skin and the shape of my belly whether the consignment within was the promised one or not. The interaction gave me a strange feeling of disembodiment, as if my womb stored an elixir that these women, like three empty pitchers, craved to be filled with. With a delicate, seemingly casual air, they asked me whether I craved for sweet or salty food and advised me various remedies for the morning sickness. Drink ginger and lemon water, chew mint leaves.

The chief queen did most of the talking. She spoke in drifting sentences, with long pauses. 'It is your good luck, too, but *ours* is the greater fortune. Be happy... think positive thoughts...we all pray that you have an easy delivery.' The second queen, a reticent, modest woman, nodded in agreement and occasionally cast sad smiles at me, perhaps to show sympathy. The third queen, who is the royal favourite, maintained a haughty air while listening without comment. Born in the Sakya clan who live in the mountains to the north, she is the best looking of the three. Petite, doe-eyed, elegant but also high-spirited, she shares Haryashva's love of horses and is a keen horsewoman herself. It is said that he visits her chamber the most, but he has not been able to make her a mother.

As the royal women were leaving, the third queen stopped. Arching her eyebrows in a calculated way, she said, 'You have been given a lot of tips and advice, but remember, no one here is an expert. They have only managed to produce girls. Do you believe it will be different with you?'

I would have liked to dodge the question, but all three women were looking at me keenly, awaiting my response. 'I don't believe anything. I only know that there are others who claim to be more knowledgeable than me.'

The first queen nodded her approval, the second merely stared at the floor and smiled, while the third puckered her mouth in a sneer.

A few nights later I dreamt of the deer. It was etched on a familiar canvas—my mother's back. A full-grown barasingha stag with broad, branching horns that grew towards the sky and drew into themselves the brightness of the sun, channelling that light straight into my body. Energizing every cell, the life growing inside me, outlined with golden light.

I woke up with a jerk. The tingling feeling from the dream remained, but it wasn't just a dream any more. A flutter, gentle as a moth's wings, was in my belly. After a moment I placed my hand on the spot. There it was again...my baby speaking to me.

I am no longer alone!

A strange new joy welled up in me. From now on I would never be alone. My own self recognized this, absorbed the knowledge and quietly exchanged its old identity for the new. Everything that had happened to me in the past few months suddenly seemed less painful. My body was changing, adapting to harbour a new life. It was natural that I was becoming a mother, but it also felt just right. The world was in the same place, but my position in it had changed. There was a life shaping inside me. Infinitely precious. My baby.

~

She has taken to visiting me every day. I don't know what to make of her friendliness. After the strange dream of the deer, the morning sickness miraculously disappeared. Now I want to eat all the time. The food I am served is cooked specially for me. There are greens on my plate every day. Cooked with lentils, fried with spices or simply boiled and mashed. I have grown to hate them. I crave tangy foods. The third queen often brings me tidbits: pickled karonda berries, slices of dried mango, a bowl of bitter gourd cooked with jaggery and tamarind. As I sample the dish she sits watching me with almost proprietorial interest. I am grateful for her companionship; I have been alone for too long. She draws me out by asking questions about how I slept, how I feel and whether I would like to get some fresh air by taking a walk with her in the garden. It's easy to see why she is the king's favourite. When she wishes to engage with one she is sparkling company. Her expression is animated, her eyes assume a flirtatious look. It is hard to resist her charm. We go out for walks quite often.

Winter lingers on this year. Consequently, spring is not the familiar slow process of the trees greening, gardens filling with new grass and fresh blossoms, the lakes and riverbanks crowding with migratory birds. Instead, it passes in a flash, but there are still some glimpses of it to be had. In the palace estates, there is a marshy area that is the wintering ground for ducks and cranes from far-off lands. The third queen and I go there frequently to watch the strange leggy birds with their long black beaks.

'Picking their way through the marsh, scrounging for food, they look like crude puppets,' says the third queen. 'The earth is clearly not their stage but have you seen them in flight?' Without waiting for my reply, she continues, 'They rule the skies. Their necks stretched in a straight line, the black-tipped wings spread out, they bring beauty and grace to the firmament. Maybe you will see them leave. It will happen soon, say in a week or ten days. I confess I feel sad when they go away.'

'But they will come back next winter,' I say. I put my hands on my taut belly. The baby has moved lower in my womb.

'Still...partings are always a bit sad, aren't they?'

I glance at her sharply. Her expression is friendly but, despite her normal tone, I see the steely look in her eyes. I grow still.

'Of course, you must not think like that,' she says.

'Think like what?' I ask blankly.

'Never think the baby is yours. He belongs to *me*.'

I stare at her silently.

'It's true,' she says in a no-nonsense way. 'The king has promised him to me. It will be our baby. His and mine.' Gripping hold of my wrist, she adds, 'Come! I want to show you the apartment.'

'But—'

'Now, don't say no. I've been dying to show it to you. It's where *he* likes to spend all his time.' Her manner is coquettish. I realize that she's talking about Haryashva and a shudder passes through me. She mistakes it for something very different—something other than revulsion—and the malice in her smile deepens. 'I insist! I want to show you something.'

A light, airy room. A cradle fashioned from gold. Soft new linen. A silver rattle.

'The king and I cannot agree on a name,' she says. 'Of

course, our son will have more than one—kings always do. Besides the name that the astrologer chooses, there will be at least two other names, so maybe the king's choice and mine as well will be accommodated. I'm sure he will be as handsome as the divine vasus. I want to call him Vasuman...don't you think it's a nice name? You must tell me what you think.' Her eyes are shining like polished black agates.

After a moment, when I am able to speak, I say quietly, 'It's a nice name.'

She throws me a dazzling smile, clearly pleased. 'And now you must help me choose the colour for—'

'I feel a bit dizzy,' I say abruptly. 'I would like to go back to my own room.'

'Yes, of course.' Her face is immediately covered in concern. 'I thought it would make you happy to see all this.' Maddened by pain I turn away, hoping to reach the sanctuary of my room before the tears come, but she bars my way. 'You must understand,' she says, firm but no longer unkind. 'Hard as it may seem to you, it is not unusual for women to give up their babies...I, too, was given away by my birth parents because the Sakya chieftain's wife could not have children. I have lived like a princess all my life. I am a queen. And I will be the mother of the next king.'

I am never left alone. It is as if they know the dread that grows in me every minute and what is now on my mind: flight. The walls are high, the gates always guarded. The prophecy of sons has incarcerated me. It has spun threads around me, and now I am trapped in this web of desire, a living prey to be consumed in slow morsels. But doesn't my own longing trap me too? I cannot bear the idea of being separated from my baby. *Yes, my baby*. I am torn. I want nothing more than to remain in this place; I want nothing more than to escape. But where would I go? Unlike the cranes who guide their little ones back home, I have no safe haven waiting for me where I could take my baby. For them the world is free, but for a woman like me it is a prison. Then why do I see my baby as a vision of a better future? Why do I crave that future?

~

The pain comes in the morning. A clamp gradually mounting and then releasing its grip. After an examination, the royal midwife tells me in a kindly way, 'This is going to take a long time.' As the frequency of the contractions increases, I am led to the birthing room. Outside, there is a courtyard where generations of women in labour, queens and concubines, have paced in the past. I add my footsteps to their numbers, a slow drumbeat towards the day's end. The sun sinks into its grave. Lamps are lit in naves. The midwife examines me again and announces to the women who gather in the courtyard that it will be an hour or two more. Only an hour, I think. *Mine for just an hour more.* Go have your dinner, she advises the waiting women. Meanwhile, my body is sluiced down with warm water, dried and dressed in a soft cloth. I am given a herbal drink. If it were not for the presence of this pain, the day would be a picnic, such is the circle of comradeship and casual chitchat that surrounds me. It is women's experience, wholly theirs, one that they never tire of, though a few of them lie on their sides and fall asleep.

The pain comes and goes as if undecided...it makes

me very tired. Suddenly, I feel tremendous pressure inside me and before I can make it to the urinal, I wet myself to my deep embarrassment. The warm liquid gushes out of me. And now, as if what had preceded it was just a light overture, the pain slams in with full force. It is everywhere. In my arching body, in my screams. In hell I am, being stripped of my very self. Not a human any more but a female creature reaching into her very core, breaking open the prison of her womb because the life within must make its way out. The birthing room is suddenly hot, overcrowded with sweaty women. Airless. I am stretched out on the raised platform. Through the thickening fog of pain, I make out the anxious, avid faces of the three queens. Behind them an army of women strains to witness this moment. Whose are the contractions? Whose are these screams? Whose are the words of advice? Who lies impaled? Whose is the rigid body with its legs splayed that must tear out from its centre the new heartbeat, the blood-and-slime-coated bald head, the tiny curled-up limbs? The baby slides out, the cord follows. Cut the cord. Cut it now. The cord is cut.

A slap. A cry.

It's a boy.

A shout of joy: Tell the king! A race towards the sabha, where the first bearer of good news will be well rewarded.

I am on the periphery again. A shell with its pearl scraped off. I listen to their excited chatter as they examine the newborn, bathe and wrap him in soft swaddling clothes before presenting him to the king. From the talk around me, I learn that the shape of the baby's head shows that it is meant to wear a crown; he has strong limbs just like his father, but his ears are his grandfather's, so say the old crones. As the temple bells ring out and prayers of thanksgiving are offered to the gods, as the news sings out across the kingdom that its new hope has arrived, the fear of the line's extinction is quietly buried. As is the umbilical cord that bound me to my babe, as is the pain I suffered...all that remains of the past is this keening inside me, this grief that is exclusively mine. The void left by an absent heartbeat.

Yet there is one more thing for me to learn. Compassion, too, lives in the human heart and even in the midst of terrible suffering it can reach out and throw you a lifeline. This time its source is the second queen. On the last night of my stay in Ayodhya, she comes to my room. 'Come with me,' she says, signalling that I should be as quiet as possible, careful not to wake up the maids sleeping in the torch-lit passages. She leads me to the royal nursery where the wet nurse is gently rocking the cradle from which tiny cries of distress are coming. The woman looks up and recognizing the second queen, says worriedly, 'He's been restless for hours...it's not hunger because he has refused milk and it doesn't seem to be colic.' Then she sees me and stops abruptly. She is a dasi, just a few years older than I, but from the looks of her, seasoned in motherhood. A peculiar expression passes over her broad, fleshy face. Suspicion that transforms into recognition. I understand that look: we are sisters under the skin. She, like me, is only a supplier. My womb. Her breast milk.

'Leave us for a while,' the second queen says to her. 'But stay outside the room.' She waits for the woman to obey and then gently lifts the infant from the cradle and hands him to me. 'He must know his mother's milk too. It's only right.'

And so I take in my arms the soft precious weight of my firstborn. His mouth finds my breast and latches on. It flows through me in delicious warm ripples, this new feeling, this wash of joy. Anguish and rapture conjoined. As I watch his face with the bud-like mouth sucking—the left breast first and then the right—I think, oh, he is a greedy one! But I know, too, that he is the liberal one. There will be paeans sung to his generosity, on their wings the fame of his dynasty will rise till it covers the entire land. But all this is so far in the future. Maybe he, too, senses that this will be the one, the only time, he will lie in my arms, because he pauses and looks up at me intently. I see that there are changes already. He has gained weight; though his cheeks are chubby, his features have become more distinct. How long his eyelashes are! He will grow up to be a handsome man. I smile. I cry. Though born of my flesh, I know he is not mine. His eyes are edged with kajal. Someone has tied a black thread on his wrist. No, he is not mine. I will never see him again. The first word uttered, the first tooth, the first step...and he too, will not know my name. Who will tell him of this fierce love that I feel right now, or how hard it is for me to leave him? Yet, a small voice within me says that letting go is what you must do. Where will you take him when you have no home of your own? He will be safe here. He will be loved. He will be a good king to his people. He will fulfil a great destiny. And all this made possible for him by you. One day, he will understand...men's dreams are built on women's pain.

When the babe has had his fill, he falls asleep. Very

gently I pull the nipple out of his mouth, but his lips continue to cling as if he is unwilling to let go. My arms lay him down in his golden cradle, my hands stroke his head, my whole being blesses him, and all the while my tears flow in a ceaseless stream. It is not just an absent heartbeat but my whole heart that has gone missing, wrested out of me—all that remains is the ebb and flow of grief.

11

Gaalav

He cracked his knuckles, waiting impatiently for the city's gates to open. He did not know which version of her he would meet this dawn—the scrawny maidservant or the elegant princess—but he was aware that he had been anticipating this moment with a mixture of eagerness, curiosity and trepidation. At last the wooden gates were flung open by a pair of sleepy-eyed guards. It was still too early for regular traffic, but special instructions had come from the palace. After a while, a covered palanquin passed through the gates and came to a stop at the majestic pipal tree under which Gaalav stood. A few minutes passed when nothing happened. His eyes were trained on the palanquin. The curtains parted and she stepped out. The bearers immediately turned around and returned the way they had come. She stood stock-still, her face as if carved from a piece of marble, eyes as if sightless. She turned her head towards the gates. Something altered in her look. A retinue of servants had followed her. Each one was bearing a casket or a covered tray. Turning her back on them she glanced at Gaalav. The baleful look in her eyes, her unwillingness to offer even the customary salutation alerted him that, despite his impatience to get going, he should be cautious in his dealings with her. The awkward silence between them stretched. Finally, he breached it himself. Glancing at the pigeon-grey clouds, he said, 'It may rain any time…we should start our journey.'

'Where to now?' she asked, her tone inert.

'Kashi.'

'Oh!' An eyebrow shot up in mock surprise. 'Are you still bent upon dying?'

Her tone made him bristle. 'Did I say anything about dying?'

'Then why are you going to Kashi?'

'To meet the king.'

She curled her lips. 'And how many white horses does he have?'

'More than enough.'

'Is that a fact or just wild hope?'

He could not see through her bravado into the wretchedness within. All he heard was the sharp, criticizing note. It made him resent her. 'Lord Brahma has recently performed the grandest horse sacrifice in the world,' he said curtly. 'The king of Kashi supplied the paraphernalia, including the ten horses. That should give you an idea of his wealth.'

'And I am to be the eleventh sacrifice!' she snarled with the fury of a trapped creature.

Taken aback by the outburst, he faltered. 'This year… it hasn't been easy for me either. I have had my own struggles.' There was bleakness in his voice. The story of his quest and the bargain he'd struck with Haryashva had spread. It had caused amusement in certain circles. He'd heard that kshatriyas were placing bets.

She met his gaze and blinked, as if suddenly stepping out of dimness. For a few moments she considered him quietly, then, in a way he found disconcerting, she abruptly altered the course of the conversation. 'Is it going to be a very long walk to Kashi?'

'We are not going to walk,' he said. 'I have brought a bullock cart for you…the last patron repaid me generously for my services. A bullock cart for you and a horse for me.' He was unable to hide the note of pride in his voice.

'Oh! Are you ready to sit on a horse again?'

He shrugged his shoulders. 'As I said, I have had my own share of struggles, and overcome at least some of them.'

The corners of her mouth lifted slightly. She went to the waiting bullock cart and sat in it.

He glanced at the line of servants that had followed her and said with a frown, 'I hadn't planned on you having so much baggage. What is all this?'

As if in response, the leader among the retainers stepped forward and placed the casket he was holding in the cart. 'The king of Ayodhya would like to show his deep gratitude to the princess,' he said and opened the casket. It contained a hoard of the finest pearls. He gave a signal to the other servants who came up too and began to place the caskets and trays in the cart, opening them to reveal ornaments of burnished gold, rich silk as well as linen garments.

Gaalav was dumbstruck at the display, but Drishadvati's reaction was the opposite. Her face working up some deeper emotion, she said, 'Take it all back… tell Haryashva from me that he will remain in my debt forever because he cannot reimburse me. Not ever.' Her eyes swept over the presents in contempt. They settled on Gaalav's face and bore into him with such bitterness that he was forced to look away. The servants glanced at each other nervously but, at a signal from him, did as ordered.

On this uneasy note their journey began. The first few hours were spent in silence. Gaalav was still reeling from the scorn in Drishadvati's words. She was behaving erratically, he thought. What had made her so furious that she had rejected the king's generosity? She had no self-restraint. She should have stopped to consider for a moment that the treasure rightly belonged to him. A firewall of bitterness began to build up in his mind. *While she has spent her time in the palace, enjoying its comforts, I've been trying to keep body and soul together by performing rituals for others and worrying about how I will gather the remaining horses. On top of everything else, I've had word of my mother's declining health. Now that my studies are over, Mother expects me to return home, but I haven't had the courage to face her. How can I tell her that I have belied all the high hopes she had? When they find out what an impossible task I am saddled with, my parents will only worry and rue the day they sent me to Rishi Vishwamitra's ashram. There are people who are laughing at me. If I fail, my name will be mud. Why doesn't this foolish girl understand my predicament?*

He glanced sideways at the cart. The creaking rhythm of the wheels had sent its passenger off to sleep. He didn't need to guard his gaze any longer and stared openly at her. The soft morning breeze teased her hair. Her face, he noticed, had remained as defenceless as a child's—tired, troubled even in deep slumber, streaked with lines where the tears had dried up. It had retained its freshness but also acquired a certain maturity. Her skin had plumped out, fulfilling the promise of shapeliness in her bone structure. The cloth cradling her breasts had loosened a little. Their fullness spilled out like firm ripe fruit, a largesse on which his eyes greedily feasted, delighting in this clandestine thing he shared with her, the nakedness of his self. He wanted her. The proof was in his body. A rush in his blood. A compelling need to feel her skin under his fingertips. It was a wild, mad dream, unthinkable, though a part of him asked why it should be so. Hadn't she been given to him? Wasn't she his? *Careful! Will you risk everything?* Yet the desire was so strong that he struggled to beat it down. Cautionary tales sprang to his mind, of other men and what had happened to them: Pururavas, Nahusha, Yayati. All three men who, lusting after women, had lost everything. No, he did not want his name to become a byword like theirs...but the fire in his blood would not die down. What had this year been like for her? How had she been treated? The questions hovered in his mind like a swarm of flies over a carcass, generating unease. And the answers to all those questions too circled back. Nothing had changed. *He* still had to pay his debt to the guru. *It's not my fault. If anyone is to blame for her situation, it is Yayati. It's her destiny that she was born to a father like him.*

The cart slowed down, then ground to a stop. The cartman turned around to look back, said something to draw Gaalav's attention and moved the vehicle to the side of the road. 'We must give way,' he said, pointing in the direction of Ayodhya, where a cloud of dust was moving swiftly towards them through the empty landscape. As the rumbling thunder of horses' hooves came closer, the ground trembled. Within a few minutes, a sea of milk, pearly with its own luminescence, rushed towards them. The wave flowed past, and all Gaalav could gather were assorted impressions of elemental forces suspended between heaven and earth—fluid manes soft as silk, light-footed grace dancing to a secret music. Boundless energy. Two hundred white horses on their way to Rishi Vishwamitra's ashram. His chest swelled with elation. He had done it! A movement in the cart distracted him. She was up, awakened by the noise, spellbound just like he was by the scene that had passed before her eyes. Still caught up in its magic she turned to him and, meeting his gaze, held it for the longest moment. The exchange had the flavour of a shared victory but there was also a humming undercurrent. His eyes on her became openly admiring. They shot a tingle across her skin. A smile, shy and soft, dawned on her face. As if welcoming it, the clouds parted and the sunlight slanted into his soul.

With the return of vibrancy, a silent truce was struck. Companionship made its way back. The cartman coughed and asked Gaalav a question about the route. Were they to head southeast? The rainy season was nearly over but the rivers were still overflowing and the fords would be dangerous to cross. Though the distance between Kashi and Ayodhya was not much, they had to make a roundabout journey. Due to the bad condition of the roads, there was scant traffic. Several times, when the cartwheels were stuck in the slush, she got off to help the men pull them out. Gaalav was secretly relieved to note that the year-long stay in the palace had not given her too many airs. He also sensed that the pent-up anger he had encountered earlier in the day had cooled a little. When it was time to eat the midday meal, she served him the food with due courtesy, and even made small talk. After a while, as if putting things behind by simply looking ahead, she asked, 'Who is the king of Kashi? Tell me about him.'

12

Divodas

It was said of him that in the kingdom he had once ruled, a lifetime ago, his name had been Ripunjaya. And that name, too, he shed when he made his way to Kashi, equipped with nothing but a begging bowl and a sturdy wooden stick. There were other nameless ascetics and renouncers in the city, who were to be identified only by the sites they frequented—the confluence of the two rivers, the forests in the south, the park of the deer herds and the burning ghats along the river Ganga. But, as he was a true seeker of solitude, even the flowing alleyways of heaving, tumultuous Kashi posed no challenge for him. He found his peace in the flow, yet reborn to the life of a drifter, he was like a rumour, here and there, everywhere and nowhere. To allow tantalizing glimpses but never be properly seen was his wont. It was a task to locate him, even for Brahma the Creator, who had undertaken the mission at the behest of the gods. Eventually, one muggy night, he managed to trace the sadhu.

'I've been searching for you high and low,' Brahma said.

In response, the emaciated ash-covered man smiled in amusement. 'Kashi is neither high nor low.'

'Right now, it's certainly worse than hell,' Brahma said, looking around at the funeral pyres spewing embers, reducing bone to ash. The air, smelling of burning flesh, made him sick. 'Too many have died due to the famine.'

'What famine?'

'You mean you don't know that there's a drought and a food shortage?' Brahma asked in disbelief.

'There is no shortage,' the renouncer said, carefully wrapping the lower end of his chillum in a small rag and raising it to his face. 'What more than this does one need?' He took a deep pull, and ganja fumes wafted from the cinders, making Brahma feel a little light-headed.

Forcing himself to think clearly, the Creator said, 'So you haven't heard a word of the riots, shops looted, and the royal granaries stormed. It's total anarchy. Babies are starved of milk, so weak are the nursing mothers. Brahmins are selling their minor daughters in slavery to old men. As for their old women, they are simply left to die. Whole families have migrated from the region. Death rules the countryside. Animals dead, humans dead. Only the hyenas remain to perform the last rites. Listen! You can hear them laughing on the far bank.'

'To be born is to suffer, unless one is born a hyena.'

Brahma's stony silence made it clear that, in his view, this sort of humour was in poor taste. The sadhu said by way of apology and explanation, 'I've loosened all my ties with the mortal world.' He looked down at his body—the ribcage sticking out, the knobby knees and stick-like legs. 'There is only this shell now.'

Brahma relented. 'The gods have sent a message for you,' he said 'They want you to take charge.'

'Of what?'

'Running this place. You were a ruler, albeit of an insignificant kingdom, an obscure dynasty. Yet you did everything right. A good king who upholds dharma is rare. If you were to be crowned king of Kashi, the gods believe that righteousness would undoubtedly return to the land. Then how could Indra deny the rains needed to end the drought?'

The renouncer chuckled. 'Ah! So Indra is angry because the people of Kashi no longer perform the old sacrifices in the right spirit. How he loves the adulation of mortals! But I see your logic and I am genuinely sorry to say no to you...I have finished with kingship and kingdoms. I never imagined that I would *like* my life as a sadhu, but I do. I'm quite attached to it now. Besides, Mahadev is the lord of Kashi. It is his universe. Ask him to sort it all out.'

Brahma almost snorted in derision but he controlled himself. Even gods must stand together. It would not do to reveal to a mere mortal what he thought of Mahadev and his indifference to the running of his so-called favourite city. Instead he said, 'He, too, is of the opinion that you are the only man who can restore order.'

The renouncer dipped his head in a gesture of modesty. 'I am humbled by this honour.'

Brahma was relieved that the matter had been settled so quickly. 'There is much to be done. Will you assume kingship right away?'

But the man still balked. 'You devas have made Kashi your home. Your shrines dominate the landscape.'

'None of us will interfere with your administration.'

'I would still be self-conscious with you watching me all the time. Besides, it would be difficult for you gods not to interfere in the affairs of us mortals. How else would you show your superiority?'

Brahma was annoyed by the man's nerve, but he decided not to take affront as there was too much at stake. 'Will you change your mind if we move out?'

The sadhu lifted his bony shoulders in a shrug. 'I would have no choice.'

'I'll give the orders right away.'

'To Mahadev as well?' asked the sadhu sceptically. 'Will he give up his city?'

'I can only request him,' said Brahma tersely, though he had grave doubts himself.

Accompanied by drumbeaters, the town-crier went around. 'Leave! Leave! All gods must leave Kashi forthwith. Go back to your own specific homes.' And so began the exodus of gods. Reluctant but obedient, one and all left. The ancient deities, benign and fierce, yakshas, nagas, dikpalas, bhairavas, matrikas, yoginis and devis—who had lived for the longest time in hills, caves, groves, fields, lakes and springs, crossroads and cremation grounds—grumbled the most. This is *our* land they cried. You can't uproot us! The mortals, too, were confused, at a loss. With the divine beings gone, whose blessings and assistance would they seek? Where would they burn incense? To whom would they make the offerings of flowers, fruit, betel leaves and milk? Whose birthdays and weddings would they celebrate with song and dance, food and ritual? Most importantly, at whom, when things didn't go their way, would they rant? Living in a godless universe was unthinkable for mortals. It was not merely the everyday life or the entire economy revolving around the gods—so many livelihoods depended on them—but the sense of continuity. Without their native gods and goddesses, who were they? And didn't the gods need them too, for without worship from mortals who were *they*? It was all about give and take, this relationship between mortals and gods. One made offerings in order to obtain. And the other bestowed favours to show their godliness. How else would their power be made visible? Wasn't it through reward and punishment that their superiority was established?

Yet there were also people who pointed out that the shining ones did not distinguish between the innocent and the guilty when they doled out punishment such as floods, fires, famines and scourges. By withdrawing the rains, hadn't they persecuted all life? Even the sacrifices of the virtuous had not worked. When the gods did not share the human condition, how could one expect sympathy from them? Good conduct, the only way to prevent chaos in the mortal world, flowed from a sense of balance. A king well grounded in dharma but who also understood the fine gradations of human nature would be inclined to fairness. He would rule honourably and thus make Kashi the most peaceful, enlightened and prosperous city on earth. Yes, a virtuous king was the need of the hour. Seeing how the general mood was developing, the gods and goddesses shook their heads and did not tarry. At last everyone had gone but one: Mahadev. And it was to him that Brahma now went.

Mahadev listened to Brahma's plea with his characteristic impassivity. The Creator chose his words with care as he did not want even a hint of reproach to pass his lips. Besides, Vasuki, the hamadryad coiled around Mahadev's neck, made him uneasy; it was eyeing him with a certain meaty curiosity. Mahadev's mysteriousness, his strange pets, the fondness for the cremation grounds had always made Brahma nervous. He found the silent mirth with which the Great God viewed the universe unsettling, as it signalled a power superior to his own. *You may create something, but I can always destroy it.* That was the underlying truth of the power balance between them. Brahma always thought that it was a little unfair that he had been made administrator of the creative portfolio. Once he'd done his job of fashioning the world and peopled it with all species of plants and animals, hardly anyone of those beings he had created remembered his name. Nobody prayed to him. He sometimes even had to use the old line—Do you know who I am?—when lesser gods acted funny with him. Why didn't either Vishnu or Shiva have to experience the awkwardness of saying that at least once?

As Brahma finished speaking, Vasuki gave a hiss and began to glide rather insidiously towards him with a transfixing stare. Brahma backed away in alarm and fought the urge to turn and run. Really! How could he have had the temerity to ask Mahadev to give up his home? He braced himself against the mysterious third eye lodged in that wide sloping forehead of Vishwanath, as the people of Kashi chose to call him. Lord of the World. The third eye, he had heard, could open without warning and incinerate the offender in seconds. But to his surprise, Mahadev merely stood up, yanked his upright trident out of the ground, reined in the wandering cobra and gave it an extra twirl around his neck. Then he picked up the damaru, his little hand-drum, and set off. His stride being long, he had already covered some distance before Brahma recovered his wits and ran after him, twittering in panic, 'What? Why? I mean, *where* are you going?'

'You just asked me to leave,' said Mahadev, without slowing his pace to match Brahma's shorter gait.

'But where are you off to?' Brahma asked apprehensively. 'You aren't going to just disappear, are you? We need you to be around.'

'I may not be wanted here, but there are other places where I am welcome.'

'Of course, of course...erm, which place were you thinking of?'

'The mountain Mandaar has invited me several times to visit him. He is a most ardent devotee. In fact, he refused to leave Kashi till I agreed to a sojourn on his peaks.'

'Well, mountains are where you and your beautiful consort, Uma Devi, are the happiest,' said Brahma. 'And Mandaar will consider himself blessed.'

'What does he call himself?' Mahadev asked suddenly.

'Who?' Brahma sent him a confused look.

'This new king of Kashi. What is his name?'

'Divodas,' replied Brahma, with unconscious irony. 'It means servant of the gods.'

Mahadev smiled as if appreciating the joke. They had reached the outskirts of Kashi. He stopped suddenly, turned to look at the city and jabbed the air with his trident. With the other hand he rattled the damaru. 'I'll be back,' he said. It was a promise. As if to seal it, he closed his eyes and silently invoked a mantra. The ground before him was parched and cracked from the drought. It split open a few feet wide. As the two edges parted, wisps of smoke emerged, undulating in the air, changing in colour to a dark black, thickening, solidifying into a smooth shape. It rose to a height of five feet and stopped: an ellipsoid stone, gleaming black.

For several minutes Brahma was too stunned to speak. 'Miraculous,' he said weakly. 'But what is it?'

'Fire,' said Mahadev, looking at the shivling with some pride. 'There's no smoke without one.'

~

Divodas was duly anointed as the king of Kashi. On the day of his coronation, it rained and the sun, too, shone simultaneously. Multiple rainbows appeared in the sky and everyone took it as a good omen that good days would surely come. Yagnas were performed again in the proper manner, sacred chants reverberated through the city, smoke carrying prayers swirled upwards till the gods declared themselves satisfied. The tide of decay which had swept over the land receded. Instead of corpses floating down the river, boats and barges laden with goods for trade began to appear. Goldsmiths set up shops and began to craft the famous studded jewellery. Weavers restarted their businesses, producing as they had for decades the famed silk, flax and cotton weaves so fine that they were coveted in lands far and wide. Gold began to fill the coffers in the treasury, allowing the king to build up his administration and restore order. Brahmins who had left the city returned, swearing that they had missed the delectable laddus for which the sweet-makers of Kashi were famous. Everyone forgot that Kashi had for a while been the saddest city on earth. It was once again the City of Bliss.

Before long, the gods began to feel uncomfortable again: Divodas was *too* ideal a king. The power he had acquired through asceticism worked to his advantage, giving him clarity, detachment and foresight. Rooted in dharma, he ruled righteously. His people were so happy that the gods feared he would become as powerful as Indra himself. What need would there be of gods then? Where would they get the worship and sacrifices that they craved?

Meanwhile, Mahadev, too, had grown disgruntled. He missed his beloved Kashi so much that it was like a disruption of the self, a dissonance, a note missing in his inner music, a step lost in dance. He had no complaints about Mount Mandaar's hospitality, but he found the ambience too exclusive. Besides, he could not forget his Ganga, the beautiful, impetuous river he had tamed, its teeming riverbank where his people bathed and prayed, where they cremated their dead in the hope that such a finale would liberate the departed soul from the cycle of rebirth. Humans wanted that final freedom, but all *he* wanted was to find a way back to Kashi. It did not help that his beloved wife Uma, too, felt the same way. Though a child of the mountains, she had grown to love Kashi. It was her home, the first home that her husband had brought her to after their wedding; as such it held a special place in her affection. She thirsted for the unique taste of its water, the creaminess of its milk. She missed the amber sunrises, the songs of the boatmen, the peacocks and deer in the neighbouring forest. Can't we go back, she nagged her husband. Not till I get that man to leave, he replied. Do it then, she said. Do everything to make him leave but take me back to Kashi. It's *my* home.

13

Drishadvati and Divodas

As Gaalav and I approach Kashi, the light changes, becoming crystalline, rippling as if energized by a new vibration. A pureness. It is like a balm to my bruised spirit. Even my lethargy fades. We join a line of carts waiting to enter the city gates which will soon be shut for the night. There is an air of companionship among the crowds in the city, relaxed, tolerant, as if everyone is certain that winding down the workday and heading towards the night's rest, they will all share the same sweet dream.

Asking our way through the maze of lanes, we arrive at a fortification by the river. This is the home that Divodas has built for himself, in which he lives alone. It has a functional, distinctly martial air. The vast courtyard is slushy from the rains. A tall stone pillar stands in the middle, with a waving flag. Within the mud walls of the fort are the thatched stables for the prized shyamkarni horses. Seeing their size and number, Gaalav appears pleased though he does not say anything to me. To one side of the courtyard, stone steps lead to the water's edge. The sky is still cloudy but there is a faint cool breeze blowing in from the river. It creates waves that attack the wide steps energetically, washing over them and then retreating. Gaalav rings the big brass bell outside the front door. We wait a long time but no one answers the summons. He pushes the door; to his surprise it opens. Inside is a small passageway that holds weapons of all types—spears, maces, swords, shields and helmets. Gaalav frowns. I can guess the questions bothering him. *Is this the right address? Where is the army of servants, the ritual welcome? Where is the king?* As if in answer, a section of the wall moves noiselessly, revealing a narrow gloomy passage lit by lamps placed in niches. Reaching the door at its far end, Gaalav pushes this open too. Inside is a long throne room with windows cut into its outer wall. They open out to the river, allowing a watery light to seep into the room. The floors are covered in simple furnishings. There are carved stone pillars, chairs to sit on, but there is still no one in sight—except for a lone man sitting on the throne and looking out thoughtfully at the river. In the distance, the white sail of a boat is visible. Noticing us, he stands up and comes forward in a leisurely way.

Of medium height, lean and supple, with a perfect posture, Divodas has the natural dignity of a born warrior. A steed, a sword and an arena seem more his native world than this throne room. As if aware of the incongruity, his manner towards us is reserved. He performs the ritual washing of Gaalav's feet, says a few words of welcome, offers us bael juice as refreshment. And still no one else in sight. To add to the unreality, I am invited to sit with the king and Gaalav. The brahmin looks shocked at this unorthodox behaviour, but Divodas gently insists on it. I think I begin to like him at this very moment.

Gaalav opens the conversation with an unnecessarily long speech. Listening to him drone on, while making several flattering references to himself, I sense that all this eloquence is aimed at turning his quest for the horses into a significant saga—with himself as the hero. It irks me that he does not once mention my role in his effort. He could just add that I agreed to help him, for that too is true. Without my support would he have got even his two hundred white horses? He ends his narration by stating his problem before the king. 'I need just six hundred horses to fulfil my obligation. A righteous king like yourself should help me. This is, no doubt, a simple request for you. Everyone has heard of the great sacrifice in which you assisted none other than the Creator...ten horses, I believe!'

'That was different,' Divodas says calmly. 'I have only two hundred of the kind you require.'

Gaalav sends him a look of disbelief. 'A man as powerful as you can procure them. It's common knowledge that at your behest the gods agreed to leave Kashi.'

'Nonetheless, two hundred horses are all I'm prepared to offer to you.'

A strained note enters Gaalav's voice. 'That will not solve my problem.'

Divodas nods, signalling that he is not unsympathetic, but remains silent.

'I am willing to wait a year while you collect the remaining horses,' Gaalav says, reluctantly. 'But I would urge you not to lose this chance.' He glances askance at me. 'The princess's lineage is impeccable. She will give you heirs. Your line will continue for a long time. You can beget as many as three sons from her.'

'However, only *one* is needed to sit on the throne of Kashi.'

Gaalav purses his lips. His hands slowly ball into fists. After a few minutes he stands up and, without wasting a word, begins to walk stiffly towards the door. He makes a cursory gesture, a nod of his head in my direction, as if I am his pet dog who is chained to him, and a mere tug will make me trail obediently after him. Though I feel the pull, something within me resists the urge to get up. His eyes are on me, the widening look of surprise in them when he senses my defiance. Yes, I am angry too. I no longer care. *If he needs any more help from me, he will have to ask for it. I am not going to make it easy for him.* He sends a quick darting glance towards Divodas. The king is watching us. Being a shrewd man he keeps an impassive expression, but there is a look of avid curiosity in his eyes, a faint glimmer of amusement. Perhaps, Gaalav, too, detects it. A heavy mask falls on his face. Only his eyes, turning back to me, are alive, fierce with loathing. Shaken by the look in them, I am the one who breaks eye contact first. Hurt, confused, not understanding...what has brought about this unexpected change in Gaalav? Suddenly I see it...from being an ally, I, too, have become the enemy. Haven't I just witnessed the exchange between him and the king? One man cleverly humiliating another man—in the presence of his woman. In Gaalav's eyes that is enough to make me too his enemy. It's all that is needed to turn everything between us into a deception. The stiff set of his back and shoulders, the grim look on his face of controlled rage mingled with icy contempt, but it is not these alone that pin me to my chair. A strange exhaustion has come over me. Was this the same man who, just a year ago, had begged me to rescue him? Though Gaalav and I came together in a strange, cruel way, I have not held him responsible for it. Indeed, I saw him as someone more unfortunate than I. There was also, I admit, an initial frisson of attraction. *Was it all my imagination?* In the months that followed, I had clung to it, or maybe it had refused to leave me because I had felt it today as well, the peculiar tension between us. As we journeyed together today, a certain warmth had returned and I had welcomed it—as a drowning swimmer welcomes a raft. We are in this together, I had thought. He suffers and I suffer for him. We have to see each other through. Now I know that we have nothing in common. He is only interested in using me. If it were not for his obstinacy, would I be sitting here like this, listening to two men bargain over me? But why do I feel, deep in my bones, that he is hurting too? I can feel the hardening knot in him of anger and helplessness. *He cares*...through the mist in my eyes, I see him leave. At the door, without turning, in a voice emptied of all feeling, he says, 'Don't fail to return her after a year.'

I have no idea how long I sit in the room. Images from the past year swamp me. All those hours in Haryashva's bedchamber. Night after night he took what he'd agreed to pay for. My body became an empty shell. I felt nothing. In the only way possible for me, I kept a part of me safe from the assault. I had promised to help Gaalav. That was how I saw our relationship, as a vow. We were bound, so I had imagined, by the trueness of it. How easy it is to fool yourself! A vow that is so unfair is not a vow—it's a curse. Am I not living this curse for him? Far from any sense of belonging, I have not received even a modicum of sympathy from him. *Why him alone? They have all used me. I have ceased to exist in everyone's eyes. I am nothing other than a mare to be bred.* His parting words, their cutting tone, have cracked open a fissure through which unsettling memories of earlier desertions—the indifference of my mother and then my father, the cold-hearted betrayals, my loveless existence—billow up like poisonous gases. A princess, yes, but there will never be a prince for me. He does not exist. That version of Drishadvati does not exist. A number of men will use my body. A year in one palace, then another year in a different palace. I will be dragged from kingdom to kingdom, my womb pressed into service to produce male heirs who will rule over multitudes, whose feats will be material for innumerable gathas that will be sung forever. And what will remain of me? To be the mother of heroes is a woman's greatest destiny. Should I then be grateful for mine? In this land of heroes, I will remain nameless, invisible. But isn't that the fate of other royal women too? Yet, no one has a story quite like mine. Who ordained it, or did I bestow this unique honour on myself? Blinded by emotions, I trusted too easily...was that my only mistake—that I, too, dreamed of love?

Outside the window, hugging the steps, the shining river flows on, peaceful, indifferent to all the detritus in her. The remains of innumerable lives, their dreams, their realities; their prayers and their sins float alike. How easy it would be to surrender myself to her. All I have to do is walk down the steps, sink in her embrace, knowing that she, at least, will not reject me. Yes, that would be simple, I think.

Look at me, she sings. I bear the ashes of kings, as well as those of their servants. In me all names lose distinction, all opposites become one. But I am not like any of them. *I* know what I am: A mother. Male *and* female spring from me. They come together to take creation forward. Life is possible because of me. I am the channel. It pours into me, and out of me it empties into the world, fills it up. It does this again and again. When it comes to Life, there is no such thing as *your* life or *my* life. I am in you, as you are in me. We are both creators and a part of creation too. Though you, born as a mortal, are subject to Time, the essence of you, like mine, is in constant motion. Never the same river, but ever the flow. This, too, is liberation.

I feel a hand on my shoulder. Divodas. A strong, princely man, seasoned and shrewd, but with an ascetic's composure on his face. The look he gives me is unexpected, as gentle as a dragonfly sitting on a lotus petal. Simple kindness: how refreshing it is to see nothing more in a man's eyes. 'I am honoured to have you in my palace, Drishadvati,' he says. 'Think of it as a homecoming. For as long as you are here, it is your home.'

Maybe it is just his quiet courtesy, but in my bewilderment and dejection that one word *homecoming* is what I grasp. A calm secures me, as if someone has unexpectedly caressed my forehead with a cool hand. I look around the room, seeing it properly for the first time. Its strict functionality, the absence of trappings, is a relief. There is nothing here that makes me feel like an outsider. The tightening rope of grief in me slackens a bit. Yet, unable to find the right words, I can only nod to show my gratitude. After a moment's hesitation, he raises me up by my arms. Looking into his eyes, at the melancholy pooling in them, I recognize that we are companion souls. Alike in some unfathomable way, but with separate fates.

~

'That bull has done it again,' he says in mild exasperation. 'Stomped down the garden and left a pile of dung.'

'Whose bull has such audacity?'

'Who else but Shiva's Nandi. He had the run of Kashi once, was welcomed everywhere, fed and feted... he misses the daily pampering.' Divodas peers out into the garden that lies in shadows. I follow his gaze. At the far corner, near a clump of banana plants I can make out a dark grey silhouette. It is motionless as if taking a moment to survey its handiwork. Then it fades, like wisps of smoke from a quenched fire.

'Nandi, too, has a grudge against you—is that what you are saying?'

'Don't laugh,' he says. 'The gods think of me as a usurper.'

'Hmm. I wonder why.'

He sends me an amused glance. 'Loss of prestige hurts them too,' he says. 'A human can come to terms with it perhaps, but the gods? Never. A god's self-esteem cannot be challenged.'

'Then why are you challenging it? Aren't you afraid of them?'

He widens his eyes in mock fear. 'I am wary...they are meddlesome.'

'Even Mahadev? One has heard that he is quite aloof by nature.'

'Not when he loves. And he loves Kashi.'

'How can anyone not? Don't you love Kashi too?'

He responds with a quiet smile. 'I am merely its custodian.'

'And hence this insistence on a son?'

His smile deepens. 'As the protector, that too, is a king's obligation.'

I could ask him: is that all it means to you? But some questions should lie stillborn. So I ask, 'What if your son is not as obliging as you? What if, when his turn comes, he doesn't want to be king?'

His reaction surprises me. 'Strange that Yayati's daughter should ask this question!' he says with a hint of disapproval. Despite myself, I flush and look away. 'I'm not mocking you,' he clarifies. 'But merely pointing out that filial devotion is in your blood—as it should be. Puru, who gave up his youth because Yayati asked for it, is your half-brother.' He pauses before adding, 'Obedience and courage, these are the two qualities that define a kshatriya. And you, a royal woman, have them. You, too, have made a sacrifice for the sake of your father and his kingdom…a son, especially a king's son, must respect his father's wishes. How else will the right traditions be carried forward? Without them, we cannot uphold dharma and there would be anarchy.'

I don't contradict him. Instead, I say, 'Puru, at least, was given a choice. I did not have that freedom.'

'Why would you want it?' He seems genuinely puzzled. 'Men need the freedom to act.'

'And women don't need any freedom?'

'It's not so important. They need understanding and respect, yes.'

How can you understand me unless you know what it is to live in my skin?

'Choosing action isn't as easy as you think,' he says. 'Particularly when you cannot manipulate the consequences. One needs knowledge, intelligence and self-control to act in the proper manner. One needs a thorough understanding of dharma.'

'And women lack all these qualities?'

'They are ruled more by their innate nature.'

'In other words, they are ruled by ignorance, stupidity and selfishness, besides not quite understanding dharma.'

'That wasn't what I said.'

'But that's exactly what you implied!'

He looks startled then bursts out laughing. 'We are squabbling, do you realize, like a long-married couple?'

'I may not be well-versed in warfare,' I say drily. 'But I recognize a feint.'

'And so you should. Women are experts at subterfuge.'

'It's a survival strategy of sorts, to protect ourselves. We wouldn't need it if we had good reason to trust men.'

He catches the note of bitterness and turns his head to look at me. 'Yayati was not fair to you—is that what you believe?'

But I'm not thinking of my father. No, not him....

Seeing me frown, Divodas sends me a curious look. 'Would *you* have chosen differently?' he asks.

Would I have? He had offered to let me go.

'Unlike Puru, I have no wish to be remembered as a hero.' I cannot help adding, 'Unlike all men.'

'Every man cares about his name, but all men are not destined to be kings.'

Beneath the grand words lies the craving that I have learned to recognize. There is also the memory of my mother's words about my father on the day we entered Pratisthan: *He owns everything you see.* Possession, pleasure. Twin lusts, one encrypted within the other. I know little of the first, but the second, the more obvious one, surrounds me like the perfume of the musk deer, a creature rarely seen but still tantalizing. An intimacy has grown between Divodas and me. We are conscious of one another. He is considerate: in his slow and careful lovemaking he has taught me that the body *can* forget, it can respond differently to touch. Desire can grow back like an arid patch greened by the rain. I look around at the bedchamber, the bed in which we sleep, our indecorous nakedness as we lie side by side. We are lovers, but is this love? Speaking almost to myself, I say, 'So what is all this about?'

'What do you think?' He turns his head to look at me.

I feel myself growing still, so quiet that even my breath stops moving. What I am looking for *isn't* there. A few hours worth of passion, a silent arrangement of limbs, like the peacock's slow dance, devoid of an inner music. It cannot amount to love, I think. Other than a sense of missing something, but I don't know what it is. How can one identify an emotion that is absent? 'I asked the question first!' I say.

'And I just answered it.'

I give him a sour look. He laughs and pulls me into his arms, where I remain, snug for the moment. We could never love one another. There are barriers in him, or maybe it is the wildness in me, that prevent us. Yet, in the time we spend together, we get along, according respect and affording a casual comfort to each other. Could this feeling, the warmth that lingers, be because we both know it's temporary? Yet, long or short, aren't all stories between men and women about the same things really, about gaining and losing? Men conquer. Women surrender—they give in, they give up. No husk clings to its kernel forever. My baby is mine only for the nine months that it spends inside me. Once out in the world, my baby will become his. Invested with a name, a gotra, a social standing to be carried forward. Divodas's son is who he will be. Kingdoms to be conquered and governed, a dynasty that will rule for a long time...all the things that have nothing to do with me. However, the ease that I felt with Divodas from the first moment has remained. We smile at each other, we talk, we do each other small favours. He gets for me the foamy dew-fresh cream flavoured with cardamom that I crave. I tell him about the deer that came to me in my dream again. He tells me of his plans for Kashi.

Beyond the open window, dawn's radiance is sweeping away the lingering inkiness. She takes her lofty place in the sky, shines her light on Kashi, but entering my chamber she is on tiptoes, a slinking tawny cat. The palace is quiet, the river still covered in patches of cloudy mist. A waterfowl's plaintive cry reaches me. Another bird, perhaps its mate, answers as it flits past the window, a silver ghost. Along the riverbank, boatmen are pushing away from land. The splash of their oars is always the first sound I hear in the morning. After a while, there are other sounds that I, lazing in bed, soak up. Brahmins chanting scriptures, a flute playing, the quiet chatter of the devout returning from their ritual bath, of women returning from filling their water pots. Sounds that embody the commitment to living, to life itself, that comes from the comfort of following long-established customs. They reflect the constant ebb and flow of the city, its quiet confidence in its timelessness. But they make me restless. In Ayodhya, I never left the palace, not once in those long months. Here I find excuses to go out every day, to choose vegetables, buy milk and curds, visit the groves in the outskirts or to simply enjoy the freedom of walking through the winding streets, so narrow that the sky is visible only in patches. No one knows me, yet people stop to speak. Taking me for an outsider, they speak with pride about their city and suggest things that I must do before I leave. Take a boat-ride, watch the evening aarti on the ghat, taste the street food. I walk through the markets, visit the innumerable shrines where once the gods were worshipped.

One day, I stop by a tattooist, a tribal woman whose skill is well known. 'On your arm,' she suggests. 'A pair of swans to symbolize eternal love. It's a popular motif.'

No, I tell her. On my back, a deer. My mother had one…I describe it to her in detail. The front hooves slightly raised, the head turned sideways so that one beautiful eye looks out at the world, the majesty of the antlers. In the backdrop, a hint of the forest.

She examines the area of my back where I want it. Too bony, she says. It may hurt.

I tell her to go ahead.

You will not be able to see it, she says.

I don't have to see it. I just want to know that it's there.

She begins. It hurts, but I don't mind the pain. That I can feel it is welcome. The tattooist is absorbed in her work. She hums softly to herself. When it's done, she sits back and views her handiwork. It's going to be dull after this to do swans and lotuses, she says.

~

Early one morning I go to the street of courtesans, a narrow lane with shadowy corners. In its best part are tall mansions with palanquins waiting outside, the bearers asleep in the shadows. Music—the strumming of a sarangi, the slow beats of a drum, the jingle of ghungroos—wafts out from a few open windows. In daylight the street has a stale air, the disenchantment of the morning after, the weariness that follows a night of passion. A woman looks out of one of the windows at me. Her eyes are dark, smudged with kajal, her stare lasts too long. There is something so specific about her look that my heart lurches. I quicken my pace. At the end of the street, when I cast a glance backwards, the window is shut. I do not go back to the street again.

~

Divodas's household runs not on servants but on self-sufficiency and magic. Those years spent as a sadhu have given him several siddhis. He uses them to run his kingdom, he says. Spells keep enemies at bay, birds bring him all the news, though, he says, most of the time it is only harmless tweeting. He also uses magic to make life easier in the palace. At a mere wish lamps are lit, floors swept, clothes washed, mirrors polished, hot puffed up rotis appear at meal times. If I say that I'm finding it warm, the breeze rushes in, bringing with it dry leaves that settle on my hair, and if I say that it's cold, a fine shawl falls over my shoulders. Even after all these months, I find it a bit eerie to be helped by unseen forces. Divodas, however, is quite blasé about it. It is not a big thing, he says. There is more serious magic, he adds.

'Why can't we live like other people who keep servants? Why do we need magic at all?'

'I need magic to fight magic,' he says.

'But whose magic do you fight?' I ask.

'Shiva's.'

'How can you fight a god? Even magic will not protect you.'

'I cannot fight him forever...one of these days he will come up with a ruse that will send me packing. However, till then, my task is to stop him from stirring up trouble.'

'What sort of trouble?'

'It started with the women,' he tells me. 'One day sixty-four beautiful women entered the city. Not all at once and not together. They came from all directions, through different gates. Two or three came by boat and one even swam across the river.'

'Beautiful, you said?'

He smiles, as if understanding the necessity of having this question answered. '*Very beautiful*. That was the giveaway—an unearthly, unconventional beauty. There was no hiding the sculpted curves, the smooth glowing skin, the air of impeccable grooming, disguised though they were in different costumes as milkmaids, hairdressers, dancers, flower-sellers, fortune-tellers, vendors of greens, betel leaves and curds. Acrobats and musicians. Female ascetics too, in orange robes and long hair left loose, playing pipes and dancing like apsaras.'

'Who were these mystery women?'

'Magic women, yoginis, sent by Mahadev. They came here to create pandemonium with their secret arts. For a year they tried every trick in the book to turn Kashi upside down. Enticing men of all ages, stealing babies, starting quarrels, sowing doubt, confusion and fear with inexplicable happenings. Kitchen fires would die suddenly leaving the food half-cooked, musical instruments would start playing on their own. The washing flew off clotheslines, monkeys tittle-tattled in human tongues and mynahs sang hymns from the Vedas. I regarded these as no more than minor disruptions and dealt with them. The town-criers warned the folks about the upheavals, the yoginis were identified and ordered to leave Kashi.'

'Did they go away?'

He smiles. 'They are still here. Some have started their own businesses as healers and palmists, while others, having married, have settled down to grow families... who has ever come to Kashi and gone back? Stay a year and you, too, will never leave.'

He holds my gaze for a second longer than is necessary. I turn my head away. After a while I ask, 'So Mahadev gave up?'

'He sent Suryadev to foment trouble.'

'Oh! Did he arrive in a golden chariot pulled by seven white horses?'

'He came here as a merchant. Throughout his stay we had rosy dawns, followed by clear blue skies. The light was blinding white. Umbrella-makers, potters and fruit-sellers did good business. The river shrank and its sandy bed became a vast sea of lush green vines yielding the juiciest cucumbers, the sweetest melons. There was a bumper harvest of mangoes. Fruits grew to twice their size and tasted of ambrosia. Fragrant mornings smelling of jasmine and lotus...the avenues were luminous with flowering amaltas trees. Everything was covered in a soft buttery light and a pleasant lethargy filled everyone. No one felt like working after ten in the morning. Midday meal eaten, housewives lowered the bamboo grass window shades, giving the rooms a soft peachy tint. Even the flies drowsed. At dusk the city sprang to life, families picnicked on the riverbank to catch the evening breeze. The sunsets were simply glorious. There were poetry competitions and musical sabhas. Sellers of thandai became rich men overnight. Suryadev was one of them—a little side business that he started. It did very well and he, who had come here to have me overthrown, he too, did not return. Instead, he stays on and thrives. Twelve shops he has, a prosperous man. And now he is building temples to himself…that's Kashi for you.'

I shake my head slowly from side to side. 'Mahadev may as well give up.'

'Mahadev never gives up. He has endless patience, the composure of a dice-player. He sent Prajapati Brahma next. The Creator himself disguised as a brahmin. He appeared in my court one day with a most unusual request. He asked me to hold an Ashwamedha yagna on a scale never imagined till today…nor will anyone in the future be able to match it. Not a one-horse sacrifice but a ten-horse sacrifice. He had, he said, selected the sacred site on the riverbank. It would become the greatest of pilgrimage spots on earth. My name would go down in golden letters.'

'And will it?'

'Yes,' he says. 'Even though Brahma watched me like a hawk, waiting to catch me for the tiniest mistake, the yagna was conducted to perfection. When one has the right intention and performs the right action for the good of the world, nothing can go wrong.'

'So you have outwitted Brahma too.'

He laughs. 'It has become a game of wits, hasn't it?'

'And now has the Creator *too* made his home in Kashi?'

'Oh yes! You may see him, from time to time, on the ghat called Dasashwamedha. He has a fondness for that spot because the horses were sacrificed there. Look out for a short portly man with a round bright face. He keeps a parrot who tells fortunes. The bird will tell you it's foolishness to leave Kashi.'

I let that pass. How could I stay?

Here we are, Divodas and I. Together, but also retreating deeper every day into the isolation in each one of us. We are careful to promise each other nothing but this friendly collaboration that will, in due course, bring forth a son. Duty he calls it, but doesn't he care about me just a little, this man who claims that he has given up his desires? He fools only himself. And I, someone who has never examined my own wishes—don't I care for him just a little? It has not slipped past me that though he says no one ever leaves Kashi, he has not spoken once of marriage. His silence on the subject reminds me that I own nothing, not even myself. I am just goods in a transaction that is entirely between men. Nothing new about that. What sets me apart—from those other women who take the seven vows—is that my womb is on lease. Even now Gaalav would be looking for the next renter. Meanwhile, Divodas, the current one, will keep, as an honourable man must, the bargain that was made with another man. Kshatriya or brahmin—men are all the same. Honourable men, that is. A breach of contract is simply unforgivable.

I will feel nothing this time, I promise myself. I will let go.

~

The baby comes in late spring, just a few days after the festival of Holi. He slips out of the birth channel with the ease of a river eel, no fuss. The midwife washes him, dresses him in soft muslin, places him by my side.

'My son,' says Divodas, lifting him up as if he were a feather. The lines of his face are soft, it is aglow with pride. I have a sudden vision of the future. This child of mine will be trained to combat as soon as he can walk. He will lead armies, win battles, the stories of his heroics will be sung all over the land. He will tread the same path, be no different...something is snuffed out inside me.

'I have chosen a name,' says Divodas.

The cord is cut again. I console myself, he will be a happy child. No rivals for his father's affection.

'But if you have a different preference, tell me,' Divodas says with the benevolence of a man who has seen his desire made flesh. 'The bards want to know.'

It is generosity and recognizing it as such, I send him a grateful smile. 'Let me hear the name you have picked.'

'Pratardan.'

'It's a good name. Pratardan, son of Divodas.'

'And Drishadvati.'

Something snaps inside me. 'Never tell him *my* name. Do not ever speak of me to him.'

His face falls. 'But you, too, will live in him. Just look at him! He looks so much like you, particularly the shape of his mouth and his nose, too, is exactly like yours....'

He will be the son you dreamed of when you planted your seed inside me. He has your eyes, the slope of your head—meant for a crown—your strength in his arms and calf muscles. His genitals will carry your name forward. He, too, will father sons who in turn will take your name even further, but who will remember me? I am the other half, the pod that carried a growing life for a while. Now dehisced, now dead.

14

Drishadvati and Ushinar

She arrives unannounced, a tired woman who has journeyed for several days. A little grubby, face pinched with fatigue, but with a queenly bearing that is unmistakeable. In her forties, tall and willowy, with a broad forehead, a resolute chin, a thin-lipped mouth. Her skin is smooth and stretched taut, hair snow-white.

'You are the one,' she says, her eyes suddenly alight with a strange glow.

The burning gaze is making me nervous. 'Who are you?'

She continues to stare at me without speaking. Divodas hurries to make introductions. 'The maharani has come all the way from a highland kingdom to the south of Kashi,' he says in a hushed, overpolite tone. Seeing my blank expression, he adds, 'It's at the very edge of Aryavarta. A much cooler place than this...you will like it.'

'But why will I like it? I'm not going anywhere just yet.'

While Divodas avoids eye contact with me, the maharani's glassy look changes to an outraged glare. She sticks out her bosom as if drawing an arrow into a bow and launches into a clipped, hard speech. 'Yes. You are going. Pack your things. And don't linger over it. We've kept our side of the bargain in full, let me tell you. All two hundred horses that my father-in-law left us as a rare legacy. By rights, we should have surrendered them only after my son was born. Yet, because that brahmin wanted them immediately, we agreed to part with the horses. Tell me, who would give up something so valuable *in advance*? It was only because *I* had the same dream three nights in a row: my deceased father-in-law looking down at me sorrowfully said, "Daughter, the throne is heirless. Will you let down your ancestors? Do something to take our line forward or else we will all hang upside down for eternity in Put". Those were his exact words!'

Divodas looks at the maharani with apprehension. 'Do not frighten Drishadvati with stories of Put. She has recently given birth and is still feeding—'

'What's so unique about that? Women have babies. Their bodies are designed for it.'

'Is yours different then?' I ask.

Pointedly ignoring me, but addressing Divodas, she says, 'Ushinar, my husband, is a simple, trusting man. Arm-twisted by that Munikumar Gaalav, he has already sent the horses to Rishi Vishwamitra's ashram; they must have been delivered there by now.' She pauses and directs a scornful look at me, 'And this one says that she will not live with us! Who gave her the right to say anything at all?'

I am numb with disbelief. *So, this time around, you even took your payment up front! I salute you, Munikumar Gaalav. You find new ways to violate me.*

'Please do not speak to Drishadvati in that tone,'

Divodas says, a little more firmly. 'She is of royal birth too. I would also urge you to remember that *she* is the giving one, and you, I and everyone else, including Munikumar Gaalav, are all in her debt.'

The maharani looks as if a crow just defecated on her head. I am touched by Divodas's protectiveness of me. It has become stronger after the baby was born. But, I remind myself that Kashi, City of Bliss, is the City of Death too. Dead flesh, dead dreams—all ultimately ash in the stream. 'I'm ready to leave,' I say.

They stare at me with identical expressions, surprised.

Divodas recovers first. 'No, you are not,' he says. 'A year was what I was promised. There are still a few weeks left.' He turns to the maharani. 'Please stay on as my guest. You will be comfortable. While you wait, there is plenty to see and do in Kashi.'

The queen opens her mouth to say something but then changes her mind and shuts it.

When we are alone again, I try clumsily to thank Divodas, even though I know that it is a reprieve only, this extra time I have with my son. The weeks that follow are bittersweet. I cannot let go of my baby even for a moment. I insist on bathing him myself. I sit cross-legged on the bed with him asleep on my lap for hours, refusing to lay him down in the carved wooden cradle. When I am sleepy I recline against the pillows with him on my chest. Divodas humours me, tries to spend as much time with us as he can allow himself.When he is with us and laughs in his relaxed, contented way, I am grateful to be a part of this, the perfect, happy family. For the first time domesticity makes sense to me; man, woman and child. Not a woman's destiny but her future.There is a pause during which I am sure I would have accepted had he proposed....

In the end I am calm. There are no tears as I kiss my son for the last time. I manage to hold my composure till I reach the door. But there I make the fatal mistake of turning back for one last look, and my resolve instantly crumbles. How tiny and defenceless he looks. What will happen when he wakes up? Will he not look for my smile, the sound of my voice? He recognizes me, I know. How long will it take for this memory of his to fade?

For some reason today Kashi is reluctant to wake up. Though the sun touches its spires, deep shadows cower in the narrow lanes. The new day draws its first breath as if learning to use its lungs. A peacock cries out. I see it standing on a white wall, its fantail spread, surveying the world with its elaborately made-up eyes. Perhaps that is the secret of Kashi's eternal beauty. It is born every day. Freshness lies everywhere. Except in my heart where sorrow rains, its saltiness the same, its loneliness the same. We are at the gates now. I hear him call my name and force myself to look at him. Divodas. The kindest man I will ever know—but he is already a stranger. The farewell is not prolonged.

~

Ushinar's kingdom lies at an elevation. Tall rocky hills surround it. On their ridges and in the sweeping valleys in between lie tracts of forest interspersed with grasslands. The air is clean and smells of wildflowers. There are deep natural caves in the hillsides, thin waterfalls gurgle down steep rock faces. Though sparsely inhabited, its people are shepherds and agriculturists, but mostly they belong to the forest tribes, the Nishadhas, whose way of life has remained the same for the longest time. Living here would be heaven for some. However, for its ruler it is hell.

He stinks of grief and alcohol. We are alone, Ushinar and I, in his chamber. Grief festoons the room, lurks in corners. Even the shadows seem to be drooping with misery.

'We had a son, we lost him.' He says it with the grey exhaustion of a failing heart. Outside the window a night bird calls, a short, sharp cry, full of pain. A last desperate cry. Perhaps it isn't a bird but a small wild creature, a hare caught by a fox. The pitcher of wine is nearly over. Ushinar calls out for more. A sleepy maid appears and refreshes his drink. In the lamplight her face is as inscrutable as marble: cool, clean, pale. As the mahua wine loosens his tongue, words flow sluggishly out of the old man's mouth, stumbling, skittering, losing their way mid-air. Displaced words seeking refuge. Straining to catch them, the shadows rustle and slink closer. The dark walls shiver.

'Perhaps I shouldn't say this but, unlike my queen, I don't care about my pitris and which way they hang in Put...that is what she told you, didn't she? That dream she claims she had repeatedly.' He gives a scoffing laugh. 'I don't know if Put exists, but even if it does, can it be as bad as this? What can be a hell worse than this, seeing your beloved child go before you?' The watching eyes blaze. Addressing them, he declares stoically, 'Devdaan, we called him, God's gift. He was all of seventeen years old, a keen archer with a passion for hunting—ironically, he got it from me...it was his first tiger kill. He drove the dagger right into the heart, exactly as I had taught him.' The words bounce off the walls. Crazed words, insane grief. 'I still recall the look on his face. Awe, but mostly disbelief, at what he had just done, at the blood spurting. He did not see the creature's mate lurking in the tall bamboo grass...in his moment of triumph the hunter was cut down! What else would you call it but a pointless death?'

As was, in another realm, the death of a tiger.

'Mortality is our lot,' Ushinar says and looks deep into the antidote, the wine-filled silver cup in his hands. As he draws it closer to his lips, a tremor passes from him to the cup. Wine dribbles out of his mouth, irrigating his short white beard. He throws the tumbler at the wall and cries out in sudden rage, 'O you cruel gods, why did you snatch him away when he was still so young?'

Deep from the moonless night, there comes a chilling sound, an echo. A keening. A snarl of pain.

'There are no thieves in my kingdom. Yet it feels like a theft....'

Silence. The swish of a tail. The shadows appear streaked. Tawny gold and black.

He turns towards me. There is a feverish tinge to his face. 'Do you know—know...?' He hiccups. 'The heaviest burden for a man is the bier of his son. No heart in the world is strong enough for that.' The words crackle in the air, a pyre torched. 'The last dragging breath, I saw it leave his chest—*I saw it!* His eyes were open, the light in them all there one second ago and then out. Just like that. Strangely, there were no wounds on his face. He looked as pure as on the day he was born. His skin was warm, still breathing, the flesh alive though he was, apparently, gone.

Seventeen years he gave us and a fistful of memories: his taste for spicy food, the speech mannerisms, a way of lowering his head in thought. Broken bits from which to remake a whole, but how do we do it? Memory never brings it all back. The sum is all wrong.' He stops speaking and stares morosely at nothing. After a while he laughs, a cackling death rattle. It gives me gooseflesh. 'So what is the meaning of this?' he asks. 'Without touch all this is a wasteland...he is alive, somewhere *he exists*—but we?—unable to touch him, to kiss his head, what are we? Dead?'

Dead we are. Dead in parts and in parts still dying. Night is spent in many shades of dark. In this room, it takes the colour of pitch, the same shade as other nights past spent in other rooms that were not unlike this one. Oppressive, dimly lit royal bedchambers, a series of strange men all staring at death, vanquished by its grinning confidence, and wanting, somehow, to deny it complete victory.

'Till now I have not spoken of him,' says Ushinar. 'I cannot bear to hear his name mentioned. But his mother—she cannot, *will not* stop...his chamber is a shrine. Every day new clothes are laid out on his bed, the flowers changed, favourite dishes cooked and served. She talks as if he has just gone out for a few days and will return any minute. He is here with us tonight—do you too believe it? You cannot live in this palace and believe otherwise. Faith is what brings the dead to life. One needs to be blind to see the dead. *She sees him.* Has he just left the room? Is that his voice? Whose footsteps are those? He is just out of sight, but he is here...it seems as if he is playing a game of hide-and-seek, just as he did as a child.

The whole palace would be looking for him. She is still looking. The retainers are loyal, a patient lot, but for how long will they support her grief? Her mind is unhinged. Else, why this insistence on my siring another child? She calls it bringing him forth, but he is irretrievable. Dead, *dead*. Yet, the foolish woman will not understand.' His mouth twists in disgust. Rancour enters his voice, igniting a quiet impotent rage. 'An old man like me who has crossed a lifetime by the strength of his dharma—and she now wants me to reawaken desire in my body so that *her* desire to be a mother again is fulfilled! A son, a son, give me back my son is her constant cry. She is the one who wants to be reborn—as a mother! Why should she get back her son? For all the love she bore, she failed to protect her child.'

I am chilled to the marrow by the extent of his love and hate. The queen has not spoken a word to me from the moment we left Kashi. It is as if her tongue has been sliced off.

'She heard, from God knows where, about how the king of Ayodhya had got his heir. She begged that brahmin to send you here. If Munikumar Gaalav had not responded to her request, she'd planned to have you kidnapped, kept a prisoner, impregnated somehow. My wife has become a ghoul, fit only to live in the cremation ground. She even gave away the horses to him so that the brahmin would not withdraw from the bargain. But, tell me, is that the solution: a son to substitute the dead one?'

A man's name connects the visible to the invisible, Sarmistha had once said. Remembrance is his fence against oblivion. But a woman has no need for a similar fence of her own. Oblivion is her life, her very essence.

From the waters of nothingness inside her is reimagined the world, her offspring. From those waters in her emerge all the relationships that make life meaningful. The first movement, the heartbeat below her heart, the soul that takes shape—blood, bone, flesh and form—from her it rises. That mother, too, is born of touch. It is all she asks, to caress, to feel, to live through her skin, to kiss, to nurse, to hold on. Is there another way for her to know eternity but in the soft warmth on her breast, the tug on her nipple, the tide of love that flows in her for a lifetime? A mother whose child is beyond her touch—where does she seek communion? I feel a stirring of sympathy for the queen; her madness is sanity too.

'At my age, I could perhaps do it,' Ushinar says. 'But I don't have the wish or the will. Having lost my son, do I care for legacy or lineage? However, I will not end my life because that will end my grief too—this spurious shape of love is all I have. For this spurious life, this living death I now endure is enough....' He sighs heavily and looks away. After a period of silence, he says, 'If I counsel her, she pays no attention. I remind her that I have brothers and they have sons. I can step down and choose one of my brothers. Thus ensuring the succession. We could make our way to the forest and live out the rest of our days together. Our marriage vows bind us and now we also have our grief.' He stops speaking and shakes his head slowly in negation of his own words. 'Who knows? Perhaps she is right. Without Devdaan our marriage itself serves no purpose. He gave it meaning. Our son was born to rule, groomed for it from an early age. My brothers' sons are good but they know nothing about kingship. They lack the mettle. It is not just in the blood, it has to be bred into the bone, built into every muscle. An heir is born but a king is made. If made wrongly, a lineage ends—sooner or later—and a culture is wiped out. Unless we know who we are, how do we know what to become? Who is the right one to be chosen as king, I cannot say. Besides, there will be comparisons, rivalries will develop. Disharmony, distrust in the ruling family has devastating consequences. I see no way out. An ordinary man has the power to bring forth life, but even a king has no power over death. What's done is done. I—' He stops abruptly as if aware of the futility of words, downs the wine and pours himself another cup. He drinks most of it then he stares at me fixedly for several minutes. I recognize that look. I know it, yet it sends a cold shiver down my spine. 'You are beautiful,' he says. A new tone has entered his voice. 'I should be drunk with desire...it can make an old man young they say. Instead, I, rendered helpless by sorrow...I cannot love you as you deserve. My eyes see your beauty but my heart has been blinded.' Grief bleeds out of his eyes, it will not be tamed. He sobs like a child. 'It gave my life meaning, this love I bore. He was my vision, he was its goal. I would gladly have sacrificed my remaining years, my very soul, if only my son could have lived.'

I let him weep, I don't know what else to do. The tears of a grown man are despicable to watch. Noisy, desolate, self-indulgent. Yet they are, undeniably, true. Despite myself, I am moved by his lament. Death is straightforward. Grief is more complex. It carries layers of ashes—guilt, anguish, defeat. He stretches his neck and his eyes bore into me. I flinch at the fierce look, I cannot help myself. Then his face falls slack, his eyes lose the momentary fire and return to their old emptiness. 'Go,' he says in a grand but hollow gesture. 'Go away. Leave right now. I cannot bring myself to touch you. I, Ushinar, give you your freedom.'

Freedom.

There is no one cure for our condition. However, there is a range of palliatives. In my tired body I seek one for both his sorrow and mine. I bring his head down to my shoulder and let him weep, drawing in his pain to fill the hollows in my being.

'You smell of lemon blossom,' he says, breathing my skin in. His eyes on my face are different. 'This crisp, clean tang.' He runs his fingers over my chin and cheeks, tuck a few loose strands of hair behind my ear. His hands move lower, pull the cloth away and free my breasts. Cupping one, he draws in his breath. 'Pure witchery...are you a sorceress?' His tone is suspicious, accusing.

'No.' I laugh sadly. 'But my mother was.'

'You are too.'

Desire creates new possibilities. His fingers lace mine. Skin scrapes skin, kindling, burning...a thousand times my boundaries are breached by probing fingertips. Tongues mesh, breaths merge and blood tastes itself. Invasions all. In the many aggressions on this body it is only the futile dying echoes of touch that have remained with me—its corpse. The cold nothingness of it. Later, when it is over, I watch him sleep. Something has shifted in him, his breathing is light and easy, the breath of a younger man. When he wakes up, the world for him will be fresh with renewed hope. A pulse will start inside me. As the old spirit fades, a new one is born. And so it goes on. Immortality.

I wrap the cloak of my loneliness around me. It is threadbare. It is all I have.

~

I am pregnant. My body adapts but my soul licks its wounds. It lies low behind a firewall, built not of resignation so much as a lack of interest in my predicament. *So be it.* My troubles no longer interest me, but still I seek solitude. Instead I find solace—in the forest. Whenever the weather is fine, I get away from the palace, spending as much time as I can outdoors. I take long walks. The forests here are like the one in which I grew up but more dense. The trees of sal and teak are very old, some of them spread their branches so wide that they seem to be like sovereigns with their own kingdoms. Their trunks are dressed in vines and ferns. The tree cover is thick, the sunlight splintering through it scatters like a fistful of diamonds, irradiating, a spider's web, the quills of a porcupine, the spots on a chital deer. Elephant herds trumpet and roam freely through the grass, langurs swing among the branches, and tigers are sometimes sighted. One day, as I am walking on a narrow path along the edge of the forest I, too, see a tiger, a huge beast with magnificent stripes, slowly walking towards me. I press myself against a tree trunk. He pauses for a heart-stopping moment, looks at me with utmost disdain, a cold callousness, before vanishing into the tall grass.

On some days, after a shower, mist drifts through the forest making the tall trunks look like an army frozen by a curse. The floor is slippery with pine needles, and I have to mind my steps. The paths have dips and climbs. One brings me to a grassy shoulder on a ridge from where

I can see for miles. Below lie the roofs of the palace, and further down the hill slopes are hamlets, clusters of round huts, separated by fields. Then a river and a small meadow...the light is soft, as if inviting you to see something special. What do I see? Families working in the fields, mothers carrying their babies in shawls slung across their backs. The villagers work from dawn to dusk, sometimes singing snatches of songs. They work till the shadows lengthen and the cows wind their way back from the meadow. Except for the silent rocks, moaning wind, stray white cloud puffs and a single eagle lazily orbiting, I am alone. My thoughts, too, dance in slow circles, tense, locked in close combat, dodging, thrusting...round and round they go, till nothing of them remains.

~

For the time I live in Ushinar's palace, I am treated by everyone with honour and respect. My food cravings are immediately attended to. I indulge. Pomegranates are my new fancy and God alone knows how they manage to obtain them. The pregnancy is the easiest one I have had, as if the soul enfleshing itself in my womb is compassionate even to me. Time and again, the queen asks if she can visit me. At first I refuse to see her. Yet she persists, and I cannot stop her from intruding. She comes in when she thinks I am asleep, caresses my belly, covers me with a soft shawl.

Spinach, something I can no longer stand—I have eaten so much of it in the past years—is served to me daily on the queen's orders; milk, almonds, fruit; venison and other varieties of game that I do not like. One day, seeing a dish that I have refused to eat on my plate yet again, I tell the maid to take it away. She looks frightened. It's been served on the queen's orders, she says. Tell *her* to eat it then, I retort. I will not touch it; this meat does not agree with me. But the prince used to love it, she stammers, and that is why the queen wants you to eat it.

Suddenly it all makes sense, all the signs that I have ignored: the flute tunes that are played every day, the stories that are told to me repeatedly, the specific flavours and colours...everything to shape the future. They are closing in on us, I tell the babe in my womb. Tell me how to fortify myself, and you too, so that neither their desire nor our dread make us lesser than what we are. And he answers me: 'The self renews constantly. In my journey, O mother, is your journey too. As I grow strong within you, so will you grow into your fullness. My father will give me a name and a place, but you, my mother, will give me my self. Whisper your dreams into my ears, Mother, I am listening.'

When he comes into this world, the queen weeps with joy. Eyes shining, she launches into a frothy speech. But I cut her short. 'He is not your son reborn,' I say. 'He is the king your kingdom needs.'

She goes quiet. Looks down at the infant for a long moment, studying him as if trying to solve a riddle. When she meets my eyes, a veil has been lowered. There is amity in her countenance. 'You are right, Daughter. I cannot trick destiny. My son is dead...this babe is very different. I can see that...he is indeed *your* son. He is our next king.'

Shivi, the name they give the babe. A gentle name for the most benevolent of kings.

15

Garud and Gaalav

'Secrets cannot be kept forever,' Garud said. 'So I am going to tell you one now. Listen carefully. *There are no more shyamkarni horses in the land*.'

The brahmin narrowed his eyes into cold slivers of suspicion. 'I was assured by several knowledgeable men that there are a thousand such horses.'

'There *were*, but not any more.'

They stood under a tree. It gave them scant shelter from the gale whipping around and the rain that fell in a stinging spray. Gaalav trembled not with cold but with a sudden white-hot rage. 'Is this a game for you? Is that all it means?'

A stony calm came over Garud's face. 'Watch your words,' he said softly. 'I, who defeated Indra and stole the pot of amrit from the gods, am no ordinary being. Last time I did you a favour, and this time, too, I have come here only to share what I have discovered...I think of you as a friend. But if you forget that, mortal, so will I.'

Gaalav turned pale. Old fears winged back in a flurry, settling in him as if they'd never really gone. 'I value your friendship,' he said stiffly. 'I'm sorry if I have offended you, but you have just given me terrible news. While it's true that I have not been able to find out the name of a fourth king with these horses, I did not give up hope. If what you say is indeed true, where do I go from here?'

'Out of this thunderstorm for a start,' said Garud. He squinted up at the wild ferment in the sky, as if assessing and then dismissing the mass of clouds with a shrug. 'Indra overdoes the optics,' he said. 'Climb on. I'm going to fly us out of this weather.' Gaalav hesitated. He had absolutely no desire to repeat the experience of flying. The agony of the last trip returned in his nightmares. He would wake up in a flood of panic, unable to go back to sleep for hours. It made him morose and lethargic all day. His mother blamed the insomnia on his poor digestion and a tendency to fret over insignificant things, but he knew it wasn't those traits alone that accounted for the dreadful roil in his stomach. It was something that he could not speak about to her, to anyone—the shame that attacked him only when he was asleep, utterly defenceless.

'Coming?' Garud raised an eyebrow. Gaalav meekly climbed on to his back and clung to his neck. He shut his eyes and kept them that way till they touched the ground.

'I hate getting my feathers wet,' said Garud. They were in a cave. The place looked as if it had been used as a shelter by a sadhu. There was a trident planted in the ground outside with a red cloth tied around it. There was a fireplace, dry kindling and a few basic utensils. The earthen floor had a smattering of bat droppings. Gaalav swept them away diligently. He lit a small fire. Spreading his wings to dry them, Garud said, 'This is one thing we never have in Vaikunth—unseasonal rain. In fact, the weather is always pleasant in eternity.'

'Let's talk about here and now,' said Gaalav. 'I have to

get the remaining two hundred horses to pay off my debt and secure my freedom.'

'I just told you, Brahmin, there are no more shyamkarni horses.'

'I could go to the place where they are bred. I need your help, Garud. Do you know where it is?'

'You will not find them *anywhere*.'

Catching the stress on the last word, Gaalav frowned. 'Why not?'

'*Because*,' Garud said with slow emphasis. 'They are mind-born horses.'

'Mind-born *horses*?' Gaalav repeated, as if trying out a new language on his tongue. 'Erm...from whose mind were they born?'

'That is the secret I was referring to earlier.'

'Does it concern a mysterious horse trader?' Gaalav asked. 'I've heard about him, but no one is able to say where he comes from.'

'Maybe he, too, was mind-born,' Garud said facetiously.

'If I could find him I may persuade him to—'

'That trader has disappeared, as have his horses...in the flood.'

'Flood?' said Gaalav. '*Where? When?*'

'My friend,' said Garud, with a slow sideways shake of his head. 'Have you forgotten the flood already? Which world have you been living in?' He looked Gaalav up and down and smirked. 'You have changed...gained a bit of weight. It must be your mother's cooking. And there's a well-groomed gloss to your skin. You look nothing like the distraught young man I said farewell to three years ago.'

'I've improved my lot since then,' said Gaalav with

dignity. 'Rich patrons invite me to preside over sacrifices. They are generous. I have acquired several heads of cattle and a few pieces of fertile land as well. With all this new wealth, my sisters have been married off. Recently, my parents had the family house repaired and expanded. I am now able to look after them, even provide a few comforts. For instance, my mother has several maids to help her in the house. When my parents go on pilgrimages they travel in a chariot. I have been invited by a king to take up the position of rajguru in his court, while another wants me to start a school in his kingdom. I haven't yet decided which offer I should accept.'

'I'm happy to hear of your progress,' said Garud, his smile benign. 'I always knew you would go far in life.'

'Thank you. But all this is just preparation. My life's journey will truly start once I have paid off the remainder of my debt.'

'Ah, yes, the shyamkarni horses.' Garud pulled a face. 'All gone! But, let me begin by telling you about the history of these horses.'

Gaalav shook his head impatiently. 'I don't have time for all that.'

'You mean to say you aren't curious to know why Rishi Vishwamitra asked for the horses in the first place?' Garud raised his eyebrows provocatively.

Hearing his guru's name, Gaalav frowned. After a moment he said in a level tone, 'Tell me, Garud. Tell me all.'

~

'This story goes back many years,' Garud began. 'I got it from an old storyteller who now resides in Vaikunth. In his mortal existence, he used to record the gathas of the Kanyakubja royal clan.' Seeing the brahmin give a start of recognition, Garud nodded. 'Yes, Gaalav, the Kanyakubja clan, your guru's family. This is one of their stories. The suta didn't call it a secret, but he did say it's not a very well-known episode. That's a euphemism for a secret. Certain tales originating in royal families are suppressed for a while, but eventually they do drift across the palace walls. This is one of those stories. It dates back to Raja Gadhi's time, before his son, who went on to become your guru was born. You may not know that Vishwamitra had an older sister. Satyavati was her name; for a long time she was Raja Gadhi's only child. This story dates back to that time. I'll tell it to you exactly as the suta narrated it.

'One day, out of the blue, an eminent young rishi named Richik came to Raja Gadhi's court and asked for Satyavati's hand in marriage. It was an unusual request from a brahmin, but the rishi said that he had seen the princess splashing about in a lake with her ladies-in-waiting and her beauty had won him over. Raja Gadhi was in a quandary. Satyavati, born in a royal household, had led a pampered existence from birth. How would she, who had been waited upon hand and foot, adapt to life in a forest hermitage? Though concerned about his daughter's future happiness, Raja Gadhi couldn't turn down the brahmin's request outright, as it would most likely anger the man. And you know what havoc an angry sage's curse can wreak on a kingdom! So, Raja Gadhi, who was a shrewd man, said to the suitor, "Rishivar, we have the tradition of bride price in our family." In response the young rishi nodded and said, "I am ready to honour your custom. Name your price." To which Raja

Gadhi replied, "One thousand horses, each white as milk, but with a single black ear."

'It was an odd request. If the suitor was alarmed, he hid it well. In all seriousness, but with a smidgen of scorn in his tone, he asked, "Would you like to specify which ear should be black—right or left?" Raja Gadhi was taken aback by the question but he wasn't going to let the brahmin get the better of him. He replied, "Oh, that doesn't matter, Rishivar—all I ask is it should be the same ear in all the horses." The sage appeared sanguine, as if conveying that this, too, was a reasonable precondition. Wasting no further time in polite chitchat, he left. Raja Gadhi believed that he had got rid of the brahmin, breathed a sigh of relief and put the matter out of his mind.

'Now, Richik knew well that the king had quoted the bride price only to put him off. White steeds with a single black ear were extremely rare, highly prized as a status symbol among the wealthiest of kshatriyas. Richik didn't think a thousand such animals existed anywhere in the world. Now what was he to do? They would have to be created, he decided. It was not just the challenge issued by a kshatriya, it was for him personally a test of strength. Only a rishi advanced in sadhana, spiritual practice, could acquire the siddhis needed to generate life. Richik would have to be a saadhak again. There was no guru to guide him this time, it would have to be the site itself, the sacred spot where the seen and the unseen worlds meet. A sangam where different streams merged was conducive to meditation. He chose the ancient teertha where the rivers Ganga, Yamuna and the invisible Sarasvati come together. Finding an abandoned shrine, he sat down to meditate. He centred his meditation on Varun, lord of the waters, from whose foam the first horse, Uchhaishravas, had arisen.

'So deep was Richik's concentration that he was oblivious to the world till a sprinkling of liquid disturbed him. A cold muzzle nuzzled his ear. When he opened his eyes, he saw that he was surrounded by a sea of horses, whinnying, swishing their tails, shaking off the water droplets from their bodies, rolling in the sand. He couldn't believe his eyes. A thousand shyamkarni horses—and he had created them! Richik returned to Raja Gadhi's kingdom and said, here is the bride price you demanded. As an honourable man, now fulfil your side of the bargain.'

'What happened to the horses?' Gaalav asked.

'Raja Gadhi performed the wedding of his daughter on a grand scale. It went on for several days. Musicians, drummers, endless processions, prayers and rituals, banquets. For a week meals were served to brahmins who, of course, thronged to the celebrations. Everyone went away satisfied with the food and the gifts. However, the purohits who had presided over the rituals were not quite ecstatic. Instead of the standard donations of gold, gems, cattle and land, the king had presented each one of with them shyamkarni horses. The junior assistants got one or three, the slightly senior ones got five or seven. And a few among the higher ranks even got as many as a hundred and one. Being brahmins, however, they had no use for horses; cattle would have been better, they complained.'

Gaalav, listening intently, nodded in agreement. 'I don't care for horses either,' he said. 'They make me uncomfortable with their energy.'

Garud continued, 'Soon after the wedding, a horse trader whom no one had ever heard of, appeared from nowhere. He went from one purohit to the next and said the same thing: "Give me the white horses with a single black ear. In exchange, I will give you wealth—gold or cattle—that you can put to better use. Believe me, it is a good bargain. These steeds are meant only for those who have more wealth than they can use in three generations. They will eat you out of house and home if you are unwise enough to keep them." He pointed out that these horses had longer lifespans than humans, and the descendants of the brahmins too would be burdened with their upkeep. The brahmins were already fed up. The horses need speciality foods, intensive grooming and regular exercise. They gave nothing in return. They also needed protection as they were attracting covetous eyes. Thieves had tried to steal them. It was too much of a strain to mount guard all night when one had to rise at the crack of dawn and begin a day packed with rituals. The brahmins needed no further convincing and agreed to the trader's offer unanimously. In this manner he gained all thousand horses and began selling them in batches of two hundred to kshatriya kings—those who could afford them. He sold six hundred, and realized that there were no more kings wealthy enough to pay the quoted price. But across the river Vitasta, in the mountainous north, there were kingdoms with rich treasuries and horse-mad kings. He set off with the remaining four hundred white horses. As he was crossing the Vitasta, there was a flash flood in the river, and the horses, according to eyewitnesses—peasants and herders on the riverbank—simply disappeared. Foam into foam, water to water. Not a single creature made it alive, nor were they confirmed as dead, for no carcasses were ever seen floating or found downstream. Where did they go? It's a mystery till today. Maybe Varun just called them back. At this point, the suta ended his story.'

'Did he say when this flood occurred?' Gaalav asked.

'Just over three years ago. Around the time I met you.'

Gaalav grew thoughtful. 'The story lends credence to your claim that there are no more shyamkarni horses, but it does not explain why Rishi Vishwamitra asked for them. He was a king. I suppose he still is...but now that he has been exalted to the status of a brahmin rishi, what good are so many horses to him? I have wondered about this too.'

'The answer to that lies in another earlier story,' said Garud. With a small laugh, he added, 'Maybe he'll tell it to you himself.'

Gaalav was unamused. 'I can hardly see him telling me a story! Besides, I don't want to go to him unless my task is complete. It's—'

'...not a total victory for you,' completed Garud. 'However, even for a partial success, your gains are substantial. Just for a minute, stop to count them: you are the only brahmin to have acquired six hundred of the rarest horses in the world. It's quite a feat and it has earned you a reputation for—' He stopped and gave Gaalav a sly, sidelong look before emphasizing the word, '*tenacity*'.

'You were going to say something more rude' said Gaalav, making a shrewd guess. 'Stubborn, perhaps? Is that how you see me? Headstrong, inflexible, mulish... take your pick of words. I don't care.'

'Actually, the word on my tongue was *ruthlessness*. I'm only repeating what others have said.'

Gaalav looked daggers at him. 'Let people say what they like. Yes, I am ruthless. So what?'

'What about the princess?' asked Garud softly. 'Don't you care just a little bit about her?'

Gaalav's face darkened but he remained silent.

'Where is she now?'

'On her way,' said Gaalav. He got up suddenly and peered out. The sky was still storm-swept, streaks of lightning charged across the heavens. The hillside trembled and the wind howled as it raced down the slope. 'Where are we?' he asked fretfully. 'I must keep my rendezvous with her tomorrow. That spot where you met me was the place I was asked to wait for her.'

'It isn't far,' said Garud nonchalantly. 'But have you thought of what you are going to do next?'

'You've just given me this disastrous news,' Gaalav said. 'I don't know what to do...what am I going to say to Gurudev?'

Garud eyed him quietly, as if weighing his next words. 'Tell him the truth. He will be disappointed, of course, but as an incentive to get over it, offer Vishwamitra the princess.'

After a moment of complete stillness, Gaalav said in a hard voice, 'That's a terrible idea.'

Garud was quietly amused. 'Why are you so offended? It was merely a thought.' He stretched his shoulders and gave a huge yawn. 'I'm off to sleep. You, too, should get some rest.' He lay down and turned his face to the wall.

Gaalav listened to the drumming of the rain beating. He had a hammering ache in his temple. Shutting his eyes, he forced himself to become calm. After a while he said, 'I apologize.'

No reply. Then Garud's voice came in the dark, 'Perhaps you *are* a little bit in love with her yourself....'

A strong gust entered the cave, the rain drenched part of the floor. The storm, raging across the whole world, was now trying to rampage its way in. But the stone walls remained unbreached. The dark made it possible for Gaalav to speak. 'She was given to me as a substitute for the horses I asked her father for,' he said, 'Through her I acquired six hundred, but it isn't enough. After all that one has gone through, it is still not enough. That is all I know, the bitter taste of failure. Then how can I afford to love her? I have no right.'

Yet you have the right to barter her. That right you have...it is what you have done and will do again.Only by winning this game that you and your guru have started can you save face. And the lesson that you were meant to learn—what of that? Knowledge of dharma strengthens a man, but he who applies it without understanding the subtle nuances, weakens dharma. Gaalav's problem, Garud reflected gloomily, was the problem of all human existence. To be born into the human race meant to be born in ignorance. Though Death came to all, humans learnt nothing from it about how to live. Life was the puzzle even for a learned man like Gaalav. For all his education, his head and heart were locked in a tussle. Obedience to dharma may quench a thousand silent mutinies, but there was always one, the secret attraction, that had the power to subvert the strongest will. Even for the most resolute of men, it was usually a beautiful woman. He sighed and said gently, 'Let me tell you the rest of the story that the suta narrated...it may help you reach a decision.

'Immediately after the wedding, the sage Richik left with his bride, the princess Satyavati, for his hermitage in the forest to begin his life as a householder. In addition to all the jewellery, fine silks, furniture and silver utensils that had been part of her bridal dower, Raja Gadhi had arranged for a retinue of servants to accompany his daughter. They would make her life a bit easy, he'd thought. But a week later, the servants returned, bringing back all the luxury goods. The message from Satyavati to her mother was, "My husband lives very simply. I have to do most of the chores myself. The finery you have given me will be wasted here, Mother. Hence I'm sending it back for safekeeping. I have a new set of garments made from bark. This is what the women in the ashram wear and my husband says that I should not dress differently, since I am no longer a princess. Though I miss my fine muslins and the gold jewellery, I have to admit that it is practical advice, given the daily tasks I have to put my hands to: cleaning out the hearth, mucking out the cowshed, milking goats, plucking greens from our vegetable patch, and a dozen other similar jobs, that you, dear Mother, probably cannot imagine...I am busy from dawn till midnight. Self-sufficiency is my husband's mantra; I too, must absorb it, he says. However, if you like, when you and my father visit us, you can bring me another set or two of bark clothes—dyed in lemon yellow (*not* off-white) or camel shade by the palace dyer. My husband joins me in the heartfelt wish that you will bless us with your presence soon." Reading it, Satyavati's mother wept a little, then consoled herself by saying that a woman's life was unpredictable, it depended solely on her luck. Raja Gadhi took his daughter's *bad luck*, as he put it, more personally. He cursed the fate that had brought the brahmin to his court and told his wife to prepare for the visit. "Ask the cooks to make my daughter's favourite sweets and savouries," he said. "Take along pickles, spices, fresh fruit, nuts, fine-quality rice and whatever else you think she will need to take care of us. Oh, and inform her that our visit will be a short one. Maybe we could persuade her husband to let her return with us to the palace for a while. She must be bored witless in that hermitage. Forests are good for hunts and short spiritual retreats but not much else."

'However, when the royal couple arrived at Richik's ashram, to their surprise, the place had everything. It was not the palace, true, but all the basic comforts were provided. Raja Gadhi and his queen were welcomed very warmly; they were put up in a charming airy cottage. The food came from the ashram's common kitchen. Though it was all vegetarian and there were fewer dishes than the royals were used to being served, it was well-cooked, tasty and easily digested. As soon as the queen got the chance, she had a private moment with her daughter. "Here," she said, pushing forward a closed utensil she'd brought from the palace. "I got the cooks to prepare your favourite dry spiced venison cooked in ghee." "Mother!" the daughter cried in horror. "If my husband smells meat on my breath, I'm in trouble." The queen frowned. "Oh! A short-tempered fellow, is he?" The daughter loved her husband, so she immediately rushed to his defence and said that Richik was a stickler for right conduct and believed in moderation. The queen looked at her pityingly. "My poor dear! Are you happy?" she asked. Satyavati assured her that she was doing just fine. She pointed out that she'd lost weight since her arrival, it made her feel good about herself. She added that she'd learned to do her hair on her own. She'd also picked up several useful beauty tips from the other women in the ashram. There was a herbal scrub that had done wonders for her skin. There was also an oil made from wildflowers: when rubbed into the scalp and left overnight, it gave volume and lustre to the hair. With a touch of impatience, the queen said, "All this is fine, but is your husband good to you?" To which Satyavati replied with a shy laugh that he was better than she'd expected. The queen was relieved to hear this. "Should we expect some good news soon?" she asked with an arch smile. Yes, of course, Satyavati said. She hoped to present her parents with a grandson in a year's time. The queen sent her a tragic look and gently warned her not to raise her hopes. "Son or daughter—it isn't a choice we mortals can make," she said. She then spoke of the fasts, pilgrimages and sacrifices that she'd undertaken so that the king would have an heir, but it had all yielded nothing. Satyavati listened, though not very attentively. "My husband *knows* about these things, and he is working on a formulation," she said, with a slightly superior air. Then delivering the coup de grâce, she added, "He has *assured* me that I will give birth to a boy."

'The queen was immediately all attention. She hadn't forgotten how Rishi Richik had turned up with a thousand shyamkarni horses. A mind that could generate rare horses by thought alone could certainly create a normal male child. The old longing that had lain low in her blood for years, but never been banished, returned in full force. She reached for her daughter's hand and holding it tight with her own two, said: "You know, child, I have been a good mother to you. We have been friends more than mother and daughter, so I can confide this to you. It is *still* my dearest wish to present your father with an heir. It is best for everyone concerned, for you as well. Imagine! Your own brother will be the next king of Kanyakubja. When your son is born, he will have the added status that comes with royal connections. Listen, dear daughter, kinships are very important, especially to us kshatriya families. Therefore, I beg you, in order to preserve our bloodline, and also for your own son's future, please intercede on my behalf with the illustrious rishi. Tell him that I, more than anyone else in the world, *need* a son." So heartfelt was the appeal that both mother and daughter had tears in their eyes. They hugged each other and Satyavati promised that she would do her best to convince her husband.

'Richik was surprisingly amenable to his wife's request. In fact, he seemed eager to supply it. "It'll have to be a different formulation," he said. "A brahmin's son, a kshatriya's son: not quite the same thing." He asked for time to work on it. Meanwhile, he said, there were a few exercises the queen could do to prepare her body and mind for the pregnancy. A few days later, he was up very early in the morning. After his ritual bath in the river, he entered the ashram kitchen in his wet clothes and indicated through gestures that he should be left alone. He shut the kitchen door firmly and closed the windows too. After a while smoke began to emerge from the chimneys, not the usual black or grey curls, but in two completely different shades, a creamy yellow and a blood red. The residents of the ashram watched in wonder and some fear too, speculating about what the learned rishi was up to and, more importantly, how long he'd take over his task; there was lunch still to be prepared and they were famished. Finally, the door opened. It was around midday and everyone heaved a sigh of relief. Rishi Richik emerged, drenched in perspiration, hair all mussed up, tired but also quietly triumphant. He held two silver bowls, one in either hand. Calling Satyavati and his mother-in-law aside, he handed them a bowl apiece. He addressed them separately but said the same thing: "This is for you, respected mother-in-law, and this is for you, dear wife. Swallow the contents without fear—it's only a special payesh—but make sure that you do it exactly at sundown." He began to walk away into the forest. "Wait!" cried Satyavati. "What about lunch?" Without stopping or turning around, he said, "Dear one, that's ready too. I've cooked my signature ghee rice. Enjoy the meal. Don't wait for me." Then, as if something had struck him on the forehead, he stopped suddenly, turned around and backtracked to Satyavati. "I forgot to tell you the most important thing. Keep the two bowls I've given you and your mother separate. They look alike, but don't, *for any reason,* mix them up." Saying this, he left.

'The two women waited for sundown. As the hours slipped by, the queen's trepidation grew. In her mind, she went back over the long years of yearning for a son, the disappointments she'd endured time and again. Though her husband had never said a word to indicate his regret, she'd been left with the feeling that it was all her fault. Despondency had eaten away secretly at her core.

Vaidyas, astrologers, holy men—everyone had promised that it would happen, a son would play in her lap, but it hadn't come to pass. She had a feeling that this time was different...destiny had taken a new turn, everything was about to change. Good news was on its way for her daughter, but *really* good news was on its way for her too. However, a niggling doubt remained in her mind. Finally, just before sundown, she voiced it to Satyavati: "Daughter, though these two dishes and their contents look identical, it's clear from Son-in-law's parting words, that they are, in fact, not one and the same. There must be a reason why he doesn't want us to mix them up. And I can think of only one: he wants his son to be better than mine. It is but natural for a parent to wish that his or her child is best. Stronger, wiser, wealthier and more famous, of course. But, Daughter, being royalty yourself, you'll agree that these are qualities that befit a king more than a brahmin. Needless to say, a man who spends his entire life in the forest pursuing knowledge has no use for wealth and prosperity. He practises simple living as he is focused on evolving spiritually. In such a man's life desire has no place. Instead, he calls it lust or greed. As if the good life was something to be scorned." Satyavati stared at her in confusion. "Speak a little more clearly, Mother," she said. "And do make it quick, the sun is about to set." The queen nodded and, without wasting any further time, grabbed the bowl that was meant for Satyavati. "Your baby brother needs this more than your son," she said quickly. Glancing at the sun which was indeed sinking fast, she downed the payesh in one shot.

'Satyavati was aghast. But there was no time for her to react. The sun was slipping away, so were the seconds. She picked up the bowl originally meant for her mother and swallowed its contents. The queen smiled her approval. "Don't worry, dear. Everything will turn out fine. Just keep this as our little secret," she said, and patted her daughter's arm. But, Satyavati, still in the first bloom as a newly wed and therefore inexperienced, hadn't quite grasped the fallacy of that oft-quoted aphorism: there should be no secrets between husband and wife. Many hours later that evening, when Richik returned from the forest, and settled down in their bed, about to fall asleep, she told him what her mother had done. He sat up with a jerk. "Foolish woman!" he said, flying into a rage. In the dim glow of the single bedside lamp, she saw his face glowering. Satyavati gaped. Who? she asked in confusion. *Both of you*, he replied. "Your mother is conniving and stupid. As for you, my dear wife, you are plain stupid...how could you not obey the simplest of instructions? Now you'll have to deal with the consequences of your imprudent nature. That mother of yours will also suffer." Worried that he may issue a curse, Satyavati interrupted him, "Forgive her...it was only mother love that prompted her to want the best for her son." To which Richik responded with complete scorn. "*Mother love!* You women have unleashed forces that will challenge the world order. You've started a blaze that only time will control. It is said that a woman cannot be trusted. How true!" Then he left.'

At this point, Garud stopped. The storm had abated but its passing had brought no relief. Inside the hut, the air had grown more dense and stifling. Gaalav's head felt heavy. He had a sense of impending doom. 'What an awful story!' he said, in a voice just above a whisper.

'You cannot choose whose womb will bear you for nine months, but *you* will have to bear the consequences all your life.'

'I wonder sometimes,' said Garud, 'what would our lives have been, my brother Arun's and mine, if our mother had quelled her jealousy of her sister, my aunt Kadru?'

'Are you still angry with Mata Vinata?'

'You have to shed anger if you wish to be anywhere close to the Lord,' said Garud. 'No, I was never angry with my mother, not even while growing up, but when I see my elder brother passing across the sky, I feel a certain ache, a sense of loss. There isn't, nor will there ever be, a bird stronger than me, but when I see him, I think about what we could have been together.'

'I know what you mean,' said Gaalav softly. '*What might have been....*' After a while, he asked, 'How does the story end?'

'Jamadagni was born to Satyavati and Vishwamitra to the queen of Raja Gadhi,' said Garud. 'Mix-ups can cause endless trouble. You know your guru well, Gaalav, but is it possible for you to understand him without knowing this story? Two powerful men: Rishi Jamadagni, Rishi Vishwamitra. Forces to reckon with. Between them they will shape the history of your world. But in each of them reside two dissimilar sets of proclivities: a strong intellect but also strong emotions. A man at conflict with his own self always makes life difficult for other people, even to the extent of being cruel. Adherence to dharma can make a man heartless. Maybe now you will see why he asked you for the horses. It could be that he saw himself mirrored in you...perhaps you were a source of pride to him but also a threat. As a disciple in his ashram you naturally worshipped your guru, Gaalav, but don't continue to make a god of him. Emulate him if you wish to, but also remember that his grain is different from yours.'

As he thought about it, Gaalav felt the weight of the story build up inside him. How much of it was the product of a suta's rich imaginings? How was it any different from the clichéd tales that were born of inevitability? Yet, wasn't it also every man's truth? How often he'd heard it said that some events simply had to happen in one's life. All that had come to reside in him—vanity, self-evasion, the secret anxieties, the perennial quest to prove his superiority to others—where had all this come from? And what lay beneath it? If it was true that Vishwamitra was a man at odds with himself, with much to prove—to himself, the world and even the gods—then would such a man's destiny lead him to freedom or would it enchain him further? He thought back to that time when, duped by the gods, Vishwamitra had brought suffering on his own head. For him, the gods had been the real challenge: bending them to his will rather than bend to theirs. Gaalav had admired him for his militancy. Was it wrong to try to be like the man you admired? Respect in the eyes of other men, but most of all in his guru's eyes...that was what he *still* wanted. In the end, every man would be judged by the consequences of his action. But thinking too was an action, and he had not been able to restrain his thoughts. When Garud asked him a direct question, he could have evaded answering it, but it was a relief to confess his feelings for Drishadvati. Once articulated, they had become a flag of surrender in his inner battle.

Desire articulated had also created new possibilities—and new fears. Success or failure: what would tomorrow bring? Like a man hanging on the edge of a precipice, to whom every passing second is both a blessing and a curse, Gaalav counted the hours to dawn.

16

Vishwamitra and Gaalav

At first he thought it was just moodiness—she had a temper, he recalled—and hoped that she would recover with the hours they would spend together. However, as they walked through the foothills, in the northwesterly direction, her silence began to unnerve him. It was incurious, as if he was invisible. It made him feel strange, as if he were left holding a loose end of a rope instead of a lifeline.

They were on the last leg of the journey. A mist lay on the path they were walking. There was no other way to reach the ashram but to cross the forest outside the kingdom of Kanyakubja, by the long, meandering path covered with yellow leaves. The light was different from what he remembered of that first journey that he had made with his father an age ago. That had been a radiant day, there had been wildflowers and butterflies, a smell in the air of fresh things growing. Now there was only the drab silence of winter, the absence of sunlight, the odour of decay. Mulch in, mulch out. Every step brought him closer to the rot in his heart, the quiet turmoil that was eating him from within. What would he say to Vishwamitra? How would he say it? How would it be received? How would it end? He was so wrapped up in his thoughts that he was barely aware that they had reached the ashram. His responses to those who greeted him were curt. Asking his companion to wait outside, he went into the sprawling house and sent word through a young acolyte: Munikumar Gaalav seeks a meeting with Gurudev.

As he waited to be called into the guru's presence, he slowly became aware of the surroundings. There were lit lamps glowing at intervals in the dark corridor. He realized with a start that it was already dusk. A cart stopped at the entrance and a man offloaded weighty sacks of rice. From one of the classrooms came the sound of young pupils reciting their last lesson for the day. The lesson ended and a crowd of seven- and eight-year-old scholars swarmed out of the room, slowing as they spotted him, sliding past in a haphazard single file, throwing quick, curious sideways glances. Watching their faces he saw his younger self. It seemed like he'd never left, would never leave this place. All the memories came back to him—each day had been the same as the one before. Days of constant hurry, the long hours of learning lessons, the gnawing anxiety that he was not performing as well as he should, the secret despair that he would never fit in. In his fearful state, he'd felt isolated for such a length of time that he had developed a permanent sense of being alone. He was exceptional, but he longed to be accepted and liked. In the end he had settled for respect. There was a way to get that in the world, he had thought. How wrong he had been! He felt wearied. *I can't wait to leave this place behind.*

His reverie was interrupted by a messenger. 'Gurudev will see you now. Please follow me.'

He was exactly as Gaalav remembered. The same perfectly straight posture, an air of supreme indifference to the world. It had always been his armour and also his strongest weapon. He was standing at his favourite spot by the window, looking out on a lake. With his back to the door, an impressive, dignified figure, hands locked behind his back in a grip. He seemed to have grown taller or perhaps it was just his silhouette that made him seem so. Slowly he turned his head and looked in Gaalav's direction. Gaalav brought his hands together in respectful salutation. Suddenly, there was a dryness in his mouth. He felt as nervous as he'd been on the first day he'd arrived here. A large stone lamp stood in a corner, at exactly the same spot where it had stood all those years ago. Gaalav remembered cleaning it, lighting it every morning and evening. How he'd enjoyed those little tasks he'd performed for Gurudev. They'd made him feel special, superior to the rest. Now someone else had lit the lamp, the light was lucid as it had been then. It made the tiger skin on the floor seem alive, the snarl on the face all too real. After a protracted silence, the guru spoke. 'So you have returned.' He moved forward, a dark shadow fell over the pool of warmth created by the lamplight. His face was inscrutable. Though Gaalav could not see the guru's eyes, he felt their hard, steady gaze on him. 'Tell me, Gaalav, what have you to say?'

'Gurudev,' he said, feeling a sense of shame only the guru could make him feel. 'I ask you to accept six hundred shyamkarni horses as gurudakshina and relieve me of my burden of debt.'

'*Six* hundred?' A faint amusement coated the guru's words.

Despite his resolve not to show any emotion, Gaalav quailed. Hadn't it always been so—the royal disdain that had reduced even the most arrogant of princes to a state of twittering terror? It was exactly these mannerisms that Gaalav had sought to imitate: the haughty demeanour, the dry tone, the hard truth that silenced every opposition. Though the words scratched the inside of his throat, he said them. 'It was the best I could do.'

'What do you want me to say?'

Fool that I was, did I expect to be let off? All I've done is given you a fresh opportunity to humiliate me.There are no more horses to be got. You know that as well as I. How can you not know?

'I'm waiting for a reply, Gaalav.'

'Gurudev,' he stammered. 'I...cannot.'

A short laugh. 'Are you telling me that you cannot keep your word?'A pause and then a softer tone, chiding but also mocking. 'How long will you cling to your delusions?'

His heart was beating fast. *It's too late.* The very words that he had not wanted to say assembled in him. They were his last line of defence. Yet he hesitated to say them. 'In lieu of what I still owe you—please accept Yayati's daughter.'

'*Yayati's daughter?*' The guru sent him a quizzical look. 'A woman...are you offering me a woman, Gaalav? Have you come to this?'

You've led me into this, Gurudev...I'm trapped. The blood drained from his face. Though he had imagined this scene a thousand times, it was turning out far worse. 'She—she is the means by which I accumulated the six hundred horses,' he said. 'Her father gave her to me. He said that she would be the mother of four chakravarti kings, so it was prophesied. He advised that in return for a bride price of eight hundred horses, I give her to an eminent royal family in need of an heir. Thrice was she given to kings, for one year at a time. Through her three royal lines have been revived.'

'And where is this remarkable woman?'

'She waits outside.'

'Go out and send her in.'

~

A lantern hung from the branch of a magnolia tree. It swayed in the breeze. Watching the flickering flame, she shivered a little. The forest lay all around the ashram, with darkness it stole in closer. The trees were no longer trees, but an otherworldliness of thickening shadows, spectres stirring to life, stretching their limbs as if emerging from slumber and starting a whispered conversation between themselves. She felt a quickening in her blood. Moonlight filtered in through the thick mesh of leafy branches. Fireflies began their slow dance. There were shadows moving near the lake; the shy deer had come to drink. In that instant she felt herself flowing backward. Every particle of that earlier existence that she had been made to give up was returned to her. An inheritance retrieved. She recognized it all, but she also knew that it was not the same—how could it be when she was no longer the same person. *I cannot return*. When Gaalav came out of the house, still rapt in the scene, she turned to him with wonder on her face. But he did not make eye contact with her. Instead, he told her curtly to follow him and turned away. Indoors, the long flag-stoned corridor felt cold under her feet, the silence was oppressive. At the door of the guru's room he stopped and, after a brief hesitation, held it open for her. She went inside alone. The door closed.

He did not know how long it remained shut. It seemed like forever. Standing on the other side, he clenched and unclenched his fists. He was torn between a growing sense of dread and anger, between the urge to flee and the desire to break down the door. *Why is he taking so long with her? What is going on inside?* Then he heard the guru call out his name. In his haste, he pushed the door too hard, but he did not apologize. The guru looked at him with a strange expression. He looked past the man, his eyes searched for her and found her in the shadows, half hidden by them, as if she were changing into one herself, slipping away from him. He had to hold on to her. To focus his mind, he fixed his gaze on the lamp. In the steady white heart of the flame, he saw everything clearly. Her plea, made three years ago in Haryashva's palace on that night, came back to him. He knew instinctively that she, too, was remembering those exact words. How foolish they had sounded then: *Take me to your guru.* But they had been the right words all along. *It's over. The worst is over. There is nothing left for me to say. Let him say what he likes to me. I'll survive.*

'Yayati's daughter in lieu of horses,' the guru said. 'Gaalav, if that was the arrangement you negotiated, then you should have brought her to me right in the beginning...instead of the eight hundred horses, you should have left her with me. I, too, am a king. Four chakravarti kings would have added to my lineage.'

For an instant, Gaalav did not understand. Then he

did and the sky came crashing down at him. But he still felt nothing. He stared at the guru. *King or brahmin rishi. The man may call himself what he will, he'll remain who he is. I will never be like him...I do not want it.*

There was nothing left now but to leave. Yet he remained rooted. She was standing a little away from the two men, head turned to one side, as if completely disinterested in them. Suddenly, he grew reckless, not caring about propriety any more. *Let him watch*. He went closer to her. She turned to look at him, a single wordless glance was all. To him it appeared as if a deep sorrow flowed from her eyes. Had she known from the beginning that this is how it would end? That, in the end, she would not want him. There was, he saw clearly, no longer any need for him in her life.

'Drishadvati, daughter of Yayati,' he said. 'You have rescued not me alone, but your father and four other kings. You have been our deliverance. O sinless one, I thank you for the kindness you have done.' Saying this he joined his hands and bowed low. Turning to the guru, he repeated the gesture silently and, without waiting for the customary benediction, left. Walking out of the house and the ashram, into the dark night.

~

The babe was born just as the rains came. Ashtak, his father named him, and announced that he would be the next ruler of his kingdom, Kanyakubja.

A week later, he summoned her. It was early in the morning. He was standing by the lake. The blue-green water was flecked with fat pink lotus buds rising on slender stalks, opening out to the sun. A rag of colts, all white with a single black ear, was playing in the water. As he watched them, Vishwamitra's expression was of repose, a fond smile played on his lips. After a while he turned his attention to her. His demeanour hardened into its usual impassivity. In the months that she had stayed in the ashram, he had barely spoken to her and she had never said a word to him. One night had been enough.

'The time has come for you to leave,' he said. 'I cannot keep you here longer than one year...what do you wish for?'

Silence.

A crease appeared on his brow. 'I meant a boon that you can use in this life. Ask.'

'Mukti,' she said.

His frown deepened as he considered the word. It seemed a frivolous request to him. 'It is not for me to release you,' he said curtly.

She nodded slowly, as if she'd known that this would be his response. 'A mare may be released from harness, but a woman cannot be set free from bondage. Why not, Gurudev?'

'For a mare bred in captivity, the stable is the best place,' he said, in a measured voice. 'It assures her survival. She has no chance in the wild.'

'And a woman too must be restricted all her life?'

'A chaste woman does not create her own independent existence. She follows her stridharma. She—'

'Accepts that she is born a daughter, reborn as wife, and reborn again as mother.' Though she'd had the temerity to interrupt, her voice remained calm. 'Does that mean she also accepts that she must die thrice and yet never be reborn to be herself?'

He did not dignify the question with a reply. Instead, he informed her that there was a chariot ready and waiting. It would take her to her father's kingdom. Yayati, he said, was now the only one who had the right to decide her future.

So now I am being returned to sender.

A salutation from her side, a blessing from him in return. No tender goodbyes; there had been no tenderness between them that one time. There was nothing to take leave of. Their son had already been placed in the arms of the royal wet nurses. His training had begun.

17

Drishadvati

My return to Pratisthan comes as no surprise to anyone. It appears that they have already heard the songs that have been composed about me. Songs that make the listeners uncomfortable. Too dark, they say. Not a popular tale, still the different titles are amusing. *The Woman Who Was Exchanged for Horses* is one. *The Obedient Daughter* is another. However, it is *The Reborn Virgin* that I find astonishing.

I ask Sarmistha, 'Where did that come from?'

We are sitting in her room. Seeing her again is a homecoming of sorts. She rolls her eyes at my question. 'That was the creation of our own sutas,' she says. 'Do you remember a mendicant who had once come home? There was the boon, you said, that he gave you...that was the basis. This whole business of being a virgin despite bearing four sons gives you a special aura of chastity. It's exactly what's needed to turn around the story from one of shame to honour.'

'Whose shame are you talking about? And whose honour? It was *I* who had to become pregnant four times. A different man each time and none of them my husband.'

She is shocked by my frankness. Perhaps she sees it as

my lack of shame. Shaking her head, she says, 'You have lived for four years in four different kshatriya households and not understood this universal truth, that a woman's chastity is her family's honour. You were entrusted to the brahmin because Yayati, your father, being in dire straits, had no choice. As king he was obliged to give...rather than send a supplicant away empty-handed, he, being generous to a fault, parted with his beloved daughter. Was there a king more obedient to dharma?'

I burst out laughing. And stop only because she does not seem amused.

'What is there to laugh about?' she asks, sounding irritated. 'That brahmin was the one who failed to do the right thing. He was supposed to marry you off to a rich king in exchange for a bride price. That was the expectation with which Yayati gave you to him. But he turned out to be a hard-nosed merchant and bartered you several times for the horses. What a bizarre idea!'

'He was thinking of his dharma too,' I say with quiet irony. 'They were *all* very conscientious men.'

But Sarmistha pays no attention to my words. 'The poets would have used stronger words for him, but we have censored them. We had to. He is a noble brahmin, after all. The disciple of an illustrious guru, and now one hears he's made quite a name for himself, as well. What is he really like?'

I shrug my shoulders. 'No different from other men.' I can see from her face that the reply does not satisfy her. I sense that there are dozens of questions she wants to ask me, but my reticence is daunting. She doesn't know what to make of it. Instead, I encourage her to talk. Sarmistha is a happy woman. At last, Puru is to be crowned king.

She can speak of little else. From her stories and gossip, I piece together what transpired in my absence.

Having run through the gamut of pleasures—the hours spent dallying with beautiful women, the delectable fruits and tender meats he'd tasted, the thirst he'd quenched with the finest wines, the gold jewellery for which he had an inordinate fondness—Yayati's ardour ran out. He was done with all that, he declared. He sent an elephant to bring Puru to the palace. When the bent and doddering old man who was his youngest son was admitted into his presence, Yayati made him sit down. Puru was still wheezing from the effort of getting off the elephant's back followed by the even greater strain of climbing the stairs to Yayati's private chamber. His rasping breaths made Yayati a bit nervous: he'd been ageless for so long, he'd quite forgotten what it was to be old. For an instant, he was tempted to change his mind, to hold on to his youthful body, but the fear of annoying his father-in-law again was stronger. Shukracharya had grown old too, he was quite cantankerous these days.

Gathering his thoughts, Yayati said to Puru, 'O son, with the youth you gave me, I have enjoyed the pleasures of life. I am sated. In fact, between you and me, I may have overdone it a bit. To get whatever you want when you want it may seem a fine thing, but indulgence is like the sacrificial fire that burns higher the more ghee you pour into it. Immoderation has played havoc with my system: the vaidya has informed me that I need to slow down. I have a fatty liver, diabetes and several of my teeth need to be pulled out...you get the drift, O son. This is what I have learnt: if one man were to own everything on earth, all her grain and all her fruit, all her precious metals and gems, all her animals and all her women, he would still not be satisfied. Therefore, one must make sure not to fall into, what I call, the Enjoyment Trap. One must maintain a healthy distance from worldly pleasures if one wishes to obtain true happiness. While there is nothing wrong in indulging the occasional wish, an addiction to pleasure is pernicious. It is the fatal disease that destroys a man. Nothing fails you as completely in the long run as chasing after your desires. They invariably outrun you. I have decided to shed mine and focus my mind on higher things. My intention is to retreat to the forest where the deer play peacefully. I'm ready now for a bit of peace and quiet, light and easily digestible food, a full night's sound sleep. A retreat of this nature will give me time to record my memoirs. I have led a colourful life. I'm sure the world will be interested in my experiences and what I learnt from them. It's only fair to share my wisdom with posterity, and it will also keep me busy. But, before I leave, I have a last duty...O Puru, let me tell you that you are indeed the lucky one among all my sons. I am pleased with you. Take your youth back. And also take this kingdom of my ancestors. You deserve it, for you are the son who empowered me so that I could taste all of life's pleasures for as long as I wanted.'

Apparently that was all it took to switch roles. When the father and son came out of the chamber, there was confusion in the palace, because neither was recognizable.

The young man—who is he? Is he Yayati?

No, that's Puru...the *old* man is Yayati.

So who stays in the palace and who returns to Sarmistha?

Apparently, they both stay in the palace for now. A chariot is being sent to fetch Sarmistha.

You mean, she and Devayani are going to finally live under one roof? Never imagined that such a thing would come to pass.

Looks like it has....

It took a few days for the excitement to settle down. Sarmistha tells me, 'When they sent the chariot to my house, I came at once. As you can see, they've given me a nice apartment. I have several maids and even a hairdresser to do my hair. It's just like the old days.' Her eyes are shining.

'Where is Devayani?'

'You mean, where is the *queen*?' Sarmistha corrects me. 'That's the proper way to address her.'

'But I'm addressing you.'

She clears her throat. 'Yes—well. The thing is, what I meant is that we have decided to let bygones be bygones. She is an old woman, so am I. I was jealous of her, then she was jealous of me. Neither of us wants to remember all that now. It's time to let go of our enmity. Though Yayati leaves for ashram life, it has been decided that she stays on in the palace. With me...I hope she'll stay for as long as possible. While Yayati was living the sweet life, the poor woman was running his kingdom. Though he will take the credit, it was she who ensured that nothing was done against dharma, the gods were offered the right sacrifices, the shraddh ceremonies for the ancestors were performed without fail, the brahmin guests were given food and drink, the vaishyas provided with protection to run their businesses and the shudras treated kindly. No one had complaints. In the times ahead, Puru is going to need her support....' She tapered off uncertainly. 'The problem is that the people of Pratisthan had never fully accepted that Yayati would bypass the four older sons and announce Puru's name as the next king.'

The brahmins had been extremely upset by Yayati's action. They had led a delegation of citizens from all sections, and spoken to the king. They reminded Yayati that his duty was to uphold the law, not bend it to his will. On what basis had he ignored the rightful claim of the four elder sons to the crown? To this Yayati replied that only he is a son who acts like a son. This meant following the wishes of his parents to the letter. A son who has slighted his father, as each one of his four elder sons had done, deserved to be punished. Only the youngest, Puru, had respected his command. Hence he was the only true son. He further added that Kavya Ushanas himself had said that the son who respected Yayati's wishes alone would inherit the kingdom. The learned sage, no doubt, wanted the best man among the five to be the ruler. It was all to the kingdom's advantage. Then joining his hands in a plea, Yayati had asked that Puru be instated as the king. He really was the best choice.

'They agreed, but one could see from their faces that they weren't jubilant,' says Sarmistha. 'The coronation ceremony is next week. All the kings in the land have been invited. The preparations are on a war footing.'

Entering Pratisthan, I had seen the tall arches, the painted walls, the makeover given to the more important avenues, the buzz in the marketplace, frenetic activity in the palace.

'There is to be a wedding too,' Sarmistha continues. 'Yayati has arranged a match for Puru. She is from a small kingdom, but the lineage is a good one. As king, Puru will need a queen by his side for all the rituals that will now become important in his life.'

'It's hard to imagine Puru as a handsome prince,' I say. 'I have never seen Puru young—or Yayati old. That will take some getting used to.'

She eyes me silently, then says in a soft voice, 'It's to be a double wedding.'

'Really? You mean Puru is marrying two princesses? Are they sisters?'

She shakes her head. Her eyes remain on me. There is an avid look in them. 'Your wedding too. Your father has invited the kings to your swayamvar.'

I am too stunned to speak.

She studies my face. The speculative look in her eyes reminds me suddenly of Supriya, the courtesan of Ayodhya. 'I knew you'd be surprised,' she says with a laugh. 'But this is a happy surprise and one that you deserve. Scions from all royal families vying for your hand! How many women have the freedom to choose a husband?'

But that is not what I want. Having a wider choice of husband—is that freedom?

'And let me tell you something more,' Sarmistha says. 'Haryashva, Divodas and even that old-timer Ushinar are coming to the event...everybody has been talking about the prophecy. No doubt there is an assumption that your next child may become a chakravarti raja too.' She looks me over with a critical eye. 'Who'd have thought that the wild creature who came to live with me would turn out this way—a prize coveted by kings? They are talking about another thing too, your magnificent looks. And I must say that you have turned out far better than I'd imagined. It's clear you've been looked after well.'

I still haven't spoken a word.

'And now we must talk of more important things,' she says. 'As I'm practically a mother to you, it's my duty—a happy one, I must say—to get everything ready. I want you to see the options for the bridal garments, and later I have asked my hairdresser to take a look at you. With a perfectly proportioned face like yours, any hairstyle will look lovely, but perhaps, a long, single plait will give you a demure look...it's needed, I feel, to stop all the tongue-wagging. Though your skin is clear, you could start with the beauty treatments to make it look brighter. A wedding day comes just once in a lifetime, child. All eyes will be on you. Imagine it! A gathering of the powerful and the mightiest men in the land and you can pick one among them...if I were you it would be Haryashva. He is all man, they say, and the Ikshvakus, besides being an ancient family, are fabulously wealthy. But the downside is that you'd have to contend with three other queens. Maybe Divodas is a better choice, though I must say, I've heard some strange things about him. I've been meaning to ask you. They say that he knows black magic. Living in his palace must have been an eerie experience.' Finally, she notices my silence and stops speaking. After a while she says, 'What is it?'

'Nothing.'

She sighs. 'Listen to me, Drishadvati. Forget him. Having got what he wanted, he is gone from your life. Think of yourself now. Here is your chance to get the things that women want.'

'What do women want?'

'Not the lofty things that men want. Women are more practical. They want what is within reach: husband, children, household. A safe place in society. This is what gives every woman an identity...Gaalav did not give you these things, but there are better men, kings, who will.'

'At one time, *you* used to sing love songs on full-moon nights.'

She smiles. It makes her look suddenly young. 'I still do...on full-moon nights a bit of sentimentality is allowed, but it has no place in the daily running of life. That is why we women need to be practical—because men never are.'

As she prattles on, I have a vision of what lies in wait for me. A week later it comes true.

~

Here I am, all decked up, holding the fresh flower garland in my hands. Alone. They have let me have a few minutes to compose myself. I stand in a hall with polished bronze mirrors. In them I see my reflections. The richness of silks, the glitter of jewels. Haven't I lived these exact same moments before? In the mirrors I see several brides, hair braided in neat long plaits, adorned with gold flowers. And clearly visible on the backs are the tattoos of deer. Of all the bridal glory on display, those deer are the most beautiful...I let out a deep breath.They are calling me now. I must go.

And here they are, these kings from across Aryavarta, seated in the hall, in two rows. I have been told that I must walk through this gathering and place the garland on the neck of the king I wish to marry. A garland for the chosen husband, a noose for me. Yes, this is what it means for me. A gathering of the powerful and mightiest men in the land, each one silently mapping my body from head to toe for auspicious marks: the six high points, the seven places of slimness, three places of depth, five spots of redness. Why did I not see it before? *I have nothing in common with these people...then how can I spend a lifetime among them? All those women before me, they were nothing but birds in gilded cages. I want to be free, then how can I spend a lifetime in a palace?*

Like a good-luck charm a memory has remained with me all these years. My mother's words come back to me, as if she herself is in the room. *The forest is yours.*

I know then whom I must marry. Whose wife I will choose to be.

Holding the garland of lotus and basil leaves in my hands, I slowly pass, one by one, the eager, ardent noblemen who have come for my hand—the kings, the crown princes, the princelings, who carry with them poems written to me and look at me with naked yearning in their eyes. I know where I go.

The forest. It will be the forest for me.

Epilogue

Her appeal had put them in a quandary. Vasuman, the eldest, stood by the window gazing out, deep in thought. Pratardan and Ashtak were shaking their heads from side to side. Only Shivi, the quietest of the four, looked at her intently, as if trying to read her mind.

'You want each of us to hand over a quarter of our merit to *him*,' Pratardan said. 'It flies in the face of all logic. '

'All men have a share in the fruits of their offspring,' she said evenly. 'There is no other way he can go back to Swargalok. And go back he must.'

Pratardan stuck out his jaw. 'I disagree. Now that he has returned to this world, he must follow its rules. He should *earn* enough merit to go to Swarga.'

'True,' said Vasuman in a placating tone. 'But it's not quite as simple as that. Where is he to start? As what? He cannot go back to being the king of Pratisthan. He doesn't know what else to be but a kshatriya. Do you see him, at his age, bearing arms? Is he capable of leading an army into battle? I doubt if he can even head a cattle raid, leave alone protect a kingdom.'

'How old is he?' Shivi asked. The question had been on his mind for a while.

'No one knows for sure,' Vasuman said. 'Determining

his age was complicated enough when he was a mortal. For instance, we don't know how old he was when Acharya Shukra cursed him, nor do we know how many years the curse added to his lifespan. Should they be included in the calculation? The sutas, whose job it was to record these details, exaggerated wildly. To give you an example, they said that he lived his second youth for a thousand years.'

Ashtak narrowed his eyes. 'What I would like to know is why was he ejected from Swarga? Did he pick up a quarrel with one of the gods? Was he rude to a rishi? Did he follow the footsteps of his father Nahusha and make a play for someone else's wife?'

Vasuman sent him a wry look. 'Nothing as dramatic as that. He merely let Indra know that no one could match the merit he'd earned from all his good deeds.'

'Bragging even in Swargalok!' Pratardan curled his lip. 'While he was here in Mrityulok, he didn't live by the rules but invented new ones for himself. Now that he's dead, he doesn't know how to remain dead. Is there no limit to his arrogance?'

Ashtak asked, 'Who is to say that having regained entry on the strength of *our* merits, he will not lose them again and land back here?'

'There's always that risk,' Vasuman said with a chuckle.

'*I* am not convinced that he deserves such a big favour from us,' Pratardan declared.

'I'm with you,' said Ashtak.

Shivi shrugged his shoulders, signalling that he was undecided. He sent his mother a puzzled look and said, '*We* owe him nothing. What's more, he was not a good father to you. In giving you away because it was convenient, he abandoned you. When he did you injustice, why do you want us to do him a good turn?'

'That is what we'd all like to know,' said Vasuman. He went close to her and looking down into her face, spoke very gently. 'You were powerless once, but you are no longer that.'

~

I owe them an answer, but what should I say? Long ago, I freed myself from all identities. I didn't know then what I now know—that some identities are indestructible.

Though it happened many years ago, it seems like it was yesterday when Vasuman first appeared in the forest in search of me. He had just turned fifteen. Even before he identified himself, I had known who he was. That astonishing rush of joy! The pride I felt at seeing him. Though I lived simply, that day I was relieved that someone had left a basket of fruit at my door. I gave Vasuman the small wild mangoes, feeling a little worried. Would he find them too fibrous or not sweet enough? He accepted them with gratitude and, indeed, seemed to relish them. It's the first time I've got something from your hands, he said. I pretended to gloss over the momentary awkwardness, but my mind winged back to the dark, cloudy morning in the royal nursery long ago when I'd held him in my arms that one time. That one last time. Suddenly I had a sense of what it was that I'd been forced to relinquish and the old grief stirred up, forcing me to blink back the tears that he, out of courtesy, pretended not to see.

He came back. Over the years, his three siblings,

too, sought me out. Though I was protective about my solitude, I couldn't help but look forward to their visits. However, I refused to accept the lavish gifts of grain, ghee, spices and fine cloth. While you are here, live the way I live, I said. They agreed without a murmur. Why did they come? Was it because within my story were nested the stories of their births? I had carried each one for nine months. In those times, the most difficult period of my life, had I seeded my pain and bitterness in the unborn life inside me? This thought disturbed me. Creatures of the forest have ways to heal themselves. While their scars are testimony to their truth—an eye torn out in a fight, a limb maimed—wild animals do not keep past wounds alive. Life does not stop for them. They do not sorrow for what has gone but simply get on with the task of living, a day at a time. By making the journey back to the forest, I too, have tried to get on. The simpler daily rhythms of my life here have dulled the intense pain I once felt, even returned to me a sense of harmony. But have I really erased the feeling of abandonment that has hollowed me from within for years? Have I passed on the shadows of scars to my sons? The unseen wounds are the most painful of all. Am I still hurting and do these four detect it? Are their visits to the forest a silent reparation? In their separate realms they are kings, here they are brothers and friends. The bonds between them are those of affection and sharing. I am mother to all four equally. My wounds have led me to myself, but it is the love that they bear each other that tells me who I am in the world. I am their mother. They seek an answer from me. It is time now for a closure.

Gathering my thoughts, I say, 'You four are worthy

kings. You understand matters of dharma better than I. As you have just pointed out, your grandfather lost his place among the celestials due to his own arrogance. He fell right in the middle of this yagna you are performing—*your* offering to the gods. I asked him how it came about. He replied that he pleaded with the gods to grant that his landing was in the company of righteous men. There are righteous men in other places too, so why did he come to the Naimisha forest? It was for a reason: peace can only be made in a liminal world. One in which the past, present and the future meet. The yagna has reached the final stage, its real fruit will reveal itself to you when you perform the ultimate sacrifice. And that is what I ask of you...you four are not just his grandsons, but also deemed to be men of virtue. Each one of you has a storehouse of merit. All I am asking of you is to give away a quarter each. You are young and will have the opportunity every single day to perform actions to acquire more merit. But he, not being of Mrityulok any more, has no chance whatsoever. Whether of this world or not, worthy of your respect or not, he remains your ancestor. Like you four, he too, followed the dharma of a kshatriya. Sometimes, following one's dharma leads one to an act of adharma. It happens more often than you can imagine. As his daughter, I entreat you to part with a fraction of your merit. It is not a small thing I ask. It means you will have to be even more virtuous than you already are—to make up what you give away to him—but if the intention is right, then everything that happens may eventually be for the best. In the process you may learn a valuable lesson that he did not learn despite his long years: One can never have *enough* virtue.'

It is a long speech but they hear me out patiently. When I'm done they respond with complete silence. Now it is up to them.

Ashtak speaks first. 'Mother, you have a way with words.'

Shivi laughs. 'If this were a philosophical debate, we might be tempted to argue, but then the question of what is to be done with him would remain.'

Pratardan continues to look sceptical. 'It's a long way up to Swargalok. What if our combined merit isn't enough to raise him to the required height?'

Vasuman, head lowered in thought, is slowly stroking his beard. After a while he says, 'We'll give it a try...let's see what happens.'

~

Yayati was very relieved that they had come up with a solution, but hid it by saying gruffly, 'Get on with it. Don't delay me. This air doesn't suit me any more. Too much smoke, too many unpleasant smells.'

To needle him Pratardan said aloud to the others, 'Shouldn't we wait for the right weather conditions? Given that our revered grandfather is no lightweight, a strong uplifting breeze would help.'

Shivi suppressed a grin and said, 'It *is* a still day. Maybe tomorrow....'

Ashtak, with a look of complete innocence, added, 'Grandfather, wouldn't you like to spend some time with us? We've heard so much about you, but to hear about your life from you would be a good learning for us.'

'The gathas sing of me now and forever,' Yayati said grandly. 'Listen to them once in a while and learn.'

'The sun will be rising soon,' Vasuman said, looking out. 'It's a clear sky.'

Escorting Yayati into the open, Drishadvati and her sons formed a wide circle around him. Vasuman stepped forward. Yayati signalled to him to stay a short distance away. He sat cross-legged in a yogic posture and closed his eyes. A look of calm came over his face.

Extending his right hand, fist upward and closed, Vasuman said, 'The merit that I have obtained by treating all the varnas in a praiseworthy manner, I give to you. The fruits of my good conduct, of being generous and forgiving, I give to you. The fruits I have gained from performing yagnas, I give to you.' He tilted his fist down and opened it.

Immediately Yayati rose in the air. He went up to a reasonable height and remained suspended there, bobbing gently.

Next spoke Pratardan. 'I have always been devoted to warfare. I have earned fame for my courage. Whatever fruits I have received through the practice of my kshatriya dharma, I bestow on you.'

Yayati ascended higher and came to a halt.

It was Shivi's turn. In his gentle voice, he said, 'I have never told a lie. Go to heaven by the virtue of my truth.'

By now Yayati, though far above, was still visible. Ashtak, the son of Vishwamitra and Drishadvati, came forward. 'I have performed hundreds of yagnas. Everything I owned by way of gems, gold and other material wealth, has been used in these ceremonies. May the gods grant that you go to heaven by the virtue of my merit.'

They expected this fourth push to send him on his way, but it did not happen like that. Yayati rose again, but continued to remain suspended. Now what? The four kings looked at each other, the unspoken question clear to all. Swargalok was still some way off. What were they to do? At this point, she stepped forward...Drishadvati, their mother.

'Whatever merit I have obtained through my actions, I give to you,' she said. And held up both her arms to where her father waited.

The words were barely out of her mouth when he sailed upwards and vanished from sight.

Acknowledgements

I am deeply grateful to Dr Pradip Bhattacharya whose landmark study, *The Panchakanya of India's Epics*, engendered my interest in the women in the Mahabharat; Murli Melwani who bore the brunt of the first draft; Shinie Antony, literary agent, and, my editor, Renuka Chatterjee.